NETWALKER UPRISING

THE NETWALK SEQUENCE BOOK THREE

JOYCE REYNOLDS-WARD

Cover art by GrinPhoto, purchased from Depositphotos

Design by Joyce Reynolds-Ward

No generative AI has been used in the conceptualization, development, or drafting of this work.

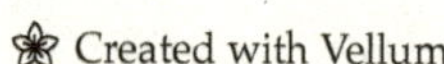

CHAPTER 1

Forget.

Melanie Fielding crouched low over her old racing skis, barely in control of her speed as she flew down the High Reach, highest run on the Mountain, trying to fly ahead of her whirling thoughts.

Forget, forget, forget.

Maybe if she thought the word enough times it would come true at least temporarily, stupid magical thinking that it was.

But she couldn't forget everything.

Not the long-delayed-thanks-to-politics swearing ceremony at the Corporate Courts Executive Council meeting in three weeks, which would place her on the Executive Council. Not her presentation to earn Corporate Courts approval of the Dialogue chip. Not the details of the damnably complex bid proposal that her company, Do It Right, was submitting to the High Space syndicate for the New Federation's space station—put together in a scramble over the last year, because the old North American Confederation wasn't supportive.

There were too many important things to remember.

Once she was part of the Exec, she would learn about the *important* secrets. Like Gizmo. The Gadget.

Corporate Courts access would give Melanie more information about Gizmo and how it tied into High Space. There was a significant connection between Gizmo and High Space and the Courts.

Melanie hadn't known about Gizmo until her mother Diana became the New Federation President fourteen months ago. She learned about High Space only nine months ago. How they tied together—hopefully, in three weeks.

That said, what Melanie already knew about those linkages was scary enough that she didn't want to think about it right now, especially after today's disclosures about how her dead ex-fiancé Liam tied into too much involving the Courts, the Gizmo, and—politics.

Three weeks and I'll get my answers.

However, personal life kept enmeshing itself with her progress toward that all-important goal of finding those answers. Like now. This close to her miscarriage. Maybe she could blame her emotions on that—but why was she so reactive?

Forget it. Forget everything but whiteness and the whisper of speed.

Just dance with gravity, up high on the Mountain with no trees to remind her how fast she was going.

But her body worked against forgetting.

Thighs ached as she fought the clatter and scratch of her skis on water-slick ice. A burn built slowly in her lower back and gut. The need to *think* about tightening her stomach muscles to hold her hips steady.

Out of shape, damn it!

It was a good thing only a handful of ski bums and racers in training were on Mt. Hood's glaciers this overcast, windblown early April day with wisps of clouds boiling around them. Fewer people to avoid. Less need to check her speed.

Her Security team followed high on the glacier above her, prudence overcoming protectiveness. Except for Nik Morley, the head of the team, who was probably cussing her out by now.

On cue, a blue circle blinked furiously in the lower left-hand corner of her left eye. When they were on the slopes, that single visual was the closest Nik would come to texting via Dialogue visual overlays for fear of distracting Melanie.

Sorry, Nik.

Skiing hard and fast was the only way she knew to outrun the demons that stalked her.

But it's not working today! Not skiing fast enough.

Her demons always came back worse on the lift ride. That was one thing that had beaten her in ski racing—she overthought her runs. And these demons—

Like this future role in the Courts. Courts management was hereditary. Both her mother and grandmother had held positions on the Exec. Gizmo factored into this process somehow. At some point Melanie's child—biological by explicit Courts preference—would step up to a management role in the Courts.

That is, if I ever have a bio heir.

She blinked back tears and gulped.

Normally she would be linked to her husband, Marty. But sharing mindspeech and emotions with him via the Dialogue wireless computer chip interface brought him into her head. Much as Melanie loved Marty, she couldn't bear that close a contact with him at the moment.

Thanks to the miscarriage. And to the fury that swept through her this morning when it was confirmed that Liam had uploaded after his death; that her ex-fiancé was not just a Netwalker but a powerful one.

Damn bastard Liam. No. Forget. Damn it, I'm not skiing fast enough!

Forget the alternating cold rage and sorrow sweeping through her. Forget that extra clutch of fear—*what is he capable of now?*

One of her tips caught on a chunk of ice. It popped off the snow. Melanie slammed that ski down hard. The ski sharply skewed sideways, almost dumping her down the steep slope as an inside edge grabbed unexpectedly. It took too long to regain control, her reflexes slower than they had been. Nearly too slow for these skis, this speed, and the wet, icy conditions. And a sharp, stabbing pain twitched through her lower back. A strain. She wasn't in shape because of the pregnancy.

Gone now. Melanie's throat tightened again. Then another edge caught. Her reaction triggered more back muscle pain and her bad knee throbbed.

She *should* call it a day after this run. That would be the smart thing to do.

And yet—and yet—*something* pulled at her, demanded that she do yet another run. In spite of common sense.

Melanie stopped at the bottom of the High Reach to catch her breath, winded from speed and the altitude.

She headed for the High Reach chair.

Swish! The snow was too wet to go flying as Nik cut sharply in front of Melanie, blocking her way. Melanie dug her edges sharply into the snow to stop.

"Damn it, Nik—"

"You're tired." He towered over her, six-foot-four to her five-foot-two. "We should quit."

Melanie shook her head. "Not ready yet."

"Mel, damn it, you're not in shape!" Nik snapped. "I saw you almost lose it. Twice."

"I recovered," Melanie said.

"Yeah." Nik slowly took a deep breath, blowing it out hard, steam clouds wrapping around his face. "You did. And you were lucky." His voice softened. "Look. We're not race kids any more. The slope's getting slicker. The racers are calling it a day. Let's do it too. Marty's been texting me. He's worried."

Melanie frowned. Skiing today was selfish.

But after this morning's news in the weekly conference with the Courts' High Space Committee, Melanie *had* to ski. She needed the ski time to banish her anger. Her fear. Clear her mind to focus.

That damned Henri Montcrief. So casually mentioning that Liam's upload has been spotted around the gadget—and being so dismissive of it. That smirk on his face when he realized I didn't know. Damn it. Damn him. Damn Liam. Is he a rogue Netwalker or does he have a host? Who is his host?

As a Netwalk Enforcer—so far, the *only* Netwalk Enforcer—she should already know that Liam was a Netwalker. She should have some idea who his host was. Hell, she should *feel* his presence, as a result of the last fourteen months spent honing her Enforcer skills under the tutelage of her paranoid, dead, Netwalker father and practicing with Marty. With all the lab work they had done. Melanie had developed enough skill to sense every Netwalker who was uploaded and online.

That they knew about.

And that was the problem. Melanie had become more aware of anomalous Netwalk presences, that couldn't be explained by what they already knew about the tech. Foremost amongst that was the faint sensation of Liam as a vague, malign, presence.

That was wrong. That was a problem. An anomaly.

The uncertainty fueled Melanie's anger and fear, more than anything else, and she didn't know how to manage it—yet.

Another Netwalk version. That makes—what? Four now, at least? Who made it? How?

She could almost hear Liam cackle.

Thought you'd get rid of me that easy, eh bitch? That I wouldn't upload?

Melanie shook her head to clear it. Just her imagination.

Not Liam's voice in her head.

"Mel?" Nik's voice softened. "Let's go down. This is enough of a conditioning run. Let's call it a day."

"Marty knows I'll be okay," she told Nik, unable to keep a bitter edge from creeping into her voice, wincing even as she heard the tone.

Damn it, what's wrong with me? I sound like a whiny brat! This isn't me!

And yet—she felt alien in her own body.

"He's worried," Nik said flatly. "Mel, *come on*."

Melanie shook her head one final time, swallowed the lump in her throat that made her unable to speak, and pushed off, blinking tears back furiously. She ducked around Nik and headed for the High Reach lift.

Nik got on the chair with her. He studied the western edge of the Mountain above them as wind blew tendrils of snow into swirling twists before letting it fall. Doing his job. Looking for problems.

He wouldn't argue with her now that they were on the lift. She counted on that. It had been their pattern for years, ever since she had been a World Cup racer and Nik her on-slope Security.

Normally Nik's wife Angela, the official head of Melanie's Mountain Security, would be here. But Angela had an urgent meeting at Do It Right's Mountain headquarters in Hoodland. Nik was in charge of Melanie's Security detail today, and Nik was not the arguing type.

Angela was. Angela would fight with Melanie about this last run until they headed down the slope.

Maybe Angela's arguments could have shut down the insidious little voice in Melanie's head that occasionally bore traces of Liam's lilt.

But Ange wasn't here, and Melanie rode the lift with Nik and her ghosts instead. Tiny ghosts that rode the tendrils of wind-driven snow.

Another baby lost.

She'd been so careful. No skiing this winter after discovering her pregnancy. Felt this baby move. Shared the movement with Marty.

Melanie blinked back still more tears, fogging up her goggles, remembering that evening when they curled together, marveling at the faint motion within her body.

Then cramps. Pain. Blood.

And last night, the surrogate who'd been a bit further along with an IVF pregnancy also miscarried.

The surrogate wasn't her idea. Her mother Diana had suggested it, in case there were unforeseen problems with Melanie carrying a child. God only knew what Netwalker toxin could do to a pregnancy, and Melanie had plenty of exposure to that—

So. A surrogate, a safe alternative, that barely fit within the Courts parameters for heirs of her own body.

Then she managed to get pregnant.

Melanie bit back a bitter laugh.

What do you do when the broodmare's compromised?

Sometimes she hated her mother's pragmatic attitude about reproduction, shaped by her years breeding championship performance stock horses as a hobby. Worse, ever since Diana took on the responsibility of being *her* mother Sarah's Netwalk host, the interactions between her and Melanie bore an edge that hadn't existed before. More like the relationship between Melanie and Sarah when she was alive. It was as if Sarah Stephens's cynical, calculating attitude infected Diana through the Netwalk chip.

The drive for a bio heir wasn't just the Courts and the weird Gizmo interface. Other reasons included family and inheritance, given how her estranged brother Andrew opposed nearly everything Melanie and her mother stood for.

Except High Space. They all agreed on the urgency of that. *And control of Gizmo.*

Gizmo. The wild card factor.

God, I don't want to think about Gizmo any more than I have to!

It was a relief to enter the tunnel that marked the head of the High Reach. As they went inside, Melanie slid off of the chair. Instead of looking around, she immediately headed down the slope, ignoring Nik's call.

Make this run the fastest of all. Blow it all out. Then I can think about the Courts and bid proposals, not Liam, not lost babies.

Edges caught on the water-slick ice. Right ski popped up. Pain shot through her back as she tried to correct. Melanie swayed. Her body twisted quickly. White slammed hard at her. Something gave way in her knee. Rolling and skidding, bouncing on the ice. Agony lancing through jaw and face.

Which way is up?

Everything went white around her.

Liam laughed.

Melanie saw his lean pale face against the sky, dark hair blowing in the wind, narrow lips twisted in a tight grimace.

Netwalker! her Enforcer instincts screamed. A copper-colored sphere with spiky protrusions glimmered behind him, glowing with a pale green light. *Gizmo!*

Then everything went from white to black.

Marty Fielding frowned at the chip grow readings. If this fix worked, then he could finally approve production. The New Fed space station contract was *huge,* even though Do It Right was a subcontractor to Johnson Space. Didn't help that Johnson bogged DIR down in endless spec and cost reduction meetings without doing much actual work.

We should be the primary contractor, not Johnson.

But Corporate Courts politics interfered with what should be. It was one reason why Melanie was only now being sworn to the Courts

—that and Melanie's pregnancy....

Marty stuck one hand in the hologlobe circling over his desk.

<Ness, what do you think of these figures?> he subvocaled to his Netwalker, a former colleague whose digitally uploaded memories and personality construct he hosted in his Netwalk chip.

Ness popped into the hologlobe, first as a falcon, then transforming to a modified version of herself in life, a gaunt, lanky woman with mouse-brown hair. One side of her face was fuzzed, a legacy of how she had died. This chip was one of her new creations, the brains of a vacuum-tolerant builder bot which allowed a user to direct remote construction processes in space.

The builder bot chip was a direct descendant of the original technology that had made DIR famous. That technology, based on externally controlled bioremediation nanobots, had revolutionized environmental recovery work, allowing remediation of chemical and radiological sites humans couldn't safely access. The first Dialogues had been headsets rather than implants, originally only a means to control biobots, but now much more than that.

<Looks good to me,> Ness said. <Everything fits the specs this time.>

<Something's not right,> Marty said. <I feel it. Can't explain why. I just feel it.>

Ness raised a virtual eyebrow. <If there is something wrong, I don't see what it could be. You sure it's not just you worrying about Melanie?>

Marty frowned at Ness's all-too-perceptive question.

Mel has too damned much on her plate between the Courts, High Space, and this push for a bio heir. Why is all of this space stuff suddenly becoming as important as it is?

He didn't like the noncommittal tone of Nik's responses to his worried texts. Nik didn't like what Melanie was doing today, that much was clear. But when Melanie was in a mood like this, better to let her blow off her frustration and rage by skiing.

Didn't mean he didn't worry. Still, she'd come back from skiing in a calmer, more settled mood, excess energy discharged and ready to focus, and that made the worry worth it. Some of her best insights popped up as a result of a frenetic morning on the ski slopes, madcap hiking, or a hard trail ride on her horse.

<Of course, I'm worried about Melanie,> he answered. <I just don't like the jumped-up deadlines. Too easy to make mistakes.>

<There's a strange feeling online,> Ness mused. <It's picked up since the High Space treaty signing.>

<Any idea what it is?>

<No. Could be new Netwalkers we don't know about, but it doesn't quite feel like that, either.>

<That's not good. Mel should be aware of them if that were the case.>

<It's like there's something looking over my shoulder all the time. Melanie doesn't see it. I've asked her to scan and she can't find anything. It doesn't feel like a Netwalker.>

<At least that's something.> A high-security message icon flashed on Marty's Dialogue overlays. <Let me take this.>

<I'll look through the stats again,> Ness said, disappearing. <Leave a line open.>

<Will do.> Marty snapped his fingers to bring up the caller in his hologlobe.

Diana Landreth, his mother-in-law and the President of the New Federated United States of America, grinned at him.

"How's things going, Marty? I tried to call Melanie, but she's not answering." A backdrop reflecting the actual view of Vancouver's current skyline framed her lanky figure.

"She's skiing," Marty said. "The only contact she's allowing is through Nik."

Diana's smile faded. "This time of year? It's April. And she's skiing *this soon* after the miscarriage?"

"Yeah."

Diana shook her head. "To be skiing in her condition, this time of year."

"We went yesterday. First time since the miscarriage. It was scary even then, and she had her slow fat skis. She took her race skis today," Marty added. "We got bad news in this morning's briefing and she didn't take it well."

"Damn." Diana's face twisted in disappointment, and was that sorrow? Marty wasn't sure. His mother-in-law had become more of an enigma over the past few months. "How's the surrogate doing?"

"The surrogate miscarried late last night. No one knows why."

"*Both* Melanie and the surrogate miscarried? That doesn't make sense."

"Mel took off skiing this morning because we learned that Liam Jeffreys managed to upload himself as a Netwalker. That news really set Mel off." He glanced down at his hands, remembering Melanie's explosive reaction. She usually kept a tight rein on her temper these days.

"Damn," Diana repeated. "What does Ness say about this news?"

"Nothing to justify refocusing on it instead of the new builder bot chip grow."

Diana nodded. Before she could say anything else, another icon appeared. Nik's ID code. Bright priority red.

Not good news.

"Priority incoming from Nik," Marty said.

"I'll wait," Diana said.

Marty snapped his fingers to bring Nik's link up, dread tightening his gut.

Red means real trouble.

Nik's blurry face stared at Marty, goggles popped up on his ski helmet, a field of white around him, sound crackling and popping from the wind on the ski slope.

"How bad?" he asked, his gut tightening because Nik was calling instead of texting.

She's hurt. Significantly.

"Bad," Nik said. "Too damned tired and upset to make that last run. Shouldn't have done it. Ski Patrol's on the way. She's out cold. Won't ski those planks again," he added grimly. "Both bindings and her right ski are broken. May have blown out that right knee. Scratched up her face. But she's moved her legs and arms a little, even though she's out. Breathing fine."

"I'll be right up."

"No. Transporting her to Portland." Nik grimaced. "She plowed a pretty good furrow in the ice when she landed."

"Sure I shouldn't meet you up there?"

"Don't waste the time. Meet us at UniHospital. We'll be gone before you can get here. I'll give Ange the details for the Medical Security team."

Marty swallowed. "Keep me posted," he said, not knowing what else to say. "Tell her I love her and I'll see her at Uni."

"I will." Nik blinked out.

Marty brought Diana back up. "Gotta go. Mel's crashed."

"Should I be there?"

"I'll call you when I know more."

Diana nodded. "I need to talk to Melanie as soon as she's able. Security issues with Netwalk. Courts as well as High Space."

"What's going on?"

"It can wait until I talk to Melanie. Sorry. I'm—not at liberty to say more."

So now what the hell is going on?

"But if it's a Netwalk issue, Ness can work on it."

Diana shook her head. "I can't disclose it. Sorry," she repeated. "Let me know what the timeline looks like for me to talk to Melanie. It really has to be her. An internal Courts matter." She switched off the link before Marty could respond.

And that is not normal. Crap.

No time to worry about it now. He checked in with Ness, who was absorbed by the chip grow stats, then grabbed what he needed before meeting Angela and the Medical Security team.

AWARENESS RETURNED. MELANIE LOOKED AT A PATCH OF BLUE SKY, FRAMED by angry gray and white clouds. She hurt all over. Head, legs, body, face.

What the hell?

Dialogue visual overlays skittered across her sight lines in jumbled order. She blinked quickly to reboot the wireless computer communication interface. The overlays stuttered several times, switched off, then switched back on. The startup settings ran smoothly, then settled into normal settings.

At least Dialogue's still working.

Nik appeared, blurry. Melanie tightened her muscles to sit up.

Ow. Damn. That hurts.

He placed one hand on her left shoulder.

"No." His voice deepened into a firmness she knew meant business. "You're not moving until the Ski Patrol gets here."

"Don't need." Her voice sounded tinny and thin. And, God, it *hurt* to move her jaw, much less talk.

"No arguing about it." Nik's voice wasn't just firm, it was angry. "You crashed hard. Your face is a mess. You plowed along on it for several feet. I don't like the angle of your right lower leg and you've been out cold. At least you're moving your arms and legs so I know your spine's not badly compromised. What the hell were you trying to do, kill yourself? Jesus!" He took a deep breath. "Marty says to tell you he loves you, and he'll meet you at UniHospital with the Medical Security team."

"Thank you."

Oh God, Marty. I screwed up bad. I got hurt.

At least this new pain drove out the dull ache that had been haunting her.

Maybe that was what I really wanted. Some physical pain to get rid of the emotional pain.

Tears blurred her vision even more.

The thunder of the Patrol skimmer interrupted her thoughts. The Ski Patrol moved in with their diagnostic tools. A few quick checks and she was strapped to a backboard, then loaded into the craft. Nik joined her.

The warm fuzziness of painkillers began running through her system. As they kicked in, suddenly the entire picture came together with crystal clarity as she thought through the sequence of events during the past few months.

First, politics delaying her induction into the Corporate Courts, before her pregnancy.

Her pregnancy.

Her mother Diana becoming sufficiently stable in her position as New Federation President that Melanie could step back, focus on research, and promote Do It Right as a contractor for the New Federation's contribution to the space stations that were part of the High Space Consortium.

And then her equilibrium thrown into disarray this morning by Henri Montcrief's sly aside about Liam being spotted near the gadget.

Liam's a Netwalker now.

Her ex-fiancé Liam had vowed, once upon a time, that she would never have a child without his consent. His, or anyone else's child, it didn't matter.

That son of a bitch is dead. But he's still found a way to haunt me. And now, with this Courts business, it matters more than ever.

But how could he interfere? How could this happen?

And what the fuck did that last vision mean? Gizmo? Why the hell did I see Gizmo?

We don't know enough about Netwalk yet. This is a danger, not just to me but to any other Dialogue or Netwalk host who's undefended.

Just what does it mean that I saw Liam and Gizmo together?

That suggested that the Courts were involved, even more than they would normally be concerning a biological heir.

Liam, Gizmo and the Courts. What the hell is going on?

All right then. Four things I need to do.

Gather enough information to decide if Liam somehow caused this miscarriage through the use of Netwalker toxin—somehow.

Capture and kill his upload or uploads.

Then neutralize his host—or hosts. Montcrief isn't supposed to have a Netwalk chip, but I'm going to find out for sure.

Finally, figure out how to prevent future attacks like this.

There's a deeper plan. A deeper problem.

And Gizmo is the key. Gizmo and whatever connection Liam has to it.

ANGELA GARCIA STOOD NEXT TO MARTY AT THE SKIMMER INTAKE AREA OF the UniHospital in Portland, waiting with the Medical Security team for Melanie's skimmer to arrive. She dutifully relayed medical data to Marty as Nik texted it to her.

Torn ACL in that right knee. Internal injuries. Broken jaw; they're running her directly to Surgery.

The white Life Flight skimmer slid into the landing space. Angela waved her Medical team forward to join the UniHospital crew waiting for Melanie. Medical Security supervision was standard for upper-level DIR staff during off-site medical procedures; especially for someone like Melanie with too damned many corporate secrets locked into her brain.

The skimmer door opened. Medics swarmed around the stretcher, transferring control smoothly from Ski Patrol and Life Flight staff to DIR Medical Security and UniHospital. Nik climbed out next. He caught Angela's eye and nodded.

"See if you can talk to her before she goes into surgery," she murmured to Marty.

Marty strode away from Angela, crossing the small space in a few long steps, gently taking Melanie's hand. Melanie's head moved in response.

Not too bad, then.

Angela joined Nik. He slid an arm around Angela's shoulder.

"It's not as bad as we first thought," he murmured as they watched Marty and Melanie. "At least the crash seems to have slammed some sense into her brain. Damn. I wish it hadn't taken something that extreme. Once the painkillers kicked in, she settled down. She put some things together on the way down."

"What about? The miscarriage?" Angela whispered.

Nik switched to the Mixteco dialect she taught him years ago, when they wanted to talk privately in public settings. "Yeah. Her Enforcer instincts are whispering to her about how it happened."

"Marty thinks there might be a Netwalk connection," Angela said.

"They're thinking alike. Just wish it hadn't taken the crash to knock some sense into her." Nik shook his head. "Let's hope she's ready for that Courts meeting in three weeks. She *has* to be there."

"If she can't be there, she can't be there."

Nik frowned, but said no more. Angela looked away from him as his lips tightened. When it came to the Courts, his Security rating superseded hers. She hadn't passed the initial aptitude screening for Courts access. Nik had.

Marty kissed Melanie's hand, and softly stroked her brow. Then he stepped back, and the team whisked her away. Marty stared after her, then sighed. He turned to Nik and Angela.

"We used Dialogue," Marty said. "Not talk. Hurts too much."

Angela nodded. "Let's go into the waiting room. Nik got the pre-surgery briefing."

"She told me that. Nik, text it to me. I need to call Diana and let her know what's happening," Marty said, fatigue settling into his voice.

"There's privacy areas inside," Angela said. "Come on. Let's clear out for the next group."

Marty nodded, moving stiffly. Angela guided him toward the waiting area.

All in a day's work, when your boss was Melanie Fielding.

CHAPTER 2

Marty sat watch by the hospital bed while Melanie slept, ignoring the pings from his messages. He snapped his fingers to shut down this latest alert about the chip grow entering a new stage. It couldn't be too urgent. Ness would use her access to alert him if things got too bad.

Melanie stirred and moaned softly. Marty rested his hand on hers, waiting to see if she woke. She shifted her weight slightly, opened her eyes, blinked in a non-command sequence pattern, gave him a flicker of a smile, then closed her eyes again.

A pattern he recognized.

Not ready to wake up yet.

His thoughts spun back to putting the pieces together, especially after what Mel had told him before she went into surgery.

How the hell could this happen? And why does she think there's a connection between Liam and the Gizmo?

Oh, he had heard Montcrief's insinuation about Liam, but Montcrief was snarky like that.

Or did he know something?

Part of Marty wanted to retreat to his lab and find an answer. Hell, he'd been doing just that this past week after the miscarriage, using the urgency of the High Space contract as an excuse. He knew better. He should have kept trying to get Melanie to talk. He shouldn't have run away to the lab. But every time he wanted to talk to Melanie, *something* inhibited him. Something that briefly blanked out Ness—but she didn't notice.

Is it at all possible that Liam's found a way to influence us?

He didn't like that thought, but Melanie's conclusion that Liam had something to do with the miscarriages—both hers and the surrogate's —was hard to avoid.

<You're thinking too hard,> Ness chided him.

<We have to trust Mel's Enforcer intuition. Liam had something to do with the miscarriages.>

<I heard her. It doesn't come together logically. Why didn't *I* sense anything out of the ordinary? Why didn't Mel?>

<It *is* one possibility,> Marty insisted. <This could be a new Netwalk model. Mel admits she doesn't know it all.>

<Are you sure you're not just making excuses? I think I could feel Liam influencing *you,* at least. You're making excuses for Melanie, Marty. She was in serious hormonal flux and anger.>

Marty didn't answer Ness, because he had that question himself.

And yet—he had to trust Mel. They'd spent the past fourteen months establishing her processing baselines, sensitivity to electronic world nuances, and uploading capacity. He *knew* she had the resources to come to that result.

Mel did things differently from nearly everyone else with the highest-level Dialogue/Netwalk combined chip. Her conclusions about Liam must have logical foundations. He had to believe that—or else the whole underpinning she had been constructing with regard to Netwalk Enforcers would fail.

Marty slumped in the chair, letting his shoulders sag against the soft back.

God. This is too much. I wish Julia was here, not still in Japan.

Julia Hawkins was the Netwalk host for Melanie's late father Will, who was DIR's original Head of Research. Will was the foremost Netwalker working as a Netwalk developer, and much more articulate than Ness about the Netwalk experience from the Netwalker side.

He could use both Will's and Julia's opinions on this.

We keep thinking and talking about Liam. But what if it's really Sarah who's found a way to go rogue?

Sarah. Melanie's grandmother, Diana's mother. Former president/dictator of the North American Confederation. Killed in the struggle that had brought Diana to power; now a Netwalker lodged in Diana's Netwalk chip. And Sarah still wasn't fully trustworthy.

Sarah had done horrible things to her daughter's family when she was still alive, in the name of control and inheritances. Who was to say that it wasn't her doing it now, instead of Liam? Or through Liam?

Marty shook his head. Things were far too complicated.

Maybe we need to go back to Nagano for a while. Let Mel recover away from the New Federation pressures.

She had to get away from the Mountain in order to recover. That much was clear. He reached over and took Melanie's hand, leaning his forehead against it.

God, Mel, I just want you to get better.

He dreaded that it might take a fight with both Melanie and Diana to take Melanie someplace where she could recover without worries.

But for once she has to let go and rest.

"Mama, see what I have!" Sophie burbled to Angela as she solemnly showed her mother the laser ball. "I push it *here* and *here,* and these lights come out! And I stop them!"

"Can you show me?" Angela asked. She looked over at her mother Brenda, Sophie's caretaker, raising a brow. Her mother nodded, smiling.

This should be good, then.

"Sure! Look! See!" Sophie triggered the activation mechanism. She bounced into the center of the room, batting nervously twice at her twin ponytails. Then she watched the ball intently, waiting.

Angela's fingers clenched into fists until the knuckles turned almost-white under brown. This was the first trial for Courts access and Security potential. It was a duplicate of something referred to as the *gadget,* something Nik muttered about in the rarest of unguarded moments after a Courts session. Angela passed the first rounds of testing but couldn't keep up with higher levels.

What can Sophie do?

She was only five. But if Mama Brenda smiled like that—

Light beams flashed at Sophie. She easily deflected them at first with her palms, dipping and spinning, occasionally throwing in a kick to bounce the beams off her feet to her hands to send them back at the ball. Then the beams pulsed faster, and faster, until Sophie couldn't keep up.

Faster than me. Already.

"I keep trying, but it gets harder," Sophie complained. Then she perked up. "But I get better each time!"

"That's good," Angela encouraged. "May I look at it? I want to check something."

Sophie batted the ball to her. Angela turned it over, punching in the command that showed Sophie's performance levels.

8.4, the level read. The equivalence of eight years, four months. Angela looked at her mother as Sophie took the ball and started another sequence.

Brenda nodded. "She definitely has Courts and Security potential. You weren't that good at this age."

"I'm not that good even now." Angela blinked away a tear. "Thank you," she whispered. "Thank you for raising her so well and keeping her safe."

"Thank you for letting me care for her. How soon will you be taking her to the crèche for training?"

"I don't know yet. She's so young. The other children are much older."

"She's *five,* Angela. She's talented. Sooner or later, she needs to venture into the world. You went into the crèche at six. She's ready now—she's learned all that I can teach her."

"I hear you, Mama." Angela turned her attention back to her eager young daughter.

Sophie could be Nik's successor in the Courts.

She shivered. Did she really want her cheerful Sophie to be a part of that grimness that wrapped around Nik every time he came back from the Courts?

On the other hand, why not Nik's daughter to succeed him? That certainly seemed to fit the Courts pattern for the leadership. Might be the same for their Security.

Angela shivered again.

May that day be long in coming.

Nik carried enough darkness for three people.

Melanie stirred slowly, aware that Marty sat beside her and held her hand, leaning his forehead against her knuckles. She wiggled a finger slightly and he looked up. She tried to smile, then flinched at the ache lancing through her face.

Yeah. Right. Facial injuries. Wonder if I can talk?

"Marty?" she tried. Sharp, fiery, twinges of pain jabbed her jaw.

Not good. Mindspeech, maybe?

She blinked to activate her Dialogue. It booted up smoothly.

<Marty?> she said, using subvocal tones. Much less painful.

<You're loud and clear,> he reassured her.

<Good. Hurts to talk.>

<It will for a while. Mindspeech and texting's what you're limited to for a couple of days; at least that's what the doc says.>

<Sorry I was such an idiot,> she said. <Shouldn't have pushed you away. Shouldn't have driven myself to this point. Couldn't see my way past what happened. God, what about the Courts? Will I be able to appear in three weeks—or is it less than that? How long was I out?>

<This is the day after your wreck. Looks like you'll still be able to appear at the Courts. No need to apologize. Should have tried harder to break through to you. Didn't. Should have. Being a coward.>

<Oh God, Marty. You are so not a coward.> She blinked back tears, careful not to duplicate any of the Dialogue blink codes. At least the upper part of her face didn't hurt as bad as her jaw. <I've been played. Didn't see it until after the crash. Sorry. So damned sorry. Should be able to recognize it by now.>

"Stop beating yourself up," Marty said aloud. "Just don't. I want you to think about getting better. Let's not try to solve any problems right now."

<I don't know if we'll have time for that. I need to get the pieces together for my Courts presentation, and then there's that contract with High Space.>

"We'll have time," Marty said, a stubborn tone creeping into his voice. "We'll make time. No matter what your mother thinks."

<Mom? Are things all right with her?>

<Just another crisis. I don't know the details. She said it was an internal Courts issue. I told her we needed some time to get you healthy first. Healthy in all ways, not just physical, Mel.>

Crap. It has to be a Gizmo problem.

<Can't wait,> she said. <Must figure out if Liam's involved and neutralize him. Neutralize his host. Neutralize that whole Freedom Army crowd. They'll do their best to kill High Space. That's their goal.>

And how does this affect Gizmo? Damn it, I wish I knew more about that gadget!

She knew just enough to know she didn't know enough about Gizmo.

Somehow, it had triggered the Disruptions of 2046, a series of catastrophic biologic attacks upon several cities which incorporated not just multiple viruses but neurotoxins, nerve gases, and mutagens. The Osaka Disruption had been so horrific that Sarah had ordered a unilateral nuclear sterilization.

Gizmo created enough of a threat that Sarah and Diana, along with Francis Stewart, the founder of the Freedom Army, had worked together to control it. Its existence was frightening enough to bring about the creation of the international Corporate Courts as a private regulatory body with real teeth, including assassination contracts and formal notices of takeover before launching corporate armies at each other. And that secret cooperation between Sarah and Diana when it came to the Courts and Gizmo was something Melanie was only now beginning to understand.

Need-to-know, her mother had said after Melanie screamed at her about keeping material secret. *You didn't have the need-to-know until you became DIR International.*

Even now, her mother and Sarah still held secrets from her.

Somehow, High Space was tied into the Gizmo control structures. Again, need-to-know? Or something that would come as she was admitted deeper into the Courts infrastructure? Melanie wasn't sure she could look at Zoë Wright in the same way ever again, now that she knew Aunty Zoë was, in effect, the leader of the Courts.

Another disclosure someone didn't feel I needed to know until recently.

"We are NOT chasing down the Freedom Army right this second," Marty shot back at her, speaking aloud again. <Even if you had the time, you're in no shape to do it,> he added.

<That's boring!> she protested.

He smiled at her. <Well, there's a bit of good news. The Johnson Space chip passed QC. Everything else can wait.>

<The Johnson production line's running? Great! Any problems?>

<Switched over from prototype to production quite nicely. Nothing more than the usual small glitches for a first run, nothing that can't be handled at a lower level with occasional bounces to me. For the moment everything's running along smoothly. Nothing so big that it can't wait for a week or so.>

<I hope you're right,> she said.

"I'll make it right," Marty said, firmly. He squeezed Melanie's hand again. "There will always be crises. Always be problems. Our challenge will be to learn how to juggle what we're doing while having time for us. Time for our family."

<If there ever is one.>

<Dearest. We already have a family. We have Nik and Ange, and their Sophie. Your mother. Mama Brenda.>

<But that's not the same!> she objected. <And I don't know if that will satisfy the Courts requirements. Or Mom's inheritance worries.>

<Dearest. It will happen. I promise. We'll find a way to make it happen.>

<How?>

<I don't know yet.> He frowned.

<And if Liam caused my miscarriage and our surrogate's miscarriage? What do we do about that?>

<We find a way to defend against Netwalker interference. Not just for you, but for others in the future.>

Melanie took a deep breath.

Time to change this subject, before I start bawling.

<So. How much longer am I in here?>

"I take you home tomorrow," Marty said. "And you'll rest. Absolutely no work for at least one week. Need to give the nanos time for your face repair to work."

<One week!> she protested. <That long? But I have to get ready for the Courts, and for High Space, and there's going to be follow-ups on that Johnson chip—>

<It's part of learning to make time for ourselves. You need it. I need it.>

<Someone or something will interfere if we stay on the Mountain. Wait and see.>

<So where do we go?> he asked.

<The Andrews Ranch,> she answered quickly. <Where Mom grew up. Over in the Reserve. You've never been there, have you?>

He shook his head. <How secure is it?>

<Enough for what we need. It's behind the No-Fence. The Andrews cousins run it in trust as a heritage ranch and conference center. It has all the com links and facilities we'll need. It should work fine for us. We'll probably even have the main house to ourselves.>

She thought about the pines, the open spaces, and the view of the Bucket Mountains from the ranch house high on a ridge in the canyon country near Blue Bucket Canyon. Yes. It would work.

As safe a place as any.

Indigenous peoples had supported her mother's bid for power, had sheltered Melanie and Marty when they'd been on the run themselves.

It would be a safe place to go until she knew what to do.

A good place to hide.

From everyone except their family, unfortunately.

CHAPTER 3

MARTY AMBLED DOWN THE STAIRS OF THE BIG RANCH HOUSE, SAVORING the quiet.

This was a really good idea.

Until late last night, they had been the only guests in the main house. Melanie and Marty stayed in the primary suite, which took up the southwest corner of the second story; big enough for a small office setup. The windows provided a stunning view of the Bucket Mountains to the south, as well as sunsets. They didn't need to leave it except for meals, if they chose.

It was too bad they couldn't have the entire place to themselves for their entire stay, but that couldn't be helped. Evan Andrews warned Marty earlier in the week that another family guest was expected, but hadn't spilled their identity.

The cousins were tight about security. Had to be, with the family connections. At least he knew the visitor wasn't Melanie's brother Andrew. *That* relative had been persona non grata within the non-Stephens side of the family for years.

And Mel's recovery was progressing faster than expected. The No-Fence's electronic protections blocked potential outside interference with Melanie's nano treatments. As a result, he could give her higher nano dosages with each treatment. Marty hadn't expected the protocol to go this well—some of that was due to his insistence that Mel *rest* and not do any work. Which meant he didn't work other than taking care of her—and that made him realize just how fatigued *he* was.

Have to figure out resting strategies, not just for her but for me.

Voices echoed from the dining area. Marty paused in the living room, trying to identify who was here.

The higher, young voice was Nik and Angela's Sophie, of course. But the two adult female voices—Diana. And Dr. Kathy Miller, Diana's personal medical consultant and black ops maven.

Marty scowled.

I told Diana seven days before we got down to business. Melanie needs the break. So what's Diana doing here? And with Kathy, of all people?

Ness stirred. <This is Kathy's home turf,> she reminded Marty. <If possible, I'd like to say hi to her.>

<Sure,> he agreed.

Of course. How could I forget?

Kathy was Ness's aunt. She had been at her hideaway on Grouse Creek, two ridges over from the Andrews Ranch, when Ness had been killed. His telling Kathy about the circumstances of Ness's death gave Kathy enough warning to prepare for Sarah's pursuit—and began the chain of events that led to Netwalk's discovery. Without Kathy's skilled shot that had brought Sarah's skimmer down, they might not be here today.

Sarah.

If Diana was here, then Sarah was as well.

Marty and Ness both shivered at the thought of Sarah.

But Sarah wasn't his major concern. Diana and her schemes were.

I won't let Diana push Mel into doing anything for two more days. Even with the Courts coming up fast.

He entered the dining room. Diana and Kathy turned to face him. Two matriarchs with brunette hair turning into silver, their lanky bodies framed against the big picture windows with the sweeping vistas of both the Buckets and the Thunders on the other side of Blue Bucket Canyon. Diana rose, plate in hand, her jeans and casual shirt emphasizing her thinness more than her usual formal office wear did.

"Hey, Marty," Diana said.

Marty took a deep breath.

"Hello." He glanced at Kathy. "Ness says hi. Do you want to talk to her? I can bring up a hologlobe for you to chat."

"That would be good," Kathy said.

"Let me set it up." He pulled the hologlobe generator out of his pocket and snapped it open. Ness gracefully slid out of his chip and into the globe.

Diana headed toward the kitchen.

"I hope you're here for some down time," Marty said as he followed. Rita, the Andrews cousin in charge of breakfast, had several warming trays prepared with breakfast meats and scrambled eggs. Biscuits, bread for toast, and fresh fruit sat in trays next to the warmers. Rita leaned against the stove, sipping coffee, her dark blue eyes measuring both Marty and Diana evenly. She met Diana's nod with one of her own.

"Ride today?" Diana asked Rita, ignoring Marty. He bit his lip and waited his turn.

"Works for me," Rita said. "Thought you'd want to check out that Challenger colt. Darn boy wants to cut anything that moves. Evan's still mad about how that colt ran the legs off of his best bull calf last year when the calf got into the colt's pasture, made the calf unfit for the big fall shows."

A quick smile touched Diana's lips. "Sounds like a date. Won't interfere with anything that you're doing?"

Rita shook her head.

"As for Mel, I thought I'd check on how things were going, that's all," Diana told Marty as she took some bacon and poured herself more coffee. "No problem with that, is there?"

"No," Marty said, reluctantly.

"Good." Diana returned to the dining room.

Marty chose fresh fruit and scrambled eggs, taking his time to pour a cup of coffee.

Just wish I knew if that really is what you are doing here.

"How's Melanie doing today?" Rita asked.

He popped two slices of bread into the toaster.

"Getting better," he said. He nodded toward the dining room. "When did she make her reservation?"

"I can't tell you that. Privacy. Works for you, works for them, y'know?"

"Yeah." His toast popped up. "Had to try, though."

"So did *she*." Rita scowled. "And she got as much out of me as you are."

"Thanks," he said, before going back to the dining room. He settled in, preparing for an argument, sipping his coffee while he decided on an approach. Kathy glanced once at him, then continued talking to Ness. From what he could tell, it was social, not technical conversation.

"How's Melanie?" Diana asked. She tapped her fingers on the table. Her face was noticeably thinner than it had been a week ago, after Melanie's crash.

Or did her face just look fuller then as a com artifact?

He couldn't be sure. Diana definitely looked more strained and tense.

Worrying about Mel—or something else?

Marty put his cup down. "She needs two more quiet days. Optimal for her recovery. You said you have Courts material to cover with her. That needs to wait."

Diana grimaced and a Sarah-esque expression tightened her forehead and brows. "There's no way to speed up the process? Damn it, things are developing and I need—"

"Di." Kathy's voice projected firmly across the room, almost as commanding as Melanie's in Enforcer mode.

Not quite Enforcer level, though.

Mel had scanned Kathy months ago. Kathy lacked aptitude for some of the virtual skills that Melanie considered important in an Enforcer. And yet—she had influence over Diana. How? Why?

Diana frowned at Kathy. Kathy shook her head in the barest of motions.

Diana refocused on Marty. "Is there any way we can speed things up? What's her current status?"

"Nano taper starts tomorrow." He tightened his lips. "Bad enough I have to wrestle her down to keep her from going hammer and tongs on the Courts presentation before the seven days are up. I don't need you pushing her."

For a moment he thought Diana was going to snap at him. Then Kathy cleared her throat. He saw the light flashes of text across Diana's eyes before she blinked a masking pattern. Kathy didn't mask. They scowled at each other, the texts flying furiously between them from the flashes in Kathy's eyes. But Diana was the first to look away.

"I get it," she said in a low voice. "But I'm struggling with the clearances. I need Mel's help for that—and the other thing."

"I *told* you I'd help with those clearances," Kathy said. "I'm as good at those as Melanie is. About the other thing—you know damn good and well that Mel will be ready. She's your daughter and Sarah's granddaughter. She'll be ready."

"God, I hope so. We didn't need this mess."

"It could mean they underestimate Mel. Let's hope for that. Andrew's the only one who knows how quickly his sister can recover."

"And thank God for that," Diana said.

What the hell are they talking about?

Must be the Courts. Something Kathy didn't want Diana discussing with him.

And just how does she fit in with the Courts?

"Ladies," he decided to venture. "Whatever this is, it needs to wait. Nothing changes on that front."

"No beating around the bush, hmm?" Diana's face softened. "Marty. Bristles down. *I understand.* I've already gotten this lecture from Angela. Kathy's gotten her licks in as well. I get the picture. Melanie still needs the rest."

"I don't think you understand how badly she needs it."

"Message received. Besides, after Rita's story about that Challenger colt, I want to give him a spin, see if he's as good as she says he is." Diana grinned suddenly. "If he is, I might just have to find a way to slip into a competition or two. Rita keeps telling me he's something good."

Slippers shuffled on the hardwood floor and Marty looked up. Melanie. He pulled out a chair as she hobbled over to him. Diana swiftly hid a quick, surprised expression as she surveyed Mel, then exchanged glances with Kathy.

Yes. She's hurting.

Melanie's face was scarred and red from her injuries. The knee brace didn't quite fit her, but he hadn't been able to get a replacement shipped in yet. Her already tiny body had dropped weight due to food restrictions and lack of appetite due to pain.

"I guess this means it's time for me to get back to work," Melanie said to her mother, moving her lips as little as possible.

Marty rested a hand on her shoulder. "I'll get you some food."

Melanie nodded. Across the room, Kathy turned away from the hologlobe. Ness slipped back into his chip. Marty snapped the globe closed. The generator still sat there but he'd pick it up after he got Melanie's food.

That is, if someone didn't get a wild idea to fire it up and suck Mel into doing virtual work. He picked up the generator and slipped it into his pocket before he went into the kitchen. One way to prevent that from happening. Diana and Kathy might have globe generators of their own, but this made them pull them out.

"Getting food for Mel," he said.

"She ready for solid stuff?" Rita asked.

Marty shook his head.

"Afraid that would be the case. Got yogurt in the fridge, also some fruit I ran through the blender. Think scrambled eggs will work?"

"Shouldn't be too much of a problem."

"Good. I've got a fresh batch right here." Rita scraped the eggs onto a plate.

"Thanks, Rita. We appreciate your help."

Rita shrugged. "You two going out again this afternoon? Weather forecast looks good."

"We're planning to do that, unless we get sidetracked by work. I'm doing my best to prevent that, but with *her* here that could be a problem."

"You won't have a problem with Diana," Rita said. "That Challenger colt will keep her occupied this afternoon. I know Diana. He's a descendant of her old Kokanee mare, who was out of her father's famous Mocha mare. She won't be able to keep away from him."

"Thanks."

"Better get those eggs to Mel before they get cold."

"Thanks," he repeated. He grabbed the yogurt and fruit from the refrigerator, put that plus the plate of eggs on a tray, then added a cup of coffee and carried it to the dining room.

Melanie frowned at Diana. Marty spotted brief flashes of color across her eyes from her visual overlays.

At least she's texting and not talking.

Melanie smiled up at him as he set the tray in front of her.

<Thanks,> she said.

<What's her game?>

<So far, she says she's just here for some downtime and to play with that Challenger colt. Like hell she is. Kathy's here, too. Something's up.>

<You are *not* going to let her suck you into doing anything just yet,> Marty insisted. <I've already told her that. So has Angela. And now *I'm* telling *you*.>

Diana cleared her throat sharply, catching their attention.

"Thank you. Now. Let's get some things straight, you two. I'm just here for planning sessions with Kathy, and a trial of that Challenger colt that Rita's been talking up to me," Diana said. "I understand the rules, okay?"

Melanie snorted. She carefully sipped her fruit puree.

Diana raised an eyebrow. "I'm serious. And I needed to consult with Kathy. You can't object to that."

Her eyes met Melanie's. Mother and daughter glared at each other once again.

Melanie put down her puree. She picked up her coffee cup and sipped it from, her eyes not leaving Diana's. Then slowly, deliberately, she placed her cup down.

"Two more days," she said as firmly as she could while moving her lips as little as possible. Still, she managed to bring up a full Enforcer tone, emphasized with the sharpness of her glance.

Marty quickly took a drink of coffee, hiding the grin that threatened to pop out.

That's my girl. Got her Enforcer tones back. That would freeze old Sarah herself!

He sent Melanie a wordless sense of satisfaction via Dialogue.

Melanie gave him a sideways grin, a mere flicker, then refocused on her mother.

Diana frowned. She dropped her eyes and picked up a biscuit. She broke it in half, concentrating on spreading the butter, then adding jam to each biscuit half.

At last she looked back up. "Two more days," she said. "I promised. But after that, we have urgent business."

"I understand," Melanie agreed. "But not until then." She looked back at Marty.

<See? I did it.>

<Good.> But he worried about Diana's urgent business.

Something about the Courts and High Space, if it's what she was talking about when Mel got hurt.

But High Space didn't involve Netwalk concerns.

Yet. And who knew what the hell was going on with the Courts?

Should I check with Mel about that?

Let it go, he decided. Melanie managed their interface with the Courts. He usually didn't have that level of clearance.

Meanwhile, he resolved to have a quick chat with Kathy about keeping Diana distracted and away from Melanie during the last two treatment days.

MELANIE LAY QUIETLY IN MARTY'S ARMS DURING THEIR AFTERNOON NAP on one of the high ridges near the ranch, gazing at the sky. He snored softly. The tall Ponderosa pine branches swayed with the afternoon breeze, and the soft roar of the wind through the branches lulled her into a half-daze that nearly eased her back into sleep.

Almost. Seeing her mother reminded her of the countdown toward the Courts meeting. Yes, she was ahead of the presentation timeline. But there were always little pieces demanding unexpected attention that wouldn't come up until the last minute. The presence of Diana—and Sarah—reminded Melanie of the lost prep time thanks to her injuries. She also worried about the Johnson Space contract. Marty hinted that there might be problems, but they hadn't gotten so huge as to break this week's hiatus from work.

The tingle in her face from this morning's nano dosage also kept her wakeful.

Supposedly, she shouldn't be able to feel them. But she did, every single day, though until today, that sensation had been a mild irritation, something she could sleep through and ignore.

My paranoia about the nanos?

Possibly. But that hadn't been a factor on other days.

Getting better?

More likely. Melanie hadn't been able to use Enforcer vocal tones since her accident. Considering how sore her face and jaw still felt, she hadn't expected to use them this quickly, this easily.

And yet, this morning, when her mother started pushing, the tones came back easily.

Unconscious threat. Polyvagal threat response. That's what it was.

Her Dialogue Enforcer capabilities ebbed and flowed with limbic system factors that neither she nor Marty fully understood. Yet. They were getting better at figuring those things out.

Probably Sarah's presence.

Sarah always lurked as a possible threat, something to be guarded against at all times.

And, speaking of Sarah—

Maybe Sarah had let something slip to Ness about whatever this urgent internal Courts business was.

<Any word from Sarah?> she asked Ness, stirring her awake in Marty's chip, careful to keep the mindspeech directed specifically at Ness so not to wake Marty.

<Not a hint,> Ness said, responding in a similar, cautious manner. <Your mother keeps Sarah tightly locked up. Problems there.>

<Do I need to intervene? Maybe Mom needs a check.> Melanie regularly ran Enforcer scans on Sarah and Diana. Sarah had been a predatory Netwalker before they tied her to Diana as a host. Netwalkers without hosts were driven to kill Dialogues to obtain energy to sustain their existence, and Sarah had been a top Netwalk predator.

<I don't think it's that bad,> Ness said.

<Maybe I need to have Kathy run some checks on Mom. Marty can ask.>

<He met with Kathy about that earlier, before she and Diana went on the trail ride with Rita. Part of Diana's consultation with Kathy. Health concerns of Netwalk. Outside opinions. Sounds like Kathy will be spending more time in Vancouver with Diana in the future.>

Well, that could be both good and bad.

Kathy served in a similar position to Diana as Nik served to Melanie with regard to Courts representation, had done so ever since Diana became New Federation President.

Damn, I wish Kathy had the aptitude to be an Enforcer. It would make things simpler with Sarah.

Marty stirred, groaning. His arms tightened around Melanie and his lips brushed the top of her head.

<You two talking shop?> he asked.

<A little,> Melanie said. <I'd like to know what's going on with Mom. Ness says you talked with Kathy.>

<Kathy's not happy with how your mom and Sarah relate. She wants your mom to do a better job of checking in. That's all that's going on—or at least what Kathy will talk about.> Marty propped himself up on one elbow and studied Melanie's face. "Ness. Let's do a nano reaction check," he said aloud.

Ness shimmered into sight, hovering above Melanie's face in miniature form.

"Ready," Ness said aloud, in the tinny, electronic voice she had when appearing outside of a hologlobe.

Melanie stared into the branches above her as Marty and Ness worked, willing herself not to flinch or move. The measurements tracked the details of the nanobot workings. She hated this twice-daily poking and prodding of her face, but it was how her healing was assessed.

Her fingers clenched into fists. She forced herself to breathe evenly and smoothly. It felt like the lines of the nanos' working had spread further across her face.

At least I'll be scarless within a week.

The discoloration would take longer to fade. But one week as opposed to months for scar healing was one good reason to go through with this process. She was vain about looking good. No. To be more precise, she wanted to look glam. Scars weren't glam.

I got that from Sarah.

Scary to consider that she and Sarah shared a desire to look good.

Finally, Marty and Ness finished.

"Good progress," Marty said. He reached for the syringe containing her next dose. Melanie closed her eyes, forcing herself to relax as he gently injected the nanos into the newest sites.

At least it's Marty doing this.

She didn't want anyone but him giving her nanos.

"I'm starting you on a quick taper tomorrow," he said. "This is your last megadose."

"How many residual nanos will I have in my system over the long term?" she asked, like she did after every treatment.

"We won't know for the next year or so," he answered.

Melanie opened her eyes and looked up at him. Marty gently stroked her brows.

"This isn't the same as the cosmetic nanos Sarah was doing at the end," he told her, as he had said at least once a day since the treatments began.

She shivered. "I know."

But didn't Sarah start doing nanos after something like this? Recovery after an accident? God. I hope I never become like her.

They'd both started with similar motivations, although hers was to heal quickly, as opposed to Sarah's battle against aging. But both of them had wanted to look beautiful.

Is looking good worth the price?

She hoped so.

CHAPTER 4

TWO DAYS LATER, MARTY WALKED ARM IN ARM WITH MELANIE INTO THE dining room, all too aware their grace period was over. Diana gazed at a hologlobe, to all appearances relaxed, but the imperceptible aura of tension in the room made it clear to him that she was just waiting for an opportunity to launch into discussion about *those issues.*

Diana looked up, brows raising as she scrutinized Melanie carefully, lips pursing in surprise.

"I didn't realize those nanos could be this effective," she said.

"I'm still on the taper," Melanie said. "There will be even more improvement."

Marty went into the kitchen.

<You tell me if they start arguing via subvocals,> he ordered Ness.

<I'm not going to mess with Sarah!>

<Not asking you to tangle with Sarah. Just tell me if Diana and Mel start fighting. Diana's on the prod. Nerves. And Mel's no better today.>

<Okay.>

Rita looked up from the stove. "Soft foods still?"

"As long as I can keep her on them."

"Diana's been in there for a while," Rita murmured as he grabbed yogurt and fruit for Melanie and a pastry for himself.

Marty froze. "I thought privacy kept you from telling—"

"Not breaking any boundaries. She's worried about Melanie, and her own stuff. Said as much to me. Okay?"

"Got it." Marty poured coffees for himself and Melanie. "Anything else?"

Rita shook her head.

Marty balanced the tray carefully on his way back to the table. Diana sipped her coffee, staring thoughtfully toward the east. Melanie looked south, toward the Buckets.

<I thought you were going to tell me if they started arguing!> he said to Ness.

<They haven't said anything much at all. It's weird.>

<Okay.> He set the tray down. <Everything all right?> he asked Melanie.

<Just wanted some quiet time. I told Mom that, and she agreed.>

<Good.> Marty settled into his chair.

Diana took a deep breath and put down her coffee. "How much longer will this taper take?"

Melanie gestured toward Marty.

"She should have two more days behind the No-Fence for safety. But she can start working now, with rest and frequent breaks."

My addition. She could go hardcore. But I'd like her to rest a bit longer.

Melanie poked at her food listlessly.

A reaction? Or just not wanting to eat at the moment, wondering what bombshell is going to get dumped on her now?

He wasn't much better, fiddling with his coffee cup and poking at his pastry.

We're both tense about this.

"I still need to do staggered treatments on her," he added. "Optimal treatment pattern."

Diana put down her fork and exhaled heavily. "Several big Netwalk issues have presented themselves," she said. "That's one reason why I met with Kathy. Melanie's conclusions about Liam's influence made me seek Kathy's feedback about any impact Sarah might have on me. Just in case."

"I think that's a good idea," Marty said.

"I'm even more concerned about Liam's potential influence on

Melanie than I was a few days ago. Let me show you." Diana slipped a hologlobe generator out of a sleeve pocket and placed it on the table, triggering it. The globe spun over the table, shimmering in the morning light. "This just happened last night. Sarah, run the latest Freedom Army vid for us, and narrate the stats."

Freedom Army.

Melanie and Marty exchanged glances. The Freedom Army was Liam's old political faction, the shards of which were being hunted down and jailed. Until last year's civil war, the members of the Freedom Army had been battling the Confederation, the business-oriented oligarchy ruled by Sarah when she was alive.

Before Sarah's death, the Freedom Army fought against her. Once she died, though, they gave their allegiance to Sarah's political heirs—first Peter Stephens, Diana's brother, and, upon Peter's death, to Melanie's brother Andrew. Andrew managed to avoid prison only because he directly repudiated the support he had received from the Freedom Army during his short tenure as Sarah's successor. But Marty suspected there were still links between Andrew and the Army.

Politics don't allow for further prosecution without any real evidence.

Not for someone in Andrew's position as president of Stephens Reclamation, and with his connections.

Marty slipped one hand into Melanie's.

I don't like this.

Sarah slowly gained shape inside the hologlobe, looking much like she had before she died. Unnaturally stiff, young-looking face, silver-white hair, and the formal cream-colored, high-necked jacket and slacks she'd worn frequently during her last living days.

"This vid was recorded at midnight two days ago," she said. "It was taken at a maximum-security National Security facility in the Midwest—Leavenworth sub B24. The site includes political prisoners from last year's war."

Numbers ran down the middle and around the edge of the sphere as the facility blinked into existence inside the globe. Marty noted the quality of the electronic monitoring, the restrictive Guard-Fence design (a proprietary Do It Right product) that controlled access in and out of the prison, and the numbers of human personnel assigned to supplement the Guard-Fence.

Movement. An unmarked truck rolled up to the main gate.

"Whoever these people were," Sarah droned, "they had the Guard-Fence codes. Not only that, but they had prearranged a delivery with the staff."

Marty nodded, resting his chin on his free hand, watching intently. <Ness, are you recording this?>

<Absolutely.>

<Good.> He wanted to watch it again later.

The truck entered unchallenged. Their perspective changed to an inside camera.

"Sarah, what's the sourcing on this?" Melanie asked.

"Pieced together from raw data of the security recordings," Sarah said.

"Who put together this clip?" Marty picked up the questioning.

"Kathy," Diana said. "This is just the latest of several incidents. I'm preparing a Cabinet presentation as well as one for the Courts because, well, you'll see."

The truck stopped. A small group of uniformed, armed men and women hopped out, led by a small woman with close-cropped blonde hair. They outnumbered the facility staff who approached them, their weapons hanging loosely.

"I'm slowing the recording," Sarah said. "Half-speed."

Slowly, jerkily, the blonde raised a hand. Even with the slow-mo, the speed at which her group brought their weapons up shocked Marty.

They're good. Well-drilled. Or are they augmented?

"Quarter-speed," Sarah said. The camera focused on the blonde. Her features transformed, and Melanie's hand tightened hard on Marty's.

"That's Liam!" she gasped.

Marty stared. The body was clearly that of the young woman's, but....

Her round face slimmed to Liam's long, narrow shape with sharp jaw, the faint scar from the skimmer crash curved down his right cheek. Black hair, not blonde. A bare hint of the blonde's original features remained underneath Liam's face.

Digital overlay. How did he do that? Netwalker for sure. But what the hell is the Netwalker version that changes a host's features? Peter did it with Andrew, but we thought it was a one-off, something unique. Hell!

Gunfire erupted. The focus pulled back. The young woman with Liam's face led the group away from the courtyard as the video clip ended.

"All twelve of the Freedom Army prisoners in Leavenworth sub B24 escaped," Sarah said. "No trace of prisoners or attacking force has been found."

"Who. Is. That. Woman?" Melanie demanded, her hand gripping Marty's tightly.

"Visual records match identifies her as Deirdre Conley," Sarah answered. "DNA traces from this site and others match that ID. This isn't the first raid she's led wearing Liam's face."

"Who the hell is Deirdre Conley?" Melanie glowered at Sarah.

"She was born into the Freedom Army and raised in their crèche," Diana said. "No data on her parents, who were apparently Army members. Our inside sources place her as someone close to Liam, a member of his inner cell. Data we've intercepted suggest that she is his Netwalk host.

"This confirms that the Freedom Army has Netwalk." Melanie's lips tightened. "Finding more potential Enforcer candidates is absolutely crucial. It's not just High Space but the Courts and the gadget. Liam with his own army of Netwalkers—god." She drew a deep, ragged breath. "What I saw when I fell—"

"Can we identify the process by which Conley changed her features?" he asked.

"It's tied to that version of Netwalk," Diana said.

"But if this is the only record we have—" Marty gestured toward the hologlobe.

"We have confirmed data from seven more incidents, with as many as ten more incidents possible." Diana grimaced. "We didn't realize they were connected until a day ago. This was the first one where the Liam transformation was actually recorded."

"And the quick response of her team? Augmentation?" Marty pressed his tongue against the back of his teeth.

"Very possible. We don't know that for certain. Not enough data available to us to analyze yet." Diana waved her hand, and Sarah faded into Diana's chip. She tapped the hologlobe generator to close it.

"They see us as a potential means to shut down High Space." Melanie's tone was flat. "What a convenient way to achieve their goals while advancing Liam's personal agenda. Use Netwalk to cause my miscarriage. Thwarts our goals for the Courts. Links Liam to Giz—" she cut it short, glancing sideways at Marty. "You know what I mean!"

"This links Liam to the gadget as well," Diana said. "Just what you said." She sighed. "Oh, *hell.* Might as well get this over with now." She pulled out a different hologlobe generator. Marty recognized it as a mechanically-locked secure generator, colored bright orange so that it was easy to see the difference between the automatically secure generator and those that had to be manually reset to a secure status.

"What needs that degree of security?" Melanie asked.

"Courts business." Diana expanded the globe. Marty shivered at the tell-tale vibration as the sphere's edge passed through him.

"Is this disclosable before I'm sworn? What about Marty?

"At this level, yes. Need-to-know."

Darkness and silence surrounded them as the hologlobe stabilized. Unlike other globes, the secure globes blocked all outside sound and light. Faint red schematics glowed from the perimeter barrier.

Melanie opened her hand and a pale blue glow radiated from it. Marty swallowed hard. He'd seen her do this before in secured hologlobes, ever since she figured out this Netwalk tool six months ago, but it still sent chills through him when she did it. Her lips moved without sound and the glow expanded until it fully lit the globe.

"Thank you," Diana said. "It takes me too long to light one of these secured globes. You seem to be able to do it without thinking."

"Enforcer skill," Melanie said. She tucked her good leg underneath her. "Now. Just what the hell is going on, Mom?"

Part of the blue glow outlined Melanie.

Stronger than before. Has she been practicing without telling me?

"First, tell me what you meant about Liam and Gizmo," Diana said. "When you said you saw something after your fall."

"No," Melanie said slowly, deliberately. "That comes after what *you* need to tell *me*."

"God damn it, you're being stubborn!"

"Like you and Sarah aren't? Damn it, Mom, I'm tired of this treatment! Of being the one who has to disclose everything first, and maybe getting half of the information I need to know—this has gone on *too long!*"

"Hey! This isn't getting us anywhere!" Marty snapped. "Diana, you've been hinting around that there's something big you need to talk about to Mel—and Mel only—since her accident. Now if I have to leave for you to talk to her, then I'll do it." He started to get up.

"No!" Melanie frowned at him. "You stay. She said you need to know." <And I want you here. For the whole thing.>

Marty sat back down. "Then let's stop the wrangling and start talking!" Usually Melanie and Diana didn't act like this. *More influence from outside?* "What's with you two? You're both on the prod. It's like someone or something is influencing you."

Melanie winced. "You're right," she said to Marty. She waved her hands and dropped them on her thighs. "Mom. I'm sorry, but chronological order makes sense to me. What comes first—my information or yours?"

"Before yours," Diana sighed. "Mel, I'm sorry. There's a lot going on, and—well—" she shook her head. "Before I can say more, I need to swear you both. Official Courts oaths."

"Will this supersede the need for me to swear later?"

"No. Situational oath."

<Situational means we have to swear every time this level of information is disclosed,> Melanie told Marty.

<I've never done it.>

<I have. Be prepared. It's—different. It feels like an unattuned hologlobe times two. And it leaves a monitoring trace for seven days. You *can't* talk about it with others who aren't sworn. Stricter than a non-disclosure agreement. And you need to shut Ness down. Safer for both of us.> "Okay," Melanie said out loud. "I'm ready. Marty?"

He shrugged. "Ready." *Where did this tech come from?* At least Melanie seemed familiar with it.

Diana grimaced. "I'll be glad when you're fully sworn and you can administer oaths, Melanie. It's harder to do than it looks."

"Just get this over with," Melanie said. The blue glow around her dimmed.

Diana closed her eyes. She sat up tall and whispered codes. Melanie tensely stared at the center of the globe.

A tingling sensation similar to that of the warning zap of an unattuned hologlobe started at Marty's toes and slowly worked its way up his body. As it rose, the prickling intensified to small, sharp shocks.

He couldn't sense Melanie's presence in virtual.

What the hell?

A malign, blood-red glow formed in the center in the globe. It changed to coppery red, backlit by a pale green light. As the coppery glow took a tangible shape and swallowed the green light, Marty quivered involuntarily. A sideways glimpse revealed that both Melanie and Diana shook along with him. Marty closed his eyes as the pain increased, biting his lip to keep from crying out as white-hot needles pricked up and down his body.

It stopped. Marty opened his eyes. A metallic sphere taller than him spun in front of them, sharp points slowly retreating inside the copper-colored structure. Green light spilled from tiny openings in the sphere.

That was more than an unattuned hologlobe times two!

Melanie stood and gestured to him. <Follow what I do. Repeat what I say and how I say it.>

He nodded.

Slowly, Melanie placed her left hand on the sphere. Her hand went inside, up to her wrist bones, green light spilling around her forearm but stopping at the pale blue light that still came forth from her. Marty swallowed hard and followed suit. To his surprise, except for a line of cold around his wrist, he didn't feel anything unusual.

"I am Melanie Landreth Fielding," she said. "I solemnly swear that the secrets we discuss in this globe at this time will not be disclosed except to another who is so sworn." She winced, then nodded at Marty.

"I am Martin Fielding. I solemnly swear that the secrets we discuss in this globe at this time will not be disclosed except to another who is so sworn." As he finished, a white-hot flash swept through his body. He couldn't move his tongue, much less subvocal.

"I am Diana Stephens Landreth," Diana said. "I observe and witness these oaths. So do we swear."

"So do we swear," Melanie repeated.

Now he could speak. "So do we swear," he said, his tongue thick and heavy, having to overemphasize the *s* sounds to keep from slurring.

Melanie withdrew her hand. Marty pulled his out.

Is there more?

Melanie heaved a heavy sigh. "Marty. Wake Ness. Netwalkers need to sleep through the oath. They—at least Sarah does—react in an odd way to the Gizmo. Let's see what Ness does."

"Melanie—" Diana began.

"I'll take responsibility," Melanie said.

"Is it safe?" he asked.

"It is with me here," Melanie said. The blue glow rose again.

<Ness?> he called. <They want you to come out.>

<I—I'm not s-sure, Marty.>

<Mel raised her Enforcer aspect. It's safe.>

Silence. Then, slowly, reluctantly. <Okay. But—but Marty. That's a Gizmo analog. I could—react wrong.>

<Mel's here.>

No response. But he felt Ness slowly easing out; not normally but in a very slow and precise manner. For a moment she hovered next to him. Then she screeched and *dove* at the sphere.

Spikes popped out of the sphere and a jagged green light sparked toward Ness from two spikes. Melanie *moved* between Ness and the sphere, shoving Ness away. Blue glow formed a shield around her that deflected the jagged green light back toward the sphere—toward *Gizmo*.

Ness keened. She changed shape into a falcon and perched on his shoulder, continuing a high-pitched screech.

"*Stop*." Melanie's voice rolled authoritatively. Jagged green light ceased dancing between the spikes. Ness stopped screeching. The green light died down and the spikes snapped back into the sphere, this time with a loud clang.

"Well, *that* was interesting," Diana said. "Marty, Ness, this is Gizmo." She took a deep breath. "Welcome to the reason that the Corporate Courts were created."

What the hell?

"There's more to it than that," Sarah suddenly said.

Marty jumped. He hadn't seen Sarah come out.

Diana scowled and bristled. "I didn't give you permission!"

Sarah laughed. Her cackle echoed around the sphere. She changed from the stiff white-clad persona she'd presented when narrating the Freedom Army video to a younger self in a navy-blue skirt suit with a red blouse and white scarf with blue stars. But the sharp lines in her face and the faint hint of red in her eyes made Marty nervous.

"Sarah, stop it," Melanie said, moving closer to her, raising her palms toward Sarah. "Mom, you know Gizmo has that effect on her. You have to watch her."

Diana shook her head. "She was too fast. I'm usually more in control at the Courts, around the real thing. Damn it, Sarah—"

"She's out now, let her speak. God knows, she's forgotten more about Gizmo than anyone knows."

"But—how?" His head was spinning. Gizmo and the Corporate Courts? "How does this device relate to the Courts? Why is Sarah saying it's more than that?"

Melanie raised a brow. "Sarah?"

"You'll let me talk?" Sarah sneered.

"*Sarah.*" Melanie's voice took on the deeper, rolling command tone.

"Oh, all right," Sarah said. She drew herself up, shape blurring slightly, until she was once again the stiff figure in the formal white suit. "The Corporate Courts were created as a means to monitor and control the behavior of the Gizmo device. These actions were deemed necessary once it was determined that Gizmo triggered the Disruptions of 2046."

"*What?*" He tried and failed to speak, words fighting to make their way out of his mouth. Melanie nodded. He realized this information was no surprise to her.

Part of the Courts' secrets? What else does she know that I don't?

"It's true," Diana said. "I was part of that founding group. As was Will, and twenty other corporate leaders worldwide."

"But—how—why—how could this thing—what?"

"You left out the point that's germane to what we're discussing now," Melanie said, a sharp edge in her voice as she raised her palms to face Sarah again. "Get on with it, Sarah."

"I'm getting there," Sarah said. "We managed to capture and disable it. That was when Francis—" Her voice caught. "The Freedom Army rose at the same time as the Gizmo. Between movements like the Army, and the chaos from the electronic, economic, and systems failures resulting from the Disruption, we decided that the only secure way to guard Gizmo was to create our own international, corporate-based governing body. Ergo, the Corporate Courts."

Marty gestured. "This—created the Disruptions? This—is why the Corporate Courts exist?"

"Yes," Sarah said.

"But then—the politics, the fighting—why is the Freedom Army what it is?"

"Because Francis Stewart was bug-ass crazy," Melanie said. "I never met him, but even *I* know that."

"I wouldn't call it exactly that," Sarah said.

Diana snorted. "Melanie speaks more truly than you'd like to admit. Stewart was crazy. Look at what he did with the Freedom Army!"

"You believed him as much as I did." Sarah scowled at Diana.

"To my regret, yes. *Then.* Now, back inside."

"I don't have any fun at all," Sarah growled. "I should be the one telling this."

"You," Diana said firmly, "lack the appropriate discretion about what can and can't be told at this stage. We're reaching limits. Soon. Back inside! Now!"

"And if I don't go?"

"You know what I'll do." Diana lifted her hands toward Sarah's head. Melanie took two steps as blue light grew brighter around her.

"I'm going." Sarah shrank down and disappeared.

Diana sighed. "You see the problem. At least Ness is compliant around Gizmo. Sarah gets downright rebellious, and it gets worse with every exposure."

<Marty, can I go back in now?> Ness asked.

"Just a moment," Marty said to Melanie and Diana. <You're sure about this?> he asked Ness.

<*Yes.* That—thing—makes me edgy.>

<Then yes, go on back.>

<Thank you!>

"Ness wanted to go back inside my chip," he said.

"Hmm." Melanie dropped into a chair, leaning her elbow on one arm and resting her chin on her palm. "Sarah gets aggressive and Ness gets nervous. Gizmo definitely has an effect on all Netwalkers. I didn't know that. I thought it was tied to Sarah's previous experience—unless Ness has had an exposure I don't know about."

Diana exhaled. "Not relevant to our current issue."

"Which is?" Melanie asked.

"Something's wrong with our containment," Diana said. "Gizmo's behavior has become unpredictable over the past six months. It's tried to escape the Cham—the place where we have it locked. Escape attempts have been escalating, stronger with a higher intensity. I needed to use Sarah the last two times to pull up old strategies from the past. The first one happened the morning you wrecked, Melanie. The old headsets won't work against it anymore. I've been on call because chipped Dialogue support amongst those with Gizmo access is limited."

"Crap." Melanie sagged back against the chair back. "And Sarah's getting more difficult as a result of that type of exposure. We need other methods to control Gizmo."

"That's why getting approval for Dialogue is crucial. And Netwalk. It may be our only chance to keep Gizmo under control."

"Or else we risk more Disruptions."

"It'd be worse this time," Diana said. "It seems to be learning. It's getting new energy from somewhere, over the past six months."

"We don't just need Dialogues, we need Enforcers." Melanie stared at the Gizmo analog.

"Yes. We need High Space. We also have to eliminate the Freedom Army as a threat." Diana clicked her tongue against her teeth. "The Gizmo breakout attempts match attempted Security breaches from outside its current storage. No one's been captured, but from what we've been able to figure out, these attacks are led by Freedom Army cells."

Melanie coughed a short, sharp laugh. "Talk about getting worse and worse. Has Conley been leading those attacks?"

Diana shook her head. "Not yet."

"She has a Netwalker. Worse, she has *Liam.* If she leads an attack on Gizmo security—" Melanie groaned. "So. Just before I passed out after my crash, I saw Liam."

"You had him on your mind that morning. Makes sense."

"No." Melanie's voice dropped. "No. I felt him as a Netwalker. *And he had Gizmo behind him. Just like we saw it right now.*"

Marty shivered.

Why didn't she tell me about this? Secrecy about Gizmo?

"You're sure of that?" Diana leaned forward.

Melanie nodded. "With what you just showed me? Yes." She uncoiled, gasping as she straightened her injured knee too quickly.

"We have to worry about the link of Freedom Army, Liam and Netwalk."

"Yeah." Melanie stood up. "How much did Liam know before he died? Not from spying on us, but from Peter?"

"He was being groomed to be Nik and Kathy's counterpart for Peter in the Courts," Diana said. "I believe he may even have gone through investiture."

"God," Melanie said tiredly. "I should not have taken this week off."

"You've been hurt," Diana said. "You needed to get stronger."

"But at what cost?"

"There's more," Diana said. "This Netwalk situation isn't the only thing I need to talk to you two about. The High Space contract with Johnson has gone to hell. Looks more and more like deliberate internal sabotage." She sighed. "As a result, I need Do It Right to take over our space station's primary contract. Johnson Space has bugged out on us."

Surprise, surprise—not. That confirmed Marty's suspicions. *Could have told you that a month ago.*

"We're supposed to step into Johnson Space's role with two weeks' notice?" Melanie asked. "We were told that we weren't big enough."

"If your brother can piece together a program with Mexico to get Stephens into the mix, you can create a program for DIR to represent the New Federation," Diana said. "That proposal for zero-gravity chip production would work, and it solves a big DIR problem with consistent production."

"That program was originally rejected because it wasn't big enough to provide financial support for a station at projected High Space production levels. That's why we were made a Johnson subcontractor," Marty said.

"Add bioremediation options for terraforming stations, maybe planetary and asteroid surfaces in the future, and space station microbe chasing, and it's now sufficiently similar to the big projects to make an independent station," Diana said. "Standards have changed as programs like Johnson's failed. Creating a matrix of specialty programs is now a feasible independent station option."

"Mmm. Possibilities," Marty said. He could see it.

"I have data on the microbe-fighting issues; it's something that's been of concern to High Space for some time but no one's working on it," Diana said. "I'm sure that DIR, especially the Rio crowd, can figure out how to deal with space station microbe overgrowth."

"So what is Andrew doing for High Space?" Melanie asked.

"Stephens is doing little bit of everything on their satellite. Transportation work with Troubadour, chip grows for Mei-lein, and pharmaceutical development for Stephens. The Mexicans are giving him free rein because they want a spot in space, badly. But his big thing is pharma."

"I need to have the numbers to make sure it works," Melanie said. "He can have the pharma. That's not our specialty area."

Diana placed two fingertip chips on the table. "I know. The New Federation has authorized me to pass this data to you. Blue one's for you, Mel. Red one's for Marty. Everything you'll need to know about the latest info needed for High Space principals." She paused, Dialogue overlays flashing across her eyes in faint blues and reds. "Looks like I need to retreat to my office away from the office here. Buzz me if you have any questions. We need to log out."

Without being prompted, Marty joined Melanie next to the Gizmo analog and reluctantly pushed his hand inside again.

"Log out Melanie Landreth Fielding."

"Log out Martin Fielding."

"This session is ended," Diana said. She whispered codes as the Gizmo analog dissolved into nothingness, then picked up the orange generator and left them alone.

"So much for peace and quiet," Melanie said. She reached for the blue chip. "At least we have two more days on the Ranch."

CHAPTER 5

Melanie pushed away from the desk in her Mountain office. One week since they'd come back from the Andrews Ranch. It felt as if she had never been away, except for niggling aches and pains in her face and the knee brace. She glanced out the big window at the tall mountain ridges to the east and sighed again. Clouds wrapped the ridgetops.

Then she eyed the file-filled hologlobe shimmering over her desk. Space station data. The latest reports on the Freedom Army investigation. Her latest version of the Dialogue Courts presentation. She looked back outside, a disjointed sensation niggling at her.

Normally, she would be coming back from skiing, or riding horses. Activities forbidden to her right now. But habit demanded that she *move*, so she could work with a clearer mind.

Walk. It's the only physical thing I can do.

<Marty?> she called.

<Yes, love?> He sounded distracted, as if he were contemplating something in the lab.

<I'm going stir crazy. Want to walk. You up for it?>

A moment's hesitation. Then, <Hell, yes. I'm getting claustrophobic. Ten minutes so I can get things securely locked down, okay? I've made augmentation tech for that Enforcer defense kit you're developing.>

<Courts stuff? Not station stuff? Shouldn't you be focusing on station stuff?>

<I'm concerned about security at this upcoming meeting. You'll see. Ten minutes, okay?>

<Okay. It'll take that long to get Security over here and ready to go.>

<Meet you by the pasture gate.>

<Don't be late.>

<I won't,> he answered.

Melanie smiled to herself. He *would* be late. That was always the case when he was chasing a hot trail on Netwalk research.

Now. Enforcer kit.

She blinked up the Enforcer tool checklist she had been developing, organized in order of recommended use. The assorted pieces of the toolkit she had assembled lay on an antique painted tin tray on top of the bookcase.

First item. *Trap door chip*. The chip that imprisoned rogue Netwalkers. A good and proven tool. Melanie slipped the chip into her left inside sleeve pocket, to be shaken out when needed.

Check. She blinked that one off the list.

Second item. *Pre-armed secured hologlobe generator.* She'd been caught without warning in a secured hologlobe with a rogue Netwalker once. Never again. Next time, it would be *her* choice, not an opponent's. With settings that protected *her*.

Melanie checked the settings. Touch-ready. Automatic opening access for Marty, Nik and Angela. She put it in her right pants pocket.

Globe first, then chip. Need to switch those items on the list.

That order fit her tool usage priorities better.

Check.

Third item. *Stun pen.* Prototype tech developed by Ness. It *might* slow or stop a rogue Netwalker, but was unproven. Belt clip.

Check.

Fourth item. *Stick patch.* Semi-tried tech. Throwable patch that stopped the target for five seconds. Designed more to calm a panicked host than as a defensive weapon. Used once in a Netwalk bonding session gone bad. Needed a clear line of access, and wasn't as reliable as a backup person with a sedative pen or a Taser. Right pants pocket.

Switch these two. Globe, chip, patch, pen.

Check.

Fifth item. *Upload blockers.*

Could have used this one when Liam died. Might have saved us a world of trouble.

New tech. Worked at least for living upload attempts, but she had no idea how well it worked on death uploads. Right pants pocket.

Sixth item. *Personal scatter generator.* Melanie slipped the scatter generator into her left pants pocket. That was personal toolkit, not Enforcer toolkit.

Check. Globe, chip, patch, pen, blockers.

That was it for specific Enforcer tools, at least so far.

I need more tools.

She grinned at the faint echo of her father's old complaint.

More tools or more toys? had always been her mother's rejoinder.

Dad and I are the same when it comes to tools.

And Marty didn't complain because he took her wish for more tools to heart, went to the lab, and came back with yet another one for her to try.

Melanie blinked up her clock. Time to get moving. She cuffed the sheath carrying her small pistol on her left wrist and clipped her short utility knife to her belt.

Now I'm ready to go for a walk.

MARTY *WAS* LATE. MELANIE WATCHED THE HERD OF SIX HORSES GRAZING IN the pasture, marveling at the concept of *ten* Security people for this walk. When had things gotten so intense?

When Mom became president. When I became more important.

Like it or not, her days of being obscure and unnoticed were gone.

Her little brown mare wandered over to beg for a treat. Melanie slipped her an alfalfa cube and scritched the mare's neck.

Marty and Keisha, one of his assistants, hurried toward them. "Sorry. Had a couple of questions from Julia."

"That's okay," she said. "Let's go."

"This first." He handed small black boxes to their Security. "Updates that Will and Julia whipped up for us. Newest upload blockers, targeted toward National Security Netwalk and similar designs. They trace keylinks to multiple hosts and break them. We haven't been able to interrupt that chain before. Give your old ones to Keisha."

Melanie swapped hers with Keisha. She checked the switches. Except for a green edging where the old ones had been red, she wouldn't have noticed the difference between the two.

"How do we tell them apart?" she asked Keisha.

"Green until you activate them," Keisha said. "Then you get the red edging. Red means discard."

"Thanks."

"Next." Marty handed out black bracelets with a small red button on them. "Reflex augmentation devices, based on a Freedom Army design. Security's been trialing these. Nik, this is the latest tweak based on your feedback. Since we may encounter Freedom Army watchers sometime soon, it's time for you to try it, Mel. I'll feel better about your upcoming public appearances if you have something like this in your kit. It could make a difference if you go one-on-one with this Deirdre Conley or anyone like her, or if you need to hustle to safety."

"Good idea. Where did you get them?"

"Will and Julia got their hands on one. Don't ask me how."

"Good." Melanie slid it on.

"Activate using the red button. But be careful. They'll run you dry pretty fast, faster than Burnout tabs can. Don't go over an hour using them, max."

"Got it," Melanie said. "Anything else I can expect?"

"You'll move faster than you anticipate when you first hit the button, so watch out for that," Marty added. "I overbalanced and fell the first time I tried it. You're better than I am at figuring out balance, so that may not be a problem for you. Nik likes them."

"They're *fun.*" Nik cracked a rare grin. "You'll like them, Mel."

"Just be careful with your knee," Marty warned. "Try it in a controlled setting first. I'm giving it to you now because I want you to have it handy for walks. Don't use it unless you have to."

"I'll be careful. Any more toys?"

"Not yet." Marty took her hand. "Let's walk."

They lined out on a trail that wandered behind the office and lab complex, past Security HQ, then down to the wetlands edging DIR property. The trail continued to an old park by the Salmon River.

An alert swept through their Security as they approached the old wooden footbridge over the river.

<Unknown group. Park,> Angela texted. <Mel, Marty, Nik, stay back.>

<What's happening?> Melanie texted Angela.

<Freedom Army attack squad,> Angela texted. <With someone who fits Deirdre Conley's profile.> Her face tightened as the Security team took off in a cadenced run. She exchanged a few sharp, quick words with Nik in Mixteco.

Melanie slipped closer to Marty as Nik and Angela moved forward protectively, unslinging their weapons.

Anger surged within her.

How dare the fucking Freedom Army come here?

They dared because Deirdre Conley carried Liam as a Netwalker. Because Liam the Netwalker had ambitions.

Melanie reviewed her equipment. Could she find a way to pull Liam out of Conley without half-killing both of them? When she captured her uncle Peter to get him out of Andrew, the resulting battle had nearly killed both her and her brother.

<Suggestions on how to separate her and Liam?> she asked Marty.

<Deep Netwalk program codes,> Marty answered. <Option that Ness and I worked on yesterday. Ness thinks they'll pull him out of Conley, get him into the trap door chip. Two possible sets so far. I'll feed them to you, depending on what you need. No guarantee that either will work.>

<Wonderful. So, assuming that they *do* work, what should I do?>

<Start with your secured hologlobe; just make damned sure you have me in there as well. The shape you're in, you're no match for her if it becomes physical. I'll tase her if I need to.>

<Taser? Why?>

<Conley looks to be in pretty damned good shape. You're still recovering from your injuries.> His hand tightened on hers as they approached the bridge.

Melanie surveyed the group facing off with her Security—apparently the Freedom Army fighters had surrendered. Paul issued an order. Every captive, including the small blonde woman—*Deirdre Conley*—had a weapon placed strategically over their implant sites.

"Damn," Angela breathed. "We caught them. But why are they giving up so easily?"

"They aren't. Not yet," Melanie said. "You know better than that. Liam's working her."

"She hasn't raised him."

"She will." She *knew* what Conley's reaction would be.

No explanation, except that the deep sense of knowing more than she realized washed over her. The same sensation she had experienced before the Netwalk battles with Sarah and Peter.

The world became sharper around Melanie as Netwalk energy lines crackled around Conley.

She'll raise him. Oh yes, she'll raise him. The question is, when?

Melanie released Marty's hand as the woman turned her head. Their eyes met. Melanie took a deep, calming breath. Soon, she'd be facing Liam.

<Bring Ness out just in case I need her,> she told Marty.

Suddenly Conley shivered, her knees buckling. Energy lines exploded around her.

It's now!

Paul's weapon bounced away from Conley's head. Conley bolted, pounding down the wooden bridge toward Melanie, shaking the planks with the intensity of her stride. Her face blurred into Liam's features.

Melanie pushed the button on her augmenter. The world wavered around her. And then it steadied before she sprinted toward Conley, the world blurring around her. Heart pounding. Reactions almost too fast.

A little like Burnout? Let's say it's Burnout times twenty.

Conley's enraged scream sounded incongruous from Liam's face.

Melanie remembered Nik's balance warning as she skidded to a halt, throwing her weight back and down to keep from falling forward. She ducked as Conley slashed at her. Shoved Conley hard against the bridge railing. Conley bounced to the other side, recovering to take up a fighting crouch. Garbled words sounding too slow came from Conley's mouth. Behind her, Melanie faintly heard Marty shouting, felt the bridge vibrate under his augmented sprint.

Liam's features grew more solid, less transparent. The sense of Netwalk *presence* grew stronger. Doubled. Energy lines around Conley trebled yet again. She felt Ness, faint tendril of Netwalk presence.

<We're here. Throw the globe!> Marty's hand brushed her shoulder.

Melanie threw the secured hologlobe's generator between them and Conley. Conley/Liam shivered again, and Conley straightened up, fingers reaching up her right sleeve.

"STOP!" Melanie projected her strongest Enforcer compulsion tones as she reached into her pocket for the stick patch. Conley paused. Melanie hurled the stick patch at her and it landed on her chest. Conley froze in place. Wide blue-gray eyes stared at Melanie. *Hers,* not Liam's. The Liam features wavered.

Marty grabbed Conley. <What now?>

<I can't see him separate from her!> Every other Netwalker she knew was a separate entity from its host. But not these two.

Just like it was with Peter and Andrew. Now what do I do?

Maybe unconsciousness would be enough.

Conley's arms twitched.

Damn it, she's throwing off the effects of the patch!

<She needs to be unconscious,> she said. <Do you have anything to do it quick and fast?>

<Absolutely.> Marty shoved an injector into Conley and grabbed her as she sagged, easing her to the ground. Ness hovered nearby, ready to attack should Liam attempt to cross into Marty.

A swirl of red and black shadows twisted out of Conley as her features returned to her own shape. Melanie warily watched as the last shadows clung to Conley, trying to get her to move. Then the shadows turned toward Melanie.

She had the trap door chip in hand, and tapped up the cage door.

<In there,> she ordered.

An electronic screech from the red and black cloud answered her. Ness changed shape, into a red cloud, and moved menacingly toward the red and black cloud.

<Marty. Keep Ness back!> The last thing she needed right now was a Netwalker battle. *Can't control that. Not now.* <IN THERE!> she commanded Liam.

The red and black shadows formed into a shape. Then Liam glared defiantly at her.

<I won't let you kill me like you did Peter!> he snarled. <I know what that cage means. I'll have you as my new host first!> He moved toward her, his eyes flaring red.

She felt a faint, hypnotic tug. She pushed the sensation away.

You have no power over me, but I have power over you.

<Stop.> She used all of her vocal compulsion tones to stop him. He did stop, for a moment. Then he pushed on.

She growled back, striking the vocal notes that triggered command reactions in Netwalkers. Again, he paused. Then he started moving.

At least his vocalizations have no effect on me.

But she was tiring. Liam knew what Peter hadn't, that the chip was his electronic death sentence. He would fight her every step of the way.

What the hell do I do now? I don't know how much more strength I have.

Codes started streaming across her left eye.

Codes! Marty's codes!

She vocalized each code. As she spoke, Liam writhed and shrieked in protest. He clawed at her as the codes compelled him to move into the cage.

<Melanie. Please. Mercy!> he whimpered as he folded in on himself, his features turning into red and black. <For the love of God, for the love we once had, mercy!>

The whimpers touched her where nothing else could. She could remember a time when those intense dark eyes made her tingle and quiver all over, when a single brush of his hand set her on fire.

Marty's hand touched her shoulder. A different warmth. Steady and calm, without the unpredictable fire of Liam, a deeper comfort.

Melanie drew a ragged breath to steady herself, and continued the codes where she'd left off.

Finally, the red and black cloud that was Liam disappeared into the cage. She tapped the codes to lock him in and shrink the cage back into the chip. She tucked the chip securely into her sleeve pocket.

It was done. Liam the Netwalker was captured—unless he had another host where he had hidden part of himself—no, that wasn't how Peter had manifested.

Melanie tapped off her augmentation bracelet.

She sank onto the bridge as she unlocked the hologlobe.

"I don't think I can walk back," she whispered.

"I *know* you can't," he said, taking her into his arms and standing up. "A truck's on the way."

Melanie leaned her head against Marty and closed her eyes as he carried her off the bridge, a great weariness overtaking her.

This was too damn easy. What if it's a diversion?

She had just enough energy to send an emergency text to her mother.

Diana responded quickly.

<Security around the gadget increased.>

Melanie closed her eyes and relaxed. Let others deal with the paperwork around finalizing Do It Right taking custody of Deirdre Conley.

She had done her part.

LATER THAT AFTERNOON, MARTY STUDIED THE RECORDINGS HE'D MADE OF Conley's capture. Ness perched in the hologlobe, monitoring the electromagnetic dataflow. Mapping the process. Gathering data.

Two of this type of Netwalker so far, and not a one safe to examine live.

Maybe some little piece of all this work would turn out to be useful.

It's a damned good thing that Ness programmed sensitivity to vocal stimuli into the original Netwalk setup. I just wish we had someone besides Melanie with that vocal ability to control and dominate Netwalkers.

There *had* to be more Enforcer prospects out there. What made his wife so different from other Dialogues? Why could *her* voice and no one else's control the Netwalkers they'd known so far? He scowled at the electromagnetic records.

He sighed and leaned back in his chair, probing Melanie to see if there was any response. Nothing. She had fallen asleep on the ride back home. Six hours later, she was still sleeping.

Should be grateful that she's getting rest. I guess.

But it worried him that she needed this much sleep. No other user of the augmented bracelets had experienced this level of exhaustion.

Still recovering. But—no one else is an Enforcer. Could that be a factor?

Red text popped up on his overlay, from Angela.

<Marty. Urgent. Need Mel.>

<Try. No promises. Still sleeping. What's going on?> he texted back, in his normal blue text.

<Possible data. Lead from tracing Army movements. *Interesting* results. Mel to Security intake ASAP. Interrogation Two.>

It took him a half hour to wake Melanie, pour some coffee down her throat, and get her pointed toward the Security building. While she was cooperative, the degree of her sleepiness and lack of reactivity worried him.

This isn't right. This is like Mel when she's crashed after a Burnout marathon. Worse for her than Burnout. That takes the augmentation bracelet off the table. Damn it.

Melanie yawned and stumbled over a small crack in the sidewalk.

Need to have her more alert for whatever this is. I hate to do it, but maybe Burnout could zap her awake.

"Do you want a tab of Burnout?" he asked.

That earned him a glare. "*You're* offering me Burnout? That's a first."

"Mel, you're running tired. It's not safe for you to be this tired."

"I'll hold up. I don't want Burnout on top of that damned augmentation bracelet."

"Did it really take that much out of you? It hasn't worked that way on others."

"It's worse than any ADHD meds I've taken," Melanie grumbled.

Yeah. That explained it. The only reason Melanie used Burnout was that it didn't act like most stimulants on her system, at least until she hit a critical dose. Burnout didn't slow her down.

So the bracelet acts like treatment meds on a hyperactive like Mel, after the first rush.

An interaction he hadn't anticipated. But at least it didn't appear to be an Enforcer effect.

"You doing okay now?" he asked.

Melanie made a face. "Now that I'm up and moving, yeah. But I'm still fuzzy. Did Ange give you any clues?"

"She just said they'd had an *interesting* result from an interrogation tip. Whatever that could be. She highlighted and underlined *interesting*. Red text."

"Likely to be big. Ange doesn't normally play with text like that." Melanie sped up, favoring her injured knee. Despite his greater height, Marty had to push himself to keep up with her.

Good. Give her something to focus on and she perks up.

Angela met them outside of Interrogation Two. "We found the Portland hideout for a Freedom Army cell. Nik and the New Fed authorities organized a quick raid. We captured seven people. Including them." She gestured toward the room.

Marty and Melanie moved to the one-way window. A heavy-set, dark-haired woman stood stiffly, arms crossed. Two small children, both boys, clung to her legs, whimpering. The woman didn't acknowledge the boys as she glowered at the window.

She knows we're here.

Melanie's quick, indrawn breath caught Marty's attention. She stared at the children, her face paling as her hands tightened into fists. He looked back at the children and understood. The taller boy looked like the woman. But the younger one resembled Liam Jeffreys.

"Do any of them have implants?" Melanie snapped. "I can't see any Netwalk effect, but that fight with Conley burned me out."

"The woman's the only one with implants," Angela said. "No uploads."

"I'll be the judge of that." Melanie scowled, crossing her arms, mirroring the woman. "You're sure about the children?"

"They're too young for implants."

"By our standards," Melanie said. "Not necessarily Freedom Army standards."

"By *most* people's standards. But we checked anyway."

"Good. Do we have a positive ID on them?"

"Yes." Angela hesitated, glancing at Marty. He read the warning in her look and moved closer to Melanie. The features of the younger boy gave Marty a good idea of what Angela was going to say. He noticed the way Melanie's nostrils flared as she breathed deeply.

Mel knows too.

"Who are they?" Melanie asked, her voice tightening.

"The woman's name is Gina Jeffreys," Angela said. "She's on record as the legal wife of Liam Jeffreys, for the past ten years."

"*What*?" Melanie whirled on Angela. "*How*? Liam had a thorough background check when we got engaged!"

Angela stood firm, not backing down. "He's good. *Was* good."

"And he had help," Nik said, appearing from behind Melanie. "The data was locked up in a private, highly classified National Security file. Highest-level classification. We haven't had access to that data until the New Feds took power. So much information that it didn't pop up until we ran a specific search on Gina Jeffreys."

Melanie sighed deeply and sank against the wall, burying her head in her hands, doubling over. "Damn it," she growled between her fingers. "Damn it, what next? *What fucking next?*"

Marty froze. He wanted to help her—but too soon and she'd just lash out.

Oh God, Mel. God. I am so fucking sorry.

At last, Melanie raised her head. She stretched one hand toward Marty. He helped her straighten up. She leaned on him for a moment, then stood.

"So *they* knew," she said, her voice hard, staring again at Gina Jeffreys and her sons. "Sarah had to know because the information was in National Security records. Damn it. My engagement to Liam was a sham all along. An opportunity to infiltrate Do It Right. No wonder he didn't want me to have his daughter. No fucking wonder." She continued to glare at the woman and her children.

The boys kept trying to draw their mother's attention but she ignored them, unbending even as the younger one's whimpering transitioned into tears.

Why doesn't she comfort them?

Marty shifted uncomfortably. Mothers should be comforting their children in a situation like this.

This isn't right.

"The children," Melanie said, finally, nostrils flaring even wider, opening and closing sharply. "His?"

"Yes," Nik said. "The older one is Donald, six years old. The younger is Alexander, three years old. We've done a gene check as part of the scan."

"Why the hell is she ignoring them?" Marty asked, finally unable to keep it back. "Why doesn't she try and calm them? Poor kids. They're scared to death."

Nik frowned. "The Army indoctrinates the children early. Bio parents don't bond closely. She's probably not had a lot to do with the kids herself; that's been the job of a surrogate parent. However. Neither boy shows signs of the Army's early imprint training. They should. They start before we do. But both boys are clear."

"There's a feeling about those boys," Melanie said, her upper lip curling slightly. "You sure they're clear?"

"They passed the tests that Marty developed."

"Then they should be clear," Marty said.

Melanie chuckled bitterly. "This Freedom Army Netwalk doesn't follow our rules. They could be the base for Liam's upload. That would explain the feeling I have about them." She shook her head again. "*I* have to scan them. And scan *her*." She took a deep breath. "God, if I have the strength." She glanced at Marty. "Still have that Burnout? I need to ride the dragon to pull this off."

Marty scowled and would have spoken but Angela spoke first.

"There's more. Gina Jeffreys isn't just Liam's wife," Angela said.

"She's Francis Stewart's daughter. She's the Freedom Army's Head of Research." She grimaced. "Need-to-know screwing us up once again. If I had known, we would have searched for her more intensely. Diana's folks have been looking for her. Hard. But not telling us."

Melanie flinched. Then she held her hand out to Marty. "Burnout. *Now.*"

Marty reluctantly pulled out the small black box with the embossed intertwined red and black dragons and pressed it into Melanie's hand. Without looking, she shook out two tabs and dry-swallowed them.

"Be careful," he said.

"Mmhmm," Melanie grunted, hyperfocusing on Jeffreys. "Just be ready to pick me up when I crash."

"If she's the Army's Head of Research, then odds are this Netwalk variant is *her* creation. We found the gold mine. How did we get so lucky?"

"They were in Portland for a quick transfer to Southern Cal," Nik said. "The New Feds almost screwed it up by taking so long to get me the warrant so we could take custody of them in the name of the Corporate Courts. Five more minutes and they would have been gone. I had the team ready—everything but the warrant and the authority for us to detain her, the kids, and Conley."

"Southern California?" Melanie scowled. "Straight into Andrew's arms, damn it." She interlaced her fingers in front of her and brought her twined hands to her chin. "There's *something* about those kids. Not her. The kids." She tapped her forefingers together, then pointed them at the kids. "Too easy. Too damn easy. I think the scan's right, it's not a chip. But there's *something* there."

"Let me check," Marty said. <Ness, what the hell do you think?> He popped up and accessed the scans. Ness slid inside the globe, moving gracefully in and around the scans. Finally, she looked back at Marty.

<They're clean.>

<Then what the hell is Melanie talking about?>

<I don't know. She's right, there's something about the kids. The mother's dead to Netwalk. Not even a Dialogue-type chip. The kids

aren't like that. But they aren't Netwalk hosts. They aren't chipped. There's *something* about them, similar to Melanie.>

Baby Enforcer prospects?

"Ness says they're clear," he said. "But she agrees with Mel. There's something about the kids."

"I'll look." Melanie stepped into the hologlobe, stopping once inside to tap her datasuit to higher levels before joining Ness. At last, she came out. He noticed she didn't tap her suit's defensive levels back down.

"Not enough," she said. "I have to scan the kids myself." She turned to Angela. "It's time to go in there." She started to push past Angela but Angela put out a hand to stop Melanie.

"Mel. Do you have a plan? Are you leaving the children with her?"

Melanie's lips tightened and her hands quivered—that meant the first rush of Burnout had hit her body.

"God damn it, part of me wants to fucking kill her and the kids!"

"*Mel.*" Mixed anguish and fear in Angela's voice.

"Oh, don't worry. I won't hurt any of them. But leave them with her? Like hell!" Who knows what twisted part of *him* they carry? Have they already been warped by their parents, by the Army? God! With what Ness and I sense, and given—the gadget—that's dangerous." Melanie gulped. "*He's* killed my babies. And now, to know this—" She shook her head. "No. The faster we get them away from her the better. Figure out what it is Ness and I feel about them."

"Give custody of them to Security," Nik said.

"You'd trust them in Security?" Melanie asked.

"At this age? Put them in the crèche," Angela said. "They're young enough to respond quickly to our structures. Besides, Sophie needs company nearer her age."

"You'd trust Sophie around them?"

"Sophie would knock the shit out of them if they tried to hurt her," Angela snapped. "As would the other kids. And if she and they didn't, I would. No. I'm not worried about the kids, as long as they're sane."

"Their sanity *could* be a question," Melanie murmured. "Given who their father was." She briefly tightened her lips. "This is the ultimate revenge. Co-opt the offspring, if we can."

"Exactly," Angela said. Their eyes met, and they nodded, grimly.

"So," Melanie said. "You want my plan. Bring the kids out here. Give me a minute in the hologlobe with them. They're kids, it won't take long for me to figure out if that something is Liam. Then I go in there to talk to their mother."

God. No.

"I don't like it," Marty said.

"I have to scan her and I can't do it out here. Not as tired as I am, even with Burnout. I need to be close to her, maybe even touch her. I'll have Ange, with a sedative pen handy. Other Security. Put her under restraint while I scan her."

"Nik, what do you think about Mel's plan?" He couldn't argue further if Nik approved.

"It'll work," Nik said.

"If you say so," Marty said. "Be careful, hon."

Melanie squeezed his hand, still focused on the woman and children. "It's worth the risk," she said. "I'll be careful. I promise."

"Okay."

"Let's do it," Melanie said.

Melanie and Angela moved next to the doorway as four Security crèche staff, along with four more Security, entered the room. The general Security staff seized Gina Jeffreys by the shoulders and arms as crèche staff gently untangled the screaming, struggling boys from their mother's legs. Jeffreys didn't fight the Security pulling at her, remaining stiff and tight, staring stonily at the window as the crèche staff took the children out of the room.

Gina Jeffreys's unwavering gaze sent chills over Marty.

Melanie would have fought if anyone ever tried to take away a child of hers in the same situation. Even Liam's child.

Melanie joined the crying boys, snapping up her secured hologlobe. She knelt before each boy, speaking in low, soft tones. The older boy managed to control his tears, stutter out his name and answer "yes" to a couple of questions Marty couldn't hear. Melanie rested a hand on his cheek. She paused, nodded, and turned to the younger boy. The younger boy continued to sob, but nodded in response to Melanie's questions. Melanie put her hand on his cheek.

She rose, patted both boys on the shoulder, and dropped the globe, tucking the generator into her sleeve.

<Clear,> she texted Marty. <Time now for Mother.>

Melanie and Angela went into the interrogation room. Gina Jeffreys straightened up as Melanie came near her, as if to emphasize her greater height. Melanie snapped up the globe. The two women stared at each other. Melanie said something Marty couldn't hear. Jeffreys remained silent, glowering even more.

"I asked you a question," Melanie said.

Jeffreys pulled her head back slightly, reminding Marty of a cobra. She spat, barely missing Melanie. Security slammed Jeffreys against the wall.

"Just what the hell do you think you're accomplishing with that?"

"Whore!"

"I could say the same about you," Melanie said. "I didn't know about you, but I'll bet you knew about me."

No answer, just the same stony glare.

"Do you know where Liam is now?"

"Bitch!"

Angela shouldered in next to Jeffreys, pressing the sedative pen against her upper arm.

"You talk to her right," Angela said.

Melanie remained immobile, matching Jeffreys glare for glare.

"Where is Liam right now?"

"You killed him!" Jeffreys snarled. "You killed him!"

"He's a Netwalker. Who are his hosts? Does he have more than one? I know your Freedom Army version of Netwalk allows for multiple hosts. Who are they?"

"What the hell is a Netwalker?"

"You know damned good and well what a Netwalker is. *Who are his hosts?*"

No answer.

Melanie sighed. "Hold her tight," she said. Jeffreys tried to flinch away as Melanie raised her hand. Melanie pressed her fingers lightly against the woman's cheek for five seconds, then stepped back, snapping the hologlobe closed.

"I'm done."

Angela moved away from Jeffreys.

Melanie limped out of the interrogation room, shaking her head.

"It's going to be a long, tough haul with that one," she said. "I'm not looking forward to Deirdre Conley's interrogation if it's like this."

"When's that going to be?" Angela asked.

"Not until tomorrow, at the earliest," Melanie said. "I can't do that one under Burnout. Too risky."

"Don't leave it for too long," Marty said. "The longer she's sedated, the more risk to both of you. She comes up too disoriented, you could get nothing useful."

Melanie nodded. "I won't leave it past tomorrow. But several things need to happen first. I need time to recover so that I don't have to touch her to scan her. We need to destroy Liam's chip. I also want more information on her background. If anyone still has a piece of Liam stashed about them, it's going to be Conley. The kids and their mother don't have it. I'm positive of that."

"That's good," Marty said.

"There's *something* about that youngest boy. He might have Enforcer potential. Less so for the other, none at all in the mother. But I've just about maxed out my Enforcer abilities. I need to rest. Right now," she said to Marty, tucking her arm in his.

Marty guided Melanie out of the Security building. Once outside, he slipped one arm around her shoulders. She leaned her head against his chest.

"That was hard. So damned hard. I thought Liam was done hurting me. But he just keeps coming at me! Having a child with her while leading me on. I thought," her voice faltered. "I still thought that he'd truly loved me. Once."

Marty bent down to kiss her.

"It's over," he murmured. "It's over."

"Is it really?" she asked.

CHAPTER 6

The next morning, Melanie scanned her mail, waiting for Marty to tell her that it was time to destroy Liam's chip. Her stomach roiled and the only thing she could tolerate was an energy bar and watered-down coffee. Even that didn't sit well.

Her office door opened. Marty stood in the doorway.

"The incinerator's ready."

Melanie slowly rose.

It's real. God, it's real. Eliminating Liam. Just wish I knew if it's for certain.

After all, she hadn't anticipated *this* manifestation. Were there others?

She forced herself to breathe as they walked to Marty's lab. Extra Security headed up by Nik stood outside the door. No one else was inside, however, not even Security.

Private. Good.

Marty handed her the clear tube that held Liam's trap door chip. Melanie turned it in her hand. She sighed and met Marty's questioning gaze. Their eyes held steady for a moment. Then he snapped up a secure hologlobe to surround them.

"Do you want to do this, or shall I?" he asked.

"It's my job." She put the tube down carefully and took the pair of datagloves Marty held out to her. Pulled the gloves on slowly, blood pounding in her ears. Opened the tube. Used thin-nosed tongs to extract the chip. Placed the chip into the electronically shielded incinerator that disposed of risky Netwalk and Dialogue chips. Hands trembled as she closed the incinerator door and secured it.

"What's our security status?" she asked.

"Highest."

She nodded and pressed the button.

Bye-bye, Liam. I hope. Will he find another way to strike back at me? A piece of him in another host?

She quivered as the timer counted down the minutes for safe incineration.

Am I going to hell for this?

Her occasional Catholic upbringing didn't come up very often, but the memory of Liam's pleas as she forced him into the trap door chip haunted her.

Am I doing the right thing?

Marty held her close. Melanie leaned her head on him.

"Remember," Marty said. "He was already dead. This is an electronic copy of his upload. You're not actually killing *him*."

"You're reading my mind," she whispered. "But I'm scared."

"Scared?"

"That he'll find yet another way to get back at me. That I'm turning into a killer. That I'm going to hell."

Marty's arm tightened around her. "He won't, love. He can't get back at you. You're not a killer, hon, and if defending yourself against him sends you to hell—well, I'll be right there with you. For what he did to you, I'd gladly kill him myself."

"Oh, love." She kissed him. "Thank you. This is just an irrational fear. But still—if he can get back at me, he'll find a way."

"Not as long as I'm around, he won't," Marty muttered.

They watched as the incinerator shut itself off. Waited as it went through the cool-off cycle. Marty opened the door and poked carefully at the remaining ashes, scattering them to check that no tiny chip piece remained.

Nothing.

<Ness?> Melanie asked.

Red clouds shimmered near the incinerator, about an arm's length away.

<Nothing,> Ness said. <No reaction at all. He's gone.>

Marty gathered up the ashes into a container. "Anything special?"

"Dispose of them as securely as possible. Whatever that will be."

"Will do. When do we deal with Conley?"

"This afternoon," Melanie said. "After lunch. Now that this is resolved, we'll take care of her."

She leaned into Marty for a kiss, then left his lab, holding her head high, fighting to keep any emotion out of her face in case she was observed.

Liam was gone. For good, this time.

She hoped.

ANGELA FROWNED AS THEY HELD THEIR FINAL MEETING BEFORE CONLEY'S interrogation. She understood that Mel needed to make sure that no traces of Liam remained in the woman, but, damn it, the woman was a terrorist. Had been raised by terrorists.

"We need to immobilize Conley completely," she said.

"Can we do that?" Melanie asked.

"Certainly," Nik said. "Whole blanket suspension field."

"Checked for weapons?" Melanie pursed her lips, half-frowning.

"Absolutely," Nik said. "Thorough exam."

"We need to treat that cybercrash. Feed her solid food, not intravenous." Melanie tapped her fingers on her chin thoughtfully. "But how the hell are we going to do that without her spitting it back out at us?"

"She responds well to threats from a weapon," Nik said.

"Yeah, and she managed to get away from Paul," Angela said. "Bet you she tries to go for Mel the minute she wakes."

Nik shook his head. "She won't be that awake and reactive."

"Her reactions aren't the norm," Melanie said. "Marty says there's something else going on. It's not just augmentation."

"Maybe you need to let us handle this, Mel." At least she had to make the suggestion. Again.

Melanie shook her head. "No, Ange. Some piece of Liam might still be in her. My job to deal with it. She's yours after that."

"Her first response will be to attack," Angela said.

Damn it, Mel, I wish you weren't planning to be within range of this woman.

"She'll be hurting," Marty said as he entered the room. "We weren't gentle in getting Liam out, and she's been under sedation. She still needs to process events. She won't have a lot of fighting energy left."

"Maybe we should just remove the chip before we wake her." Melanie continued to tap her fingers on her chin thoughtfully. "That'll slow her down even more."

Marty shook his head. "It's as decommissioned as possible. If we need to do more with that chip later, we can reactivate it, or pull it out. I don't want to muck around in her brain too much more at the moment. She and Jeffreys are our best sources on how this Freedom Army Netwalk variant works, and I'd like to keep Conley's linkages fairly intact in case she will work with us."

"All right," Angela sighed. *I don't have to like it.* <You be fast,> she texted Nik.

<Always am,> he answered. But she noticed the quick unconscious pat Nik gave all of his personal security devices. One of his tells.

He's more worried than I am.

MELANIE EXTENDED THE SECURED HOLOGLOBE TO COVER THE WHOLE ROOM.

Showtime.

She took up her position at the foot of the bed and glanced at the others, catching Angela's gaze before nodding, clenching her fists. Angela picked up the sedative antidote. Nik stood at the head of the bed; his weapon drawn in case Conley managed to fight free of the suspension field.

Angela administered the antidote. She stepped back and picked up an injector of paralytic, in case they needed it.

Conley stirred, but her eyes didn't open.

Getting her bearings before she reacts. Exactly what I would do.

Melanie considered the steps *she* would take if it were her in that bed.

First, she'll try to wake her implant.

Next, she'll try to contact Liam.

Then she'll panic.

What happened after that—ah, that was the question. And whether Conley would be disconcerted enough by lack of connectivity to give them useful information.

Won't know for sure until she wakes.

"She's awake," Angela said, eyeing the monitors.

"As scheduled," Nik said. "She's playing possum on us."

"I could do something about that," Angela said.

"No need," Melanie said. "She'll wake for me." Conley's muscles tensed as Melanie moved closer, and Melanie had to force herself not to react. "Isn't that right, Deirdre Ellen Conley? You've got questions for me, I'm sure, including the whereabouts of your precious Liam. You won't get your answers by pretending to be unconscious."

Conley's slight body jerked off of the bed. She nearly managed to sit up before the restraint field slammed her back down hard with a loud *thump,* rocking the bed. Her body shook from the impact. She struggled briefly, then stopped, her body sagging, gasping for breath.

She still glared at Melanie, eyes stony and cold. Melanie matched that glower with one of her own, not looking away.

I can do this all day, woman. Can you?

Angela chuckled, the sound breaking the tension between Melanie and Conley.

"I won this one, didn't I, Nik. Told you that her first move would be to go after Mel." Conley's focus switched from Melanie to Angela.

Nik shook his head, a rueful smile touching his lips. "Girl, what would I do without you?"

"For one, you owe me a massage. I won the bet."

"We're not done yet."

Conley continued to focus on Nik and Angela's banter rather than on Melanie.

Marty's hand brushed against her arm. <Sit down,> he said. She felt a stool pushing against her.

<Thanks.> She settled onto the stool, watching. <First probe. Back me?>

<Always.>

It was easier to slip into Enforcer mode with Marty leaning against her.

Melanie blinked. Scanned once. Twice. A third time to be certain.

The electronic fields around Conley didn't betray any traces of Liam.

<I don't see anything on surface scan,> she said. <Do you?>

<Love, you know I can't see what you do.>

<Never hurts to ask. Okay. I have to take this to another level.>

<She needs feeding before you do anything more, Mel. Look at how she's shaking.>

<Fighting the restraint.>

Marty was slow to respond. <That's part of it. But you're also seeing cybercrash. Gotta feed her before it gets worse.>

Melanie studied Conley.

He's right. Damn it.

She knew far too well what that felt like, and an unwilling thread of sympathy stirred in her. "Nik, Angela, time to feed her. Nik, you feed her, Angela, stand guard."

Nik nodded. He picked up the tray holding a plate of protein cubes and a tube of protein drink and set it on a table next to Conley's bed. She focused on him.

Hunger or looking for an opening? One way to find out.

"So you know this is safe," Nik said, keeping his tone emotionless and professional. He ate one protein cube, then sipped from the tube of protein drink, carefully cleaning the tip after he used it, showing Conley each step of the process.

Angela crossed to Conley's other side and placed her weapon over Conley's implant.

Nik held the first cube to Conley's lips. Conley tried to spit it out.

"I'd eat it," Angela said. "Cybercrashing is a bitch. Seen it with Melanie. But whatever you do, *don't bite him.* I'd take that action really personal, seeing as he's my bondmate. You know who I am. You know I'll shoot. Got it?"

Conley nodded slowly.

"Okay," Angela said. "But my weapon stays where it is."

Conley nodded again, then ate delicately and carefully.

"So what the hell do you want with me?" Conley snapped when she was done.

"You've earned the right to sit up," Melanie said. "Nik?"

Nik made the adjustment to the restraint field and raised the front of the bed. Angela followed Conley's movement, keeping her blaster placed firmly over Conley's implant site.

"Let me show you where you stand." Melanie snapped up a second hologlobe, summoning the capture video. "This is what you probably last remember."

She watched Conley for her reaction at the end, when her men had tried to rescue her and been killed.

Conley blinked hard, faint wetness shimmering in her eyes.

She's not a complete Freedom Army martyr bitch, unlike Gina Jeffreys. Good to know.

The thread of sympathy broadened, but—too early to show it.

Save it for the possibility of cooperation.

"That video has been released to the media," Melanie said. "I prefer to discourage assassination attempts. I've experienced too damn many of them in the past year. No more playing around. You try to kill me—you're likely to die."

"You bitch!" Conley snapped.

"You might want to save your spew for the rest of this update," Melanie said.

She brought up the video of the capture of the Army cell, complete with the screaming kids.

"What the hell have you *done with them?*" Conley tried to launch herself at Melanie again. The suppression field shoved her roughly against the bed, cinching down so hard that Conley gasped for breath, mouth half-open.

If Liam was still in her, he'd have appeared by now.

"It seems," Melanie said, "that one of those folks we captured, Gina

Jeffreys, is Liam's wife, dating back to before he was engaged to me. It also seems that this same Gina Jeffreys, daughter of the Prophet who founded the Freedom Army, is the scientific mind that implemented the technology your people stole."

"You bastards would have kept it for yourselves!" Conley growled.

"That's not at issue here," Melanie said, keeping her vocal tones mild, saving her sharpest tones for what came next. "What I *have* discovered is that Gina Jeffreys is a potential source of information. But. There's a slight issue of the children. Liam's sons."

"You *wouldn't*," Conley said, anguish creeping into her voice. "No. *No!* You wouldn't use them too!"

"And who are you to be telling me what I will and won't do with them?" Melanie snapped, using her sharpest Enforcer tones.

The kids. Why is she so interested in the kids? Is she their real mother and Gina just a façade?

No. Couldn't be. The DNA match was for Gina Jeffreys.

Conley's voice faded to a whimper. "Dear God, they're just *children*." A tear ran down her cheek.

Not the detachment that Gina Jeffreys displayed.

Is this interest a sign of Liam in Conley? Or are the kids a possible key to turn her? Why would they matter to her?

Melanie probed gently. No response. She went deeper into virtual, and poked at the electronic signatures hovering around Conley. No trace of Liam.

But there was something she didn't recognize. She clipped an image of it to take back to Marty.

<Do you recognize this?> She sent him the image.

Marty hesitated. <Let me check with Ness.>

Melanie turned her attention back to Conley's electronic signature. She pushed more deeply. Something about that unrecognized segment seemed familiar. She touched it. Different, and yet so familiar. She couldn't explicitly identify why it attracted her, and yet it did.

If we can ever get to a point where we can trust her, I want to test her for Enforcer potential. God! What do I do when I encounter an enemy with Enforcer potential?

<Mel.> Marty called her focus back.

Melanie reluctantly pulled away. <What does Ness say?>

<She's a potential Enforcer.>

<So how the hell do we turn her so we can trust her?>

<I don't know, Mel.>

<We have to figure that out. Meanwhile, we sure can't risk her getting free. Not with Enforcer potential.>

<Absolutely not.> She became aware of his hands tightening on her shoulders. <Wrap it up, Mel. I don't want you getting overtired. Not this close to the Courts presentation.>

<Understood.> Now that Marty mentioned it, her face *was* beginning to ache. She had to rest after this.

Or do more Burnout.

Not a good option.

She checked Conley one last time, then unlocked the secure hologlobe and tapped the command for it to retreat back into the generator.

"All right," she said to Conley. "I have my answer. Liam's not in you anymore."

"I could have told you that!" Defiance in Conley's voice again.

"I had to be certain."

"What about the kids?" Conley's voice switched to pleading. "What are you going to do to them?"

"What does it matter to you?"

Conley tightened her lips firmly, glaring at Melanie.

"Answer me!" Melanie snapped, pushing her vocal tones.

Conley's lips tightened further and her jaw worked. For one moment Melanie thought she would speak. Then Conley breathed out softly and shook her head.

She threw off an Enforcer compulsion tone. For a moment Melanie doubted. *Did I check deeply enough?*

"What do those children mean to you?" she asked again, this time without compulsion tones, just a plain voice to see what Conley's reaction would be.

Hesitation. "They. Are. Children. Of. The. Army." Conley forced each word out slowly, laboriously. Her eyes widened, bulging slightly as she strained to speak.

Is that fear or anger?

Fear, and deep conditioning. Not going to be overcome immediately.

This problem wasn't going to be solved in one session. How on earth could they win Conley over? She clearly wanted to cooperate, for the children's sake.

"If they are children of the Freedom Army, then they are prisoners of war," Melanie said in a quiet, reasonable tone, again not using any Enforcer elements. "The Freedom Army are agents of a known enemy of the New Federated States. Of me and my family."

"Incestuous bastards that you are!" Conley blurted.

"Mel, I suggest we wrap this up," Marty said before Melanie could respond. "She still needs time to recover from the cybercrash." <And you're getting tired.>

"Understood," she said. "So. Are you going to tell me why those kids are so important to you?"

"I told you!" Conley snapped.

"All right," Melanie said, letting herself sigh with just a hint of exasperation that she took and twisted a little bit. It gave her some satisfaction to see Conley wince at that nuance. "Since you won't tell me any reason why you should be concerned about the fate of those kids, then you don't need to know."

Distress crossed Conley's face. "But what are you going to do with them?"

"Their father owes me a debt. A big debt. His sons are the payment. Rest assured that they'll be cared for. They won't be abandoned. But make no mistake, they will be paying the debt their father owes me. If you want to know more of their fate, then you'll tell me what your interest is."

Conley remained stubbornly silent.

Melanie rose.

"What's happening to me?" Conley asked.

Melanie shrugged. "I have the authority from the New Federated States to dispense justice of my own choice here in Hoodland when it comes to my personal safety; and the Corporate Courts give me the authority to do what is needed to protect the integrity of my company. Your actions threaten both."

"So much for the justice of the Courts and the New Federated States!"

Get this over with.

"This is what will happen to you. You will be questioned and confined, given work to do. At some point in the future, you will be released, when and if it is determined that you are no longer a threat to my safety and the safety of the New Federated States. If you're lucky you'll get to keep your implant."

"And...Liam?" Conley showed more humanity than Melanie expected.

She sounds like she truly loved the jerk.

Melanie looked at her steadily. "Dead. Finally. Completely. No part of him remains as an upload."

"No. You can't guarantee that."

"I can guarantee it, and I have, to my own satisfaction." *Let her know where she finally stands.* "Nothing remains of him." Melanie allowed herself a faint smile. "I had one question left, as to whether he'd managed to store some little piece of himself in you. He has not."

"You can't know that!"

"Ah, that's where you're wrong." Melanie limped toward the door—another sign of fatigue. She half-expected a further comment but nothing came.

She sagged against the wall once she was safely outside.

Marty slid his arm around her.

"Damn," he said.

Melanie ran her fingers through her hair. "We might be able to turn her. But it will take a lot of work. What do those kids mean to her? That's the key."

"Yeah," Marty agreed. "There's something there."

I just wish I could figure it out before the Courts meeting.

On the other hand, figuring out the ties between Conley and the Jeffreys kids was a situation best not rushed.

CHAPTER 7

What am I facing?

Melanie braced against the slight tug as Angela tightly braided her hair. Her gut roiled with tension and she wanted to pace. Run. Ski. *Something.* An hour spent swimming in the pool at Courts headquarters wasn't enough exercise to put her at ease.

"There," Angela said. "What do you think?"

Melanie stared at the mirror. Her thick, fine brunette hair lay smoothly in place, neatly French-braided without a hair straying, just like Angela's heavier, thicker hair.

Security hair.

And, today, full Courts dress uniform to go with it. Black instead of Nik and Ange's forest green.

First time I've worn Courts blacks.

She had her own set of Security dress greens, as a sworn Do It Right Security adjunct. However, at the Courts, every Corporate leader wore black. Or so she had been told. Her previous position as a Courts consultant only required dress greens and *not* the special black coat.

Why?

"It looks great, Ange," she said. "Thank you."

"Ready for the coat?"

"As ready as I'll ever be." Melanie rose and slid her arms into the sleeves of the knee-length tunic coat that went over the form-fitting black pants, grateful for Angela's help. "I don't know how you two manage to do this on your own. It's so tight." The wrap front was so snug she could barely move her arms to button it.

Angela laughed. "Once the nanofabric adjusts to you, then it becomes easier to move and talk. You'll see. This coat has built-in defenses, so it's stiffer."

A reason to wear the blacks, then, I guess. As well as a signifier of power.

Light rap of knuckles on the door. "You two ready?" Nik asked.

"We're clear," Angela said.

Nik entered and surveyed Melanie. "Looks good." He handed something to Angela. "Hold this. Mel, look here." He held up a small blue and gold pin. It flashed. Nik pinned it to her coat collar. He repeated the process with the small gold pin Angela held. "Courts-specific ID pins. They stay on this collar from now on. We'll initialize them next."

Melanie looked into the mirror, studying the two small, round pins. One was gold. The other was a swirling mix of blue and green with gold trim. The blue and green pin matched those on Nik and Angela's collars, though theirs lacked gold trim. But Angela's other pin was white with gold trim, while Nik's was black and silver with gold trim.

"What do the colors mean?" she asked.

"Blue and green for Do It Right—organizational ID. Gold trim for company presidents. That's universal ID here at the Courts. Your gold means Executive Council. My black and silver with gold trim means I'm your approved Security representative. Ange's white with gold means Head of Security. Allows for quick visual ID."

"Makes sense."

Nik cleared his throat. "Ange, what's on your schedule?"

Angela grimaced. "Head of Security meetings. I won't see you two until evening. I need to leave now." She gave Melanie a quick hug. "Good luck on your investiture."

"Thank you," Melanie said.

Angela kissed Nik and left. Nik took a deep breath. "Ready?"

Melanie nodded, unable to speak.

"You'll do fine. Your pins aren't just visual IDs, they're quick access IDs. Let's initialize them now."

"How?"

"The pins will take a blood sample from your thumbs. Very miniscule." Nik waited while she put her thumbs on the pins. "Repeat this after me. Initialize. Melanie Landreth Fielding." He blinked and she saw teal text flash across his eyes. "MeDrethF 29. L34. WDLSES30."

She repeated the code phrases. Something pricked her thumbs. The pins grew hot.

"That's good."

Melanie dropped her hands, then glanced quickly at her thumbs, expecting to see some sort of mark on them. A single pinprick on each thumb faded away as she looked.

"What does this do?"

"Once you swear your oath in front of the Executive Council, you have full access to Council facilities and structures worldwide. ID via retina scan, DNA link, thumbprint. Full Gizmo access. That's done at the Council swearing. No more situational oaths."

"That'll be a relief."

Nik scowled. "We'll see if you say that afterward. Those pins are now locked into your coat."

"So someone could take my coat and pretend to be me?"

Nik shook his head. "Once you're done with this meeting, the coat is locked into your biometrics. No one else can use it. If they try, it might kill them, might disable them. Random."

"Pretty serious Security. Has it been tested?"

Nik's face grew darker. "The results haven't been pretty. It works. That's all you need to know. Let's go."

Melanie took a deep breath of her own and stepped out. An overlay icon popped up over her right eye and she blinked it up. A map.

<Trust the map?> she asked.

<Yes.>

She blinked the overlay to a smaller size so it wouldn't obscure her vision, and continued down the hallway.

Her mother and Kathy Miller waited for her around the corner. Diana wore the same black uniform as Melanie, but her organizational ID was the red, white and blue of the New Federated States, edged with copper and silver. Kathy Miller's uniform was navy blue with a

Security pin like Nik's, and the New Federated States pin like Diana's, without the copper and silver edging.

"You come in with me," Diana said. "I introduce both you and Andrew."

"Andrew? Too?"

"High Space and—other issues you'll understand soon."

"So why the hell couldn't I know this before now?"

"Yes. What the hell is *she* doing here?" Andrew snapped from behind her. Melanie turned, clenching her fists. The jagged scar down the left side of her brother's face showed brightly and she bit back a smile. Her mark. She'd given that one to him when extracting Peter the Netwalker from him.

His ID pin sported the Stephens Reclamation brown and green. At his side stood a slender, tall blonde in an olive-green uniform with Stephens and Security pins—Celina Mariskova, Andrew's Head of Security. Her pale blue eyes glanced over Melanie and focused on Nik. They nodded at each other.

"I'm being sworn to the Courts Exec," Melanie said.

He bristled. "Mother, how can you do this? Both of us? On the same day?"

"It's required for the initial swearing," Diana said. "You are siblings. My children."

"Both of us for Exec," Melanie said, keeping her vocal tones flat. "I can't see how that's going to be productive. Why weren't we told?"

"Part of the process!" Diana growled.

"It's not productive." Andrew's gaze met Melanie's. "Agreed?"

She nodded unwillingly. He was right, damn it. They should have been told.

"You two are adults. Be professional, damn it! I raised both of you better than this!"

Andrew pressed his lips together tightly. "Mother, there's been a lot between us."

"Everyone else puts aside differences once they pass through those doors!" Diana snapped. "Your companies are now major High Space participants. Stephens and DIR sit on Exec at the same time. There are —reasons for that. As you'll see. Your uncle Peter and I made it work;

hell, your grandmother and I cooperated when we walked inside those doors. I expect nothing less from *my* children."

"Understood," Andrew growled.

"Agreed," Melanie muttered.

"Here's the protocol. One of the Courts judges will escort us inside. I'll be in the lead. Melanie, you're on my right side. Andrew, you're on my left. Both of you have initialized your pins?"

"Yes," Andrew said.

Melanie nodded.

"You'll feel something as you walk in the door. Should be minor if the initialization worked properly. After that, we'll sit in the three seats provided. At that point you'll swear your oaths. Then—well, we'll see."

Melanie swallowed. "When do I present the Dialogue final?"

"You're on the agenda. You won't present until you're seated. I'm not sure when you're presenting because I'm not at that level. I'm not at Exec status any more. Can't be, as the New Federation President."

"Okay."

Diana looked at both of them. "Any more questions?"

Melanie shook her head, mirrored by Andrew.

"Then let's take our positions." Diana turned. Kathy Miller took the lead. Melanie fell into place at her mother's right side, Andrew at her left. Nik and Mariskova followed them.

They walked to this hallway's end. Two thick blast doors kept them from going further. Melanie licked her lips, making herself breathe deeply.

The doors rumbled open slowly. A small, gray-haired woman wearing a white uniform limped out to meet them. Relief welled up in Melanie as she recognized Zoë Wright, the Corporate Courts judge and family friend she'd known for years as Aunty Zoë.

Not Aunty Zoë, Judge Wright.

"Hello Diana. Melanie, Andrew," Judge Wright said, smiling. "We've waited for this day for a long time."

What the hell does she mean by that? Especially since it's taken so long to get this swearing to happen?

"It *is* a momentous day," her mother said, her voice neutral.

Judge Wright bowed, first to Diana, then Melanie, then Andrew. "Follow me."

Kathy Miller stepped to the side as Diana, Melanie and Andrew followed the judge into the chambers. A quick flash of heat pulsed through Melanie, followed by cool pinpricks. Bright light dimmed out everything around her save for three chairs set in the middle of the large chamber. She heard others in the room but could not see them.

"Who is being presented to the Executive Council?" boomed a deep voice.

Artificial, modified with distortion.

Zoë Wright bowed. "I present the third generation from the Stephens family to serve on the Executive Council of the Corporate Courts of the Gizmo Protectorate."

What the! Gizmo Protectorate?

Applause rose around them. Judge Wright waved them forward, then continued on, disappearing into the darkness that surrounded them.

A chime sounded and the chamber fell silent.

Diana strode forward two steps. "My name is Diana Stephens Landreth," she said. "I present Melanie Landreth Fielding and Andrew Landreth Stephens to the Executive Council of the Corporate Courts of the Gizmo Protectorate."

"Verification?" the hidden voice rumbled.

Kathy Miller joined Diana. "Security Representative Kathryn Patricia Miller for Diana Stephens Landreth."

Nik joined Melanie. "Security Representative Nikolas Andreas Morley for Melanie Landreth Fielding."

"Security Representative Celina Marina Mariskova for Andrew Landreth Stephens."

"Be seated."

Melanie sat in the right-hand chair. Nik stood behind her, hands on her shoulders. A low hum resonated in front of them. The floor opened. Slowly, a copper-colored spiky sphere rose through the opening. A deep bass growl that vibrated into her bones took the place of the hum, continuing as the floor closed. Alternating pinpricks of ice and heat raced up Melanie's left side and down her right side, repeating.

Gizmo itself.

Her hands tightened on the arms of her chair.

"Andrew Landreth Stephens, come forward!" The voice echoing from Gizmo lacked the deep vibrato of the previous speaker. Andrew stood.

"I am Andrew Landreth Stephens," he said. His chin jerked twice—something he'd always done when nervous.

"Who speaks for Andrew Landreth Stephens?"

"Celina Marina Mariskova."

"Diana Stephens Landreth," their mother said. "I am the natural and only daughter of Sarah Elizabeth Stephens and Daniel Kenneth Andrews. Andrew Landreth Stephens is my natural and only son, my oldest child. His father is William Parker Landreth."

Silence. Then Gizmo spoke in a deeper tone. "Truth. Descent confirmed for Andrew Landreth Stephens. DNA connection to Diana Stephens Landreth and Sarah Elizabeth Stephens confirmed. Andrew Landreth Stephens confirmed. Celina Marina Mariskova and Andrew Landreth Stephens, come forward."

Andrew slowly walked to the Gizmo. The spikes glided apart, creating two openings. Mariskova guided Andrew's hands inside them. She whispered something to him. Andrew nodded curtly. She slid a mouthguard into his mouth. Andrew chewed on it a couple of times, settling it. The openings closed down on Andrew's wrists.

Bright green light flared around Andrew. His body jerked irregularly, legs kicking, torso twitching, head lurching back and forth. His arms remained stiff, constrained by the Gizmo.

Then the light flared out. Andrew sagged, then straightened up. The openings snapped wide again, and Celina stepped forward to remove the mouthguard, then ease his hands out of Gizmo.

"Andrew Landreth Stephens is now approved for Executive Council," Gizmo boomed.

Oh. My. God.

Melanie took a deep breath, only now realizing she had been holding it while Andrew was connected to the Gizmo.

Do we control it or does it control us?

<What about Dialogue? Should I shut it down?> she texted her mother.

<It's okay,> Diana answered. <Netwalkers can be a problem. Dialogue only is okay.>

Andrew stepped back slowly, pausing after each step, in careful control. His pale gold hair glowed in the bright light. He raised his chin defiantly, tightening his jaw, close to falling into his chair as he sat.

"Melanie Landreth Fielding, come forward!"

She stood, heart pounding like it used to do while waiting for the countdown to start a ski race.

"I am Melanie Landreth Fielding," she said, firmly keeping her voice from quavering.

"Who speaks for Melanie Landreth Fielding?"

"Nikolas Andreas Morley."

"Diana Stephens Landreth. I am the only natural daughter of Sarah Elizabeth Stephens and Daniel Kenneth Andrews. Melanie Landreth Fielding is my only natural daughter and my second child. Her father is William Parker Landreth."

"Truth. Descent confirmed for Melanie Landreth Fielding. DNA connection to Diana Stephens Landreth and Sarah Elizabeth Stephens confirmed. Melanie Landreth Fielding confirmed. Nikolas Andreas Morley and Melanie Landreth Fielding, come forward."

This is it.

Melanie walked up to the Gizmo, swallowing hard. Nik guided her right hand into the opening. She felt a padded grip and closed her hand around it. The grip warmed and expanded to wrap around her hand like a glove. Nik guided her other hand inside and the same thing happened to it.

No turning back now.

<Want a mouthguard?>

<Should I?>

<I didn't use it during my investiture. Relax.> Nik paused. <Been through worse. Both of us.>

<Then no.>

<Good luck.> Nik stepped back.

Bright green light flared around Melanie. White-hot pain shot through her, ten times worse than anything she'd experienced in a situational oath. Sharp needle points pricked up and down her arms while mild electric shocks twitched through her.

Steady. Steady. Breathe. Relax. Don't fight.

<INTRUDER ALERT!> flashed across her eyes in bright flashing red text.

Crap! Enforcer alarm! Forced virtual!

Her eyes snapped open and she stared right into the green glare of an unfamiliar virtual space. No Gizmo. A shadowy male figure reached for her.

"NO!" she yelled, projecting every ounce of Enforcer compulsion she could summon into her voice. "Back OFF!"

The shadow-wrapped figure startled. It poked at her again, but this time she fended it off with raised hands. It stood still for a moment, then shot a ray of green light at her. She bounced it back.

More lights came at her.

Like the dance game.

One light grazed her cheek, and it burned.

Only this time it's for real!

"STOP!" she finally screamed. It rarely worked in the dance game, but maybe here it would. Rules changed between virtual and sims, unpredictably so.

This time it worked.

<*Submit,*> the shadowy figure intoned.

"No. Not until you reveal yourself," Melanie gasped.

The shadow moved closer. A single green ray beamed from its hand and took on a rapier shape. The tip touched just under her chin, the point burning and poking at the same time. Pressure increased until she stood, chin raised.

<*Submit,*> the figure repeated.

"No," Melanie said. "Reveal yourself first."

Could I use the blue light as a parry?

She'd never used her blue light as a weapon before, but if those green lights had that power in this virtual setting, maybe her own tools might.

Manipulating blue light's too new a skill to be certain. But worth trying.

She began to whisper the codes.

<*Stop that*>

"No." Damn it, did that break the code cycle?

She repeated the last sequence, relieved as the familiar tingle that meant she had blue light in her hands prickled.

<*Submit or die.*> The green light started to trace a line from her chin to her throat.

"Never!" Now how could she shape blue light into a tool?

Need something long and solid. Staff. Think of it as a staff of light.

Staff formed in her hands. Solidified. She knocked the rapier away from her throat, suddenly free from all restraint. She sparred with the figure, staff against rapier, until she found her opening, sending the rapier flying.

Flash.

She blinked asymmetrically, momentarily blinded by that bright white light.

No longer in virtual. The staff of blue light had disappeared. She knelt on the floor before Gizmo, gasping for breath.

How the hell did I get here?

Melanie rose, breathing hard, staring at Gizmo. Murmurs arose in the shadows surrounding her. Then, slowly, coming from where she'd seen Judge Wright disappear, the sound of a single set of hands clapping. Others took up the beat. Melanie looked around, bewildered, still unable to see past the shadows.

"Melanie Landreth Fielding approved for Executive Council," Gizmo whispered, its tone somewhat less intimidating than it had been before.

Louder applause, coupled with cheers. Nik rested his right hand on her shoulder.

"Holy crap, Melanie," he whispered. "Are you all right?"

"I think so," she gasped. "What the hell just happened? What did you see?"

Her mother joined Nik. "None of us has seen a human form connected with Gizmo. Until now."

"Was it identifiable?"

"No," her mother said. "Think about it later. Still more to do. Need help sitting?"

Melanie shook her head. She drew three more deep breaths, then turned to face the chairs, choosing not to back away from the Gizmo like Andrew had.

Don't show fear to that damned thing.

Her mother and Nik stood close, ready to help if she needed it. Andrew glowered at her but Celina gave Melanie the faintest smile, then a quick nod of respect.

Step one. It didn't hurt.

Step two. A little wobbly.

Step three. More confidence. She'd felt worse after a morning of training.

Step four. At the chair.

She turned around, put her hands on the chair's arms, and eased herself into the seat, tightly controlling every aching muscle in spite of wanting to thump down hard into the seat like Andrew had.

Judge Wright re-emerged from the darkness.

"Congratulations, Andrew. Melanie, that was spectacular. Congratulations. Your mother's reports on your abilities have certainly understated what you're capable of doing. Impressive. This bodes well for your later proposal."

"Thank you."

"Now it's time for your actual oaths." Judge Wright snapped her fingers. Three men stepped out from the shadows. Melanie recognized them as Henri Montcrief of Troubadour, Zhao Mei-lein of Mei-Lein Enterprises, and Satou Hisuko of Tobai Heavy Industries. Montcrief stood by Andrew while Zhao stood by Melanie, giving her a quick smile before he took his place.

Thank you.

He'd always been a good friend and ally. Satou stayed by Judge Wright.

"Andrew Landreth Stephens." Judge Wright turned to face Andrew.

"Yes." Andrew stood, intensely focused on Judge Wright.

"You are the principal leader of Stephens Reclamation?"

"Yes."

"Who recommends Andrew Landreth Stephens for the Executive Council of the Corporate Courts of the Gizmo Protectorate?"

"I do," Henri Montcrief said firmly. "I solemnly vow that Andrew Landreth Stephens is eligible for this position."

"Second?"

Diana rose. "Andrew Landreth Stephens is my natural son. I second the recommendation of Troubadour for his placement upon the Executive Council."

"Moved and seconded." Wright looked around the room. "Are there any objections?"

Silence.

"Satou, do you hear any objections?"

"Most honorable judge, I do not."

Wright walked to Gizmo. "Andrew Landreth Stephens, come here."

Andrew's lips tightened but he joined Wright.

"Place your right hand here." Wright pointed to a different space on Gizmo from where they'd placed their hands before. Andrew slowly, reluctantly, obeyed.

Melanie watched him, trying to determine if the device wreaked any further toll.

"Repeat after me. I, Andrew Landreth Stephens, accept this most high office of member of the Executive Council of the Corporate Courts of the Gizmo Protectorate." Wright waited for Andrew to repeat the words, then continued. "By this oath, I most solemnly swear to keep the secrets discussed here in highest confidentiality." Another pause for repetition. "Should I breach this oath, the penalty is death."

Andrew's voice faltered on this repeat. He coughed, then repeated the phrase in a steadier voice.

"I will take any conflict with any other member of this body to arbitration rather than seek satisfaction through filing Intent or Contract."

Oh crap. What does that mean? What happens when one of us breaks this part of the vow?

Again, Andrew's voice faltered. His eyes darted toward Melanie. Then he swallowed hard and repeated.

"I will extend my best efforts to protect Gizmo and keep the full range of its abilities secret."

No hesitation.

"To your knowledge, do you have any natural heirs, sons or daughters, either acknowledged or unacknowledged?"

"I do not." Andrew's lips tightened.

"Then you will swear the following. I will extend my best efforts to conceive my own biological heirs." Pause for his repetition. "When these children are born, they will be presented to the Corporate Courts for genetic recording."

Andrew hesitated, then repeated this phrase.

Why is this so important?

"Should I not conceive my own biological heirs, I will present suitable close kin to the Courts to be my eventual successor."

Again, Andrew hesitated before repeating this phrase.

Oh God. In a few moments I have to make this oath. Does this mean any kids Andrew has might end up being my heirs?

"So do I swear."

As Andrew repeated the final phrase, Gizmo flashed. Melanie swallowed hard.

I'm next.

She kept wondering about the requirement for an heir throughout her own swearing. This time, when Gizmo flashed, she thought she caught a glimpse of the shadowy figure she'd just fought.

But nothing further happened. As she dropped her hand from Gizmo, the bright lights dimmed. Softer light illuminated the galleries surrounding the central stage. Her mother shook hands with Andrew, kissed Melanie, then faded into the galleries.

"Let me show you your seat," Zhao said, offering an arm. Zhao guided Melanie to a seat next to him, Nik following them, while Montcrief took Andrew and Celina to another seat directly across from her. Judge Wright returned to an elevated stand at the front of the chambers, joining five others. Satou Hisuko followed Wright and sat in the high seat.

"This regular meeting of the Executive Council of the Corporate Courts of the Gizmo Protectorate is now called to order," he said. A viewscreen shimmered to life in front of Melanie. "Congratulations to our two new members. If you have any questions about procedures or protocol, please ask your sponsors. In the future, you will receive advance briefings on meeting topics. Please refrain from votes today unless you are certain you understand the issues at hand. If you are unsure, please check with your sponsors. At this time, agenda items and supporting documents are on your viewscreens. Item One."

Melanie quickly scrolled down. Her Dialogue presentation was next to last on the agenda. She looked around quickly for her mother and didn't see her.

Guess she must have left after our investiture.

She scrolled back up and pulled up the first item, a presentation by Henri Montcrief reviewing the most recent Courts filings.

The Dialogue approval process would be anticlimactic compared to what she had just gone through.

Why are heirs of my body so damn important?

Whatever the reason for her own heirs, it was important enough that she had to present them to Gizmo. *When will I learn more about this?*

Melanie sank back in her chair, sick dread rising in her, along with fatigue and the beginnings of a headache. She slipped the box of Burnout tabs out of her pocket and took one.

Burnout had more than one use—and right now she needed this headache *gone.*

I WONDER HOW MELANIE'S INVESTITURE WENT?

Marty hurried back to their quarters after he finished his High Space meetings. Not a lot of time before the formal reception in Melanie and Andrew's honor tonight. Enough time to quickly debrief Melanie about his meetings and whatever she could share of the day's events. From what little buzz he heard, she had made quite the impression at the Executive Council.

<Hon?> he called via Dialogue.

No response.

Surely she'd be done by now?

She was safe here. Wasn't she? He didn't even know for certain where they were. They had been brought in under cover of darkness last night, in a shaded skimmer, all location tracking disabled.

<Nik. Where's Mel?> he texted.

<In quarters.>

<She's not answering me.>

<She's not answering anyone right now.>

<Is everything all right? Did something go wrong?>

<Dialogue went well. Tired. I think. Needed down time.>

<Thanks.>

Something's wrong.

Marty ran the rest of the way to their quarters.

"Melanie?" he called as he burst into the main room.

A faint noise in the study, the only room with an outside view. He hurried toward it. A single, narrow window let in light through the three-foot-thick walls. Melanie still wore her dress blacks as she sat on the ledge in front of the window, legs pulled in tight, head buried in her knees. She didn't look up at him.

"Hon?"

Melanie slid over so he could sit next to her, but kept her face buried. She was crying. He slid his arm around her and held her close. She turned her head toward him. He murmured softly and stroked her forehead until he felt the tension ease from her body. She finally raised her head.

"What's wrong?"

She shook her head and buried it in her knees again.

"Mel, talk to me. What's wrong?"

She shuddered and sat up, leaning her head against the wall. "Godawful headache. Took a Burnout hours ago. Several. Didn't touch it."

"I have stronger stuff."

"No," she sighed. "I have that damnable reception in less than half-an-hour. I need something to knock me out after, though. It's Gizmo."

"There's been some buzz about what happened this morning."

Melanie snorted. "It was pretty damn dramatic. But I can't tell you about it. Tight secrecy." She closed her eyes and grimaced. "Oh God,

Marty. Natural heirs of my body are important for some damned reason. No one will tell me why. " She clenched a fist and pounded her knee as she continued to speak. "No. One. Will. Tell. Me!" She slammed the wall on the last word, wincing as she did it.

"Do you have any idea at all what's going on?"

Melanie shook her head. "I thought I'd get answers today. I got something." She put her forehead in her hands and rubbed it. "Gizmo and Liam are tied together. *And I can't talk to you about why I know this without this damn headache cinching tighter around my head!*" She slammed the wall again. "Ow! Fucking Gizmo!"

"Oh Christ." He reached around and started to rub her shoulders as best as he could. "How much Burnout have you taken?"

"I can't take any more without the dragon turning on me," she groaned. "I have to get the fuck away from here. From it." She drew a deep sobbing breath. "I need to eat. I've not eaten for hours. I don't know if it's the headache or the Burnout or that I'm cycling again or what. Or if it's everything all together. But I'm just not hungry."

"Maybe we should leave now."

"No. I can't. It's not—politic." Melanie leaned her head back again, shuddering. "And maybe, just maybe, I'll learn what I need to know at the reception tonight. I have one more meeting tomorrow morning. High Space ratification. You can be at that one. Between now and then, if I can corner my mother, maybe she'll give me some answers. But as soon as we're done, we're out of here." She rolled her head from side to side, then worked her shoulders. "How did High Space go?"

"We're approved to replace Johnson Space. Easier than I thought. Your mother was very persuasive."

Melanie laughed harshly. "Dialogue final certification was the same way, minus Mom. Zhao complimented me on being over-prepared."

"That's good. I guess."

"They grilled me pretty good. I didn't feel like there was anything I couldn't answer, so that's good." She laughed bitterly. "After my investiture—ow!" She grabbed her head, sucking in her breath quickly.

"You okay?"

She nodded, wincing. "Yeah. Just—figuring out these Security limits. *That* word is off limits. Definitely. Anyway, after—what happened this morning—I don't think anyone wanted to give me too much grief." She straightened up. "God, I really want to take a pass on this reception, but I'd better splash some water on my face."

"Not going to change?"

She shook her head. "Formal dress blacks are mandatory for onsite Exec meetings and activities. There are—identity keys—built into the coat."

"Oh." He slid out of the alcove. Melanie stood up and went into the bathroom.

"At least my hair looks good," she said. "This Security style is amazing. After everything I've done today, it still looks like it did when Ange braided it this morning. I don't have to fix it. That usually doesn't happen."

Marty heaved a sigh of relief.

If she can talk about her hair, she's starting to pull out of this funk.

WILL THIS DAMN FUCKING DAY EVER END?

Melanie stared into her wineglass as Zhao told a joke. The uproarious laughter at their table added to the overwhelming overstimulation of the day. At least alcohol took the edge off of her headache. Food still didn't look good.

Andrew and his consort Renee sat with Andrew's Mexican partners, as well as Montcrief and the rest of the Troubadour party. Alliances seemed to play a major part of socializing tonight, more than she remembered from previous Courts meetings.

I wasn't on the Exec then. Maybe that's part of it. Damn it, why haven't I felt Gizmo like this before? Something about that looming presence still lingered close by. *It shoved me into virtual easily, as if I were just a piece of fluff.* That scared her, the more she thought about it. *I have to figure this out before the next Exec. But how? I can't talk to Marty. Can I talk to Mom?*

Her mother wasn't in the seat she had occupied just a minute earlier.

Damn it, Mom, don't cut out on me!

Kathy Miller still sat at the table with Diana's party, laughing at something Zoë Wright was saying.

So Mom will be back.

And if she isn't, Kathy has clearance. I can talk to her.

So did Nik, but he didn't know enough about Netwalk and Liam's potential ties to Gizmo to be of use.

"Mel." Her mother touched her shoulder. "Let's talk."

Melanie put down her wineglass, relieved. <Marty. Be back soon. Cover for me.>

He squeezed her hand. <I will. Take care.>

She followed Diana out the door and down the hallway. "Mom, I can't take another Gizmo session today. Maybe not even tomorrow."

"This won't be a Gizmo session. Sarah wants to talk."

Melanie rolled her eyes. "I don't know if I can handle an Enforcer discipline session, even. My head is splitting."

"Initial exposures to Gizmo do that to you. It gets better."

"Well, I'm glad to hear that," Melanie grumbled.

Diana stopped and traced a figure on the wall. A door silently slid open. As she followed her mother through the opening, Melanie's headache faded.

Diana faced Melanie. "This is one of the few places you can get away from Gizmo on site. You can't stay here for more than half an hour, but it's a break." She scowled. "It's also very popular, especially in the evenings. We can't be too long."

"Thank you." With the headache fading, the combination of Burnout, alcohol, and little food made Melanie's legs wobbly. She sank gratefully in the closest stuffed chair. "So what does Sarah want?"

"What happened this morning?"

"You were there."

"She was deep inside the chip." Diana snapped up a hologlobe. "We just looked at the vid and she has questions. Sarah, come on out. Mel, what happened?"

Melanie shrugged. "What's to say? Flashing lights, lots of pain. I got into a fight. I won. End of story." Melanie buried her head in her hands, rubbing her eyes.

"More went on than that," Sarah said. Melanie looked up. Sarah looked younger than the usual guise she chose, closer to Melanie's age. "Diana, run that video again." She peered intently into the globe. "Stop. There."

Melanie shuddered at the sight of the shadowy figure. "I don't need to relive that experience."

"No one gets free from Gizmo during investiture like you did!" Sarah said abruptly, a tone so much like her own in the midst of deep analysis that Melanie sat up straight in shock. "*No one.* It hasn't been possible—until now. Did you feel anything?"

"Run it backward and focus on me, not the shadow," Melanie directed. "There."

Sarah took her hand. "Show me."

Melanie rebelled. "You're dancing pretty close to the edge. That's Enforcer territory."

"I need to know. Tell me if you won't show me."

"I was attacked," Melanie said slowly. "I won't tell you the specifics. There was an attack. I reacted."

"Okay," Sarah said. "Slow-mo the recording."

The video advanced frame by frame. "There!" Diana snapped. "Do you see it?"

Sarah stalked into the hologlobe. She peered closely. Delicate finger traces reversed the video, slowed it even further. "I can't see how you did it, Melanie."

"Unless she thought herself free psychokinetically," Diana said.

Sarah and Diana stared at each other.

"That could be," Sarah said. "She's very strong."

"Strong enough to control Gizmo?"

"Maybe. Maybe more."

"God, we've got to have those genes! If not her, then her daughter."

"What the hell is going on?" Melanie asked. "And will someone tell me, *please,* why having an heir of my own body is so damned important?"

They turned to face her.

"We don't have a lot of time," Diana said.

"Then make it quick. All this stuff is making my head hurt."

Not to mention that I'm really feeling the booze and Burnout, and I'd just as soon not be this vulnerable around Sarah!

"Two things," Diana said. "First, Gizmo manipulates the epigenetics of humans around it. It appears to be a factor of age at initial exposure as well as direct line descent from those exposed to it. It activates the genetic expression of certain traits."

"I already know that."

"What you don't know is that we—Sarah, me, now you—show distinct genetic tendencies toward skills that enable us to work with and control Gizmo. Those skills improve with each generation, predominantly amongst women."

"Wouldn't that mean that you and Sarah would have similar abilities? After all, Mom, you were an adult when you were exposed."

"My exposure was different from Sarah's. More intensive. My skills are stronger than hers. And you were exposed in utero, after I spent several years working with Gizmo. Your father was exposed to Gizmo, too, so you and Andrew are the first children of exposed parents. You've also had Netwalker toxin exposure."

"What does this mean?"

"You and any child you bear—especially a daughter—might be the key to understanding and controlling Gizmo," Sarah said.

Melanie laughed. "Don't we already control it?"

"You have to ask, after your fight with it?" Sarah began pacing the room. "The other thing. That shadow you saw. You can't bring it up in more detail?"

Melanie shook her head. "I haven't the faintest clue who or what that was. I thought it was Liam."

"Damn it!" Sarah growled. "No, Melanie, *it's not Liam*. He's in there but he's not that powerful."

"Then who is it?" Melanie asked.

"It may be Francis Stewart. He uploaded himself to the Gizmo while he was still alive, in an attempt to control it," Sarah said. "Figuring out what Francis did, and trying to find a means to counter it, is how I got the original idea for Netwalk."

"Francis Stewart? *The* Francis Stewart? Just what the hell is his connection to Gizmo?"

Is this what's different about Liam's children? They're descended from Stewart through their mother—but did she have exposure? Or was it Liam?

"He may have created the Gizmo," Sarah said. "We don't know."

"If Stewart didn't create it, then who did? And why did I get a feel of Liam when wrestling with that damn thing—oh."

Suddenly it made sense. Of course, Liam had gone through a Gizmo swearing. She had seen him at the Courts, wearing the same olive drab Security uniform that Andrew's Celina now wore. Liam had been Peter's vowed Security representative.

Oh God. I have to check the kids again when we get home. No delay. Liam is tied to Gizmo. But how deep does that tie go?

"Stewart understood the most about Gizmo. He never would explain his knowledge. Next to your late grandfather Parker Landreth, your father knows more about war machines and their functions than anyone else—and he couldn't explain the Gizmo. He thinks it may be alien in origin," Diana said.

"What?" Melanie stared at her mother. "Are you serious?"

"Alloys. Abilities. Technological capacity," Sarah said bluntly. "Trust me in this even if you don't trust me in anything else, granddaughter. I know what weaponry we humans are capable of. I concur with your father—because of the role he once held in Landreth Technologies."

"Mom?"

Diana exhaled. "Either Gizmo is an interdicted war machine, far beyond any tech your father could comprehend—or it's of alien origin and Stewart somehow made an alliance with it. If it's alien, we're in big trouble if more of them find us. Now do you understand the High Space stakes?"

"I need another drink," Melanie said, instead of what she really wanted to say.

Why wasn't I told this sooner? How much can I share with Marty?

God. No wonder her mother and grandmother were in alliance when it came to the Gizmo.

And they want to make certain I have a kid. So what does that make Liam? The Freedom Army? Are they in alliance—

Melanie shook her head. "My headache is coming back just thinking about all of this."

Her mother studied her. "I think it's about time you learned the *other* way to get rid of a Gizmo headache. Come on, I'll have that drink with you."

CHAPTER 8

LATE THE FOLLOWING AFTERNOON, MELANIE STRODE DOWN THE HILLSIDE at DIR headquarters, headed for the crèche. Her head pounded with a hangover from last night's epic drinking session with Zhao, Kathy Miller, Nik, and, eventually, Andrew, Montcrief, Judge Wright, and her mother.

At least I can still drink Andrew under the table!

The tricks she'd learned as part of Ski Patrol and the race tour still worked.

Transfers very nicely to Corporate competitive drinking. Still, it's a good thing I don't do that too often anymore.

This morning's meetings had required a double dose of Burnout, but the hangover counteracted the Gizmo effect.

Have to find something besides alcohol to block that damnable Gizmo headache. Takes too much alcohol to get that effect.

It *did* explain why everyone drank so heavily at the Courts.

She blinked her access code to the lock at the Security crèche building. It took a few minutes to locate the classroom for the youngest crèche residents. Melanie looked through the one-way window to observe before stepping in. Sophie pored over a pad with the older boy, now called Donnie by most of the staff, while the younger boy, Alex, sat in the middle of a pile of blocks, frowning as he arranged them by size and color.

<May I enter?> Melanie texted to Helen, the supervising teacher.

<Of course,> Helen answered. <Ready for reading time. Want to do it?>

Melanie hesitated. She had hoped for just a quick screening, no prolonged contact.

On the other hand…if I eventually want to make a case for the boys as my potential legacy, I need to get to know them better. Considering the possibility that they're a possible alternative Gizmo-controlling bloodline, I damn well want to keep an eye on them.

Early bonding was important. She had learned that about horses from her mother. Why would kids be any different?

<Yes.>

She pushed the door open. Sophie looked up.

"Auntie Mel!" she squealed, dropping the pad and running hard toward Melanie. Melanie managed to fend Sophie off before she smacked into her bad knee.

"Easy there, girl!" she laughed.

Both boys watched her with wary eyes. Donnie stood protectively by his brother.

Scared of me. Can't blame them. Last time they saw me….

Sophie hugged Melanie hard. "Are you going to read to us today?"

"Yes."

"Goodie!" Sophie bounced up and over to a pile of books. "Come *on*," she said to the boys. "Auntie Mel's a *good* reader. She's *fun*."

The older boy scowled at Melanie. "What did you do with Deedee?"

Deedee? Oh. Deirdre. Conley.

"She's—well, we're still working things out," Melanie said. *I'm not going to lie to them.* "She's okay. But we don't agree on a lot of things." She made herself smile at him. "Our first meeting was not the best. I'm sorry about that. I would like to get to know you better." She spread her hands wide. "I'm really not that scary."

"Don't be stupid," Sophie said. "Auntie Mel is fun! She'll take you skiing, and riding horses. Hiking. Fun stuff!"

"Horsies?" The younger boy perked up at that.

Melanie grinned at him. "Yes. I have a horse. Would you like to meet her?"

So little Alex likes horses. Not like his father.

"Yes!" Alex stood up and toddled over to Sophie, who was sorting through books. "Want horsie book."

Donnie watched Melanie warily. "When can we see Deedee?"

"Honey, I really can't say. I'm sorry. I didn't realize how much she meant to you."

He nodded, frowning thoughtfully. Melanie chose not to push it.

"Here!" Sophie crowed. "Here's a horse book!" Alex grabbed it from her and carried it over to Melanie.

"Read?" he asked.

"Yes," Melanie said to him. She looked at Donnie. "Is that all right with you?"

Donnie sighed. But Alex took Melanie's hand as she walked to a rocking chair. He climbed into her lap as if he had a right to be there, grumbling when Sophie pushed in.

"Make room for Donald," Melanie said.

"Donnie!" he insisted. Still, as she shifted the kids around on her lap, Donnie unbent and slid between her knees, forcing Melanie to change the angle of the book so he could see it.

Perfect.

Sophie tired of the picture book quickly and slipped off of Melanie's lap, lying at her feet and staring up at the ceiling, making Security fingersign to go along with the story. Alex slumped against Melanie while Donnie sat up, barely touching her knees.

Melanie managed to do a quick, non-globed scan of Alex as she read. As she blinked up the crude electromagnetic overlay viewer, she spotted the stirrings of an outside influence. A subtle trace. But no hint of Liam. A very slight whisper of colored green and copper, tinged with a bitter coppery taste in her mouth. Melanie withdrew her probe, blinking away the viewer.

That trace is Gizmo-based. Dear sweet Mother of God. Does that mean he's going to be vulnerable to Conley—or if there's a trace of Liam—or their grandfather Stewart?

Melanie adjusted Alex's position. He blinked sleepily at her.

Donnie continued to eye her suspiciously. She didn't think scanning him would be as easy.

"Time for another book," Melanie announced as she closed this one. Alex roused and followed Sophie over to the book pile. Donnie continued to glare at Melanie.

"You did something to Alex," he said quietly. "Why?"

"Because I'm responsible for keeping you safe, and I needed information that lets me do that," Melanie said without thinking about it. She startled at the words. Where had that come from? It was true enough.

"Why?"

"Because of who your parents are, and who your grandfather was."

"Deedee kept us safe."

"She can't keep you safe from everything. There are things only I can protect you from."

She can't keep them safe from Gizmo.

"Want this book!" Alex insisted.

"No! This one!" Sophie argued.

"Alex. Sophie. You need to take turns." Melanie automatically put a slight Enforcer emphasis on her words.

Donnie studied her further. "Deedee used to do that when we fought."

"It's what we adults do to teach you how to share."

Another datum toward Conley having Enforcer skills!

He considered her words. "Are you doing something to me, like Alex?"

Careful, Melanie!

"I need to find out some things that I can't see otherwise."

"Is it part of keeping us safe?"

"I won't do it if you tell me not to. But it will help keep you and Alex safe."

Donnie frowned, the considering look on his face suddenly reminding Melanie of Liam. He glanced quickly at his younger brother, chewed his lip, then nodded.

"Okay." His voice held a fearful undertone.

Melanie rested her hand gently on his shoulder. "I promise I'll be careful. You shouldn't feel anything."

He nodded again, jaw tense and tight.

Sophie danced back with another horse book and Alex clambered back into his spot. Sophie settled at her feet next to Donnie. Sighing, Donnie leaned back against Melanie's knees. She felt the tension slowly ease out of him as she read.

She didn't do it right away. The trick was to find a page with detailed pictures and enough text that she could pay half-attention to the story, half-attention to the scan. To her surprise, Donnie's trace was weaker than Alex's.

Perceptive kid, though. I think Nik's right about Security potential. He notices things.

<Mel.> Angela's text was muted in color.

<Yes?>

<Marty needs to talk to you when you're done.>

Why didn't he text me himself?

A sick feeling came over her.

Something's wrong.

She forced herself to finish the book without changing her affect. Donnie gave her a careful look at one point when her voice broke slightly, then relaxed more than he had before. Melanie found that oddly reassuring.

"Got to go now," she said once she finished the book. "Need to get back to work!"

"One more!" Sophie pleaded.

"More!" Alex echoed.

"Sorry, not today. I really have to go."

"Tomorrow!" Sophie demanded.

Despite her worry, Melanie laughed, detecting resonances of both Angela and Mama Brenda in Sophie's firmness. "Yes, Sophie. I'll read to you tomorrow, and maybe we can plan with Miss Helen to take you guys to visit the horses."

"Yes!" Sophie danced around them. Alex cheered and joined Sophie in her dance. Donnie gave Melanie a shy smile and joined them, elbowing Alex out of the way as he grabbed Sophie's hand and danced with her. Alex tagged along behind them, surprisingly not objecting.

Melanie watched the kids, smiling.

"Come on," Helen called to the kids. "It's time for gym practice. You'll come tomorrow?" she asked Melanie.

"I promised the kids. Do you think it'd be okay to take them to the barn?"

"I'll go with you. Sophie and Alex have been asking, but none of us here have horse skills, and it takes time to set up an expedition otherwise. That'd be really great if you could do it."

"Then I will. Maybe we can set up something regular, because I wouldn't mind doing that."

Something fun to look forward to.

She hugged each of the kids. Melanie kept a smile on her face until she left the room.

<Marty?>

<I'm outside.>

She left the building. Marty sat on a bench, staring at seven older crèche kids running through a set of training drills on the field.

"Hey," he said. The grim look on his face tightened her stomach.

"Hey yourself. What's up?" She tried to keep her tone light.

"I didn't realize you were spending time with the kids."

"I needed to do another scan." She smiled to herself, remembering the way Alex had inserted himself into her lap.

"That's pretty quick after our return. Find out anything more?"

"That trace I found in the kids? Definitely the gadget." The faint throb of pain that wasn't her hangover warned her about saying more.

Marty looked at her questioningly. She shook her head.

He sighed and leaned back on the bench. "These damn restrictions are going to play hell with our research. If you can't talk to me about things related to the gadget and Netwalk, or the gadget and Dialogue, how are we going to get anything done?"

"Patience," she said. "I'll figure it out. That damn gadget isn't going to rule my life! I'll get approvals. There are ways. Marty, what's going on?"

He rubbed his face. "God, Mel."

"Just tell me, damn it." It felt like her gut kept tightening down on icy shards. This was bad.

Marty dropped his hands from his face, staring at them. At last he straightened up. "Before we left for the Courts, Ness and I started a sim. Electronic comparisons of your routine morning scans, ranging back to before your pregnancy."

"And?" Her heart pounded in her ears.

"Small traces of Netwalker toxin were released into your system just before the miscarriage, enough to kill the fetus."

"How?"

"We found programming codes. Ness thinks a Netwalker left something we're calling a preprogrammed poison pill at one of the virtual nodes you've intersected over the past year. We still haven't completely figured out the triggering mechanism. We do know it demonstrates characteristics compatible with what we know about the capabilities of the Freedom Army Netwalk build."

Melanie stared at Marty, stunned.

Liam. It was Liam after all. The fucker!

"What does this mean?" she asked. "Was it a one-time thing?"

Marty flung himself back and looked at the sky. "No. It has a long-term residual effect. Until we can find it in your system, you're going to be at risk for miscarriage in any pregnancy."

"Why did the surrogate miscarry?"

"The triggering mechanism is locked into the zygote," he said. "We can't pull the poison pill out of you because it's too thoroughly integrated into your body. Ness thinks you can get away with one more pregnancy before the pill's programming codes adapt. You would have to stay behind a No-Fence for the duration of the pregnancy."

"But would the baby be safe after it's born?"

"We think so. She's running models on the process now. It appears to release enough toxin in the fetus to kill it during early second trimester, but it's not consistent. What's consistent is that the pill is based in your system. Once past the second trimester, the models show toxin levels degenerating."

"Would a surrogate behind a No-Fence be safer?"

Marty shook his head. "The last testing suggests that the toxin has already adapted. It appears to have evolved to need feedback from your body to stay viable. It's unlikely any future surrogate pregnancies would last even as long as this one did."

"So it's learning," Melanie said slowly. *Hell. It's some sort of fucking Gizmo effect.* "God damn it. Damn it to hell!"

"Mel. We're still researching. We're still trying."

She couldn't sit any longer. She started pacing.

Is this how Gizmo manages to resist the genetic expression of those who would control it? Or is this a Liam or Stewart scheme?

She opened her mouth to ask Marty about this then remembered. Headache. Pain. She whirled away from him to avoid the temptation to speak despite the pain. A whistle blew and the kids gathered around their two teachers.

I'm getting approvals to talk to Marty. As soon as I can. We're working partners as well as spouses!

"Mel?" Marty's voice snapped her out of her thoughts. "We'll keep trying. If that's what you want."

"I don't have a choice," she said. "The Courts require that I do my best to produce a natural heir. We keep trying." She couldn't turn back to look at him. "You and Ness keep researching it when you can." She took a deep breath. "It's a priority." She closed her eyes so she couldn't see the kids streaming by and to hold back tears. "A Courts priority."

"I understand." His hands gently turned her to face him. "We'll get through this, Mel. Somehow."

"Thank you," she said. "Three more weeks until I can start intensive fertility treatments."

Liam. God. If I can ever find a way to make you pay for this—may you rot in hell forever!

CHAPTER 9

"GOOD GOD. IF IT WASN'T FOR ALTITUDE AND THE LACK OF HUMIDITY—" Cat McCauley stopped to cough as they marched up the slender wildlife trail behind the main house at the Andrews Ranch. "I'd think I was back at an illegal slash and burn site in the Amazon," she finished. "Whew!" She took a long drink from her water pack.

"Welcome to late summer in the Bucket Mountains." Melanie sipped on her water. An angry red sun glowered through the low smoke clouds. "But it's not much better at the Mountain right now. August is the height of our fire season."

"Worse on the Mountain," her assistant Janine said, stopping behind Cat. "Morning report from Regional Fire Authority pinpoints new fires on Hood from last night's thunderstorms. At least none of them are near HQ this year."

"Evan, how much farther should we go?" Melanie asked. This morning's hike before the DIR business meeting had been Evan Andrews's suggestion. Cat McCauley and Grady Keeney from the Rio Bravo DIR division had been the most interested and, well, she needed bonding time with both Cat and Grady. Especially Grady, who headed up DIR Rio Bravo.

Evan strode back down toward them. "The trail flattens out after this. We'll go around the tip of this ridge and through a stringer of trees in a little draw. I saw some fresh elk sign so we might be able to tiptoe up on them."

"Raptor." Cat pointed at a golden eagle rising effortlessly in the thermals rising from the canyon.

Evan squinted. "That's Number 245. Her data is accessible via Dialogue. She's one of my favorites."

"Oooh," Cat said. "She's raised ten clutches successfully? Nice."

Melanie studied Cat.

You may want to consider her as a potential Enforcer, her mother had said last night. *But good luck getting her away from Grady. She's his Head of Dialogues.*

Cat was too sensitive to the virtual world for Melanie to scan her surreptitiously, but her profile carried many of the markers Melanie considered important.

The key is virtual reaction speed.

Virtual reaction speed killed the eligibility of too many prospective Enforcer types—and that wasn't something that showed up in profiles.

Maybe I need to back off on that criterion—no, speed is crucial.

Sifting through the higher-performing Dialogues to find those with Enforcer capabilities revealed the wide variance in virtual reaction speed amongst Dialogues. Melanie *had* thought that it would be easy to find others with reaction rates like hers.

No luck so far.

But it was a matter of time. Only three busy months since her investiture to look for Enforcers. Few of the Rio Division Dialogues had been tested yet.

Timing and Grady.

Grady was used to working independently, and guarded his autonomy jealously. He got results from his Rio team. Melanie hadn't wanted to interfere with his success as she moved from President of DIR North America to DIR International President. She needed his cooperation, so she had to move delicately.

And yanking Cat McCauley away without preparation impedes a positive relationship in the future. But, damn it, if she has Enforcer potential, I need her on deck. With me. How am I going to get there?

Melanie rolled her shoulders, masking her impatience. Her heart pounded more quickly than she liked after the steep uphill hike. A function of the new fertility regime.

Not that it's made any difference yet.

But it had only been three months since she started treatment.

Just makes me more irritable. Especially with each month's failure to conceive. Maybe this week.

"Okay. Let's get going," Grady said.

Cat wryly grinned at Melanie. Melanie let Grady push past her to join Evan and hung back, hoping Cat might take advantage of the widening trail to talk a little. Another advantage of using the Ranch instead of Hoodland HQ for the quarterly update meetings was the possibility for occasional hikes with only one of the cousins as guide—no need for a major Security presence.

Granted, Melanie was pretty damn sure Nik and a few Security trainees were skulking nearby, within easy range, along with the occasional protective drone. A squad of newbies was working this conference, and from what she had seen, both he and Angela were giving them plenty to do. Surveilling this morning's hike would be a perfect training sequence.

They picked their way through the last tight series of rocky switchbacks around the ridge's point. The path took them into the stand of trees, a park-like mixture of Ponderosa pines, aspen, and brush. Evan and Grady flushed a blue grouse and Melanie admired its mottled mix of blue-black, white-tipped feathers as it barreled past her to perch on a high Ponderosa pine branch, where it scolded them with worried clucks.

"This is pretty country," Cat said. "Have you spent much time here?"

"Not as much as when I was a kid. This was my grandfather's ranch before the tribe took it over. My cousins manage it for them."

Cat nodded thoughtfully. "Bet it was fun."

Something crashed in the brush ahead of them and Melanie froze, Cat along with her. Evan held up a warning hand to stop Grady. He peered down toward the bottom of the draw, then pointed. Melanie spotted the cow elk.

"Gorgeous," Cat breathed. "So different from Rio."

"It is." Melanie thought back to the six months she'd spent training in DIR Rio Bravo. "Both places are beautiful in their own ways."

"Yes."

Melanie started to say more but paused as something *stirred* in the low-level Enforcer Netwalk monitoring utility Marty had installed in her chip last week.

What's that?

She sent out a small inquiry to the *stirring* and the sensation went away.

"One place I'd like to go—" she started.

<Melanie.> Her mother's text was urgent red. <We need you folks back at the house. Fast. ASAP.>

The Enforcer monitor stirred again. Stronger this time.

Ahead of them, Grady talked quickly to Evan. Cat and Janine stopped, Cat rapidly blinking through text.

<What's wrong?> Melanie asked her mother.

<Biological attack on Charleston. South Carolina. Leaving ASAP. Need coordinated DIR response. Talk to you first.>

<We're on our way.> Melanie switched text links. <Nik. Bring your kids in. Crisis.>

<Got report. Join you in five.>

She turned down the trail, striding past Janine and Cat. "What info are you getting?" she asked Cat.

"Scattered reports," Cat said. "It sounds like a biobomb out of the Disruptions."

That's not right—Gizmo's contained!

Footfalls behind them. "Biobombs are exactly what they are," Grady announced. "Explosive rockets, nerve gas, coupled with pathogens and some particularly nasty biotoxins."

"Origin?" Melanie asked.

"No idea yet." Grady stumbled and she steadied him.

"Take it easy," she warned. "Last thing we need is for any of us to get hurt now."

"Plenty of opportunities for that ahead," Grady growled. "Cat, you're faster at Dialogue spidering than I am. I need you to pull up everything from Brisbane May 2046, San Francisco July '46, Osaka

September '46. Do a sim plot, retrieve post-surgical measures, targeted bioremediation actions, proprietary bioremediation biologics and treatment recipes. Identify any similarity patterns. There's others but I think those are most relevant from the early data I'm getting."

All sites sterile nuked during the Disruptions.

Cold fear ran through Melanie's body.

Has Gizmo gotten loose again?

Probably not. Her mother would have told her.

Wouldn't she?

"On it as soon as I find steady footing," Cat said.

"I'll support." Melanie placed one hand on Cat's elbow, guiding her along the trail so Cat could focus without worry about the uncertain footing.

"Thank you."

As Nik and the Security kids scrambled up from the rimrocks below the trail, Melanie fought back the instinct to turn Cat over to one of them and run to the ranch house. At best, that would only save a few minutes.

And if I fall again, it'll be worse.

<Smallcraft en route for pickup,> Nik texted.

Thank God. Speeds it up.

<Thanks, Nik.> She heard the rumble of the small skimmer even now.

Hopefully it isn't too late.

She poked at the Enforcer monitor. Nothing, now.

DAMN IT, I WISH I WAS BACK IN MY LABS ON THE MOUNTAIN!

Marty scowled at the hologlobes he had running. The Ranch's labs lacked some of the tools he needed to make this massive multitasking task run more smoothly.

But this is a safer location. We get some time, this gets upgraded.

<First analysis says mutated airborne hemorrhagic flu,> Ness reported. <Match for Brisbane-46. Fast incubation, 90% mortality in first four hours. Limited vax available, start with injecting all on-site

rescue teams. Other pathogens present, analysis running. Local EMP interference with the drone samplers makes it hard. High casualty rate already.>

<Cat's finding correspondences with Osaka-46,> Marty said. He turned to another hologlobe, where Cat's research popped up. He spidered through the globe to find Cat's link, copied, tossed it into Ness's globe. Then he pulled his hands out of that globe to turn to the third one that Janine maintained for strategic assignments from Mel and copies of official response notifications.

He startled as Melanie touched his shoulder. <Finish this task. Gotta talk quick.>

He nodded acknowledgement, warned Cat and Ness of his brief inattention, set his systems to alert status, and turned to Mel.

"I'm Site Command," she told him. "Leaving in ten minutes with Grady, Cat, and folks Grady's grabbing from the Nagano and Hoodland teams here for the conference. Angela's already left with her team to secure my HQ so it'll be ready once I get there. Nik and Paul are my personals en route." She made a face. "I have to take the time to jump into Courts formal blacks. Mom's orders. We're stopping at Hoodland HQ to pick up as many finished high-end bots and more team members as we can before beating feet cross country. It'll slow down the shipment of High Space bots but that can't be helped. Gotta do this."

"Osaka-46," he said.

Melanie nodded. "If we can shoot for a different outcome, we will. Mom's giving me the full briefing en route." Her hand tightened on his for a brief moment. "*God,* Marty. That Enforcer monitor tweaked just before Mom called. Should I trust it?"

"Is it flaring constantly?"

"No. Flashes."

"Then be careful. Don't depend on it. It's still beta."

Melanie sighed. "Wish it were further along."

"So do I."

"Can't stay any longer. But I had to see you before I left."

"Glad you did. Wish I could come with you. Take care of yourself."

"I'm not on the front lines," she said.

"Close enough. If the wind turns—" He waved his hand at the admin globe. "Still an offshore flow. If it changes—"

"If the wind turns, Mom will call in the nuke. No alternative with that 90% fatality rate—can't have it spreading. She's made that clear. I'm going to do my best to keep that from happening." She paused. "We'll miss this fertile cycle. Unless I time the treatments differently. Can't be helped."

"It's a reality. There's time enough afterward." He kissed her.

She smiled as he pulled away. "Thanks. Love you. Got to go now."

"Love you. Do it right!" he said.

Her faint smile turned into a bigger, brief grin. "Do it right," she said back to him, leaning in for another quick kiss before leaving. As she left, he heard her arguing with someone via vocal link in a tagalong globe about safe perimeter lines and zone resources.

Keep her safe. Please. Not just for me. For all of us.

RIDICULOUS.

Melanie twitched at an imaginary piece of fluff on her dress blacks while waiting at Hoodland for their bots and staff to load.

Taking time to get formally attired instead of other prep. What a waste.

But she needed the Courts access. And the coat augmented her online presence—unexpected.

Normal function or unanticipated interface between it and my chip?

A fascinating consideration. Not one she had time to think about, since a growing sense of malign presence loomed over her. Almost like the malaise she'd felt just before her accident. But it could be her dread at what lay ahead.

She reviewed Osaka-46 while waiting. Ugly stuff, requiring frequent breaks from the data's unrelenting grimness. Melanie had studied Osaka in brief during her initial training. That had been dark enough. The detailed review was a horror show.

Sarah *did* have legitimate reasons to order the nuking of Osaka.

Hopefully this isn't as bad.

She disciplined herself to turn back to the task at hand.

Focus.

The Burnout box rested in her pocket, but she was still riding the curve of her first dose.

<PRIORITY INCOMING> flashed on her overlays, adding in the code for a Courts connection—Andrew. Melanie opened it in her com hologlobe.

"Mel." Andrew also wore his dress blacks. "Stephens Reclamation has teams handy in the Florida War Zone and on site at Gulf Reclamation. Can you use them?"

"Absolutely. Thank you. Link your team leaders to mine. If your teams can set up a perimeter, deploy your bots for early measures, we can speed up response."

"Done. Sending team leader links to you now."

The links popped up in her globe and she routed them. "Routed. Thanks again, Drew."

He smiled grimly. "Gotta stop this one. Any clue what's coming down in the upcoming Courts briefing?"

"Mom's not talking to me or anyone else at our level about it. Other national leaders only, not Corporate."

"Damn, I wish I had your Dialogue access," Andrew said. "Slows my response down."

"Yeah, well, there's reasons."

Andrew winced. "I don't want to risk any more of the brainburn I experienced after you got Peter out of me. I'll get my logistics folks moving so they can join up with yours. See you at the briefing."

"Thanks. See you." She switched off the link and turned to coordinating the logistics on her side.

<Activate cooperative Stephens Reclamation protocols,> she sent to Janine.

God, how many years has it been since those were last activated? Not since before I was born. How many updates will I need to do?

"ACTIVATE INITIAL SECURITY PERIMETER, EXTERNAL RING," ANGELA snapped at her console. "Keying in parameters now."

Getting that EMP pulse transmitter knocked out had taken too damn long, and data said there were more of them. She set up the inner Security Perimeter with its own power and its own shielding. Even if the external ring went down, the internal ring would hold and protect Mel, short of a direct, targeted attack.

That's Nik's job—and Diana's Security.

<EXTERNAL RING PERIMETER ACTIVATED.> Angela blinked the schematic into her globe, checking for potential breach sites. None. Good. She took a deep breath.

Next step.

"Activate filters. Sim first." Too tight and air passage could be a problem. Too loose and they risked pathogen exposure. Again, she typed parameters into her keypad. "Bring up sim." She studied this one carefully, checking areas of contact. Several areas needed minor corrections. Angela fixed those, studied. Nodded. "Full activation."

She clenched one fist and waited until the filter field stabilized.

<Bonnie's team, test filter reliability.> She released that fist.

<Clear,> Bonnie texted.

<Ready to activate full Security Perimeter,> she broadcast to her team. <Check in.> She waited until everyone checked in.

"Activate." Angela watched her screens as the system went live. She plunged her hands into the globe and scanned through the links, muttering as she encountered odd anomalies from the archaic Stephens cooperative protocols.

Hope to hell Andrew's team is clear of malign intent because I don't have enough time to check them!

She'd done the next best thing, though, and attached minders to anyone who would come remotely close to Melanie. Meanwhile, either she or Nik would be at Mel's side 24/7.

<SYSTEMS GO,> popped up on each of her checklists. Angela checked them a second time. Good. She could shed the mask now—except that she had to go back out to meet Mel. Might as well keep it on.

Now if only they had located *all* of those damned EMP generators....

<We're good to go here,> she texted Nik. <Access codes now.>

<Ten minutes out. Just about perfect timing. See you soon.>

She reviewed her checklists a third time, signed off, handed over monitoring to Juanita, and pulled together her squad to meet Melanie at the skimmer pad. As she got there, Raul finished clearing the pad for Melanie's arrival.

The fleet of skimmers was impressive in number.

Glad coordinating those landings aren't my logistics.

Melanie's skimmer was first down, the others hanging back until she was clear. Nik hustled Melanie and Janine out, followed by other masked figures that Angela disregarded. She signed her team to surround Mel and Janine.

"Ange." Melanie took a moment from a vocal link to nod at her. "*Hell* of a mess."

"Yeah. Be careful, EMP generators are flaring and you're not protected until you're inside."

"Got it." Melanie strode off toward her HQ, damned near at double-time pace, the flared bottom of her dress coat whipping from side to side as she hurried. Two small hologlobes floated after her, connected by portable tethers. Angela fell in next to Nik.

A chime warned her just before the systems went dark. Two seconds. Three seconds. Then the shielded generators kicked over, and systems shimmered back into place.

"WHAT in the HELL?" Melanie snapped.

"EMP generator!" Her responsibility. "I'm on it. Nik, you're on Primary. I'm tracking down that electromagnetic pulse generator!" She peeled off from Melanie's group, running for her own control room.

When I catch whoever's kicking off those EMP generators....

Meanwhile, she had shields and perimeters to recheck.

<Mel's in Inner Ring,> Nik texted. <Unmasking now.>

<Good. Tightest security around Primary,> she ordered. <No one unauthorized comes near Mel without two escorts and clearance from me or Nik! *Everywhere,* including the Inner Ring!>

God, if this is the Freedom Army....

"East perimeter clear and clean for two miles inland," Cat reported to Melanie.

"That's good." Melanie palmed another Burnout, her third? fourth? since her last nap. Sleep was odd snatches of naps in a secure off-duty room just off her situation room for the last twenty-four hours. Or was it forty-eight? She paced around her Inner Ring control room, not daring to sit down for fear she'd crash.

Getting tired. Getting groggy. This has to be my last Burnout before another nap.

But they were so close to getting it clear. So. Damn. Close. As long as the offshore winds continued, they had a fighting chance. That is, if those damnable EMP generators could get shut down.

Every time we catch up, they knock us back two hours!

That sense of malign presence hadn't gone away. But it felt different from before.

At least this wasn't Gizmo. But it was the Freedom Army. Ange's team had found one cell and shut it down before they could fire off their EMP. Janine was publicizing that link, getting it out to the media, coupling it with images from the devastation.

God, the casualty rate.

And refugees who needed to spend the next few years in isolation camps for treatment and support, because of the other nasty viruses.

If this isn't the damned Gizmo, then where the hell are they getting these mixes?

"Not fast enough," Grady grumbled. "Nowhere near fast enough. This one's more potent than Osaka-46. And forecast says the wind changes soon."

"We hold until the wind changes," Melanie said. She pulled up the weather forecast, frowning.

She tapped in a call to Marty. Too far to use Dialogue under her current shielding. Voice was what she had.

"Love," he said, face softening at the sight of her. "How's it going?"

"Touch and go. Every time we knock down an EMP pulse generator another one pops up. I'm on tight lockdown. Have to be. But we're making some headway."

He nodded. "Your dad sent through a schematic for a counter to those EMP generators. Didn't want to say too much or dedicate too many resources until we knew it worked. It's solid. First ones can be en route in two hours."

"Thank God. Get them here as fast as you can." She would have said more, but the floor rocked under her feet. Darkness fell.

"DAMN IT!" MARTY YELLED. "NESS, WHAT THE HELL JUST HAPPENED? Mel? MEL!" He frantically tried to establish the connection with Melanie, first through the hologlobe, then conventional links. Nothing.

"What the fuck is going on?" he screamed into his local Security link.

Dean's shaken face popped up in his viewscreen. "Charleston got hit with a tactical nuke. Not from the New Feds or the Courts. Estimating potential yield, fortunately *very* small."

"Oh crap," Marty murmured. He collapsed in his chair, covering his eyes. "Tell me when you know more."

<Ness. Can you reach Mel at all or is it too far?>

<I'll try.>

Static, then resolution on his viewscreen. "Marty?"

He shot up, leaning close to Melanie's static, broken, half-formed image. "Mel? Are you okay? I just got told Charleston got hit by a tactical nuke."

"That's—we—too," Melanie said, the connection dropping words.

"Breaking up!"

"Got." Pause. "It." God, but she looked pissed. "Safe." Pause. "For." Pause. "Now. Contact. Soon. Going." The image winked out.

He sagged back again, in relief this time. <Ness, still try to keep a trace on Mel.>

<Very faint. Not reliable. Will try.>

<Do what you can.>

"God. Damn. It!" Melanie snarled, struggling with a recalcitrant screw on the monitor console after replacing the chip with one that had been shielded. The screw popped loose and she tossed it to Ange. "Get me another one like that!" She paused to gasp for breath through her mask.

Hate this fucking suited protocol.

But there was no choice, not since the nuke went off.

Angela rooted around in a bowl of screws, found a replacement, and dropped it in her hand. This one fit and with a few more twists, Melanie had it in place. She booted up the console and heaved a relieved sigh as it shimmered back into life.

That one's done. What's next?

She straightened up and looked around her control room. This appeared to be the last console that hadn't been worked on yet. Cat, Grady, Reiko and Yesenia worked on the others.

"Status check," she barked, blinking up Dialogue overlays. The status check scrolled through her overlays. "Looks like we're back in business."

Her com buzzed. Andrew. Also suited.

"Drew, your folks okay?"

"All except those close to the probable location. Yours?"

"Same here."

"My team is working out a plan of attack to contain this one. We gained some ground, but now we have radiation to deal with."

"If you can manage that—" Stephens's specialty was radiologics, after all.

"We can. Link sent to your people. Thanks for swatting down those pathogens."

Do It Right's specialty.

If we could only work together regularly….

"De nada."

<HIGHEST PRIORITY COURTS INCOMING> flashed across her Dialogue.

"Did you get that?" Andrew asked.

"Courts priority? Yeah. What the fuck's going on?"

"I haven't the faintest idea. Can I link in through yours? We're still getting our control room restored."

"No problem." She toggled the needed switch.

Satou Hisuko came up, exhaustion showing on his lined face. "Melanie. Andrew. Thank you for checking in so quickly. We appreciate the work you two are doing. Zhao. Do we now have quorum?"

Her screen split into twelve different pieces, three cells by four, each cell containing an Exec member's face, including her own.

She and Andrew were the only masked participants.

"We do," Zhao said.

"The Corporate Court Executive Council is considering a request from the President of the New Federated States of North America. Diana?"

Her mother looked haggard. "As you may have heard—Drew, Mel, I'm glad to see you two are okay—Charleston has been hit by a tactical nuclear weapon. Our sources tie it to continued action by the Freedom Army."

"What the hell is going on?" Henri Montcrief demanded.

Diana said something to someone off-screen. "We now have demands from the Freedom Army. They want a prisoner release in one hour." Her face twisted. "That includes a demand for Gina Jeffreys."

Jeffreys but not Conley or the kids? Interesting.

"Or what?" she asked.

"They have another big biobomb in Charleston, and nukes elsewhere. We're—reasonably confident we've been able to pull their teeth in those places. Nukes are easy compared to biobombs." Diana took a slow, deep breath. "From our best estimates of what we know about the Freedom Army resources, Charleston is their big shot for biological warfare. For now. They need Jeffreys to build more devices for them."

"Crap."

"We are not handing anyone over," Diana said grimly. "As the President of the New Federated States of North America, I have a request, approved by my Cabinet. We request permission from the Corporate Courts to implement the Osaka protocol."

Melanie's skin crawled.

Sterilization nuclear attack.

"I object! Stall the Freedom Army. We can turn this around!"

"Out of order," Satou said.

"Says who?" Andrew demanded. "Give us a chance! We can turn this around! *We've not had enough time for full implementation!* Stephens and DIR teams just reached full deployment twelve hours ago. We need at least six more hours!"

"Out of order," Satou repeated. "Montcrief, has the situation deteriorated to the Osaka requirements?"

"No!" Andrew yelled. "Six hours! Just give us six more hours!"

"The situation can't be so bad that twenty-four hours will make that much of a difference," Melanie said, wondering if she dared try an Enforcer compulsion tone.

"Landreth. Stephens. One more outburst and your coms will be silenced," Satou said. "Montcrief?"

"The situation meets the Osaka requirements," Montcrief said. "I move to invoke the Osaka protocol."

"Seconded," said Othman al-Faisal from Saudi Oil.

"Opposition to the motion," Melanie said. "How will postponing implementation of Osaka for six hours negatively impact our desired outcomes?"

Montcrief shook his head. "By definition, Osaka is the last-ditch protocol. Both you and your brother are too young to remember those circumstances. Your mother and some of us here do. We cannot spare six hours. Move to end discussion."

"Seconded," al-Faisal repeated.

"Members vote," Satou said.

Melanie keyed in her vote. The results came up.

10-2 in favor.

Me and Andrew against.

"Osaka Protocol to be implemented," Satou said. "Immediate evacuation. Thirty-minute countdown. Isolation screen for all within twenty klick range of the ops perimeters established by Do It Right and Stephens Reclamation. The Corporate Courts formally subpoena Gina Jeffreys, currently in the custody of Do It Right, International, for immediate interrogation. Does Do It Right have an objection?"

"No. I would ask a stay of this verdict for six hours while you interrogate her. We offer full cooperation."

"Thank you, but no. Begin evacuation procedures immediately. Good luck, Melanie, Andrew."

The Courts screen winked out, leaving only a sick-looking Andrew.

"*Christ*, Melanie," he moaned. "We're so damned close."

"Can you get your people out?"

He straightened back up. "Some. The rest are mixed in. They're not all responding. Our Dialogue linkages aren't restored yet."

"I can reach them."

He stared at her. "How?"

"*I can reach them.* What's your recall code?"

"It's—I'm breaching my own Security if I give it to yours. But I have to reach them. Renee's with one of your teams. Deep inside."

"You won't be giving it to my people. You're giving to me. Personally. I'm Netwalking. I can reach all of our Dialogues, linkages or no. Yours and mine. We'll make sure Renee gets out with the rest of our teams."

God, she's not supposed to have a Dialogue; she's too close to Andrew.

Hope flared in Andrew's face. "How? I mean, you're still alive—Mel, you're not—that'd be crazy! You can't reach her, she has a headset, not a chip."

"It's proprietary and it works with headsets and chips. *I can do it, Drew.* Me. Personally. No one else."

"After your performance at the Courts—yeah. Okay." He tapped in a code. "Got it?"

"Yes. Do me a favor. Facilitate the logistics to get my folks out as well as yours! I can't be on direct supervision while I do this."

"Absolutely. Good luck!"

"Thanks."

One more Burnout for the road!

She pulled out the box of Burnout tabs and straightened up.

"Janine. Angela. Cat. I need you here. Now."

Guess this is the time to find out if Cat has Enforcer potential. I need a backup and she's the only one I've got.

They filed over. Melanie pulled out an Enforcer globe generator.

"The Courts have implemented Osaka," she told them. "Thirty-minute countdown."

"Will that be enough time to evacuate?" Angela asked?

"That's what you and Janine need to coordinate. With Andrew. He's in charge of DIR and Stephens evac systems. We'll sort it out later. I—I need to go. Inside."

"Not to Charleston!" Cat protested.

"Not physically. I have the recall code for Stephens as well as our own folks. I'm going virtual. You're going with me."

"How—" Cat began.

Angela cut her off. "You'd do this without Marty here? Mel, that's stupid!"

"I'm taking Cat virtual with me as a safeguard. You'll make sure we're settled and safe. You have the globe keys. You may need to pull our bodies out before we're done. Transport us in the globe. You'll have the keys to adapt it."

"I don't know—" Angela started.

"We don't have time to argue! Cat, I'm sorry. I wanted you to have a better intro, ease you into Netwalk. But you're the highest performing Dialogue I have on site. I need you for backup going virtual. Will you do it? I'll go alone if need be, but I'm tired and on the edge. It'll be safer for me to go virtual with you there."

"I've never done this."

"It's not that complex. You'll follow me."

"What do I need to do?" Cat asked.

Melanie shook out two Burnout tabs and gave one to Cat. "Take this. This virtual process sucks a lot of energy." She sat on one of the comfortable chairs Angela dragged over. "The other chair is yours. Activate your datasuit to its highest level if it isn't already." She picked up two pairs of datagloves and tossed one pair to Cat. "Put those on."

"Done."

"Good."

Angela scowled at her. "What am I going to tell Marty?"

"I'm doing what's necessary to save people. We'll be fine, Ange."

Angela sighed. "Good luck. Do it right, Mel, and come back in one piece."

"We will." Melanie waited until Angela stepped back to activate the secured globe. She waited until it was stabilized.

<Hear me?> she said to Cat.

Cat startled. <Voice, not text?>

<Yep. I'll gather you once I'm fully virtual.> She knew she could do that easily for herself. But taking someone else virtual who wasn't Marty?

I can do it. I have to do it.

She closed her eyes. Visualized turning sideways, stepping out of her body—

Virtual space came alive around her, much more vibrant than what she could access through viewscreens and hologlobes. She turned to Cat. Tapped on Cat's shoulder, took her hand. Carefully helped virtual Cat separate.

Cat screamed once. Fluctuated. Then settled.

<So this is Netwalking?>

<As close as we can get and still be alive. Follow me. I need you to back me up.> She sent a quick briefing code. <Unpack this. Follow me. Should have time to review before we finish the first trace. Not perfect but will give you what you need.>

<Done.>

Melanie pulled up Andrew's link. Traced it to its furthest distance, zipping through the links with Cat tagging behind her. Began the process of broadcasting the recall, contacting each Dialogue, issuing Stephens and DIR codes. Identified the dead links and flicked them over to Cat for storage and later identification.

Only way we'll be able to positively ID our dead other than them going missing.

Directly contacted Andrew's Renee and ensured she was on a fast skimmer out of the sterilization zone, though she needed to shout to reach the poor-quality headset.

She'll have to go through isolation protocols but not too long.

<Melanie!> Cat said. <What's that?>

Melanie turned from checking the squad she'd just routed to see what Cat meant.

A gray nothingness hung behind them. One malign tendril whipped toward them, but pulled back before it struck too closely.

<Let me deal with this!> she told Cat. <Continue getting staff out!> She consolidated the DIR codes and the Stephens codes in separate packets, quick-labeled them, handed them over to Cat.

Not waiting for acknowledgement, she strode toward the spreading gray, calling up the blue light.

Marty and I stopped Sarah when she was like this. Codes.

She blinked up her recording of those codes. Whispered them as she traced a blocking line using the blue light.

Gray shoved against the line. Backed off. Pushed on and through.

<NO!> Melanie projected her full Enforcer vocal command tones. <STOP.> It halted. Then it pushed again, forcing her back three steps.

<Not enough!> Sarah materialized next to her.

<What the hell are you doing here?>

<You haven't the faintest clue what you're up against, girl!> Sarah's shape changed, forming a black cloud that swarmed around one of Melanie's hands.

<What is it?>

<I don't know but it's something to do with Stewart! Now do it again!>

<You aren't recording these codes!>

<Damn it, Melanie, we have to shut Stewart down! They've figured it out and we've got to stop this leakage! *It takes a Netwalker to shut this down!*>

That's Stewart—no time to argue. But later—

Melanie encrypted the codes as best she could.

Not that this will stop Sarah if she really wants them.

<Ready?> she asked Sarah.

<As ready as I can be.>

Melanie muttered the codes again, this time using the hand that Sarah swarmed around to draw the line. As she drew, the black cloud joined with her blue light to draw a barrier.

Sarah's barrier held. Melanie saw the difference between them. Sarah's barrier was less porous than hers had been with blue light alone.

So that's a Netwalker difference.

She recorded it quickly to pass on to Marty.

Sarah took form next to Melanie, not as clear as she had been before. <Now let's get the hell out of here, girl.>

<I still have linkages to rescue.>

<You're getting out of here. NOW.>

<But my linkages—>

<Your partner's done what's possible! You need to get the hell out of this linkage because it blows in thirty seconds! For her good and for yours!>

Cat. She won't be able to find her way out. Too new.

<You cover us!> she snapped at Sarah.

<I will! Damn it, run!>

Cat was wavering as Melanie grabbed her. They ran back through the electronic pathways, Sarah trailing. At last, they reached the marker Melanie set for their virtual access. Melanie shoved Cat through and turned to ensure Sarah had returned to her mother.

The gray shapelessness had broken through Sarah's barrier and followed them. Sarah stood boldly in front of it. Melanie joined her.

This reminds me of Sarah when I first saw her on the Net after her death. Only she was blackness. This is grayness. Who is it?

<You get out of here,> Sarah said.

<You get back into Mom.>

<Can't. Not until that nuke goes off.>

<Why?>

Sarah didn't answer.

Brightness. Suddenly Sarah grabbed Melanie. The two of them were flung backwards, rolling away from the grayness that had caught flame. Melanie screamed as flame seared into her brain.

<That's why you needed to get out, girl!> Sarah screeched. Then she faded.

A momentary darkness. Then she was back in her body, lying on the floor in recovery position on her side, the world swirling around her.

Cybercrash vertigo, damn it.

Angela and Cat knelt over her, Cat relaying information to Angela.

Melanie blinked. No Dialogue access. She blinked more firmly, trying to bring up her displays.

"Marty says don't do that," Cat said.

"How?" Melanie gasped.

"He's linking through me," Cat said. "This Enforcer stuff is pretty dang new. He says your chip is most likely fried."

Melanie groaned. "And Charleston?"

"Gone. We're on our way home."

Melanie sat up slowly, only now aware that she was in a skimmer instead of her site HQ.

No wonder the floor's moving. That part's not vertigo, at least.

Melanie sank her head onto her knees. "We failed. Damn it, we failed!"

"We got our surviving people out. Stephens people too. You did good."

Melanie shook her head. "Not good enough."

Nik pushed past Angela. "Mel. Just don't go there. Trust me. You did what you could. You saved more people than you realized. Think of what you did do."

"But I didn't save Charleston," she whispered.

"You rescued a lot of people anyway. Rest," Nik said. "Just rest. This will help." He held the sedative pen up, waiting for her consent.

Melanie nodded. She closed her eyes, waiting.

CHAPTER 10

"She pushed pretty hard for the past forty-eight hours," Angela said.

Marty nodded, studying Melanie's still form on the Hoodland HQ infirmary bed. "How much Burnout did she take?"

Angela shrugged. "God, I haven't the faintest clue. None of us had time to pay attention, including Mel. Pretty damn close to Redline myself. Nik's not much better."

"She's probably at Redline. Crap. On top of a cybercrash."

"I'm leaving her in your hands," Angela sighed. "You know the cybercrash and Redline treatment drill. Nik and I need to get some rest."

"Not a problem. You guys did what you could. And you brought her back safe."

Angela grimaced. "I don't call bringing her back with a fried chip and in Burnout crash mode particularly safe."

"She's alive. That's what matters. Thank you."

He studied Melanie's vitals again after Angela left. They looked better than they had when she arrived. Nothing that triggered his alerts as Head of Dialogues.

Recovering fast. A good sign.

Wait a few more minutes before he woke her.

Diana reported that Sarah came back and holed up in her chip. No stirring. But she's still there and quiet. Wonder what the hell happened?

<You've reviewed Cat's report?> he asked Ness.

<I can't make sense of what Sarah did. You have to retrieve that from Mel's data storage.>

<Which is most likely fried. Damn.>

<Give the nanos time to regen her chip. It's worked before.>

<True.>

"Need help with Melanie? I'm done checking Cat."

He looked up, relieved to see Reiko from the Nagano labs. Most of his support staff had gone to Charleston with Melanie and hadn't made it back yet. Reiko had been part of the HQ evac so she came in with Melanie.

"I could use help checking out her chip functions."

Reiko nodded. As the assistant to Julia Hawkins, Nagano's Head of Research, Reiko had overseen the reprogramming of Melanie's original combined Netwalk/Dialogue chip under Julia's supervision, and provided continuity monitoring for subsequent upgrades. More than that, Reiko was one of DIR's best Dialogue and Netwalk techs—and she had been Julia's representative for the big DIR meeting at the Ranch.

"Scanners?" she asked.

"Lab's the same layout as Nagano. Make yourself at home."

Reiko grabbed a scanner and began to check Melanie's chip. Marty turned to post-cybercrash prep combined with Redline Burnout crash. The routine, methodical preparation settled his nerves as he checked her vitals again, laid out a tube of liquid supplement, ripped open a packet with protein cubes, and shook up a fruit drink package to mix it. He added Dragondote and some lesser Redline recovery meds to his tray. He wouldn't know whether Mel needed them until she was awake and talking, so that he could run diagnostics.

"Chip is regenerating nicely. She'll still have to reintegrate, but she's had worse."

"Let me see."

Reiko handed him the scanner. Marty scrolled through the readouts.

"Memory's in good condition. Great. She didn't take that bad a hit. Regenerating functions are slower than usual." He scowled, scratching his chin as he studied the results. "This is a weird pattern."

<It looks like a Netwalker partially shielded her. But only partial,> Ness commented.

"Partial shielding from a Netwalker?" he said out loud.

Reiko raised her brows at him. "Explains the anomalies."

<Do you think that's why Sarah's hiding out?> he asked Ness. <Could Sarah have been the Netwalker shielding Mel?>

<If that was what Sarah did, odds are she's in pretty damn bad shape herself.>

"We need someone to check out Sarah. Cat. Mel was going to introduce her to the Enforcer skill set—" He caught himself, uncertain.

There's no way Cat's going to know what to do to check Sarah.

"Mel did do that. It's posted in official Netwalk records. But Cat's green as grass as an Enforcer and she's not likely to spot subtle anomalies in Sarah," Reiko said. "Could Ness check Sarah?"

"Once Sarah's awake." He thought about possible options. "I'll text Diana to keep Sarah under wraps until either Ness or Mel can talk to her."

<I can check Sarah,> Ness said. <At least I can ping her. Though I wish Will could back me. Nagano's just too far for a reliable connection.>

<We can wait for Mel. Or—perhaps you can take Cat as a backup.>

<Will she know what to do?>

<She will if Mel preps her.>

<I'll—try.> Ness sounded unsure, but that was her standard response to anything to do with Sarah.

"Texting Diana now," he said to Reiko.

"Mel's about ready to wake," Reiko said.

"Good."

Even better that she's waking on her own.

He rested his right hand on Melanie's to help orient her as Reiko mirrored him on Melanie's other side. Melanie blinked and groaned. Her muscles tightened. He quickly pressed on her shoulder to keep her from jumping up.

Melanie relaxed. "I remember I'm not supposed to move." She squinched her eyes tightly closed. "Everything's spinning around me. Redline plus cybercrash. Not moving until you say so."

Marty let out his breath. "You're oriented. Good."

"Hard to miss the stink of the Mountain's forest fire smoke. Charleston smells—*smelled*—different. That sedative dose Nik hit me with must have been max. What I needed. God, do I ever have a headache. Everything's spinning even with my eyes closed. How bad is my brainburn?"

"Not as bad as it could have been," Marty said. "You were protected."

"Thank Sarah for that. And—Charleston?" Her voice quavered.

So Sarah was the Netwalker shielding Mel.

"Contained." He winced at the sharpness in his voice.

Melanie tightened her lips. "We failed to save it."

He squeezed her shoulder gently. "It—" His voice faltered.

"I know," she said bitterly. "Only choices and all that damn fucking crap. But bottom line, we failed."

"We saved who we could," Marty said. "Between Stephens and DIR, we contained a potential outbreak. That counts for something."

"Unless the you-know-what is behind it."

"We can't do anything more, Mel. You did what you could."

Melanie shuddered. "If this was what 2046 was like—"

"It's a pretty damned good taste of it," Reiko said.

"Who's the media blaming?"

"Your mom and the Courts are billing it as another Disruption incident. They figure that's safest; hopefully enough to stop further Freedom Army blackmail attempts and calm the public down."

"Unless the whatchamacallit *is* doing this."

"How do we predict that, Mel?"

Melanie sagged into the bed, relaxing again. "We can't. Unless Sarah sees a pattern. Let's hope that one city lost is enough. Cat. She got out okay?"

"Better shape than you," Reiko said. "I've checked her."

"I could use something to eat, Marty."

"Here." He touched her lips with the nozzle of the liquid supplement. Melanie sucked hungrily at the supplement. When it was dry, he put it aside. "Ready for some cubes?"

Melanie started to nod but winced. "No. Best not. My head's still splitting. They'll come back up."

Not surprising with Redline. Wish we could have avoided this.

"Reiko, hand me that tube of Dragondote."

"I don't know that I need that one." Melanie's voice quavered.

"After sucking down that RecoverNow supplement as fast as you did? Hon, Redline plus your brainburn says Dragondote comes next."

Melanie moaned inarticulately. Reiko handed Marty the tube covered with the black and red dragons twining around each other, mirror reflections of the red and black dragons on the Burnout tab boxes. Marty uncapped the Dragondote and held the tube to Melanie's lips. She sucked down the painkiller/supplement/sedative slowly, with longer pauses between each swallow, clearly waiting for him to tell her to stop.

No way. Not like this. Whole thing for you this time.

"Better?" he asked once she had finished.

This time she didn't try to nod. "Much. But getting sleepy."

"It's what you need."

Melanie waved a hand in protest. "No time for this, damn it." She sighed. "Can't be helped. Drew. What's the follow up like?"

"He's running cleanup and the isolation setup. Still sorting out DIR and Stephens personnel from the recovery records you gave Cat."

"Gina Jeffreys?"

"New Feds picked her up twelve hours ago."

"Been out that long?"

"Yes."

"Sarah?"

"Incommunicado in your mom's chip. We'll have Ness ping her with Cat as backup, if you can tell Cat what to do."

"That would be best." Melanie stirred, still keeping her eyes closed. She fumbled to find the edge of the bed, then slowly turned to her side and faced Marty. He helped steady her as she settled in, taking quick advantage to stroke her cheek.

"I've got her now," he told Reiko. "Thank you for your help. Get rested because when the rest of our folks get here, we're going to get slammed."

"Thank you." Reiko left.

"God. I'm beat." Melanie opened her eyes, then shut them quickly.

"Still spinning?"

Can't give her any more meds. She'll have to sleep it off.

"Yeah. What was Conley's reaction to the news about Charleston?"

"Neither she nor Jeffreys were told about it."

"Good. Keep it that way until I can talk to her."

"Another Liam connection?"

"No. That is—I don't think so." Her voice faded with each word. Melanie coughed, then continued, her voice starting out firmer but fading. "But. I can tell you more. Later. Not sure why Sarah got involved. Need talk to Mom."

"She didn't answer my page to tell her to keep Sarah locked up until we could check her."

"Mmhmm. Marty?"

"Yes?"

"Do I hafta stay here? Our bed comfier. With you. You need rest too."

"You're not walking." He was firm on that point.

Her laugh turned into a cough that shook her body and ended in a moan. "Can't. Won't. Exhausted. Floater. Please."

"Coming right up." He texted a floater request.

"Good." Her voice trailed away. Marty let her sleep until the floater came. Melanie barely roused enough to cooperate with Marty and the Security who brought the floater, keeping her eyes tightly closed. He let Security guide the floater while he stayed on it with her, keeping her upright.

She sighed with relief when he eased her into their bed, rolling over onto her stomach right away, sprawled widely across the bed. He grinned as the beginnings of a snore came from her mouth.

Honey, a few minutes and I'll be right there with you.

He snapped up a globe and dealt with pressing organization matters.

There. Done. I can rest now.

Melanie roused as he climbed into the bed. "Good thing missed fertility round. God knows what exposures I got. Plus Dragondote and all that Burnout."

"How much did you take?"

"No idea." She rolled onto her side and snuggled into him. "Lost track. No time. Sheesh. Stupid. Enough for Redline."

He wrapped his arms around her. "But not a bad one. Nik did the right thing."

A snore answered him.

Fought it as long as she could.

He settled in next to her and closed his eyes.

She survived. God.

It took him only slightly longer to fall asleep.

TWELVE HOURS LATER, MELANIE TOOK A DEEP BREATH AS SHE WAITED FOR Cat McCauley outside the DIR Security lockdown wing.

Can't put this off any longer.

She was mostly recovered from Charleston. However, while the pain from cybercrash and Redline was mostly gone, leaving a sour taste in her mouth and a trace of headache, she was still tired. Full integration of her regenerated Dialogue/Netwalk chip was still in progress.

But talking to Deirdre Conley couldn't wait any longer, and Melanie didn't *need* Dialogue or Netwalk access to interrogate her further, especially if Cat was also there.

She wanted to see Conley's reaction to the news about Charleston. Despite Conley's isolation, the segregation wasn't perfect—and they couldn't keep her segregated forever. Charleston was being discussed everywhere at DIR today, and Conley was savvy enough to pick up bits and pieces of information, given the amount of buzz.

"Melanie." Cat entered the foyer. "Sorry, but I was debriefing with Marty and Ness after scanning Sarah."

"How did that go?"

"Ness did most of the work. I didn't know enough to be able to tell much. Sarah's okay, just charging. She's not saying much."

"Sarah is the most devious Netwalker we have on our side. She's a hard read. Ness is probably the easiest to understand. Spend training time with Ness. That's a good start for learning Netwalker management."

Cat nodded. "I have a week before we go back to Rio Bravo."

"Good." Melanie coughed. "Hopefully I can give you some direct coaching about virtual navigation that is less abrupt than your introduction was. I'm glad you didn't let that put you off taking on an Enforcer role."

"It *was* pretty intense," Cat admitted. "Debriefing with Marty and Ness helped a lot."

"I'll send a training program with you. Check in regularly. Once you're a bit more solid, I'll send you the recruitment profiles. We need more Enforcers, and I don't have the time to scan everyone."

"Okay."

"Meanwhile. I need your help with this interview because I am not going to see things in virtual, at least not until I'm reintegrated. The additional catch is that Deirdre Conley may have Enforcer-level potential."

"You'd recruit someone from the Freedom Army?" Cat scowled.

"I'm desperate for any and all Enforcers. I think we can turn her to our side. I just don't know how long that will take. We may need to isolate her in research and training for a while."

"What are we doing?"

"I want you to observe and record in virtual mode. Look at the changes in the electromagnetic fields around her, if any, and show them to me after. Good?"

"Yes, got it. But how will I go virtual without her noticing?"

"Distraction. You'll settle in your seat, then give me handsign when you're ready. I'll throw the cube and distract her while you slide into virtual. I'll give you a three count. Work for you?"

"Yes, except that you'd better give me a seven count to get out."

"Seven count it is. Let's go." Melanie led the way to the interrogation room.

Conley didn't look up as Melanie carefully opened the door, her attention focused on a book lying on the plain steel table. A sideways glance and stiff tightening of her body was the only indication that Conley was aware of company.

Melanie waited, leaning against the wall, while Cat settled herself at a chair across the table from Conley. Conley ignored Cat and turned a page. She stared at it, but Melanie was willing to bet that Conley wasn't focusing on the words.

Cat signed her readiness with a casual flick of her fingers. Melanie brought out the secure hologlobe generator.

Another sideways glance from Conley.

"I'm throwing the globe," Melanie said. She flipped the generator into the center of the cell. The globe shimmered open, expanding slowly until it took up the whole room. As the perimeter passed through Conley, she shivered and closed her book.

Showtime, Melanie.

"Must be an interesting book."

Seven.

"What do you want with me?" Conley didn't look at Cat or Melanie.

Four. Three.

"Are you comfortable?" Melanie asked.

Two. One. Cat should be in virtual now.

A quick sideways glance at Cat confirmed it. Cat sat so that she was looking down, but Melanie recognized the tightness of her body.

Left part of herself behind to monitor. Good. She's been reviewing my reference files.

"What kind of stupid question is that?" Conley snarled. "I'm locked up. I have no freedom. True, there's no bars on this jail and I have things to do, but it's a jail nonetheless. No electronics. No outside news. Minimal contact with others. How comfortable do you think I am?"

"There are ways to improve your situation," Melanie said.

Conley snorted. "Right."

Melanie sat down next to Cat. "Cooperation will get you outdoor walking privileges. Maybe others."

Conley shrugged, averting her face from looking directly at Melanie. But something about the way she twisted her lips suggested she was fighting back saying more.

Discretion on her part? Or—something else?

"How about news access? So you can hear about things—like how your Freedom Army buddies destroyed Charleston."

"Charleston? But that's where—" Conley broke off.

"Where what? What's the big deal about Charleston?"

"What happened in Charleston?" Conley parried.

"Biobombs. Two tactical nukes. One a probable suitcase nuke from your buddies, the other a sterilization bomb." Melanie leaned back. "We can show you if you'd like."

Shock flitted across Conley's face briefly. She closed her eyes, then reopened them. Her expression went blank, emotionless, but it was clearly an effort of will.

"I'd just as soon remember it as it was. It was...a very important place to me at one time."

For a moment her face softened.

"How so?" Melanie asked.

"That's personal!"

"What does Charleston mean to the Freedom Army?"

"Remember your history?"

"Which part? What ties does that have to the Freedom Army?"

Conley eyed Melanie, a sardonic smile briefly twisting her lips before fading. "I forgot. You aren't as knowledgeable about the Army history as I am. Charleston was the site of Francis Stewart's Great Revelation."

"I knew that."

"And did you know the prophecy about it?"

"That I don't know," Melanie admitted. "Tell me about it."

Conley smirked at Melanie. "Congratulations. You've brought about the first steps in the New Uprising. The destruction of Charleston is the sign that our day has come. The Last Days when freedom will ring from shore to shore, and every man is free, answering only to the memory of Francis Stewart."

"Oh really?" Melanie suddenly felt sick.

Gizmo. This has to be Gizmo-related.

She strove to keep her tone light. "So you're telling me that your Army activists were consciously bringing about these Last Days."

"The signs had to be right," Conley said. "Stewart must have spoken to the cell leaders in Charleston."

"But Stewart's dead!"

"Is he? Or is he as dead as Liam was?"

Deep breath, Melanie. Don't let her see your reaction.

She met Conley's gaze directly, not looking away. "You're telling me Francis Stewart is alive."

"I didn't say that," Conley said. "What I said is that he must have spoken to the cell leaders."

"If he's dead, then how can he do that?"

Is Francis Stewart a feral Netwalker? Mom and Sarah thought he uploaded to Gizmo before he died. That might mean he's a Netwalker. If he is, he has to be crazier than hell. No human contact. Unless he's got a host somewhere I don't know about—God. If he is a Netwalker, then he's been at it for years. What does she know about Stewart that she isn't telling?

"A machine helps him."

"A machine called Gizmo?" Melanie guessed, wincing at the direct mention.

Conley paled. She pressed her lips together firmly and stared down at her hands.

"A machine called Gizmo?" Melanie repeated.

Can't risk saying anymore.

Conley swallowed. "I don't know what that machine is."

"So tell me what you do know about that machine." How much of Conley's stubbornness was actual resistance, and how much was her trying to cover up an outside-imposed block on what she could say?

"I don't know anything!" Conley shoved away from the table and began pacing. Melanie noted the jerkiness in her movements.

Block. But is she riding with it or fighting it?

"The way you're acting, you know something. Are you blocked?"

"I. Don't. Know. Anything," Conley insisted, stopping to glare at Melanie. Her hands clenched into fists. She blinked hard. "I won't tell you anything more!" Her face twitched and her mouth opened. "No!" She jammed both fists into her mouth and turned her back on Melanie to stare at the wall.

Can't tell me, you mean. Blocked from speaking. Don't need Dialogue or Netwalk to see that. Damn it.

Next to her, Cat jerked, and looked back up. Out of virtual. Cat shook her head and mouthed the word "no."

So no Netwalk-related anomalies from her. Yet.

"Gina Jeffreys is now in the custody of the New Federation. Should I send you to join her?"

"No!" But Conley continued to stare at the wall.

Melanie rose. "Then I suggest you think harder about cooperation. I need answers. Otherwise, you're just taking up space here."

Conley shuddered. She blinked harder, then took a deep breath. "Heard anything about a fella named Tim Conley?" she asked, speaking quickly, flinching as she said the name.

"Is he someone close to you? How close was he to Liam?"

More blinking and another deep breath.

She's fighting the block.

"Nobody. But a nobody you need to find if you're going to solve some problems. He's—he's someone I need to know about." She swallowed hard, eyes widening again. "Need to know if he's dead or alive, before I can talk."

Melanie sighed. "I—understand. I'll see what I can do."

"Thank you. I—"

"Don't. *I understand.* Can you tell me how hard this is?"

Head shake.

Melanie shrugged. She picked up the globe generator and manually shut it down.

"Let's go." Melanie motioned Cat out first. She lingered for one moment longer, giving Conley a chance to say something.

Nothing.

"So did you pick anything up when you were watching in virtual?" she asked Cat.

"She's under a stiff block," Cat said. "I'm sorry I had to pop out so soon. She's very resistant because of that, and I was, was," She frowned, obviously thinking about her word choice. "I want to say tired but I'm not certain that's the exact comparison. But I had this very distinct feeling that I needed to get out. And now I'm starving."

"That's normal. She didn't show any Netwalk traces or odd electronic shifts when we were talking about Gizmo and Francis Stewart?" Melanie asked.

"No." Cat frowned. "No, that's not quite right either. She was *too* quiet on that one. Is it possible to block reactions so that they don't show up in virtual electromagnetic fields? Because she reacted to the Charleston news. At first, I thought maybe the lack of response about Gizmo and Francis Stewart was just control on her part, but now I don't know."

"Download your records to Marty's lab. I'll give you the address—oh, dang it, I don't have access! Go to the labs. Download the record. Tell Marty I'll be by in half an hour to look at it."

"Will do. Do you want me there when you look at it?"

Melanie chewed on her lip thoughtfully. "I don't think so," she said finally. "I have to watch it and think about it."

"Okay." Cat went to Marty's lab. Melanie headed for her own office.

I need that custom headset I used in Nagano after Ness fried my chip. Maybe I can get away with using that.

She needed every advantage she could get because she was more than certain she would be the one tracking down data on Tim Conley.

Who is this shadow named Tim Conley and just who the hell is he to you, Deirdre Conley? And is he the key to opening you up?

"No," Marty said firmly. "No headset. Not even that one."

Especially not that one! She'll go too far and too hard with it for her current condition.

Melanie scowled but she appeared to accept his ruling. She delicately set the headset down on the table, slow, controlled, precise.

She is oh-so-pissed about that!

"Mel, we can't risk it."

"I know." Melanie let out a long, hissing breath. "But, damn it, Marty. I think Cat missed some nuances."

"She's green at this. And she may not operate at your level even with more experience. We might not find anyone else who is as proficient as you are."

"True. But it's still frustrating."

"Let's both look at it. I'll bring Ness out and see what she says."

That earned him a smile. He popped up a secured globe to enclose both of them. Ness popped out, adopting her falcon guise and sitting on his shoulder, the side away from Mel.

Not her usual style.

He ran the interview. Mel slumped in her chair, chin resting on her interlaced fingers as she stared at the last frame of the interview. Then she sat up and snapped her fingers. Nothing. She snapped her fingers harder.

"Mel, you're not integrated yet," he reminded her.

She sagged back. "Damn. I'd forgotten. Crap. I need to see into those electromags!"

<Ness, what did you see?> he asked.

<Conley's been blocked, no question about it. There's one segment where her electromags flatline. Outside tampering. Nothing else could do that.>

"What does Ness say?" Melanie asked.

"Ness says there's a flatline section."

Melanie nodded. "Was that when I asked her about Stewart getting help from the gadget?"

<Tell Melanie yes.>

"She says yes."

<Tell her about the tampering,> Ness's tone took on urgency. <She needs to know about the tampering!>

"Ness also says that the flatline section is a result of tampering," he added.

Melanie shot out of her chair. "I thought so! Ness, can you see anything deeper about that flatline section?"

<Sorry. No.>

"No," he relayed.

Melanie began to pace. "I thought this was all Liam. But now, with this Francis Stewart piece, and the gadget, and Sarah, I'm beginning to wonder." She stopped and whirled to face him. "How soon before I can go virtual? I have to talk to Sarah."

He hesitated. "Mel, if you rush it, that'll be even more of a setback."

Her lips tightened and he thought she would snap at him. Instead, she shook her head. Then she walked back over to her chair and sank down into it again. She took two deep breaths.

"You're right," she said in a low voice. "Plus, what would happen if I started talking about the possibility of Francis Stewart uploading himself as a Netwalker? Who'd believe me besides our inner circle? Sarah didn't talk. Now maybe that was a gadget effect working on her." She winced. "And we're getting close to my Exec limits. God, Marty. Am I going too far out on a limb to tie this Charleston attack to Francis Stewart?"

"Before you do anything further about that notion, you probably should talk to your mother and Sarah."

Melanie made a face. "And that means waiting until the next Courts session for this conversation to be absolutely secure from the device's interference. I don't trust that thing, Marty."

"There has to be a secured hologlobe level that will keep the gadget out," Marty said. "I'll work on that."

"Thank you." Melanie got up. "Damn, my head hurts after this."

"Don't overdo," he cautioned.

She smiled bleakly at him. "I promise to do nothing more than dull, boring paperwork that needs to be managed. God knows I have enough of that stuff to do. New searches as a result of that interview with Conley. Figuring out what to do with her to keep her secure until she'll talk—or can talk. As well as pick up the post-Charleston pieces, at least what I can do without a chip."

"We'll get it figured out, Mel."

"I just—I hope we figure it out in time to prevent more Charlestons." She kissed him. "Going now. Sending what I know to Mom; get cracking on my work. Maybe we've gotten lucky and this piece from Conley will prevent more incidents."

"Let's hope that's the case."

"I'll make it so," she said firmly. "Somehow." She squared her shoulders and left the room.

If determination could solve this problem, Mel would have it fixed already.

CHAPTER 11

It was one of *those* ski days.

It shouldn't have been.

Fluffy, powdery snow blew hard around Melanie. The first of the season, starting atypically late in February. It should have been glorious and wonderful.

It wasn't.

Melanie fought her boots, her skis, the slope. Nothing worked right. She skidded to a stop at the bottom of Designer, muttering when she crossed her ski tips.

She herringboned over to the chairlift. The snow level was low enough that she had to climb the slight rise to the ramp. It didn't help that her gut roiled nervously, with multiple moments when she thought she was going to vomit.

I don't feel sick. But the gut sure doesn't want to settle. Nerves or toxin issue? Another damn thing to check.

"One more run?" Nik asked as he pulled down the safety bar.

'Yeah. Sure. There's time before we leave for Seattle." She sank back, slamming the bar with her left hand. "I can't find my rhythm!"

"Your form looks good," Nik said mildly. "But you're overcontrolling. You need to relax into the flow."

"I can't find it."

"It'll come. Mel, just relax." Nik scowled. "I wish it were clearer so I could take you up on the High Reach. That's what you need. A couple of more challenging runs, and you'd find the flow again."

I wish I had your confidence, Nik!

Part of the problem was worry about non-skiing things. Today was pregnancy check day. If not pregnant, another fertility treatment.

Followed by that damn Seattle High Space meeting. Another reason to play it careful. I can't risk getting hurt this morning.

Still, one more run might make the magic work. It seemed as if she had been jinxed during the six months since Charleston. Research forays fizzled out, whether connected to products in development or to the Freedom Army and Tim Conley.

Oh, there was a prophecy about the destruction of Charleston in Stewart's quasi-mystical ramblings that formed the foundation of Freedom Army belief. But it didn't seem to fit the actual events.

Deirdre Conley continued to dole out small chunks of information, but she kept asking about Tim Conley, as best as the block set on her would allow. It seemed that obnoxious, rude behavior allowed her to work around the block for short periods of time, and damn, that behavior got tiring to deal with.

Finding out if Tim Conley was dead or alive proved to be much more difficult than anticipated. Still, even though she kept coming up with the wrong Tim Conleys, every time Melanie gave Conley a new chunk of data, Conley fed her more information in return.

There hadn't been any sign of renewed Freedom Army activity since Charleston. The flurry of arrests afterward seemed to have destroyed much of their organization.

But I don't feel like it's settled. We've missed something. The only ones who seem to understand my worries are Marty and Sarah. Andrew can't or won't talk about what happened.

They unloaded from the chair. Before she pushed off for another battle with the easy Designer run, Nik put a hand on her shoulder. "Wait." He went off by himself, calling someone.

Melanie leaned on her poles and studied the snowflakes falling on the half-dead firs around her.

"All right!" Nik grinned as he joined her. "We've got clearance for Trina's."

"Trina's?" Melanie winced.

Not her favorite run. Steep with odd placement of lift line poles, a few uphill stretches that required skiing faster than she wanted right now, and a couple of long, curving tricky runs with possible exposed stumps, to enhance the difficulty. "Sure there's enough snow?"

"They're opening it *now*. C'mon, let's get first tracks."

"You put it that way, we've gotta do it." First tracks, always the lure of first tracks.

Melanie followed Nik, taking advantage of the relatively flat slope to drill her turns one last time before Trina's. Even on the flat, her edges kept grabbing in that sickening way that reminded her of last spring's wreck. But there was also no way she would duck a challenge from Nik.

Just need to screw up my nerve and do it.

She expected Nik to pause at the end of the flatter slope to let her catch her breath. Instead, he immediately tucked into the tight, speed-seeking crouch needed to gain enough momentum for the first uphill section. Melanie grabbed a deep breath and tucked hard, balancing low over her skis.

She stayed curled up tight and didn't stand until she was certain she had enough momentum to take her over the top and into the first short, tight, steep pitch. Nik pushed off as she caught up. Her angle placed her on the difficult side of the lift pole. Instead of a leisurely, careful traverse, she had to turn right quickly and sharply.

Damn it.

Melanie fought through those first two turns.

Then, suddenly, it clicked.

Faster I ski, less I need to turn.

She pointed her tips directly downhill, shifting her weight easily from ski to ski, riding her edges without stuttering or stopping. Melanie breezed right by Nik, rounding the corner for another small dip, catching her breath on the next uprise for the last big drop.

There, she chose the most challenging line and rode it hard and nearly straight down the slope, marveling that it had been so difficult on Designer but so easy here. At the end of the run, she stopped smoothly and waited for Nik.

He grinned at her.

"Better?"

"Absolutely," she said.

"*Now* let's go home," he said. "I told you that it was a matter of relaxing."

"Hell of a way to do it," she said.

As they rode up, she thought back to how things had been ever since Charleston.

It's not just skiing where I've been tense, overcontrolling, and lost my confidence.

TENSION ROILED OFF OF MELANIE SHE SLIPPED INTO HER SKIMMER SEAT next to Marty, enough to make him edgy.

Thought she would have blown it off skiing!

Apparently not.

"Anyone else?" Nik asked Melanie. "I thought Janine was coming today."

"She's on her way," Melanie said. "We had a last-minute situation. She's finishing it off—there she is."

Janine climbed aboard and settled in her seat. "All done," she said. "Grady sent Cat for this meeting."

Melanie scowled. "It wouldn't hurt for him to come to this one. Ah well, Cat and I can work on some drills, and she'll know their presentation better than he will, anyway."

The skimmer rose.

<There's something roiling in Netwalk that doesn't feel right,> Melanie said to Marty. <Nothing big, but it's like something just keeps poking at me. Maybe it's not Netwalk. Maybe it's to do with High Space.>

<Have you said anything to Nik or Angela? Could be you're picking up on a potential Security breach no one else can see because of your linkages in Netwalk.>

Melanie scowled at him. <Yes, and Mom's people as well. I think

everyone's tired of me crying wolf. They all think the Freedom Army's gone away. I don't.>

He wanted to reassure her that it wasn't the case, but they had this discussion far too many times since Charleston. Melanie's moods kept spiraling darker and darker.

She was supposed to see the doctor today.

<What did the doctor say?> he asked.

<Had to put off the appointment. Vijay Gupta called right after I got back from skiing, about our proposal on his subcontract to Troubadour. That took priority. Left me without enough time to keep the appointment so I moved it. Couldn't be helped. I'm close to getting his signature on the contract. It's just a matter of a few terms, and Sandra in Legal is cooking up the framework for a contract I can plug details into.>

<That's good.>

Melanie nodded. She snapped up two small globes. The smaller of the two she put to one side while she expanded the larger and brought up a contract. <Good. Sandra sent me the contract draft. Sorry, Marty. I have to work on this. Won't have any time once we get to Seattle. I need to find Vijay and get this settled right away.>

<Understood.> He pulled up his own globe and began work.

THIS ROUND OF THE HIGH SPACE MEETINGS TOOK PLACE ON THE OLD-fashioned corporate campus of a Tobai Heavy Industry subsidiary. Mock-ups of the various High Space contracted stations were in the galleries leading to the auditorium. While waiting for Nik and Angela to clear them from the skimmer, Melanie blinked up the layout schematic she had been sent that morning, looking for the Troubadour station model. Vijay would meet her there.

Ah. Next to Stephens.

DIR's station model was close to the auditorium door, so she could take care of business with Vijay, hopefully have time to chat with Zhao at the Mei-lein model next to DIR, then check in with DIR staff before going to the auditorium. She snapped both her globes closed, then set up a quick link for the Gupta Research Institute contract. Her presentation was already linked. All her pieces were together. No need for the roiling in her gut.

Wonder if Andrew will want to talk?

As she had expected, post-Charleston he'd backed off of close association.

Wish we had debriefed before drifting apart. I'd like to know his take on the Freedom Army. Does he think they've disappeared, like everyone else?

"Mel?"

"Yes, love?"

"I'm going to head straight for our model once we're cleared to go. I want to make certain everything's set up. Cat will meet us there."

"Good. I'll be along as soon as I meet with Vijay. You're coming to the opening session?"

"Wouldn't miss it," he assured her. "Especially your speech."

"It's just a small piece," she protested. "Not a big one."

"Big enough."

"All clear." Nik opened the skimmer door.

"You stay with your Security," Melanie cautioned Marty. "Just enough outsiders here to get me worried, especially since I can't figure out what's bugging me. Freedom Army's been quiet too long. Ange, who's in charge of Marty?"

"Erica and Rick." Angela waved them over.

"I'll see you after the opening session." Marty kissed Melanie. "Do it right, Mel. Knock them dead."

"It's just a little piece on biologic nanotech modifications for chip interactions," she protested. "Nothing big."

"Still, good luck."

"Thanks. Be careful."

"You too." He walked off with Erica and Rick.

"I'll set up your materials," Janine told Melanie. "I'm bringing Crispin with me for the prelim Security clearance."

Melanie glanced at Angela. She nodded.

"Okay. I'll see you in there."

Nik finished briefing the remainder of the DIR Security team and joined them. "I've placed extra shadow Security on our Primaries," he reported to Angela. "Sent you the list."

Angela nodded sharply. "Looks good."

"So we're clear to go?" Melanie asked. "I need to settle this contract with Vijay before I do anything else."

"We're clear," Nik confirmed.

Melanie strode off. She sensed Angela and Nik next to her but her focus narrowed to finding that Troubadour setup. She spotted it at last —the schematic was not quite true to the actual display layout—and headed for the Troubadour station model. This station was designed primarily as a transit hub to service shuttles, interstation transport, and eventual interplanetary transport. Troubadour was working aggressively on overcoming the radiation hazards posed by out-of-Earth atmosphere stations and bases while keeping the needed shielding light, to reduce liftoff and travel energy costs.

Vijay stood near the model. They moved out of the main flow of traffic.

"Did you get those numbers into the contract?"

"Here it is." Melanie snapped up her globe. She pulled on datagloves and highlighted the portions covering the bot specs, plus the cost numbers Vijay had been concerned about earlier.

Vijay skimmed the contract, borrowing one of Melanie's datagloves to manipulate it. He tweaked several provisions. Melanie reviewed them silently, leaving several as they were, but modifying six of Vijay's counterproposals. Vijay accepted four of her tweaks, and modified two, as they had discussed. Melanie countered. Vijay studied them carefully, then approved them.

He signed the contract with a flourish. Melanie added her signature and saved the contract. She registered it with DIR Corporate, the Courts, and High Space. Vijay followed suit for Gupta Research.

Business concluded, she pulled off her dataglove and closed the globe. Vijay gave her back the borrowed glove.

"It's always a pleasure doing business with DIR," he said. "Other companies would drag out these negotiations."

Melanie shrugged. "I don't see a lot of gain in wrangling too much over the details, especially for one of our proven products. I want a profit but I don't want to gouge you." She smiled at him. "And you're pretty reasonable about the details. It's a real pleasure."

"Thank you. I look forward to your presentation at the opening session. Perhaps we can talk further, later on?"

"I am certain we can find time." Melanie texted the request to Janine to plug into her schedule.

They shook hands and Vijay moved on. Melanie nodded to Henri Montcrief, currently talking to her mother, and started toward the DIR model.

Ten minutes to go.

She spotted Andrew and Renee, talking to Othman al-Faisal. A faint sadness crashed over Melanie as she noticed the slight curve rounding Renee's lower body.

Not the time to think about this, Melanie.

As she joined them, al-Faisal bowed politely to Andrew and dismissed himself.

"Andrew," she said.

He frowned slightly before speaking. "What's up?" The frown faded, replaced by a smirk. "Busy wheeling and dealing?"

"Andrew!" Renee snapped, her tone lacking any real reproof. "Melanie, thank you for your help in Charleston."

Andrew's expression softened. "Yes, Mel." He slid an arm protectively around Renee's shoulders.

"Thank *you* for *your* help," Melanie said. "I didn't hear back about those replacement bots we sent. Satisfactory, I hope?"

"Sufficiently so," Andrew said sharply. "Did I need to say anything?"

What's got him on the prod?

"No, not really. You'd already paid for them."

"I guess you're sharing some of your latest whiz bang biologic devices with us in the opening session." Again, his voice had that sharp edge.

About like he was when Peter was riding him.

Melanie stifled a shudder. Since Sarah had become a Netwalker she had discovered a few redeeming qualities in her grandmother. But her murderous uncle?

He's dead both in the flesh and as a Netwalker. Or is he?

No. Don't go there. You have no evidence, and enough worries about Liam.

"I was asked to do that," she said. "It's an offshoot of what we did in Charleston."

"I am looking forward to what you have to show us," Renee said. She reeled slightly.

Melanie automatically reached out to steady her with both hands. Static electricity shocked her. "Oh! Sorry."

"This sweater has a lot of static," Renee said. "Thanks, Melanie. I get occasional vertigo with this pregnancy."

She sounds almost too casual about it.

Melanie's thought was echoed by a fleeting concern on Andrew's face, replaced by that scowl. The *something* that had been nagging at her flared larger.

Renee would normally be asking more questions about the presentation.

She chanced a quick scan. Nothing. Nonetheless, something about Renee bothered Melanie.

Maybe it's just an aftereffect from Charleston. Or jealousy that Andrew is ahead of me in producing an heir.

"Um, looks like congratulations are in order," Melanie said.

"Thank you. Renee, we'd better be getting our seats. The Exec is seated at the high table," he told Melanie.

"I know that," she said. "I got my notice, same as you."

"I'm going to get Renee settled," he said, taking her arm and moving Renee away.

Melanie frowned after him.

Now that is absolutely weird.

Or was Andrew simply being protective of his pregnant partner?

Suddenly she felt warm, like she was about to break into a sweat. For a moment the room swirled around her, then steadied.

What the hell is this? Anxiety? Or am I getting sick?

"Something's not right with Renee," Nik said softly into Melanie's ear.

<Yeah,> she texted back. <What do you see?>

<Body movement doesn't fit last profile I took.>

<Can you spider data with Dialogue's Security subroutines?>

"No," Nik said aloud. <Not without a Netwalker,> he added by text, then continued out loud. "But they're in the clear and not paying attention to us at the moment. Look for yourself."

Melanie turned her head slightly, and let her eyes drift, watching as Renee walked with Andrew. For two strides Renee jerked like a marionette manipulated by a clumsy puppeteer. Then Andrew started talking to someone Melanie couldn't see. Renee's motion changed from jerky to smooth.

<You sure?> Melanie texted.

<Been watching for a while. Movement like Freedom Army fighters with Conley. Periodic. Not regular.>

<Any way to prove connection?>

<Not yet. Need to watch.>

"Yeah," Melanie said aloud. "The Courts plus Mom and her people need to know about this."

"Absolutely. I've already warned Sergio and Courts staff."

"Thanks."

Melanie spotted her mother. <Mom,> she texted, muting the text color so it wouldn't flash brightly across Diana's visual overlays.

<Not a good time,> Diana texted back.

<Need to conference. Urgent. What Nik told Sergio. Ask him. Meet you by the head table in auditorium.>

<Okay. Couple of minutes.>

<Marty?> she said.

<Yes, love?>

<I have to go to the auditorium *now*. Please let our folks know I appreciate their hard work and I'll talk to them after the opening session.>

<Be careful.>

<I will. Please. If you see Andrew and Renee, be very careful. Please?>

<I will—what's up, Mel?>

<Later,> she promised. <Things moving too fast now. Suspicious about Renee. Love you.>

<Love you. Be careful.>

Melanie fretted as they wandered toward the head table, careful to acknowledge others as she walked, hiding her worries.

Did Renee transmit some problematic nanos to me? Toxin? This doesn't feel like Netwalker toxin. Not even that weird Freedom Army variant.

<Here she comes,> Angela texted.

<Get us private,> Melanie texted back.

<Got it,> Angela acknowledged. She and Nik joined Sergio and Erica in forming a protective cordon around Melanie and Diana.

"What's going on?" Diana asked.

"Have you taken a look at Renee lately? A *good* look?"

"I know she's pregnant," Diana said cautiously.

"Not that. Something else is going on. She's moving like those Freedom Army fighters. Can Sarah take a look?"

"I'll pass it on," Diana said.

A series of chimes called them to order. Melanie took her assigned seat on the Corporate side, to Zhao's left, while Diana joined the other heads of state seated on Zhao's right. Melanie kept one eye on Renee, who sat in a front row seat across from Zhao. Marty was a few seats away from Renee.

<Marty. Watch Renee. What does Ness say?>

Sarah broke in. <Melanie.>

<Yes.>

<That consort of Andrew's isn't what she appears to be. Or who she appears to be. She's not even pregnant.>

<Sarah's right,> Ness chimed in.

<What *are* you two saying?> Melanie's gut tightened.

<She's wearing a Netwalker guise. And I'm not completely sure the host is Renee. Hard to tell. Doesn't feel right,> Sarah said.

<She's a Netwalker?> Melanie was incredulous.

<She's a host, but I can't separate her out from her Netwalker's guise.>

<Freedom Army Netwalk, then.>

How the hell did she pick up a Netwalker, much less a Freedom Army Netwalker? She's not supposed to have any chip that allows her to do that. Not and remain close to Andrew. Damn it. What if she's passed on toxin to me? Is that why I had that flush of heat?

Renee hadn't had a chip in Charleston. Why now?

<Yes. It has all the tags of Freedom Army Netwalk. It's a long-term guise,> Sarah said.

<I didn't know that long-term guises were possible. Any idea who they really are?> Melanie asked.

<I haven't the faintest damned clue,> Sarah growled. <Andrew managed to keep secret any relationships he had with that crowd while I was still alive.>

<Do you think he *knows*?>

<It's hard to hide a guise from anyone who's Dialogue savvy, especially someone who's a former host. That's what you want to hear, isn't it?>

<It's the truth, isn't it?>

<As far as I know, it is. With shadings.>

<Ness?>

<Sarah's right, Melanie. Andrew *should* know,> Marty answered instead of Ness. <But it's entirely possible that he doesn't see it because his chip's gone.>

<Shit.> Melanie sagged back against her chair, keeping her focus on Zhao. <Sarah. Mom knows?>

<Not yet. She specified that I was to report whatever I found directly to you.>

<Tell her,> she commanded. <Run an ID scan on both Netwalker and host. Quietly. Think they suspect we've figured it out?>

<No. Not yet.>

Melanie's stomach roiled and a sick bitter taste briefly oozed into her mouth. She swallowed hard, forcing the ooze down, and sipped from her water glass. Toxin? Something else?

<Why the hell would Andrew do this?> Melanie asked. <Does he think I'm blind? I'm an Enforcer, after all.>

<He doesn't know what an Enforcer is. And he's without a Dialogue,> Sarah said. <He never was a perceptive or strong host. I could walk him around by the nose when I popped into him, and Peter was even slicker at playing Andrew than I was.>

<What are you saying? That doesn't sound like what you just said about him being aware of her Netwalker guise. Are you playing me?>

<No, no, no,> Sarah equivocated.

<Then what *are* you saying?> Melanie rubbed her head, the early twinge of a headache coming on. <Do I have to play Enforcer to get you to spit it out?>

<I'm not that certain of his virtual awareness levels!>

<Then check his Dialogue status,> Melanie ordered.

<I can try.>

<Ness, you do it along with Sarah. And get Mom in the loop. Sarah, are you *sure* she's not pregnant? Andrew won't play around with *that*. It means too damned much in the Courts.>

<She's far enough along that there should be brain activity, plus a heartbeat. Neither are there.> Sarah hesitated. <Okay. More data. That woman's brain waves don't match Renee's brain waves. Someone's pulled a switch on Andrew.>

<How can that happen without Andrew knowing?> Marty asked.

<Perhaps he's not able to tell,> Cat said. <Melanie, Sarah just told me what's going on.>

<Here's another complication. I'm feeling sick. Started just after I touched her. Poison pill again? Another toxin dose?>

<What's happening?> Diana texted. <Sarah told me about suspicions.>

It was disconcerting to switch back and forth between mindspeech with Ness, Cat, Marty and Sarah, then texting for Diana.

<Mom. Talk through Sarah? Whatever's happening to me, swapping texting and mindspeech makes me sicker. Need mindspeech only.>

<Can you borrow Sarah?> Diana texted. <I'll text, she'll translate to mindspeech.>

Melanie shivered at the thought of Sarah so close, so intimate inside her chip.

Stop fooling around and do it!

<Okay,> she texted to her mother. To Sarah, she spoke, in her best Enforcer command tones, <Don't get any damned ideas about being too comfortable.>

<I won't,> Sarah grumbled back at her. <Don't kid yourself. I

haven't the faintest intention of settling into *your* chip unless it becomes necessary. Now. Here I come.>

A swimming feeling, and the room spun briefly around her. Then everything settled, except for that sense of an additional presence in her head. Melanie struggled against the instinct that made her want to shove Sarah out of her brain.

<I'm here,> Sarah announced. <Now. I *know* that's not Renee.>

<You sure?>

<Data spidering results came back while I was popping into you. Not a match at all.>

<Andrew *has* to know that.>

<Could be,> Sarah said. <Or—she could be influencing him.>

Melanie tapped her fingers, watching the woman out of the corner of her left eye while keeping her main focus on Zhao. Cat discreetly changed her seat so that she was sitting directly behind Renee.

Freedom Army Netwalk means I need to take the host out first. Then go after the Netwalker. One of these days I'll have a standard protocol for dealing with rogue Netwalkers. I just hope nothing happens.

Zhao began to wind down his speech.

<Her muscles are tightening,> Sarah reported. <Watch out.>

Renee rose from her seat, moving toward Zhao.

<She's moving!> Melanie texted, broadband. She jumped onto the table, ignoring the gasps and yells from her neighbors.

"This for the cause of anarchy! Death to all government fascists!" Renee screamed, reaching under her maternity shirt and pulling something out, snapping it into shape. Melanie recognized it.

Pocket rifle!

Melanie slid off the table and landed on the floor, running for Renee. Nik and Angela beat her. Nik wrestled with Renee for control of the weapon while Angela looked for an opening. Cat crouched slightly back, waiting to make her move.

"Get away from her! Clear the room!" Melanie shouted as she skidded to a stop five feet away from the woman.

Renee shifted guise from female to male, changing from starched blonde to fiery redhead. Renee plus Netwalker fought back skillfully against Nik as they wrestled for control of the gun.

Angela dove for the knees and took them down, but the Netwalker/host wrestled free and sprang back up, quicker than they should have been able to do.

Augmenter!

"Get Nik *back*, Ange!" Melanie yelled, as Nik reengaged the Netwalker/host while it tried to point the rifle at Zhao.

I have to catch this one without a globe, too many people, too close!

Nik wrestled the weapon free and hurled it at Angela. The Netwalker/host screamed and turned on him, lunging at Nik with teeth and nails.

Dear God in heaven, no.

Melanie leapt, grabbing at the Netwalker/host's head. She missed and slammed hard on the floor.

Nik ducked away from the Netwalker/host, but he was too slow. The Netwalker/host ripped at his throat with its nails.

Melanie flung herself against the Netwalker/host's legs as hard as she could, pushing them back away from Nik. Cat grabbed the Netwalker/host's shoulders from behind, pulling them off balance. Melanie staggered back to her feet as Nik collapsed.

<Fucking Freedom Army anarchist,> Sarah muttered. <I'm going to get him!> Melanie felt Sarah slip out of her chip.

<No! Sarah! No! Back to Mom! Get back to Diana! Cat! Marty! Ness! Help!>

Sarah ignored her, shimmering into visibility near the Netwalker.

Damn it, Two Netwalkers to manage now!

Ness stirred and popped out.

God, no, not three Netwalkers!

<Marty, for the love of God, keep Ness out of this!> Melanie tried to call up the blue light. Nothing.

<I've got her!>

Ness shimmered out of sight.

Melanie tried to raise the blue light again.

Why isn't this working?

<Cat!> Melanie said. <Get Sarah out of here! Get her back to Mom! She'll hurt more than she'll help!>

Where is Mom, damn it, she needs to take charge of Sarah!

"Stop!" Melanie commanded, moving toward Sarah and the Netwalker/host, desperately projecting every ounce of command she could into her voice.

The Netwalker/host snarled at Melanie, now focusing solely on her.

"What can I do to get that motherfucker disabled?" Angela hissed.

Melanie slammed the sedative pen into Angela's hand. "Sedative. Get the host out of this crap. I can't do anything more until they're separate. But for God's sake, don't get hurt!"

Bad enough Nik's down. Damn it, we haven't practiced these protocols enough, and we should! Damn it, damn it, damn it! Too fucking complacent!

"Got it." Angela moved away from Melanie. The Netwalker/host's attention switched from Melanie to Angela.

Recognizes her as a foe. Got to distract them. Where's Sarah?

Melanie chanced a quick look around. Cat was facing Sarah down, herding her back toward Diana. She switched her attention back to the Netwalker/host.

"I said *stop,*" Melanie said, growling her deepest command tone. *"Leave your host!"*

That caught the Netwalker/host's attention. They snarled at her.

Why aren't they capable of speech?

Angela darted in and pressed the injector against the host's neck. As the host sagged and collapsed, the Netwalker swirled out of—*her*—another skinny blonde like Deirdre Conley who looked nothing at all like Renee. So who was the redheaded male?

Melanie slipped the trap door chip out of her sleeve pocket and formed the cage, watching warily as the clouds took on shades of black and red shadows.

Another Liam shape.

The clouds didn't take a human form.

Not typical. Hope this works outside of a globe.

She gestured toward the cage.

"Inside," she ordered.

The Netwalker pulsed at Melanie, then swarmed toward her.

"Inside," she repeated, using her full command voice.

Not working. Codes!

She blinked up the generic Netwalker command codes she and Marty had devised after they captured Conley, transmitting them to Cat just in case.

The cloud hit Melanie full in the face. The world disappeared around her, becoming shades of black and red. Melanie couldn't breathe. Black and red tightened around her face. She flailed at it but her hands couldn't gain purchase.

It's going to kill me. I'm the real target.

"*Inside,*" Cat's voice commanded, full, rich and strong. "*Inside, now!*"

The Netwalker disappeared. Melanie looked around, her vision blurring and fading. No sign.

"It's in the cage," Cat said.

"Thanks." Melanie tapped the cage closed and locked it into the chip as her world went completely blurry. She collapsed to her knees, then fell onto her hands, rocking slightly on her hands and knees.

Tired. So damned tired.

And more, as sourness filled her mouth. Her head pounded and her body tightened. She threw up, gagging as she tried and failed to hold it back. Her entire body tightened and released as she emptied her stomach, and kept on spasming even after her stomach was empty.

"Melanie." Cat's hands were on Melanie's shoulders, supporting her.

"Toxin," Melanie gasped between heaves. "Overload. *Get Marty now!*"

"Mel, I'm here." Marty's hands replaced Cat's. "Here's a painkiller."

Melanie nodded, unable to speak any more as pain joined the nausea wracking her body.

God. Oh God. What a mess.

The fuzzy warmth of the painkiller pulsing through her was a welcome relief.

CHAPTER 12

WHAT A FUCKING MESS OF A DAY.

Angela shook a tab of Burnout into her hand and dry-swallowed it.

And it's not over yet.

Mel had been right to worry about the Freedom Army.

Why didn't anyone listen to her? I should have. Nik. God, is he all right?

No time to check on him yet. He had a mild dose of Netwalker toxin, but what did that mean?

The Security Center frenzy around her was slowly starting to settle down. Fewer bodies milling around and shouting. No more muttered consultations between different Security branches. Order slowly returning from the chaos caused by the scramble to assure the safety of multiple Primaries.

False Renee here. Successful assassinations of the Brazilian President, the Japanese Premier, Neuroleap's President, Johnson Space's CEO. Attempt on Grady but he managed to duck it. Rio Bravo, Tokyo, and LA. All by fake support staff, in supposedly secure office settings. Except for us.

Angela heaved a sigh.

I hope Marty can talk now.

She tapped the code into the globe and sat back, waiting for it to connect.

Marty popped into view. "Nik's doing fine, Ange. He got a light dose." He scowled. "Keeping him down is about as tough as keeping

Mel quiet. Cat's using nanos on him to clear the toxin. Things must be calming down on your end?"

"Yeah. For the moment. But it's still a fucking mess. How's Mel?"

Marty scowled. "That's entirely different. Ange, she got a major dose of toxin that triggered that poison pill—and she's pregnant."

"What? She didn't think she was—"

Marty nodded. "Six weeks along. Sarah and Ness both picked it up while we were treating her. Don't know yet if the toxin will trigger a miscarriage. Don't know why Ness and Sarah didn't see it until after the attack. Ness says timing."

"Oh God, Marty. Can you use those nanos Cat's using on Nik to treat her?"

Marty shook his head. "Cat's not certain what they'd do to the embryo." He took a deep, shuddering breath. "The irony of it is, we might be able to use these nanos to clean that poison pill out of her. But we don't dare do that while she's pregnant."

"If she loses this one—"

"Exactly. And even though Mel's deep under, she keeps muttering about the gadget. With both Mel and Nik down, though, no one will tell me about why she's worried."

"I don't know much either. Nik doesn't talk."

"They *can't* talk," Marty said. "Our one best hope at keeping the pregnancy is to ship her to the Ranch. Get her behind the No-Fence. Perhaps it'll shut down the mechanism of the poison pill. I wish I knew how it got triggered. Best that Ness and I could figure is that it happened when Mel touched the host before the opening session. That slowed her down enough that the Netwalker was able to hit her. Thank God Cat was there. Even though she's still a novice Enforcer, that still helped. If I hadn't had my hands full keeping Ness from reacting to Sarah and that Netwalker—"

"Marty, you did what you needed to do."

"I know. Doesn't make me feel better. Nik will benefit from being behind the No-Fence as well." He paused to take a breath. "Kathy Miller is en route to set up an obstetrics Medical team." His lips tightened. "I'll talk to Diana, suggest that further meetings of High Space and the Courts be held on the Ranch, under strict screening and No-Fence protections."

She nodded, for the moment unable to speak.

"Good. One more thing. I'll bring the kids—Sophie and the Jeffreys boys—to the ranch. It might make things easier on Mel. They helped her before. And they can use the ranch experience, all of them."

Angela half-grinned. "The kids will love the chance to ride horses regularly! I guess it's their new favorite thing to do."

"I'm sure Rita will get them out there as much as they want. I'll keep you posted about timelines and who's going where and when. I have to get the kids from the Mountain, so I want you to stay with Mel. That work?"

"I can handle it."

"Good. Lot of stuff to get started. We'll talk later, once I know more. Later." He reached out and clicked off the screen.

Angela sank back in her chair.

Next time we'll all listen to Mel when she says there's a remaining problem. I know damn good and well the Courts leadership will do so now.

She just wished it hadn't taken this to make it happen.

MARTY STOOD WITH KATHY MILLER AT THE SKIMMER PAD ON THE Andrews Ranch, looking south down the canyon where the skimmer would appear. The kids had wanted to come with him, but Melanie was still unconscious, and he didn't want them to see her like that.

"It's a good thing you didn't let the emergency team try those nanos on Mel," Kathy said. "They're the fast solution, but *my* team doesn't agree that it's the best. Given Mel's medical history, and whatever residuals she might have from that treatment for her injuries last year, I'd not chance using them on her again this soon. Odds are her nano counts still run too high, and you'll risk them antagonizing each other."

"I know those nanos too well." Marty blinked slowly into the wind pushing the gray-blue clouds above the high, grassy plains around them, and the snow-covered mountains. He shivered, marveling at how lightly Kathy was dressed, not seeming to notice the sharpness of the cold wind.

He should have grabbed his heaviest ski jacket instead of leaving it at home. February at the Ranch was colder than February on the Mountain.

The black shadow of a skimmer whispered up the canyon toward them.

"I'm tweaking a datasuit to give her more protection," Kathy said. "She'll need to exercise extreme caution in the virtual world throughout this pregnancy."

"What does the team think we should do for the toxin overload?"

"Regular blood work and monitoring of the embryo as it develops. From the data about her last miscarriage, and that of the surrogate's, the issue may be development-stage related. Second trimester is going to be the problem." The skimmer jockeyed in the stiff wind before landing. "We'll do the standard treatment for toxin recovery. More aggressive, actually, as there's some thought—disputed, but we have to consider it—that physical activity may raise her risk factors for toxin activation in pregnancy. We want to watch out for the development of autoantibodies. Very conservative management, overall, when it comes to virtual. Double datagloves for any globe work, and *no* full-body globe work. Period."

Marty grimaced, imagining what the next few months were going to be like. "That's going to be tough."

"She wants that baby bad enough, she'll do it," Kathy said. "She *could* abort the baby, and hope that the nanos clear her system so she can try again."

"I'm skeptical about that working."

"I am as well. I'd rather do a slow, systematic, *careful* filtered flush combined with meds. It'll take longer but have better results, in my opinion."

"I understand," Marty said, as the skimmer door opened.

The beginning of a new chapter in our lives—I hope.

MELANIE LAY WITH HER EYES CLOSED, GATHERING UP THE STRENGTH TO push up her heavy eyelids. For once, she didn't want to rouse her Dialogue right away. She hurt all over. Not the kind of ache that came from physical injury.

Toxin overload. Crap. How did that happen and where am I?

She assessed the clues. Big, soft bed with old-fashioned quilts. Dry but cold. Distant raven calls. Sudden lowing of hungry cattle who had spotted the feed wagon, mixed in with impatient hungry horse nickers. The Ranch, either morning or evening feeding time.

Why am I at the Ranch rather than Seattle?

IV in one hand. PICC line for feeding. Oxygen cannula in her nose.

Bad toxin overload. What the hell happened?

Oh yeah. Anomalous Netwalker at the High Space meeting. Andrew's consort Renee—*no, not-Renee.*

God, what happened to her? What happened to Nik? Is he okay? What about Ange?

She shouldn't check Dialogue, not with this level of toxin. The aches and nausea alone indicated one king-hell of an attack. Odd that she still felt this sick behind the No-Fence.

I need to find out what happened. Fast. Keep it short.

She blinked up her news. Urgent message in Courts code warning all Exec members to get to safety after four out of five Netwalkers had successfully assassinated targets.

Gizmo stirring, frantic note from her mother because Sarah had gone deep after Gizmo and come back in shreds. Cat needed Marty and Ness's help to get Sarah calm and back in Diana's chip.

No news of Renee, no news about Nik. Melanie dreaded what that might mean. She hoped that the frantic message about Sarah meant that Marty and Ness had come through the attack unscathed.

Melanie's head ached harder than ever, and she reluctantly shut down her Dialogue.

Pushing it. Okay. Time to get data by traditional means—if anyone will tell me anything.

She opened her eyes. Kathy Miller put down her book and got up, diagnostic pen in hand.

"Glad to see you're awake," Kathy said. "Let's check things out."

Melanie relaxed. Kathy was in charge. Good.

The door opened as Kathy examined her. Melanie recognized Marty's shambling steps on the creaking floorboards before she saw him.

Thank God. He's okay.

He sat on the other side of the bed from Kathy, and took Melanie's right hand.

"Damn it, Mel, you're not supposed to be using Dialogue after a toxin overload. Ness told me."

"Had to find out what's going on. *Four* Netwalker-based assassinations?"

"Possibly more," Marty said. "All Freedom Army Netwalk types. Grady dodged an attack thanks to Cat's second. We're not announcing that one, but I'm betting we're not the only ones keeping silent about internal attacks. Nothing at Nagano; Will fingered several potential attackers before they could do anything. Sarah got shredded by the gadget and we had one hell of a time getting her back to your mom. Cat's reviewing your recruitment protocol for Enforcers. That project's now on the front lines."

"Nik?"

"Doing well. He's back to work, albeit limited. You, on the other hand—how's she doing, Kathy?"

Kathy straightened up. "Slow declines in the toxin levels. Too early to tell with the other stuff yet. But the slow flush appears to be working so far."

"Good." Marty took a deep breath, looking at Kathy. "I need to have that talk with Melanie. If you think now's a good time."

"It's a *great* time for it," Kathy said. "You'll be able to sit with her until I'm back?"

"Of course. What do I need to know?"

"I'll show you what needs to be monitored." Kathy put down her diagnostic pen and snapped up a display. Marty gently rested Melanie's hand on the bedcovers and joined Kathy on the far side of the room. Melanie was too tired to try to make out what they were saying.

That's not usual. Kathy must have me on some strong meds.

Then Marty returned to the bed.

"What's that all about?"

"You're undergoing a touchy treatment protocol right now." Marty said. "It's as aggressive as we dare get at the moment. Needs regular monitoring at this stage."

"What's going on?"

"It looks like you're pregnant. But you had one hell of a Netwalker toxin overload."

Pregnant. How? Oh my God, that explains a lot.

"I'm pregnant?"

"Six weeks into the pregnancy," Marty said. "We're checking your blood levels daily, and that includes monitoring your hormones. We're not doing any virtual diagnostics with you for—reasons."

"I can't believe it," she whispered, now daring to hope. One hand slipped down, covering the area where she thought the embryo would be. "I don't believe it's true. Is it?"

"Yes." He squeezed her hand, smiling at her. "It's true, hon. Believe it. But there are challenges because of the new dose of Netwalk toxin. We can't use the nano-based treatment Cat used on Nik without risking the pregnancy. You have to go through a very slow treatment protocol. And there's more."

"What?"

"Data suggests that too much movement triggers the toxin. So you're on significant bed rest for several months, at least. Kathy and the obstetrics team are focusing on getting the toxin flushed out of your system first, slowly and carefully, or at least as much as we can do while pregnant. Then we reassess what we do with you next."

"The toxin won't affect the baby?" Melanie asked.

"The issue isn't necessarily the dose of toxin, but the fetal developmental stage when the toxin is triggered. We may be able to let you up after a few weeks. Or not. We just don't know yet."

Bed rest. Melanie squirmed just at the thought of it.

But this might be my last chance to have a child of my own.

She pressed her lips tightly together.

"Any ideas about how to keep me still without going crazy?" she asked in an even smaller voice. "God, how am I going to work? Cat can't do full Enforcer recruitment."

"Cat does the initial screening, and you do the final, with exterior tools. You have to be extremely conservative in accessing the virtual world. Limited hologlobe access, with two layers of datagloves. No full-body access. I'll devise a double firewall. Plus a new datasuit, with tighter security. The key is to keep you safe from outside triggering of the poison pill, and aggressive management of any increase in toxin levels."

"If I have to, I have to. What about Renee? Andrew? What did he know?"

"He's cooperating. He's in shock. What the hell else can he do? Otherwise, he risks getting charged as an accessory. They found Renee's body in California. We've not IDed the substitute yet, but it seems that the substitution took place during this last week while he was away, before the fake Renee flew up last night." Marty sighed. "And the original Renee *was* pregnant."

So now Andrew's lost his heir, too. I need to call him and offer sympathy.

"Sounds like there's been a lot going on."

Marty nodded. "One hell of a lot, darlin'. I've been putting out fires connected with Dialogue and Netwalk."

"Oh God, Marty." Melanie blinked back tears. "How long do you think I'll have to deal with this toxin?"

"The entire pregnancy, most likely. You can do a lot of work from your bed. I'm getting that set up. No globes in here. Screens only. No more use of Dialogue without Ness there to shield you. That may help stave off the poison pill."

"It's the worst possible time for me to be out of commission."

"Hon, given our lives, I don't think there ever will be a good time."

"What about the High Space and Exec meetings?"

"Postponed until we get more capacity set up here. Right now there's a lot of interest in No-Fence secure meeting facilities, with tight Security screening. Angela and Cat are prepping trainers to teach Dialogue safety and Netwalker spotting techniques.."

She turned carefully on her side to face him. "I'm afraid of all this.

Afraid of losing the baby. Afraid I've let you all down by being sidelined like this."

"Hon, you're not superhuman. I think your mother spent too much time in the past years thinking you were. This'll be good for her, too. Cat is learning how to manage Sarah and Diana. Cat might be a better match as a monitor for them than you are."

"But still—"

"No." He stroked her cheek. "Hon, *let it go*."

Melanie heaved a deep sigh. "I feel so damned helpless."

"I'm betting it won't take you long to be back at work hard as you can. I know you will. And besides, we have a baby to think about."

"If I don't lose this one." Her voice faltered.

"You won't." His voice was firm. "Not this one. I promise you that."

She smiled back at him, her eyes growing heavy-lidded.

"I'm getting sleepy," she said.

Marty grabbed the pad from her nightstand. He contemplated it for a moment. "Yeah. Right on schedule. Go ahead and sleep. If I'm not here, Kathy will be. Okay?"

"Okay." She let her heavy eyelids close. "Just—stay with me for a while—right here. Okay?"

"I'll be here. You know that."

Then his arms slid around her and he pulled her close.

CHAPTER 13

I THOUGHT MORNING SICKNESS WAS SUPPOSED TO END AFTER THE FIRST *trimester.*

Melanie closed her eyes and swallowed hard, fighting back nausea. This time she won.

Five months along today. Over halfway. Little one, hold on.

At least this nausea didn't feel like a toxin overload.

We can make it through. It's a bad morning. Just part of the pattern of good days and bad days.

She nibbled on some crackers, gritted her teeth and went back to her morning isometric stretches, followed by the High Space muscle maintenance sims she was trialing for Mei-lein's medical staff.

When she finished her exercises, Melanie carefully crawled out of bed to shower and change into a lighter pajama set, to reflect the forecast for a warm July day. After showering, she munched on more crackers, sipped flat soda, swallowing hard as the nausea roiled, then pulled up a hologlobe. Morning review was a lot tougher when she couldn't do more than online fingertip access.

She highlighted reports to prioritize them. Cat's most recent report on Enforcer recruitment and training. High priority, red.

Current Freedom Army incident reports. Medium priority, but she was the person with the most time to scan these reports for patterns. Orange.

High Space production stats. High priority, red. Quick and easily dealt with.

She continued to rank her reports until she was done, then turned to review.

She was halfway through the reviews when Kathy and Dr. Mitzuko from Nagano, the obstetric toxin specialist, came in for the morning scan and bloodwork. Melanie put her reviews on hold and waited for their report.

"Going to be a hot one today," Kathy said absently, gazing at scans. "Zuko, what do you think of this result?"

Dr. Mitzuko looked over Kathy's shoulders. "Hmm. Yes."

Melanie noted the intensity of text flashes between them.

"I'm calling Marty," Kathy snapped. "Zuko, we need to run more tests, *now*."

"Is this a miscarriage?" Melanie asked, tensing. "It doesn't *feel* like one."

"Don't know," Kathy muttered, poring over her tablet. "This damn data—"

The door opened. Marty strode in, face set in hard, grim lines. Her gut roiled even more.

"How bad is it?" she whispered, forcing the words past the sudden tightness in her throat.

Marty rubbed her shoulders.

"We're worried. But we're waiting for data," he said softly.

"She's not miscarrying—yet." Kathy didn't look up from her tablet. "But there's some suspicious spikes in your toxin levels, Mel."

"I'm nauseous but it doesn't feel like toxin. Marty, it really doesn't feel like toxin."

"*Good,*" he said fervently.

Melanie burped and her gut tightened. Sour taste in her mouth. Stomach spasmed, a pattern far too familiar over the past months of morning sickness. She fumbled for the pan and vomited. Marty took the pan away when she was done and Kathy silently helped her clean up. Melanie collapsed onto her side, fighting the stomach spasms.

Marty returned and started rubbing her back and shoulders. Melanie breathed in slowly and carefully. The spasms eased, then surged. Unlike the toxin flares she had before, though, relaxing and breathing didn't help. She groaned as the nausea rose in intensity. Her head throbbed.

Now this feels like toxin.

Zuko and Kathy carefully checked the leads on Melanie's abdomen and head, then returned to their tablets, text lights flashing brightly in their eyes and reflecting in her water glass. The flashes added to her headache.

"I'll do it," Marty said. "She'll be better with me here, anyway."

"What's happening?" she croaked.

He squeezed her shoulder with one hand while he took an infusion pen from Kathy.

"Caught the poison pill just as it kicked off. We're infusing you with a low dose antitoxin regime rather than a big one—that could trigger a miscarriage. Low dose means you'll need consistent in-person monitoring with someone trained to administer and monitor antitox using non-virtual tools. Can't use more complex automated tools because that can trigger the toxin. No more virtual exposures today. Maybe even longer."

She nodded as a bigger wave of nausea crashed over her.

"Do it," she muttered.

"Steady," Marty murmured. He rotated her forearm to expose the veins in her wrist. Whistling softly, he found the one he wanted, cleaned the skin, and injected the infuser. Once he was satisfied, he expanded the infuser's cuff around her arm to hold it in place, then attached the antitoxin bag and set the programming.

Nausea slowly ebbed away, replaced by drowsiness. The spasms subsided to twitches. Marty stroked her forehead gently while he talked to Zuko and Kathy.

"We caught this one just as it started. Should we increase the number of times we do labs?" Marty asked.

"Now that we know the profile of an attack, we can program it into the alerts," Kathy said.

"Wait minute," Melanie said through thick lips. "Can spot pattern?"

"Yes. A distinct spike in both the drop and resumption, strong match to your vitals," Marty said.

"And intensive virtual use," Kathy said. "Time to cut back on your virtual time again, Melanie. It's a factor."

"But Enforcer finals!" Melanie protested.

"Not today, not even as early as next week," Marty said. "At least not virtual."

Melanie wanted to argue. But the roiling in her gut and the ache in her head kept her quiet.

Another damn misery you owe me, Liam Jeffreys.

By afternoon Melanie felt well enough to eat and look at her reports in hard copy. Marty ran back and forth between their suite and the other bedroom suite where he set up globes to relay messages. She couldn't share a room with a globe now.

They set up individual in-person interviews with the prospective Enforcers for the following week using this roundabout method.

When the kids burst into the room for their afternoon reading, it was a welcome dose of semi-normality. Donnie and Sophie curled up at the foot of the bed, practicing Security fingersign while she read aloud. Alex grumped at having to change sides because of the infuser, but before long he'd settled in his usual place with his head on her belly.

"Baby talk me," he had told Melanie matter-of-factly three weeks ago, once her daughter had started moving. "Baby like talk me."

The baby *did* either settle or become more active when Alex was around, depending on what Melanie was doing before he came. It didn't seem to hurt anything one way or another, so Melanie noted it as an observation point and wondered what it meant. Nothing about either the baby or Alex's behavior triggered any of her Enforcer instincts. The baby just seemed to have a preference for certain voices—Alex and Marty in particular.

Marty made a face as he carried a tablet into the room. "Sorry Mel, sorry kids, but there's an urgent call."

"Who is it?" she asked.

"Andrew. Courts code."

Melanie frowned.

Dismiss the kids or not?

The call was unlikely to take very long, and if she kept the kids nearby, that gave her an excuse to end it quickly.

Kids here.

She reached for the tablet. "I'll take it."

Marty raised a brow and nodded at the kids. She shook her head.

"You stay here too," she said. He nodded again and settled on the bed. She glanced at Donnie and Sophie, who were engaged in a long fingersign conversation.

Good that they're practicing.

The occasional verbal phrases she heard sounded like Sophie was teaching Donnie Mixteco.

Wonder what Ange thinks about that?

Alex appeared to have gone to sleep. Melanie took a deep breath and accepted Andrew's call, adding in the sigil which indicated the conversation was unsecured.

"Melanie." Andrew scowled at her. "Are you attending the next Courts meeting?"

"No. What's up?"

"We have infringement issues."

Damn! Has to be Jeremy.

Jeremy Halstead's research into bioradiologic sensors took him dangerously close to Stephens proprietary interests, and had ever since Charleston. Melanie had hoped that perhaps they could collaborate with Stephens, because that research was sweetly promising.

Didn't sound like that now.

"We could cooperate on the combined bioradiologic sensors," she offered. "There is a precedent for a combined patent."

Marty frowned at her and reached for another pad. He scribbled a note and passed the pad to her.

Andrew shook his head. "That's not acceptable."

"Give me a moment," she said. *Jeremy won't support that,* she read.

There's been issues with Stephens. It's our process, not theirs. She looked back up.

Andrew smirked at her. "Lot harder to do things slow like the rest of us mortals, huh, Melanie?"

The headache began to throb again. "Andrew, we have to work together on this. The product has good potential, and we could get past this family BS."

"We tried that in Charleston. Nothing happened."

"That wasn't our fault."

"Fault doesn't matter. It's a Stephens process. Your researchers are impinging upon ours. Call your guy off."

"There's no way we can negotiate this?" Damn it, they'd come so close to cooperation. Renee and Jeremy had a compatible vision, and he had her notes. "Renee's notes show the path but she and Jeremy had worked out the techniques together. I still think they could have turned it around in Charleston if we'd been given more time."

"Renee's *dead*," Andrew said bitterly. "And Charleston's gone too. What could have been didn't happen. I want those notes back, and your promise of no further research in this direction."

How much of this behavior was Andrew still being locked into grief? Her fault that this accord had failed. She hadn't gotten back to him with condolences since Renee's death had been confirmed—all the craziness around her pregnancy coupled with old habits.

Andrew cared about those sorts of social niceties. It had caused many problems between them over the years because she didn't always think about it. She should have remembered. Sick as she had been, as complicated as things had been, she still should have found a way to talk to her brother. Her mistake.

"We can do that," she said. "But Drew, shutting down productive research—"

"She's *dead*!" he snapped. "And I'm not going there!"

"Drew, I'm sorry about her death. I really am."

"Sorry because you mean it or sorry because it interferes with your research? Bit late with your condolences, aren't you?"

"I'm sorry," she repeated. "I didn't know her very well. But I'm sorry it happened."

"You should be." His face twisted. "If you and Sarah hadn't pushed that Netwalk stuff—Shut that research down. Or I'll take it to the Courts."

Melanie's gut roiled. Tension this time, not toxin.

We can't take this to the Courts. We'll both be censured—we can't afford this.

"I'll shut it down. But Andrew—"

"Thank you." He closed the connection.

Melanie dropped the pad and leaned back against her pillows. She slammed the bed with her unencumbered arm. "Damn it!"

Sophie and Donnie gave her cautious looks, then returned to their handsign. Alex stirred, stretched, then snuggled back into his spot.

Marty retrieved the pad. "Jeremy won't like this."

"I don't see any way around it. We can't afford Courts sanctions, and I just don't have the strength to wrangle with Andrew today. I fucked up. I should have followed up with Andrew after Charleston. After Seattle. Both times I didn't. Now I'm paying the price for my mistakes."

"Jeremy may appeal to you."

"Let him," she said quietly. "I'll explain why."

Marty got up and squeezed her shoulder. "Okay. I'm going to do my best to keep him from bothering you."

"If he needs to talk to me, he can," Melanie repeated.

Helen appeared to collect the kids, Sophie and Donnie got up without argument, but Alex needed some persuasion.

"Baby feels better with me here!" he insisted when Helen tried to pull him away.

As if to emphasize his case, the baby kicked wildly until Alex settled back down against Melanie's abdomen.

No. Don't risk it. Not today.

"He's been napping," she said. "It's okay. The others can stay as well. The baby is quieter with him here, and today that's a good thing."

Sophie and Donnie climbed back on the bed. The baby's movements calmed. Helen frowned at them.

"Another hour," Melanie said. "All right, Alex?"

"Mmhmm," he murmured. "Go with Helen when nap done."

Melanie smiled at Helen. "Then we'll do it in an hour." She sighed and leaned back against her pillows, closing her eyes.

Four more months to go.

MARTY WAS BACK AT THE MOUNTAIN, AND DID HE EVER MISS MELANIE. HE rarely spent nights here when Mel was at the Ranch, but tonight was an exception. The discussion with Jeremy had gone long into the evening. Then, thunderstorms. Nik vetoed returning to the Ranch tonight because of the weather.

The loud rolls of thunder fit his mood.

I promised Mel I'd talk to Conley, give her the latest possible Tim Conley variant. Tonight, or tomorrow morning?

Timing wouldn't make a difference, save for the new Enforcer from Security. Karl, one of Cat's finds of high-level Enforcer skills in the first Enforcer class. Melanie had tagged Karl as the onsite Enforcer to deal with Conley, especially when Marty talked to her.

I want Karl's perspective when you talk, she had insisted. *Record it. Cat just doesn't see details in Conley's reactions. Karl's Security, maybe he'll spot it.*

Marty contemplated the options. He was tired. Not the best state to be around Conley. But tomorrow morning he'd be rushed and wanting to get back to Mel. Equally bad. However, Karl was rested and beginning a new shift this evening.

Tonight.

If he sent the recording to Mel afterward, she would have time to review it before he got back to the Ranch. One less thing hanging over his head for tomorrow.

He texted Karl and Nik. Better to get it over with.

They met outside of the detention wing. <You've reviewed Melanie's notes?> he asked Karl. It still felt odd to mindspeech with someone other than Melanie or a Netwalker.

<Yes. She's given me details.>

<Then let's do it.>

"Let's go," he said aloud for Nik's benefit.

"A word of warning," Nik said. "She's on suicide watch. Shoshana's not certain what's going on, but Conley's been irrational over the past few weeks even with increased freedom and research tasks. She's verbally abusive and on the prod. Shoshana thinks she's saying provocative stuff in order to get someone to beat on her. It—" he hesitated. "It fits the profile of someone raised in the Freedom Army, like Conley was. If she can't kill herself, she'll try to get someone else to do it."

Marty nodded. "Point taken. It could also be the behavior of a former host deprived of her Netwalker."

"I wouldn't know about that," Nik said.

"It's entirely possible," Karl said. "I'll know more after this interview."

Ness stirred. <I think it's host-related. Netwalkers go crazy without the sensory link of a host to charge with and tie into the living world. Why wouldn't hosts have problems when cut off from Netwalkers? Andrew didn't get any treatment after Peter was yanked out of him.>

"Ready?" Nik asked.

<We'll talk about this later,> Ness added.

Marty nodded. Nik gestured to Karl.

<I'm acting like I'm just the new Security watch staff,> Karl said as he opened the door to Conley's room.

Marty flinched as he entered the room. Bandages covered Conley's arms and she jumped up, slamming herself against the wall as Nik entered.

<Don't react!> Nik texted. <She stops if you don't react.>

<She's cutting herself,> Karl added. <Doesn't need a sharp edge, she'll find something and rub her arms and legs against it until it bruises. They've tried tranqs and other meds to stop her. No luck. Meds just agitate her.>

Crap. That's what Mel would do. Fight until she's unconscious. She's a lot like Mel.

Marty activated the secure globe. The familiar colors and light flashes of virtual world expanded around them. Karl slipped into virtual with an ease that matched Melanie and Cat's prowess, though his movements lacked their grace.

<She's trying to access her chip,> Ness said.

<Got it.> Another thing Mel would do. Not give up, in spite of continual failures.

Okay, then, how would I start things with Mel in a situation like this? Confront her straight on.

"So why are you trying to hurt yourself?" he asked Conley.

Conley's face contorted slowly, her mouth opening wide. She lunged at Marty as if to bite him but Nik intercepted her. She shrieked and struggled against him.

"She's faking," Karl said laconically, projecting *boredom, bored, boring.*

Damn he's good. Almost as good as Mel.

Marty shook his head to toss off the unspoken *boring* projection.

Boring, bored, boredom.

"I am not boring!" Conley screamed, wrestling with Nik and lunging at Karl.

<She picked it up even with her chip disabled!> he said to Ness.

<Residual effect,> she responded. <Fascinating. Theoretically possible, but I hadn't thought it that likely. Wonder how else it manifests?>

Karl yawned, a long, slow languid yawn that seemed to take twice as long as it should. "Could have fooled me," he said.

Boredom, boring, bored.

<She's good,> he said.

<Good enough to go up against Sarah,> Ness said.

Marty shrugged. "When you're ready to talk, let me know." He dropped into a chair and snapped up a short report to scan.

As if a switch had been flicked, Conley stopped. She stood steadily, not straining against Nik any more, breathing deep and hard. "Wouldn't you try to hurt yourself if you were locked up like I am? Given excruciatingly boring routine tasks?"

Marty shrugged again, filing the completed report away. "We can't let you go, and your latest behavior is worrying. Are you a danger to yourself and others? Right now, I'd say the answer is *yes.*" For the first time, he looked directly into Conley's eyes. Green, with golden flecks.

Conley sniffed as Nik lifted his hands and freed her. She swayed over to one of the chairs and kicked her left leg up and over the back before sitting, easing into the chair with a controlled grace.

She's staying in shape.

Not a behavior that matched the self-destructive nature of her cutting.

<What do you think about her cutting?> he asked Ness.

<Stereotypic behavior can be a part of a Dialogue withdrawal. Could be the same for former Netwalk hosts. Could also be a conditioned Freedom Army female reaction. Or some combination of all three.>

Conley glared at him. "What kind of cooperation and information do you want?"

It can't be this easy!

<Still faking,> Karl told Marty. <Her patterns match behaviors that Melanie has identified as avoidance or evasive answering patterns.>

"Tell me about Freedom Army Netwalk," he said to Conley.

Conley's jaw dropped. Then she burst out laughing. "You think I'd tell you just like that? What do I get in return? Can I leave?"

"Leave this site, no. More access to research, yes."

"Not worth it." She leaned back in her chair. "I want more. You have that authority to give me more, brown man boy-toy?"

Marty flinched at the sneering tone, more than he expected. Too late, one of Mel's warnings came back to him.

She's good at compulsion tones.

And even though he accepted that he had a significant role in DIR that wasn't tied to his marriage to Mel, the casual bigotry still hit him hard. Conley had never done this before.

But this is the first time I've talked to her away from Melanie.

Conley's comment brought up too many memories of Liam's knifing remarks, when Melanie, Diana or Will weren't around to hear. Was Conley another of the same ilk?

She kept looking away instead of studying his reactions.

Wouldn't she want to watch me squirm if she meant it?

Liam had visibly savored every moment of discomfort his remarks brought.

Nik's hands clamped down hard on her shoulders. "You be polite."

"He's brown, isn't he? And he's *her* man."

Nik's hands tightened. Conley winced but didn't cry out, staring down rather than at Marty.

"Nik," Marty warned, swallowing hard to overcome his own reaction.

"Okay. Sorry," she finally muttered.

Nik released the pressure and stepped back. "Don't do that again. You won't get what you want from us that way."

"Next time you want to get a rise out of me, get it right," Marty said. "You can call me a dirty Kalapuya Siwash half-breed Indian. That's what your Liam used to call me. Along with other things. But Kalapuya is my people. If you're going to be a bigot, at least call me the right thing!"

He took momentary satisfaction in snapping out the last sentence. It lacked the subtle twist Melanie would put on it, but it was sharp enough to make Nik wince.

Conley flinched. "He's not *my Liam* anymore," she said, almost choking on the last words. For a moment he thought she was going to burst into tears.

"And even if you get a rise out of me, we're not going to kill you. Maybe send you to the New Feds along with Gina Jeffreys instead."

Conley shivered. "No. Not that. Sorry. I mean it. Sorry."

Silence hung between them.

"*Are* you going to tell me anything?" Marty pressed.

She laughed defiantly, her face changing swiftly from softening to brief resistance that faded into a desperate stare as she looked up without meeting his eyes. He caught her eyes and she flushed, staring back down at her hands.

<*Now* we have an interesting electromag pattern,> Karl commented. <It's different from the previous patterns I've been shown.>

<Marty, Karl, the pattern change is because she's looking to find her chip connection,> Ness said. <Look here. Both of you!> She pointed to periodic yellow flashes around Conley's implant site that Marty could

only see when Ness touched them. <Has that been part of the pattern, Karl?>

<No.> Karl moved closer to the flashes. <New.>

<Marty, I think it's because she senses me. Have we brought Netwalkers around her since her chip's been disabled?>

<Not that I know of.>

Something we can use?

"You don't have enough activity left to your chip to do anything, so looking for your connection isn't going to do you any good," he said.

Conley's lips tightened. "You can't tell that!" But the way she sagged encouraged him.

"That Netwalker you're sensing and trying to contact is in my chip. Do you want to see her?"

"No!"

"I don't mind."

<I do,> Ness said. <Marty, this is foolhardy!>

<She won't take me up on it,> he told her confidently.

<I'd prefer to have Mel around if we do this.>

"I. Don't. Want. To. See. Her." Now she dared look at him, but her expression lingered between fear and longing.

Maybe it's time for the tidbit Mel wanted me to give to her.

Marty pulled out the chip reader Melanie had given him. "Here's some information about a Tim Conley," he said. "What will you tell me in return for it?"

Conley blew hard, staring as Marty twirled the reader in his fingers.

"Have I told you the details of what happened at Leavenworth?"

Marty blinked up Melanie's database of Conley's disclosures. Not there.

<Mel categorizes it as a medium priority,> Ness said.

<Thanks.>

"We don't have that information," he said.

Conley licked her lips and extended both hands. "Let me see that chip. Then I'll tell you."

Marty dropped the chip reader into Conley's hands. She switched it on, body tight, scanning the record intensely. Then she sighed, body collapsing in what appeared to be relief.

"Not the Tim Conley I'm looking for. Tell *her* to keep looking. Now. Leavenworth. It was an inside job. Your whole operation there is compromised."

Marty sat back, listening as Conley spoke. He almost thought she seemed relieved that this wasn't the Tim Conley she was looking for.

What's going to happen if—when—we find him?

CHAPTER 14

GRAVID. THE WORD DIDN'T ADEQUATELY DESCRIBE THE WAY HER BODY WAS weighed down. Melanie slowly rose from the massive oak desk in her grandfather's old office.

At least I can get up and work now.

She walked with steady, measured steps into the dining room to watch the sun set and wait for dinner, rubbing her aching back. A line of dark clouds hung above the Bucket Mountains, warning of an incoming storm. Typical October weather.

Thirteen months since Charleston.

She thought the Freedom Army would have done something on the anniversary of Charleston's destruction. But things had been stubbornly quiet.

Only two. They'll go for a third. This close to the High Space launches, I'd much rather see more activity rather than less.

Especially in the Florida War Zone, where international teams were busy securing Canaveral in time for the launch two months from now.

I'd feel a hell of a lot better if we could pin down Tim Conley. Or get Deirdre Conley to tell us more.

Deirdre Conley was deathly afraid of Tim Conley, and didn't dare speak until she knew where he was. Why?

The scent of broiled chicken wafted from the kitchen as Rita came into the dining room to set the table.

"How you doing, Mel?"

"Glad to be able to move around."

"Want something before dinner?"

"If it's not any trouble, perhaps some mint tea?"

"Easy enough. I can do that." Rita disappeared back into the kitchen.

Melanie leaned against the window frame, one hand resting on the curve of her belly, the other rubbing her back. The baby stirred against her hand.

No Marty at dinner tonight. High Space meetings in Seattle all day. Contact through visual screens and keyboards, a long and tedious process. He was spending the night in Hoodland working on lab-based chip redesign, returning to Seattle for the next batch of meetings in the morning.

More wrangling at these damned meetings.

But, bit-by-bit, they made slow progress.

Rita came back out with a steaming, fragrant cup of spearmint tea. "From my herb bed."

"Thanks, Rita." Melanie held the cup to her face and took a deep breath. The scent of spearmint soothed her. Almost enough to help her regain her scattered focus.

Today's meetings had been a struggle with brain fuzziness and a distinct lack of desire to think.

"Hey Mel," Angela said, coming up behind her. "Meetings done for today?"

"Yes." Melanie sipped her tea. The warmth spread throughout her body. "I want to pee all the time and I feel huge."

Angela nodded. "Yeah, I remember that from being pregnant with Sophie."

Melanie sipped her tea again. "I didn't think it would be like this—aah!" A sharp pain lanced through her abdomen. She doubled over, hot tea spilling on her hands, barely aware of Angela grabbing the cup and putting it on the table. She gasped, hands on her knees. The pain went away.

"You okay?"

"I don't know." Melanie straightened up. Another sharp pain

twisted through her body, muscles tightening hard over her abdomen. Melanie groaned as she rode this one out, dropping to her knees. "God, Ange, is this labor?"

Angela knelt next to her. "I'm texting Kathy now."

Another pain struck, this one harder than the last one. This time it was in both her back and her stomach. The back pain continued after the abdominal contractions ceased, fierce and hard instead of the dull ache it had been just moments ago. Melanie collapsed to the floor, fighting to control her breathing.

In. Out. Stabbing pain in my back—breathe. Breathe.

Angela placed her hand on Melanie's lower torso. "Pain here?"

Melanie nodded. "And back," she gasped. More pain. This time she couldn't keep from crying out.

Angela took her hands. "I'm here."

Wetness between her legs.

"Think. Water. Broke," Melanie panted against the pain. Against her will she screamed as it hacked through her again, blinding white light worse than when she'd fought Peter.

I can't do this. I can't. I have to. God.

"Sweet Mother of God," Angela moaned. "Damn it, Kathy, hurry up!"

"What? Wrong?" Melanie tried to sit up but Angela pushed her down. Another wave of pain took her. Once again she screamed, every nerve in her body on fire. When it was gone, she tried to struggle back up. And then another wretched contraction shredded through her.

"Stay down, Mel!"

Running footsteps, Kathy barking orders.

"Ange? What's wrong?" Melanie gasped.

"There's blood."

"Is my baby all right?" She lost control of her voice and it came out as a sob.

No, no, no, oh God, no, we've tried so hard not now not now. Too soon and too fast.

Kathy's hands steadied on her shoulder. "It's okay, Mel. We've prepared for this. It's one of the contingencies in our plan. *It's okay.*" She turned her head. "Get her on the stretcher."

"Operate?" Melanie asked. "Or is toxin an issue?"

"No surgery unless we see fetal distress. Let's do something to help you with the pain. Looks like we're having a baby today." As she talked Kathy injected something into the port placed inside Melanie's elbow.

"Marty," Melanie groaned.

"Calling him once you're upstairs," Angela said. "I'll get him here ASAP."

"Thanks," Melanie murmured. The pain receded. Then the next contraction struck. White hot pain. But a veil lay between her and the pain twisting her body. Just enough that she could groan instead of scream.

"Now," Kathy said. "Before the next contraction." Hands eased her onto the stretcher.

Another contraction. This time she half-cried, half-screamed through it, every nerve on fire despite the cloaking curtain. As it stopped, the team hoisted the stretcher. Three steps and another contraction that flamed through her body, sharp hot pins twiddling on every nerve. But Kathy and Angela's hands were there, holding hers. Melanie gasped for breath as the pain receded, lapping at the edges of her awareness, regrouping for another assault.

Please let my baby be all right. Please.

MARTY SCOWLED AT THE CHIP DESIGN SIMULATION IN FRONT OF HIM. Melanie was much better at this sort of full-body immersion and manipulation. He could visualize it but not always maneuver the design pieces effectively, while she could manipulate the pieces to his direction with much more ease. Too often Ness had her own ideas, which slowed things down if he had to explain what he wanted to do. Right now, she held the one piece he wanted to insert into the 3-D structure. And he had to move three pieces to make it work. The last four times he'd tried, he'd messed it up and had to start over.

<Move X-b93 first,> Ness suggested.

<Tried it. Has to be a-29 first.>

<But then J-293 twists.>

<I *know* that! I have to move a-29 while shifting b-93 and then keep J steady!>

Ness didn't respond. She knew better at this point.

Marty chewed on his lip, then put one hand on a-29 and the other on b-93. Carefully, he slid under the structure and supported J-293 with his shoulder.

God, I wish Mel were here.

Ness couldn't hold the pieces in place. Something about Netwalker interaction with virtual skewed a design build in process, though a Netwalker could handle the individual pieces. He got the pieces steady, twisted his left hand to hold a-29 and b-93 in their new place, and reached out for the piece Ness held.

An urgent message alert flashed through the hologlobe.

"Damn it!" Marty muttered. <Ness, can you get that?>

<No. Tight secure from Angela.>

Mel.

<It needs to wait.> He forced himself to focus, ignore the bright flashing green light despite the dread clawing deep into him. He eased the piece into place. Paused. Sagged his shoulder. It held. He backed his hands slowly away from the design.

It held.

Good.

He saved the design, then blinked up the message.

"God, it's about fucking time you answered!" Angela blurted.

"Sorry, I had to finish a design and I couldn't drop it. What's wrong?"

Angela swallowed hard. "Mel's in labor and it's tough. Kathy says get here fast."

"Oh God. How bad?"

"Placental abruption. Moderate severity. Hoping to avoid surgery."

"They're still okay?"

Angela looked back up and nodded. "Kathy says it'll be fast." She blinked. "Crap. Oh fucking hell. As if this wasn't enough."

"Mel?"

Angela shook her head. "Get the fuck out of there, Marty! Shut down and *move*! This isn't a drill, it's for real! ACTIVATE DIASPORA!"

The link broke off. *What the—?*

Diaspora.

He automatically whipped through his routines for safe shutdown.

<Ness, what the hell is going on?>

<Security. Netwalker-based attacks at the High Space Conference Center. Vijay's down but still alive, not sure about others.>

I'd still be there if I hadn't needed to work on this process.

Marty shoved globe generator and data chips into his go-bag, heart pounding.

Diaspora. Attacks at High Space. Crap.

He looked around the lab.

Anything else? No.

He hit the clear button to let Nik know safe entry into the lab was possible.

"Let's go!" Nik slammed the door open.

"On my way." Marty picked up his go-bag. "Ness told me about the attacks. We see any action?"

"Sensors quiet so far but I'll be one hell of a lot happier once we're safely at the Ranch." Nik's hand on Marty's shoulder hurried him along. Karl shouldered in on Marty's other side.

<See anything, Ness?>

<Not yet. Linking with Karl. Priority to get you safe to Mel.>

"Careful now." Nik steered Marty away from the outside door and toward an internal access. Marty lost track of the twists and turns as Nik led him to the shielded skimmer pad.

"Go!" Nik yelled at the driver once they were inside the skimmer.

Marty sagged back in his seat.

An attack just as Mel goes into labor. Coincidence or more Freedom Army bullshit?

<Freedom Army takes responsibility for the act,> Ness said. <Cat says keep your online presence down until you're behind the No-Fence. Netwalkers tracking targets through virtual. You're shielded, but for how long?>

<Understood.>

<Don't shut down completely but no more talk.>

<Understood,> he repeated. Marty threw his hands over his head and stared at the ceiling.

If they're tracking by virtual, then no work while I'm in transit. Nothing to do but worry about Mel.

And wonder just how bad it had gotten in Seattle.

THIS SHOULD NOT BE HAPPENING.

Angela's attention was split between soothing Melanie and supervising the fallout from the Seattle attack.

Contractions too strong and too fast.

Alarms tore her attention away from the Seattle situation.

"Got her!" Kathy snapped, beginning chest compressions on Melanie.

"Clear!" Dr. Yaros yelled. Kathy stood back as a shock jerked through Melanie's body. Melanie drew in a sobbing, deep breath and the monitors resumed their typical beeps and clicks. Angela grabbed Melanie's hand and squeezed it.

Hang on, Mel, hang on.

There was so much blood. Mel's skin was bone pale with gray tinges around her nose and lips. And Kathy had said that a C-section was the absolute last option because Mel's blood clotting had gone to hell, thanks to the toxin. But it had been several hours of excruciating labor.

God, Mel, a baby just to lose you? I'll take you any day.

"Crowning," Zuko announced. "Just a few more contractions."

Melanie moaned. Angela found the moans easier to take than the screams. Melanie never screamed until the pain got too much to bear. *Never*. The fact that she screamed throughout this labor was unnerving.

"She may not have the strength to keep pushing," Kathy said.

Angela squeezed Melanie's hand again. Relief washed over her as Melanie pushed against her hand.

"Suction," Yaros said.

Melanie groaned through another contraction. She sounded feebler than ever.

God damn it, Mel, we're not losing you too.

"And here's a baby," Zuko announced.

"Okay?" Melanie croaked, eyelids fluttering slightly.

Faint cry. "It's crying, Mel."

"Go—" Melanie's body tightened and her eyes rolled back into her head.

"God, not again!" Kathy growled as alarms sounded.

The baby's faint cry quadrupled in volume, changing from a faint wail to a full-out angry, frantic shriek. Then Melanie's body eased and she took a deep breath.

The alarms faded. The baby's shrieks diminished.

Melanie's eyes flickered open.

"Don't talk," Angela said urgently.

Melanie nodded.

"Angela, step back and let us clean them up?" Kathy suggested.

"You okay with me stepping back, Mel? I'm still here. Don't talk. Just nod or shake your head."

Faintest of nods.

"I'm right here." Angela squeezed Melanie's hand before easing it onto the bed. Once out of Melanie's sight lines, she sank into a chair and let herself have a moment of the shakes. Then she blinked up statuses and ran checks. Marty and Nik were still an hour or so out. Cat reported tentative containment of the Netwalkers involved in the High Space attack. Pattern similar to the last one, with guised attackers replacing third-tier support staff.

Angela shook her head.

Similar but not as high a profile. Crap.

"Can I see my baby?" Melanie's voice was surprisingly firm. Angela clicked off her reports. Mel lay on her side, still pale but not the bone-white blue-gray she had been during labor. A faint pinkish tinge now colored her cheeks.

"You're not sitting up," Kathy said.

"Put her next to me."

"I can do that." Kathy lay the baby next to Melanie.

"You're here," Melanie breathed to the baby, her face softening. She brushed her right index fingertip across her daughter's cheek. The baby turned her head, quickly grabbing at Melanie's fingertip with her lips. "You're all right," Melanie choked, sobbing. "Oh honey. *You're all right.*"

The baby focused on Melanie, gazing intently at her mother. Melanie reciprocated with her own steady gaze, her sobs fading.

Chills went down Angela's spine as she watched the two of them looking at each other with an uncanny intensity.

I think the game's just changed, though I don't know how.

A Mountain Security guard opened the door for Nik and Marty as they reached the darkened ranch house. Nik headed for the Security office and Marty turned toward the stairs, not knowing what to expect as he climbed the staircase. He had anticipated more activity.

Instead, it was silent and still. The small nightlights set into the steps clicked on as he approached, then switched off as he passed.

Angela waited for him at the top of the stairs, her face tight with exhaustion. At least she wasn't as pale as she had been when she called.

"I came as quickly as I could," Marty said. "But between Security warnings and the weather—"

"No blame. Get in here, Dad."

Marty walked into the primary suite and paused just inside the door, taking in the scene before him. A clear plastic bassinet sat next to the bed, but nothing other than blankets were inside. Melanie lay in the bed, propped up sideways, her dark hair illuminating just how pale her skin was.

God, she's almost translucent tonight.

A small bundle wrapped in white was next to Melanie. Marty's throat tightened.

Our daughter.

The bundle snuffled at Melanie's breast while Melanie smiled down at her.

He took a step closer and the floor creaked under his feet. Melanie looked up. He couldn't see anything but the glow in her face as he walked across the room to join her and gaze down at the baby.

"I'm sorry," he said. "I should have been here."

"She got impatient." Melanie's voice was deeper and huskier than he had heard from her before. "No blame. It happened so quickly."

Marty slid onto the bed next to Melanie, leaning into her, watching their daughter nurse.

Our daughter!

Red-faced, with more dark hair than he'd expected for a newborn, a long, lanky baby with dust-brown skin just a few shades lighter than his.

"Lucky for Melanie she came early," Kathy said. "Another four weeks more, and she'd be a huge baby. Big girl for her length of gestation. Probably going to be tall and skinny, like Diana."

"She's okay?" Marty asked. "No toxin aftereffects?"

"None that I've seen so far," Kathy said. "She's healthy and strong. Lungs in good shape; glad I had Mel on those meds ever since she was eight weeks out from delivery because I suspected the baby would come early. Good suck reflex. Good color at birth; everything seems to work all right despite the delivery being a bit touch and go. Not overly fussy."

He smiled at Melanie. "How are you feeling?"

"Tired. Sore." But her smile belied her words as she beamed down at their daughter. "One hell of a lot lighter. Such a tiny thing for as big as I was feeling."

"You're both beautiful."

The baby's sucking slowed and stopped.

Marty gazed down at his daughter.

She's here. She's really here. All the work and effort to keep this one, and she's here.

"What's her name?" he asked. They had been tossing around several possibilities.

"She looks like an Elizabeth to me. Funny. I wasn't wild about that name, but looking at her, I'd say Elizabeth. Bess." <That is, if Ness doesn't mind the similarity,> she said to Marty.

Ness startled inside Marty's chip. <Bess. That's a good name. Mel, I don't mind.>

<You sure we should start talking like this again? Might not be completely safe,> Marty cautioned.

<We can do it just for this,> Melanie said. "Yes," she said out loud. "Bess. That fits her."

Bess stretched and yawned, smacked her lips a couple of times, then settled back in. Melanie's eyes drooped, fading fast. He closed his eyes, listening to the steady breathing of his wife and daughter, his muscles relaxing, worry fading away. He was here. With his family.

He jumped at the touch of a hand on his shoulder. "Let's put you three to bed," Kathy said quietly. "Put the little one in the bassinet first."

Marty nodded, and carefully eased Bess off of the bed. Melanie was sound asleep. Kathy took Bess from him and placed her in the bassinet under a warming light, then set up a breathing monitor.

"She's okay?" he asked again. "What about Mel? You said it was a hard birth?"

"Oh yeah. Baby's fine, Marty. We just take precautions," Kathy whispered. "As for Mel, she's recovering quickly. Medical team's next door, monitoring her and Baby."

"How bad was it?"

"Bad enough but they're okay now, Marty. Let's talk later. What matters is that both Mel and the baby are fine. You just need to take care of them. Melanie shouldn't be moving very much. Change diapers and help her get set up for feeding, okay?"

"I can do that. Where's the diapers?"

"Buzzer's by the bed if you need anything. Diapers on the cart underneath the bassinet. Change her when she wakes. You do know how to change a diaper, right?"

"Nephews," he mumbled. "Years ago. Probably hasn't gotten all high tech yet."

"The basics are still the same. Changing table's over there—" she pointed. "Disposal's next to it. Wipes are on the changing table. I'll set the floor touchlights on when I leave. Change Bess and bring her over for her next feeding when she wakes. If you're lucky you'll get a few hours' sleep."

Marty nodded. After Kathy left, he slowly slipped into his sleepwear and slid in next to Melanie. She stirred slightly, then tucked herself into the curve of his body.

I'm a father now. My God, what am I gonna do with a daughter?

Fatigue overtook him before he could think too much about it.

ANGELA LEFT THE BEDROOM. NIK SAT ACROSS FROM THE DOOR WHILE PAUL and Steve stood on duty on each side.

"You're off-duty?" Nik asked.

Angela nodded. He rose, and opened his arms. She leaned against him.

"Let's go," Nik said. "I posted the new rotations for you and took care of the urgent Security issues from Seattle and Diaspora. Nothing new. We're covered. We can take a few hours off."

"Good." She leaned into him as they walked down the stairs. Nik steered her into the dining room corner set up for casual seating.

"I'd say it's time for a small celebration," he said. "Didn't lay in any champagne, but I have some nice brandy stashed here."

"That'll be fine," Angela said, dropping into one of the comfortable armchairs. Nik went into the kitchen and came back with a couple of glasses and a bottle. Angela raised her eyebrows as she recognized the brand and the vintage.

Nik grinned at her. "I figured this birth deserved something good."

"God, how long has it been since we got into that stuff?"

"At least once since Sophie was born, after we got those two married. Not much otherwise." Nik set the glasses on the table, then poured them each a generous helping. He placed the bottle between the glasses.

Angela picked up her glass. She was more than ready for a drink.

"So," Nik said. "What did they name her?"

"Elizabeth. Bess, for short."

"Elizabeth," Nik mused. "I like it. So. A toast to young Elizabeth."

They clinked glasses. Angela tossed hers back quickly, then poured herself another one. She had put the bottle down when she heard footsteps and tensed, whirling to her feet.

"Just me," Kathy Miller said. "They're tucked in. I heard your voices, and came to see who was still up."

Angela dropped back into her chair.

God, I'm nervous. Tired, but jumpy.

"Pull up a chair," Nik said. "I'll get you a glass."

Kathy grabbed another comfortable armchair and drug it over to face Nik and Angela.

"We did it," she sighed. "But God, I'm too damn old for this."

She took the glass from Nik, then, like Angela, tossed her first one down quickly. She poured herself a second one and slouched back in the chair.

"That was a fast birth," she said. "Scary fast."

"I wondered about that," said Angela.

Kathy frowned at her glass. "The speed might have been a toxin effect. I don't think Melanie should go through another pregnancy. Not after seeing what the toxin does to her. I suspect the abruption is part of the toxin."

"You'll have your hands full convincing her of that," Angela said. "Mel's produced an heir; she needs a spare."

"Toxin effect has completely screwed up her blood clotting. A second pregnancy might not go this well," Kathy sighed. "Sorry. Shouldn't be talking about this to you for confidentiality purposes. But I need to work out what I'm going to say, and for God's sake, you're her Security. You'll need to know this anyway."

"We'll keep it to ourselves," Nik said. "Meanwhile, there's more news from Seattle. Mel may need to go virtual to deal with it. Diana got injured, and Sarah went a little crazy before Cat and Diana reined her in. Cat's not wanting to share details with anyone but Melanie right now."

"Dear God in heaven," Angela breathed. "I hope you told Cat that Mel has bigger things to deal with?"

"I did, but I'm not sure how much time that'll buy. She didn't grasp the idea that Melanie was in labor. She's frantic. Not dealt with Sarah in this mode by herself."

"Send them to me until Mel's rested," Kathy said. "Diana will listen to me. I can screen and relay what needs to get passed on."

"Thanks," Nik said.

Kathy finished her second drink and got up. "I'm off to bed. Just keep in mind that I can give you a hand with Security details. If you want." She pushed her chair back into place and left the room.

"Black ops if Kathy gets involved," Angela said. "Is that what this is coming to?"

"I'm afraid so," Nik said. "I had an odd conversation with Andrew's black ops guy today. I didn't expect the degree of cooperation we're suddenly getting from them. For a while, when Mariskova moved on from the position, they were stinky. Now they're cooperative again."

"That bad a situation?"

Nik nodded. "They're worried. Andrew's okay, but several of his people were injured. Plus he's scared. He doesn't have a Dialogue, but he's still a target."

Angela stared thoughtfully into her snifter. "Who *are* we going to recruit against the Freedom Army?"

Nik shrugged. "We have Deirdre Conley."

"Yeah, with her wild goose chase for this Tim Conley."

"I have a new lead, and if it's what I think it is, then Deirdre Conley's right on the money to be pointing Mel at him."

"Oh?" Angela eyed her empty glass, thinking about a third drink. "You trust it?"

"Can't say more," Nik said. "Boundaries. But it is every bit as bad as it could be. Sorry, love. You look tired," he said, abruptly changing the subject. "Why don't you come over here and keep me company?" He grinned at her.

Angela grinned back at him, not fooled by the swift switch in topic.

He's tired and had enough of the discussion for a while. What the hell, it's late and I am tired, after all. We're not going to solve this mess tonight.

She sat in Nik's lap. He wrapped one arm around her and she

leaned against his chest. They sipped their brandies quietly, each lost in their separate thoughts.

"Was the delivery as bad as Kathy made it sound?" Nik asked.

"Yes."

Nik shifted his weight. "At least that's over. I'm ready to go to sleep. You?"

"Yeah. Let's do it."

Maybe she had consumed enough brandy to relax after the events of this day.

CHAPTER 15

Bess's lips slowly stopped moving as she fell asleep at Melanie's breast. Melanie burped her. Bess belched surprisingly loud, spitting up a small dribble. She whimpered slightly, yawned, and went back to sleep.

"I'll take her." Marty held out his hands.

Melanie clung to Bess for a moment, oddly reluctant to hand her over. Somehow this tiny being had caused the world to stop swirling crazily. She couldn't explain why, but ever since that first gaze into Bess's eyes, focus came much more easily.

Protect. Protect Bess, protect Marty, protect DIR, protect—the world?

She knew one thing. To protect everything she loved, she had to pull Gizmo's teeth. For good.

That may be the work of a lifetime. But it's what I have to do.

Too many threats popping up without warning.

If Marty hadn't been on the Mountain....

Melanie pushed aside those thoughts. She kissed Bess's forehead and handed her over to Marty. He smiled at their daughter, the tight tension lines in his face softening, crooning wordlessly as he carried her to her bassinet.

She clicked open the hologlobe and tapped up the Seattle vid she had been watching, pulling on her hologloves. Until Melanie got full clearance from Marty and Zuko, she was limited to non-virtual tools to prepare for the Enforcer meeting in response to Seattle. Melanie clucked once to restart. The vid picked up with Vijay Gupta grabbing at his chest, panic tightening his face, but there was a piece missing.

Damn it, I forgot the notes!

Melanie froze the vid. She tapped up the syndrome notes Marty and Karl had pulled together for her. Karl had broken his analysis down to tenths of a second.

I'm glad he's a Security Enforcer.

But even with Karl's notes, analyzing the Seattle events went too damn slow, compared to virtual.

"Any chance I can get cleared for virtual work sometime soon?" she asked, rubbing her forehead. "This process is giving me a nasty headache."

Marty joined Melanie on the bed. "Tomorrow, love. Kathy's not happy with the toxin traces in you and Bess. Matter of time and flushing your systems. I don't like the way Bess reacts when you do limited virtual, or when Ness is out."

"She accepted my use of datagloves in the globe this morning, after I wrapped one of my datasuits around her. No screaming, though she was alert and a little anxious. She needs her own datasuit."

Marty nodded. "I can have a design ready by this afternoon."

"Good." Melanie thought for a moment. "I'd like to have a front-pack carrier with datasuit protections built in as well. Can't hurt."

"True. Doubled protection will provide more of a defense to her than just a datasuit," Marty sighed. "Just wish we didn't have to think this way."

"Me too."

Angela came in. Marty got up. "I'll work on it now." He kissed Melanie. "Hang on, darlin'. It won't be that much longer before you can go virtual again."

"Thank you, love."

He kissed her again, then left.

Angela settled on the bed. "I talked to Mama Brenda."

"And?"

"She's excited that you want her to be Bess's nanny."

"Oh *good.* Thank you for talking to her, Ange. I—well, I didn't know if she'd want to travel."

"The travel part was a bit iffy, but she didn't argue about it," Angela said. "She's bored now that Sophie's in the crèche, and she misses her granddaughter." A wry grin twitched the corners of her lips. "Hermano mio keeps treating her like an old lady."

Melanie laughed. "I can't imagine your mother putting up with that from your brother for very long."

Angela chuckled. "Ramon can be overbearing, plus Mama's happiest when she's working."

"It will be all right for her, won't it? You did explain I just got spacey and didn't ask her myself earlier? Ange, I really hated to load this request on you but—it's okay?"

"She understands. She did say she wasn't surprised. Fits who you are."

"She knows me too well." Melanie shook her head. "So. How's the Enforcer meeting prep going from the Security side?"

"Karl is in charge of electronic security." Angela blinked up an overlay. "He's scheduled to talk to you about that this afternoon."

"Good. And the tribal liaisons?"

"Security is at its highest level and has been ever since Seattle."

"Do you have an arrival schedule yet?"

"Your mother and Cat come in tonight or tomorrow morning, depending on your mother's schedule this afternoon. Julia and Reiko from Nagano tomorrow night. Then the rest trickle in all day, the day after."

"Can't be helped." Melanie shrugged. "Our new Enforcer cadre is in high demand."

"Very much so."

"I also want to take care of this issue with Conley." Melanie chewed on her lower lip. "Once your mama is here to take care of Bess. Whatever it takes to break that block of hers. If it takes me, Karl and Cat to break it, then that's what it takes."

"Nik thinks he's found the Tim Conley she's looking for. But he's dead."

"Dead doesn't mean he's without influence in a Netwalker world. Dead would actually be worse."

Until we catch his Netwalker form. And if he's a Freedom Army variant, there's no guarantee he's not cloned somewhere. I want to kill that Freedom Army Netwalker variant completely. It's too unpredictable and it may not be controllable.

But getting answers to that particular question also meant a significant interrogation of Sarah.

Sarah. Still in pieces after Seattle.

Cat's done her best, but she's not the best Enforcer manager for Sarah.

Melanie ticked through her options. Karl wasn't a possibility—too heavy-handed and not the type that Diana liked in her Security. If only Sergio had Enforcer potential! Diana trusted him without question.

She sighed.

Me. Has to be me.

Not ideal, because Melanie was Diana's Optioner, the designated backup host for Sarah.

What happens when Mom dies and I have to take over Sarah?

Hopefully that wouldn't happen soon. Juggling a baby and Sarah didn't sound optimal—and that didn't address Diana's fate after death. Her mother *had* said she wouldn't choose to upload. But if she changed her mind? Who would manage *her* as a Netwalker?

Mom will be as much of a pain as Sarah to manage if she goes Netwalk.

"Mel?"

Melanie realized Angela had been speaking. "What? Sorry. Lost in thought."

Angela chuckled. "Spacing out again?"

"Thinking about long-term Enforcer and Netwalk issues. What did you say?"

"I said that Tim Conley being dead and a Netwalker might be enough to have Conley throw in with us. She seems to be worried about him."

"It might." *Unless she allies with the Freedom Army against us. The kids. I need to find out why the kids are so important to her. Why won't she talk? If she would just talk, then maybe we wouldn't need to keep her secured.*

"I want her here, Ange. Tight Security. When she arrives, make sure she sees Sophie and the boys. Those boys mean something to her."

"That should be easy enough to stage."

"Just—be careful, okay?"

"We will be." Angela got up. "Mama Brenda arrives tonight. Conley can come in tomorrow, before we sequester the kids from the rest of the arrivals. That gives me and Nik time to talk to Sophie and Mama about what we want them to do."

"Sophie will get the boys to cooperate?"

Angela snorted. "Mel, the bond between Sophie and Donnie already looks like a long-term Security linkage. Alex follows along but he's a third. She's teaching Donnie Mixteco. Not Alex—just Donnie. Sophie and Donnie are probably going to grow up as a Security team. Sophie leads, Donnie will follow her, and Alex trails after them."

"It'll be interesting once Bess is old enough to join in."

"For sure." Angela stretched. "Anything else this morning?"

Melanie shook her head. "Let's just get this conference going."

"On my way." Angela left.

Melanie resumed her scanning.

God, I hope I can go virtual soon.

She was more than ready to return to peak working efficiency.

"There!" Marty grinned at the virtual baby datasuit model.

He loaded the cartridges with the nanofiber components into the printer. Now to do the final tweaks with Bess. He had based the original sizing on one of her larger sleepers. He started to text Melanie to let her know he was ready. Then he remembered. She was still on quarantine. He texted Angela to let her know instead.

Be glad when she's off of that restriction.

This last flush of toxins should clear both mother and daughter. Netwalker toxin didn't seem to cross into breast milk. But they still needed to monitor Bess and Melanie for a few weeks.

<Mel's at the lab door,> Ness said.

<Thanks. You'd better go inside my chip until we get that suit on Bess.>

<Doing it now.>

Moments later he felt the light mental touch that was Ness awake and aware inside his chip, but fully shielded from the outside.

"Safe to come in?" Mel's voice squawking through the lab com startled him. Between texting and mindspeech, he didn't use it much anymore.

It took him moments to remember that he had to go to the door to push the button to activate the com and open the door.

"It's clear. Ness is in my chip."

The door slid open, and Melanie entered the lab, Bess in her arms.

"Let me take her and you sit down," he said quickly, taking Bess from Melanie's arms. She smiled briefly at him before walking to one of the softer lab chairs and carefully easing herself down. "You're feeling okay?"

"Tired and a little light-headed. Kathy says it's normal, I still need to be resting." Melanie scowled, sagging against the back of the chair. "But I don't have time to rest!"

"You don't have time *not* to rest."

"I know." Bess started to fuss. "Is she reacting to Ness?"

"Ness is in my chip. I think this is just baby fuss." He turned Bess over so her stomach rested on his forearm and rubbed her back. She settled, after a loud burp. "What do you think?" He jerked his head toward the 3-D sim of the baby datasuit spinning in its secured globe. "I can bring it closer if you'd like."

"Yes, please." Melanie pulled out a pair of datagloves she'd tucked into her waistband. As she put them on, Marty carefully guided the globe over to Melanie with one hand. Bess whimpered. He stopped the globe next to Melanie and stepped back. As his hand fell away from the hologlobe, Bess stopped fussing.

"Codes?" Melanie asked.

"20-Z, 396-lower case w, 594."

Melanie repeated the codes, then slid her fingertips into the globe. She turned the suit one way and then another, stroking it as she frowned thoughtfully.

"Marty, it's beautiful. But how do we test it without her going ballistic?"

"I don't know any other way," he admitted. "She's going to fuss and cry."

Melanie sighed. "Can I hold her during the fitting?"

"You have to do that anyway. You won't be able to manipulate the model with your current restrictions. Maybe we should wait until Mama Brenda is here, let the toxin levels in both of you die down."

Melanie chewed her lip. "I want to walk out of this lab with Bess in a datasuit."

Of course.

"Put a tertiary datasuit on over your clothes. There's an old-fashioned hoodie suit amongst the unfitted ones. The hood should give both of you more protection than usual. It'll be big on you."

Melanie nodded. She pushed herself up and shuffled over to the datasuit storage cubby, fumbling through them until she found the old hoodie suit and pulled it on over her pajamas. The larger-sized datasuit hung loosely on her small frame. Melanie tapped the fitting tabs, taking it down as far as it would go, shrinking everything but the hood.

"I can partially shield her with the hood," she said, grabbing one of the smaller datasuits. "I'll also use this one as a blanket for her. Extra protection."

"Good idea."

Melanie carefully wrapped Bess in the datasuit. She pulled the baby close to her chest and pressed her cheek to Bess's, so that her datasuit's hood fell over their heads, covering Bess's head and shoulders.

"Expand the globe," she said, her voice muffled.

As the hologlobe boundary brushed through Bess and Melanie, Bess fussed. Melanie murmured and Bess calmed.

He maneuvered the model next to Bess. "Time to try the fit."

Melanie drew a deep breath and straightened up. Bess whimpered as Melanie pulled back the hood and unwrapped the datasuit. Then she held Bess out so that Marty could fit the model to her. Marty carefully eased Bess's legs into the virtual model, sliding it on over her sleeper.

"Not a perfect fit putting it on over her sleeper, but I want some room for her to move without having to replace these on a weekly basis. This stuff is spendy, and we need several copies at a time."

"A few centimeters of ease will help."

"I've already calculated for that. It's the diapers that might be the problem. That's the only piece of clothing I'll want the suit to cover." He adjusted the leg fit.

"Agreed." Melanie's voice rose over Bess's fussing.

Marty gently pulled the suit over Bess's arms, leaving her hands exposed. He pulled the hood over her head and adjusted the settings.

"That should work," he said. "We'll have to keep resizing these suits frequently as she grows. But it should be easier now that I have the proportions correct."

"She's fitted?"

"Yes."

"Let's get the damn thing printed and on her for real, then."

Was the edge in Melanie's voice due to worry, or Bess's continued fussing?

Marty carefully slipped the model off of Bess. Melanie rewrapped her in the datasuit and sat down, bending low over her again with the hood on.

He uploaded the revised design into the printer. The datasuit slowly took form on the printing table. Marty monitored the suit's proportions, inserting virtual supports as the suit's framework rose higher and wrapped to form legs, arms, hood. At last, the print job ended. He sprayed the suit with a curative.

"Now we wait," he said, setting the timer.

"Mmhmm." Melanie didn't look up from soothing Bess, murmuring softly. Marty recognized the edge of an Enforcer tone in Melanie's soft, wordless humming, a gentle *relax, all is well* note that rose slightly when Bess's voice grew more frantic. Bess quieted momentarily, then started again. But the periods between Bess's fussing grew longer, and her complaints were less intense and shorter.

Mel's training her using Enforcer tones? What impact is that going to have? Is this action a conscious choice by Mel? She wasn't doing this when they first came into the lab.

He didn't think it would have a negative impact right away, but he could see potential problems if Enforcer tones created a too-compliant child.

Bess needs the freedom to make her own choices, with all the responsibilities she'll have descending on her.

Then again, Bess was Mel's daughter, Diana's granddaughter, Sarah's great-granddaughter. Odds were good that it would take more than Enforcer tones to create an overly compliant child.

The timer went off. Holding his breath, Marty removed the virtual supports. He picked the suit up, visually inspecting for flaws before running a scan. Minor variations, easily within error margins. The suit remained flexible and non-restrictive, allowing for free movement and a certain amount of baby growth. A good print.

"Ness needs to do the final suit check," he said.

"Okay." Melanie wrapped herself protectively around Bess.

<Ready to check?>

<I'll make it quick,> Ness answered. She slid out. Bess cried. Ness formed a smaller shape than usual and Bess's cries softened.

<It's good,> Ness reported. <I'll go back in.>

<Thank you.>

"Ness says it's good."

"Thank you." Melanie sat back up. "Let's put it on her, then check with Ness again."

"You sure?"

Melanie nodded; her jaw tight. She set Bess down on a lab table and removed the sleeper. "Bring it over." She checked Bess's diaper. "Wait a moment."

He waited while she changed Bess, then handed the suit to Melanie. She carefully slid the suit over Bess's legs, then eased it slowly and delicately over Bess's diaper. It held, with no tearing. He let out the breath he hadn't known he was holding. Melanie pulled the suit the rest of the way on, and adjusted the hood to fit smoothly over Bess's head. With a careful stroke, she made the hood transparent.

"No need to advertise that she's wearing a suit."

"Good idea."

Melanie sealed the front of Bess's suit with a fingertip. "There! Bring out Ness and see what happens."

Melanie picked Bess up as Ness eased out. Bess fussed. Ness came close. Bess stared at Ness for a couple of moments before whimpering again, her lips moving as she changed her focus to Melanie, for the first time more concerned about food than virtual intrusions around her.

"That's good," Melanie said. "I'm getting this old suit off. Too awkward. Here." She handed Bess to Marty and peeled off the hooded suit.

"What about your exposures?"

Melanie opened her regular double-layered datasuit, took Bess back and began to feed her. "I don't think a lab hologlobe exposure long enough to nurse Bess will make that big a difference in my toxin levels at this point. Or hers, either."

She was probably right.

MORNING WAS A RELATIVE TERM WITH A NEWBORN, AS MELANIE WAS learning. She pulled back the west window curtain to look outside as she burped Bess, wanting to see what last night's storm had left behind. She had heard the storm blowing through during an early morning baby feeding, but was too tired to check then.

Snow. A small skiff of white covered the dried grasses, already melting in the bright sun.

The storm hadn't delayed her mother's arrival. There was a commotion outside their room, and Marty had told her Diana was at the Ranch. But Bess had just gone to sleep after the excitement of meeting Mama Brenda, and Melanie was almost asleep, so she postponed the inevitable.

Wish this wasn't the first time for Mom and Cat to meet Bess. Wish they arrived sooner last night.

Something worried her about the first encounter between grandmother and granddaughter.

Maybe it's the Netwalker great-grandmother that worries me the most.

Melanie sighed. Best to get it over with. Besides, she was hungry. She put Bess down and pulled on the shielded frontpack, then carefully maneuvered Bess into it.

"Time for us to go to *my* breakfast, young lady!" she said. Marty had offered to bring it up, but she wanted to start moving again. She wouldn't regain her strength just lying around.

She took the stairs carefully. Baby in the frontpack was a higher balance than baby inside of her. Melanie stopped at the bottom of the stairs, surprised at how much more tired she was than when heavy with child, just a few days before.

Just temporary. An effect of childbirth.

But as she walked, it seemed as if the house had grown bigger in the past three days. Melanie ached as she walked toward the kitchen. She paused in the entry to the dining room as she spotted her mother. Diana faced the windows, a hologlobe spinning in front of her, chin on her hand.

At least she's alone.

Melanie couldn't see if Sarah was in the globe. She extended a virtual feeler to check and Diana jumped, startled, half-turning in her chair.

"What the—Melanie! I didn't know you were in virtual! Let me get Sarah back in the chip."

"Thanks. I want to eat something before we expose Bess to Sarah."

Her mother hurried to Melanie's side, peering delicately into the frontpack without reaching in to touch her. "That will be okay? From what Marty said, baby's very responsive to virtual influence."

"Better now that we've got her in a baby datasuit." Melanie slowly walked to the table. "Still, if you're not doing anything urgent, it might be a good idea to dismiss the globe. Bess has both suit and frontpack protection, but I'd just as soon not push it."

"Of course. Of course."

Melanie had to hide a smile as her mother hesitated, obviously struggling between a desire to help her sit down and worry about closing the globe quickly.

"I can sit down by myself, Mom. Close the globe."

"You're sure? From what Kathy said, it was one hell of a labor."

"Thankfully I don't remember much of it. Though I still hurt."

"Wait," Diana said as Melanie leaned on the table before sitting. "Do you want a pillow to sit on?"

"I'm fine. I just have to take it slow." Melanie used the table to support herself as she eased into the chair.

Hurt if I thump down too hard—ah, there.

"Can I see her?"

"But of course!" Melanie fumbled with the straps and carefully extracted Bess.

"She's beautiful," Diana breathed as Melanie settled Bess. She reached out to Bess but stopped, frowning, her hand hovering two inches above Bess's head.

"Sarah is nervous as hell about this, Melanie," she reported. "Why?"

"I don't know," Melanie said. "Let me ask her." She switched to mindspeech. <Sarah. What are you seeing? Is she aware of you?>

<Let's just say I don't think it's a damned good idea for Diana to touch her while I'm inside and awake,> Sarah responded. <There's—something about that kid. Don't tell me you've already put an implant in her?>

<No, she's way too young. We don't do implants until puberty!>

<She's projecting like she has an implant,> Sarah said.

<She *is* aware of Ness, and she seems to track our mindspeech. Is she using words?>

<No,> Sarah said. <But she's sending a strong *stay away!* feeling to me. It's very uncomfortable. Kid has a pretty good defense mechanism without an implant.>

<Thanks. Tell Mom.>

Now that's an interesting data point.

"What are we going to do?" Diana asked, after a pause. "Sarah really is spooked, Melanie. She's not been the same since the last attack."

"Either sleep Sarah or send her out so she's not directly in you," Melanie said.

"Okay," Diana said. "Sarah's asleep now. Can I?" She held out her hands. Melanie carefully handed Bess to Diana. Bess stirred awake, staring at her grandmother with big eyes. Diana cuddled Bess for a couple more minutes, then handed her back.

"She's beautiful, Melanie."

"Thank you."

Marty rested a hand on her shoulder. "I'll get your breakfast."

"I don't need—"

"Sit," he said more firmly. "Let me take care of you."

"Okay," she said. "The usual."

"A little bit more than usual," he corrected.

"Yes, dear," she said, her voice sliding into sharpness. "Sorry. Just getting impatient with everyone treating me like I'm made of glass!"

<Save your energy for Sarah,> he advised. <Ness picked up that she's still pretty shattered after this last attack. I want to be present to support when you do your diagnostic, along with Cat. Do it in the lab, and do it with support.>

"Where is Cat?" Melanie asked out loud.

"Getting the lab set up," Marty called back from the kitchen. "Brenda's organizing the nursery space and having Cat set the virtual protections."

"Sarah's worried about this upcoming process," her mother said in a low voice. "Cat patched things up pretty well, but it's a veneer."

"I've been away too long. But we'll deal with what I can do today. It may take a couple of sessions. Thank you," Melanie said to Marty as he set the plate heaped with scrambled eggs, potatoes, a small breakfast steak and toast in front of her. "I don't know if I can eat that much."

"I'll finish off what you don't eat. Let me take Bess."

She handed Bess to Marty and dove in. To her surprise, the first bite of food made her ravenous. When she was finished, Melanie felt full, but not bloated. She leaned back to sip her coffee, only to catch her mother's quizzical look.

"I don't think I've ever seen you eat like that for a long time," Diana said.

"I was hungry. I guess."

Had it really been that long since she had been a hearty eater?

"Glad to see it."

"I am too," Marty said. "Suggests that you're throwing off the toxin effect. Mel, once Bess is weaned, I want you to undergo the same nano treatment we did with Nik. That should banish the last dregs of the toxin effect."

"At least until the next time I get attacked by a Netwalker."

And then it'll probably be time to think about a second child. Not that I'm in any hurry!

"If you're ready, let's go to the lab," Marty said.

Melanie drained her coffee cup. "I am."

Marty helped her get Bess into the frontpack. "I'd put a jacket on," he suggested as they walked toward the door. "Still a bit nippy outside."

"Could you get Grandpa's old sheepskin?" Melanie asked.

"Of course."

Melanie waited while Marty got the old jacket she had worn during her last weeks of pregnancy. As Marty helped her into it and wrapped the front around Bess, Melanie glanced at her mother. A curious expression crossed Diana's face.

"The last time I saw your grandfather wear that was just before he died," she said. "How did you find it?"

"Rita brought it out when I needed something to wear outside in late pregnancy. It just felt right."

"It looks very good on you," Diana said. "He hadn't had it that long when he died. I'm—glad to see it back in use again."

"Should I not be wearing it?"

Diana vigorously shook her head. "Wear it. With my pleasure. It was my last gift to him."

"Then I'll take extra care with it."

Her mother half-smiled and gently ran her hand over one sleeve. "Your grandfather always liked a good shearling sheepskin coat. This one could last quite a while. Maybe a lifetime."

"I'll cherish it as part of my heritage. It's not often I have something from the Andrews side."

They left the house as a group. Melanie wrapped her arms protectively over the front to keep the chill morning breeze from reaching Bess.

The walk to the Ranch labs was no further than the comparable walk on the Mountain, but once again fatigue pulled at Melanie as they walked. Still, it was good to get outside. The crisp bite of October chill coupled with the faint tangy scent of pine needles and freshly fallen leaves invigorated her. The slightest hint of damp air from the melting snow reminded her that winter wasn't that far off.

Will I be able to ski this winter?

A low priority in her new role as a mother, at least for this winter, but at some point....

Brenda and Cat waited for them. Bess remained quiet as Melanie took her through the open space of the room-sized shielded hologlobe.

"How do you want to handle Bess?" Marty asked.

"Brenda, do you mind keeping her in the frontpack? Less exposure."

"Not at all," Brenda said.

"We can just slip the pack off of you and transfer it to Brenda," Marty said.

"Probably the easiest way."

He took hold of Bess through the frontpack, holding it and Bess steady. Brenda helped Melanie ease out of the pack, then took Melanie's place. Melanie attached the straps over Brenda's back, checking each one. Marty slowly let go of Bess.

"We'll sit over here," Brenda said, nodding toward a rocking chair Melanie hadn't noticed yet.

"Perfect. Thank you, Brenda." Melanie ran her fingers through her hair, ruffling it up.

She drew a deep breath, straightening up. It felt odd not to have baby weight pulling at her front.

<I think a second globe is a good idea,> she told Marty. <Let's open one up and have Mom put Sarah in there.>

<With me and Cat along with you.>

<Not arguing that one, love!> Melanie snapped the second globe open and set the attunement. Despite months without much practice, the skills came back quickly.

Bess started to cry as Melanie stepped inside the second globe.

Melanie quickly stepped back out. "Shh, shh," she hummed to

Bess, projecting a calming tone as she hurried over to Bess and stroked her head. "It's all right, little one. I'll be back soon."

"It'll be okay," Brenda reassured Melanie. "I've got her."

Bess quieted as Brenda rocked her. Melanie hesitated, then turned back to the second globe.

She has to get used to this. I have to get used to it.

She hummed a soft reassuring tone. Enforcer tones seemed to communicate with Bess when words wouldn't.

This time Bess didn't fuss as Melanie stepped into the globe.

Marty and Cat joined Melanie. Diana stood at the opening to the second globe. "Should I come in?"

"No," Melanie said. "Send Sarah into the globe."

Her mother nodded. Sarah slowly eased out of the chip and into the globe. Cat closed the globe as Melanie focused on Sarah.

Melanie immediately spotted Sarah's problems.

Sarah's virtual presentation was always a reflection of her inner state. Not every Netwalker's image reflected their moods and condition so accurately—doing diagnostics on Will and Ness were challenging in that respect.

The Sarah that Melanie now saw resembled the feral, unbonded Sarah who had run wild online, sucking charges off of several hosts and a posse of wild and braindead Netwalkers. But while feral Sarah looked vampiric, with elongated fangs, claw-like fingernails, albino coloring and sharp features, this Sarah appeared strained and blurry. Her facial angles were still tight and sharp, but about midtorso her image blurred. Melanie couldn't make out individual fingers or legs.

<Wow. That's quite the hit you took,> she said.

<I feel stretched.>

<I see that.> Melanie pulled on datagloves for a further protective layer. <Full scan. Hands and forearms.> She stepped into full virtual, gasping at the moment she made the transition from body to virtual presence.

Uploading this time. I'll have to kill this upload when I'm done. Missing that fine touch. Need to get back into virtual practice.

Sarah hung back. <I don't know— >

"Do it." Melanie projected her strongest command tone. At least she had been able to practice her tone usage during pregnancy.

Sarah flinched. Then, carefully, delicately, she pressed fingertips against Melanie's. Sharp, pointed, irregular shocks vibrated across Melanie's fingers, a sensation almost like touching Gizmo. Tell-tale sign of Netwalker misattunement.

How the hell could Cat let her get so scattered?

Melanie closed her eyes to aid in visualizing a regular, consistent energy pulse. She opened her eyes as the shocks became sporadic. One pulse was a flash of feral Sarah, the next the strained, blurry Sarah.

<Sarah. Pulse with my breath.>

Sarah shuddered. Feral. Strained. Strained. Fainter Feral. Strained. Strained. Strained. Even fainter Feral.

Working but not fast enough. Time to change tactics.

<Beat. Beat. Beat,> Melanie said.

<beat. beat. beat,> Sarah murmured back.

Feral grew fainter, until Strained Sarah was all that was left. But what came through the fingertips now was a softer, regular vibration instead of irregular prickly shocks.

Got the foundation. Now to address the integration.

<Deeper now,> Melanie commanded. <Hands, then forearms.>

<I don't know— > Sarah seemed more hesitant now that she was stable. <Are you sure you want to deal with this?>

<We have to do it, Sarah. We need you to be right.>

<I—there—something not right. Something dangerous in me, something not me.> Sarah faded, looking more strained than ever.

<Marty. Cat. Back me. Marty, best have Ness out and watching.>

<Like when we caught Sarah?>

<Yes. Only don't let her touch you.>

<Like I'll let *that* happen again!>

Ness slipped out of Marty and took a falcon's guise, hovering over Melanie and Sarah. <What am I watching for?> she asked.

<Not-Sarah,> Sarah responded.

Moments later Melanie felt Marty's virtual hands on her right shoulder, Cat's on her left. <Did either of you create uploads in the process?> she asked.

<No. You're the only one with an upload to kill,> Marty answered.

<Good.> With Cat and Marty backing her, she felt more confident. Melanie pressed her palms against Sarah's. Sarah tried to twist away.

How much of this is Sarah and how much of it is the not-Sarah?

Sarah always offered minor resistance to diagnostics. But this was more than usual. Melanie spotted the faint shards of not-Sarah twisting deep inside of her, an indistinct grayish crystalline shape.

How could it have gotten so deep?

Cat couldn't manipulate deep structures yet. That was why. It had taken Melanie several months to develop this skill, so it was reasonable that Cat wouldn't have. Plus Cat hadn't developed the trust needed between her and Sarah to do this sort of intensive repair.

Melanie shuddered.

Might be more than I can do right now. This isn't typical. But the eight months I was out of virtual can be a lifetime in virtual evolution.

How could she best do this?

Delicately. Precisely. <Sarah, I have to go deep.>

<I don't know,> Sarah repeated.

<Relax.> Easier said than done. Melanie extracted one hand from Sarah's grasp. She placed her index finger on Sarah's chest. <I need to go inside.> If she could directly pluck those shards out, then they could reintegrate Sarah.

Sarah suddenly bent over.

What the—?

<Melanie!> Cat cried out.

Melanie turned her head. Marty yanked her away from Sarah. Before she could snap at him, a red and black cloud exploded from Sarah's form.

That can't be Liam!

Melanie turned to face the cloud. Still cloud-shaped, no real form. Like the last feral Netwalker she'd encountered, at the beginning of this pregnancy. No quick grab for this one.

A trap.

But it was good to know that color mixtures weren't necessarily unique. This wasn't Liam; couldn't be Liam. Liam was *dead*, both physically and virtually.

We drove that last one into a trap door chip. Just have to do it again, this time without it nabbing anyone physically or virtually.

<Cat, get that trap door ready— >

The cloud and shadows coalesced into a human shape. Melanie froze, shocked at the guise this one was taking. It was less-than-perfect, a fuzzy, nearly transparent version of the usual solid, almost-lifelike, appearance of the typical Netwalker.

Liam grinned at her.

<Told you that you couldn't get rid of me easily,> he sneered.

Behind him, a small spiky copper-colored globe formed, emitting a dull rumble. *Gizmo!*

And, from the sonics making her tremble, this guise projected enough of Gizmo's essence to be dangerous.

CHAPTER 16

"*Stop*," Melanie commanded out loud, not trusting her subvocal tones with Gizmo present.

What do I take on first, Gizmo or Liam?

Gizmo.

<Cat, Marty. Try to herd Liam into a chip. I'll take care of the device.>

<What the hell is that thing?> Cat asked.

<Something we don't deal with,> Marty answered. <Mel's job.>

Faint angry cries from outside the globe momentarily distracted Melanie.

Bess crying, damn it. Why?

Before she consciously considered it, she thought <*be still!*> at Bess. The cries faded.

Liam laughed. <Convenient of you to bring your kid along this time, Mel. She'll be *mine*, soon. Let's see what an infant Netwalker could do.>

<You're dead,> Melanie growled. <We tracked down all possible upload copies. You aren't Liam. You're just someone else's lousy guise. How funny.>

<Is it?> He advanced on Melanie. Cat leapt at him, grabbed one shoulder and tried to drag him back. Liam lunged at Cat. She evaded

his grasp. Ness stooped on him with a loud screech, raking him with her claws and sending pieces of the cloud flying.

<No, Cat!> Marty snapped. <Codes and vocals!>

The rumble from the Gizmo guise grew louder. It doubled in size. The loose pieces of cloud from the Liam shape floated toward it and melded with the larger form. It expanded, the rumble pressing against her.

Sonics.

Melanie experimented with a clear tone. Gizmo paused, then continued to grow.

Tone is good. But can I project enough to stop it?

Alone, maybe not. Marty and Cat to help? No. Marty and Cat were busy with the Liam guise.

Black cloud stung as it brushed against her hand. <What we did in Charleston. These specific codes.> Sarah sent Melanie the codes. <Plus that tone.>

<You recorded those codes, didn't you?> But she couldn't scold Sarah now, not when they would be useful.

<Not full codes. You still need to say them. And fast! With your blue light trick.>

If it worked, she wasn't going to argue.

The Gizmo guise moved toward the hologlobe wall.

What the—?

Melanie snapped up the blue light. The guise blasted through the side of the hologlobe, shattering its integrity as if the barrier didn't exist. As the globe broke open, Bess started screaming.

<NOW!> Sarah shrieked, her black cloud breaking into shards that darted toward Gizmo like little knives, swirling between it and Brenda and Bess.

Body!

She managed to jump back into her body without vertigo. Melanie drew in a deep, sobbing breath and projected a strong, full high A note. The blue light shimmered into a curtain surrounding them, strengthening as she pushed the tone.

Sarah's black cloud reformed just short of Gizmo, emitting a tone a half-step higher. The Gizmo guise wavered. But it continued to advance, even as Brenda backed away from it, raising a blaster. Diana joined her, shakily raising a blaster as well.

"Mom, Brenda don't shoot!" Melanie screamed. "It won't work!" She raced to Brenda's side, grabbing the frontpack. "Give her to me! I'm the only one who can protect Bess now!" The blue light faded as she touched Bess.

The Gizmo shape bore down on them. Marty, back in body, turned from Liam and dove toward Gizmo. Jagged green light flashed out from Gizmo, zapping Marty in the chest and slamming him back several feet.

"Stay back from it! All of you!" She and her mother and Brenda managed to wrestle the frontpack onto Melanie's chest. Bess's screams escalated into full-voiced baby hysteria. "Sarah, god damn it, what the fuck is this?"

<Use codes and tones! Get that blue light back!>

Red and black dove toward Marty. Ness fiercely drove it back. Cat knelt by Marty, fumbling with the trap door chip.

Gizmo needed to be removed. Melanie sounded the high A note again, her entire body quivering from the Gizmo vibrations. She brought out the blue light.

Sarah's black cloud formed around Melanie's right hand, flowing inside the blue light like she had done in Charleston, black cloud lined with blue. Melanie lifted the hand high, letting the Sarah shape guide her movement as she traced a blocking line.

Bess's cries matched Melanie's tone. Gizmo moved away from them.

<Sing the codes,> Sarah directed.

As the codes streamed across her visual overlays, Melanie articulated each one, her hand with the Sarah shape tracing a boundary around Gizmo.

The Gizmo shape shrank. It disappeared. The sonic vibrations were the last manifestation to leave. Melanie sank to her knees as her body stopped shaking.

God. I'm exhausted.

Not done yet. Now she had to help Cat and Marty catch Liam. Marty was back on his feet, apparently unharmed.

Brenda and Diana shakily helped Melanie up. Melanie rubbed Bess's back.

Little one, I am so sorry you're experiencing this.

"Should I take her now?" Brenda asked.

Melanie shook her head. "Not in a Netwalker situation. Gotta be me or Marty. Mom, get you and Brenda in a shielded globe, until we get this Liam guise under control!"

"You'll need me for Sarah."

"Whatever. Protect Brenda!"

No time to waste arguing.

The Liam guise focused on Marty and Cat. Maybe with Sarah's help, she could drop the chip's restraints over it from behind.

<Can you cloak me from his awareness?> she asked Sarah.

No answer. The black cloud pulsed around her hand, then faded, taking the blue light with it.

God, now what?

Melanie thumbed the trap door chip open. They'd have to pry Sarah out from Diana's chip to finish reintegrating her, most likely. She raised the trap door chip, ready to throw it.

<Not that easy!> The Liam guise whirled away from Cat and Marty, leaping over Melanie and dodging the chip's cage.

<Stop,> she commanded.

<I'm immune to your orders now. You can't touch me!> the Liam guise sneered.

A black cloud swirled toward Liam. Sarah's shape formed quickly, standing between Liam and Melanie, eyes red, fingernails glowing and clawlike, skeletal in form, the white shards of the stealthsuit she'd died in hanging from her.

Sarah in feral, predator form.

<*I* can touch you,> Sarah snapped. <And I *will*.>

<Traitor to your own kind!> Liam growled at Sarah. <You could join us—>

<And be killed the final death for my pains? No!>

Sarah struck at Liam, sending bits of shadows flying through the globe as she ripped into him.

Liam shrieked. He retreated from Sarah, his eyes darting between Melanie, Marty, Sarah and Cat.

<Aha!> he crowed suddenly, and lunged toward Diana. <An open host—>

Sarah slammed into Liam before he reached Diana, tearing at him with fingernails and teeth. He twisted away from her and tried again. Sarah shoved him into the side of the globe. He crashed into it. Melanie activated the trap door chip.

Gonna be tricky. Have to catch him but not Sarah.

Once again Liam dodged away from the chip's field.

Damn it! Slippery son of a bitch.

Melanie shut down the chip so she wouldn't catch Sarah instead. At least this generation of trap door chips could be activated multiple times.

Liam grabbed at a link, following it out of the globe. Melanie dove after him, back in virtual, tracing the link, determined not to let him get away.

Liam disappeared.

Melanie stopped hard, suddenly keenly aware of her virtual surroundings.

And Bess. Oh God. Bess.

She patted the frontpack. Bess was still there. In virtual.

I went virtual with Bess! She extended a quick nonverbal feeler toward Bess. Fear choked her. She projected *I'm here, Mother's here, it's all right, we're here together,* reducing the words to holding, hugging, contact, safety, warmth.

Fear subsided. Consciousness grabbed at her, as grabby as a brand-new Netwalker seeking a host.

What the hell have I done?

It—Bess—shoved hard against her, calming, settling.

Now what?

Melanie looked around. Deeper in virtual world than she expected, further down the link than she'd anticipated.

Trap!

She whirled in place, all senses acute, alert.

<Mel?>

Marty! Thank God.

<I fucked up. Bess is here with me. Was she all right in body?>

<I don't know. We took off after you.>

Sarah appeared, even more skeletal and glowing than before.

<Do you see it or perceive any sign of it?> Melanie asked Sarah.

<No. But I'll try a trace.>

<Leave it,> Melanie ordered.

I need to get her back to Mom. And figure out what I've done to my baby.

<I can find him,> Sarah insisted.

Melanie shook her head, uneasiness rising in her. What was Sarah's game right now?

Something transmitted to her from Liam! Virus, most likely.

<Back to Mom. Back to Diana,> she ordered.

<I can find him.>

<Do you have a clue? A solid link?>

<No.>

<Then you have nothing. Get back to Diana!> Melanie pushed, glad that Marty and now Cat stood next to her.

<No.> Sarah bristled tall.

Melanie took a deep breath. *This* was the trap, intended to lure the strongest Netwalker predator into attacking her.

<Get back!> Melanie growled at Sarah.

<Get back!> Cat echoed Melanie, adding a push in her tones.

Sarah snarled at them, her features thinning and becoming more skeletal. <No. I won't.>

Melanie advanced a step, Cat shoulder-to-shoulder with her. <Go. Go back.> Repetition was the key.

Don't let Sarah be goaded into attacking.

And the blue light was once again stubbornly not cooperating.

Codes. She had to use the codes, and hope Sarah didn't twist them against her.

But it was what she had. Melanie started to recite codes, Cat following her lead.

Nothing.

Sarah advanced toward Melanie. She swiped at Bess's frontpack, making contact with the material.

Bess screamed, an angry, frightened, full-voiced mad baby yell that carried Enforcer tones. Sarah skittered away, momentarily turning into the black cloud, then reforming in even more erratic predatory form, oscillating between cloud and predator. Melanie advanced, trying to match the predominant note in Bess's screaming with her own vocal tones. The combination sent Sarah back down the links.

<Follow me!> she subvocaled to Cat and Marty. <I can get us back!>

She chased Sarah until they returned to the globe. With a twist she slid back into her body, shoving the Bess presence back into baby body. Bess kicked hard against Melanie's torso, still screaming, but this time a normal baby howl.

Thank God. But is she going to be all right?

"Mom, get Sarah in your chip, fast!" Melanie yelled. "She has a virus!"

Sarah tried to turn away from Diana, but Melanie and Bess blocked her way. Sarah crouched, snarling, falling further into her disorganized state.

Shit. She's too far gone for codes.

If she didn't do something, *fast,* they would lose Sarah. And they had grown way too dependent upon her to control Gizmo.

"*Inside,*" Diana ordered, advancing toward Sarah.

Sarah turned on Diana, clawing at her. Diana used her forearms and elbows to block Sarah from tearing at her face and neck with her fangs. She kicked at Sarah with her left knee and grabbed at Sarah's head.

At last Diana gained a grip. With a sharp, quick, twist, she jerked the head free from Sarah's virtual body, just as she had when they captured Sarah. Melanie flinched at the violence of the action.

We have to find a better way to manage Sarah!

The shadows making up Sarah's body faded away as Diana lifted the head high.

"You *will* upload into my chip," she snarled at Sarah's head. "Now!"

A thin black line streamed from Sarah's head back into Diana's chip, the head fading and collapsing into nothingness. Melanie stood back, trembling, jiggling Bess in her front pack as she watched.

As Sarah faded, Bess's cries trailed off into hiccups and whimpers. She continued to wail softly, but she sounded more like a hungry, wet baby than an angry baby.

I'd better check her. Oh God, I will so not make that mistake again!

Melanie wrapped her arms around Bess, crooning softly, fear churning deep inside of her.

What have I done? Oh God, what have I done?

Diana swayed, dropping her arms to her sides, a dull glaze covering her eyes, bleeding scratches on her face and arms.

Damn. Sarah nailed her good.

"She's in," Diana said, her voice slow and sluggish. "She's in the chip."

"Mom, you have a dose of Netwalk toxin. We need to get you treated. Now." Melanie hurried toward Diana, snapping to release the globe that protected Brenda.

"Can' get toxin from my own Netwalk—" Diana's eyes rolled back in her head and she collapsed.

"Like hell you can't," Melanie muttered, dropping to her knees next to her mother, left hand still jiggling Bess while she sought Diana's pulse with her right hand.

<Angela!> she texted. <Medic! Here! *Fast!* Mom's down. Netwalk toxin!>

<How bad?> Angela responded.

<Condition Red bad. Unconscious. Pulse slow. Irregular.>

<On our way!>

"Mom," Melanie said out loud, not daring to use Dialogue for fear of stirring Sarah awake again. "Mom!" She shook Diana.

Diana's eyelids fluttered. "Wha's going on?"

"You got hit with a nasty dose of toxin."

"Mmm. Tired. So tired."

"Listen to me. Look at me. Don't you *dare* zone out!" Thank *God* Bess was whimpering, still sounding like a normal baby. One crisis at a time, even though Melanie really wanted to curl up and scream in terror. Oh God. Bess.

Please let her be all right despite my stupidity. Please.

"Sarah's *pissed*," her mother drawled. "Irrational. Doesn't feel right. Wants out."

"She picked up a virus from that other Netwalker. Don't you fucking *dare* let her out, not until we regroup. Make her sleep!"

"Sleep? How?"

A further chill ran through Melanie. The sleep sequence was the first technique they'd developed to control Sarah.

Bad toxin overload if she doesn't remember this.

"Repeat this code sequence," Melanie ordered. "S-12, lower case g-49, star-12, X-20, lower case g-z-x, X-29."

Diana obediently recited the code after Melanie. "She's sleep now. Not happy, but sleep. Can I sleep now?" Her voice had the petulant rhythm of a tired toddler.

"Not yet."

Kathy was beside her. "I have her, Mel. Bess okay?"

"I don't know. I need to check. Damn it, I took her virtual! Sarah made contact with the pack but I don't think she got through it!"

"Go check her. We can handle your mom."

"I also have an upload to kill. Mine only but maybe Bess."

"No Bess upload," Marty reported. "Just yours. Don't do it until we know what's happening with Bess."

"Thanks." Melanie staggered to her feet. Brenda steadied her. "I need to check Bess," she repeated to Brenda. "Sarah made contact with the pack."

Brenda guided Melanie toward the small nursery. Melanie's hands shook so badly that she couldn't manage the clips and hooks to remove the frontpack. Brenda took over, her hands steady.

"You okay, Mel?"

Melanie shook her head, forcing herself to go at half speed and take her time. Brenda helped her lift Bess out of the pack. Melanie pulled Bess tightly to her chest, murmuring soothing tones, shushing her daughter. As Bess made contact with Melanie, her whimpers quieted, though she trembled.

Melanie lay Bess on the changing table, keeping up a steady flow of soothing, nonsense words as she fumbled with Bess's clothing. Brenda helped her slip off the outer clothing, the t-shirt, and then the baby datasuit. Melanie eased Bess onto her side, looking closely at her back. No marks there. She ran her shaking hand over Bess's head, scanning her scalp. Nothing.

"She's clear," Melanie said. "At least from the direct contact. But I-I-I took her virtual. What's that done to her?"

"Sit down. I'll change her," Brenda said. "You look like you're going to pass out."

"You sure you didn't get nailed?" Angela asked.

"Positive. Just nerves. Liam's back. *And I fucked up and took Bess virtual after him!*"

"Damn. Son-of-a-bitch just doesn't stop coming at you, does he?"

"Liam? That son-of-a-bitch is dead, isn't he?" Brenda's experienced hands moved through the diaper-changing routine. "Even as a Netwalker. At least that's what I was told in the briefing."

"It appears the briefing was wrong," Angela said. She and Brenda started talking in Mixteco.

Bess began to fuss, looking around for Melanie. "You'd better keep physical contact with her." Brenda changed back to English. "I think she'll be happier."

Melanie slid her hands onto her daughter's chest. Bess settled, although she kept looking for Melanie. Melanie leaned forward into Bess's range of vision, murmuring nonsense words to her daughter, her voice breaking and quavering. Brenda and Angela continued talking in Mixteco.

"There." Brenda slipped a fresh baby datasuit onto Bess, then clean clothing, and handed Bess back.

Bess rooted toward Melanie's chest, smacking her lips. Melanie adjusted her clothing and put Bess to her breast. Bess latched on and eagerly began to nurse.

Good. She's nursing normally.

Marty's hand rested on her shoulder. "All okay?"

"She's physically clear. Nursing okay. God, Marty, what did I do?"

Ness, still in falcon form, landed on her shoulder. Bess paused in suckling, eyes darting toward Ness. Her slight body tensed. Ness emitted a soft, soothing chirrup. Bess relaxed, and resumed her eager sucking.

<She's calmer with me than she has been,> Ness said.

<I'll scan her while you're nursing,> Marty said. <Kathy took baseline scans at birth and we've been doing it every six hours, ever since Bess started reacting to virtual.>

<Thank you. How's Mom?>

<She's responding, but Kathy wants to take her to the infirmary. Diana won't cooperate until she knows you and Bess are okay.>

<Tell her Bess is okay.>

<Done. She's going now.>

The commotion around her faded. Melanie focused on Bess as Marty knelt next to them with a scanner, frowning as he stared at the functions. Melanie forced herself not to look at the scanner.

At last, he put it away.

<Cognitive functions normal.>

<Dodged a bullet. God, Marty, what do I do next?> Tears rushed into her eyes.

<You finish feeding Bess. Once you're done nursing, you'll kill your upload. And then it's back to bed. Too much excitement for both of you.>

<Oh God, Marty. Oh God.>

He held her tighter. "It's okay, Mel. I'll take her while you kill the upload. When Julia and your father get here, we'll spend more time figuring this out before you take on Sarah again. *Something* happened in there, and Bess is a part of it. Our little girl is not defenseless. I don't think *you* would have gotten away without harm if she hadn't been with you. She has Enforcer tones, Mel. Already."

"My God, what have we created here, Marty?"

"Our little girl might be the key to—the gadget," he said.

He held Melanie until Bess stopped nursing, then eased her out of Melanie's arms. She wobbled away from Marty and Bess and threw a globe around herself and the upload. Once she killed the upload, Melanie staggered back to Marty, Bess, and a waiting floater controlled by Brenda.

Questions still kept spiraling through Melanie's thoughts as Marty steadied her and Bess on the floater.

Gizmo. Bess. Liam. Sarah. What the hell is going on here?

It was almost enough to make her wish for simpler days, when all she had to worry about was protecting DIR and its staff from raids by Sarah and her National Security blacksuits.

NIGHTTIME. MARTY SIGHED DEEPLY AS HE CLIMBED THE STAIRS INTO THE house, heading for the dining room rather than upstairs to Melanie and Bess. Kathy Miller had sent a message asking for a face-to-face debriefing.

Kathy sprawled in an armchair, reading a projection. Another armchair faced hers, and two empty glasses plus a bottle of bourbon sat on a side table.

Kathy looked up.

"Marty." She gestured toward the chair. "Come into my lair." She gave him a quick wry smile. "Want something to drink?"

"Sure." He dropped into the chair. She was offering bourbon. Not good at all, not from Dr. Kathy Miller. "How's Diana doing?" A lesser subject, but safer.

Kathy poured; her hands steady. "I want to clear her from more toxin before we try tinkering with that virus in Sarah again. At least Melanie's being sensible about this incident. What happened with Bess scared her."

Bess. The as-yet-unresolved question. "Is Bess going to be all right?"

"We won't know for sure until she's older," Kathy said, tapping her fingertips on the chair's arm, "I'm not seeing any cognitive abnormalities. I think we made it through this incident without harm. *This* time."

"Psychologically?"

"What's the psychological impact of neonatal surgery and the use of anesthesia on a fetus?" Kathy sipped her drink. "What's the impact on infants of formal presentation to the gadget? Melanie and Andrew both experienced that."

"It's not the device that Mel and I are worried about."

Yet.

"The doubled combination of datasuit and frontpack appears to be the key for Bess's safety should Melanie go virtual with her. Melanie reported skill impairments during the conflict. She shouldn't have had problems manifesting that blue light she uses as a virtual tool. Something blocked her, and it wasn't any of our usual suspects."

"The device or this Liam guise?"

"No. Bess blocked Melanie. Bess already has a virtual presence. She may have been exerting it even before birth. That presence could have been a factor in Melanie's pregnancy complications, as much as the poison pill."

"Whoa. Where did you get that theory from?"

"Bits and pieces that started coming together after Bess's birth." Kathy stared down into her glass, swishing the brown liquor around. She put her glass down and added more. "I think Bess was sensitized in utero by multiple factors. Toxin—Melanie's gadget exposures—Melanie's virtual skills. Singly or in combination, the result made Bess so reactive to virtual that Melanie couldn't be exposed further without risking a miscarriage. It's as likely an explanation as that poison pill."

"Doesn't explain what happened with surrogates. Unless you think this is at the egg level."

"It could be." Kathy sipped her drink. "Whatever the case, we have a baby who is reactive to virtual exposures. The effects aren't fatal, thankfully. Bess is a strong little girl. All the same, I wonder what this means for her future."

"I don't want to make any assumptions without Will and Julia's opinions. That's what Ness recommends." Marty finished the rest of his drink and poured himself more.

"Bess appears to have Enforcer tones in virtual. She seems to have an effect on the device. The gadget—at least the analog we saw—wanted to go after her." Kathy winced, an expression he recognized from talks with Melanie. "Damn."

"Device limits?"

"Yes."

"Will doesn't have links to it."

"That might be our salvation." Kathy grimaced and tossed back her drink. She set her glass down firmly by the bottle but did not pour herself more. "Here's another datum. Bess isn't the only young child here who shows toxin exposures on the scans."

"Who else?"

"The Jeffreys boys. Alex more than Don. It's very minor, but enough for a keen observer to notice. Sophie even has a tiny trace."

Marty digested this piece of information.

What does this mean? God, I don't know!

He tossed back the rest of his bourbon and shook his head when Kathy offered more. "I'm tired. It's been a tough day."

"Go," Kathy said. "I just wanted to debrief. I'm still processing the info."

"We all are." He rose. "Thanks, Kathy. You've talked to Mel?"

"I have. But you need to repeat it to her. Bess took no harm from this exposure. As long as she has both datasuit and frontpack protection, she can have brief virtual experiences. It's not optimal, but she has parents who can help her orient to the difference between body and virtual. Damn it, we need Melanie's help with this latest manifestation—" Kathy winced again. She poured herself a stiff shot and gulped it down. "Bess is a new generation, with new abilities."

"And that scares me."

"She's going to be a little girl for a while yet!"

"But a little girl with virtual skills? That could be scary."

"Bess is what she is. Let's hope it turns out to be what we need."

So much to worry about with one little girl.

"It still scares me."

"It should." Kathy rose, picking up the bottle and the glasses. "Go. Take care of Melanie."

"I will. Good night."

"Good night."

He trudged up the stairs, nodding at the guards outside the bedroom door. Melanie looked up from the bed as he entered the room, her worried expression softening into a smile.

"Hey, darling," he said. He eased on the bed and kissed Melanie, then caressed Bess's head. She stirred slightly, then settled back into sleep, mumbling tiny baby coos. "Shall we put her to bed?" he asked Melanie. "Or are you still worried?"

"I'm not sure," Melanie said, uncertainty in her voice.

"Kathy's checked her. She's okay."

"*I took her virtual.* What did that do to her?"

"She's been exposed to Netwalker toxin. The device has performed epigenetic modifications on you—probably me as well. What does *that* do to her?"

Tears trickled down Melanie's cheeks. "I'm so worried."

Ness roused faintly from her recharge sleep. <Tell Mel it's okay.>

"Ness says it's okay."

"You're sure?"

"Yeah. I'm sure. Now, if it's okay with you, let's put the princess in her bed. I'm ready to crash. You?"

"I could rest," Melanie said. "Now that you're here."

Marty carried Bess over to the bassinet. She smacked her lips, and settled into deeper sleep.

He returned to the bed, taking Melanie into his arms.

"It's okay," he whispered. "I'm here. I'll take care of both of you."

She quivered against him. He kissed her forehead.

"I was so worried," she whispered.

He kissed her again. "Understandable."

"I fucked up so bad," she moaned. "What's she going to be?"

"Our daughter," he said firmly, and meant it. "Our daughter, who will be fortunate if she is even half as brilliant and beautiful and intelligent as her mother."

"Flatterer."

He was relieved to hear the joking tone in her voice. "True, every word of it."

"Still flattery."

He kissed her to quiet further commentary. At last Melanie sagged away, blinking away the last of the wetness in her eyes.

He held her until she slept, lying awake for some time after she'd turned away from him and her breathing had steadied into a restful rhythm.

Dear God, what have we created in this child?

CHAPTER 17

The skimmer jockeyed gently over the landing pad as Angela waited. The stiff morning wind was cool enough to chill her, but she welcomed the dry cold. It snapped her further awake, keyed her senses into higher alert. And she sure as hell needed to be alert right now.

The skimmer settled. The hatch popped open and Karl guided Deirdre Conley out. Conley stood unsteadily, blindfolded, thick gloves over her hands.

She's still cutting herself.

But Angela also noted the ease with which Conley regained equilibrium, even blindfolded, and the fluidity of her motion.

She's also in good condition. Remember that.

Karl removed the blindfold. Conley blinked in the bright light.

"Where am I?" she asked.

"The Andrews Ranch. Don't worry, there's not much chance of escape," Angela said.

"I wondered when I'd see Melanie's dark angel again."

"Knock it off." Karl shoved her.

Angela raised a hand. "Stop it. I can deal with her racism."

Conley shook her head. "Not meant that way. She's Melanie's Angel of Death."

Despite herself, Angela grinned, because Conley's half-mocking, half-subdued tone was *so right*. "That's not me. You want the Angel of Death, that's Nik."

"But you control him. He's your instrument."

"Not always." Angela shrugged. "Let's go inside. Had your breakfast yet?"

"Offering me breakfast, even. That's a step up from our usual interactions." Conley faced into the east wind, studying the snow-capped mountains.

"Would you eat it?"

"Oh hell yes. One thing I'll say for Do It Right, you folks serve good food. Better than the New Feds or the old Confederation."

"Come on, then." Angela gestured to Conley. They walked toward the Security building. <On our way,> she texted Nik.

<All ready,> he answered. <Sophie's got them riled up and ready to run.>

<Good.> She quickly texted details of the plan to Karl so he was ready in case Conley tried anything.

Happy kid squeals alerted Angela. Sophie led the boys, giggling as the three of them ran toward the main office building where their morning school took place.

Conley stopped short, her hands rising to her mouth as the boys and Sophie capered by.

Donnie stopped. Stared at Conley for a moment.

"Auntie Dee!" he yelled, and charged toward her. Alex hesitated, then followed. Sophie turned back, looking first to Nik and then Angela for guidance. Angela smiled and signed *it's all right*. Sophie grinned and ran to Angela, hugging her.

Conley dropped to her knees as the boys slammed into her, wrapping her arms around them.

"Oh my darlings, my darlings," she cried, her voice catching. "Oh my darlings, I've missed you so much!"

There was no mistaking the genuine affection between Conley and the boys, so different from their occasional visits with Gina Jeffreys before she was shipped off to the New Feds. The boys babbled happily at Conley.

"We get to ride horsies!" Alex.

"Stories every night from Melanie and Marty!" Donnie.

Conley didn't answer but kept hugging the boys, murmuring their names.

Nik stepped forward, nodding to Angela. She gave Sophie one more hug. "Better go. It's time."

Sophie hugged her fiercely back. "I thought they'd *never* get it and I'd have to lead them closer."

"Thank you, honey." Angela kissed Sophie's forehead. "You did it just right. There's Miss Helen now."

"Alex! Donnie! Miss Helen's here!" Sophie bolted toward Helen.

The boys pulled back from Conley. "Auntie Dee, you've got to meet Miss Helen! She's so much fun!"

The boys pulled at Conley's mittened hands, half-dragging her to meet Helen. Nik and Karl moved close but the encounter happened without incident. Then Helen herded the three children away.

Tears trickled down Conley's face as she stared after the boys. "They've gotten so big."

"Children tend to do that," Angela said.

Conley glanced sideways at Angela. "The girl that ran to you. Who is she?"

"My daughter. Nik's daughter."

"With the boys?"

"They're part of a Security cohort."

Conley nodded, her face contracting back into control, lips pressed together so hard that they almost disappeared. "You said something about breakfast?"

Angela gestured toward the Security building. "In there."

"Well, let's get to it, then." Conley's voice carried a thread of bravado, though her chin quivered.

And two thin lines of wetness steadily trickled down her face.

Not quite the break we've been looking for—but Mel's right. The boys are the key to opening up Deirdre Conley.

<Mel. Kid gambit worked. Spectacularly,> she texted.

<Karl sent me images. On to the next step,> Melanie answered.

MARTY ENTERED THEIR SUITE. MELANIE'S BACK WAS TURNED AWAY FROM him, her head propped on one hand, voice soft as she talked to Bess.

Feeding time must be over.

"It's me," he said. He came around the bed. Bess stared myopically up at Melanie's face, aimlessly waving her tiny fists. Melanie murmured to her and Bess responded in similar tones.

She's teaching Bess tones already, Marty realized, listening closer. Melanie hummed a non-Enforcer tone and Bess echoed. Then Bess cooed and Melanie mirrored the dominant tone back to her. *I didn't know you could do this so young.*

Marty sat on the edge of the bed. Bess's eyes turned to him. For a moment her eyes locked into his, and she stared with more focus. Melanie hummed and Bess turned back to her.

<Marty. Bring Ness out. See what she does,> Melanie said.

<Ness?> he asked her.

<She was looking for me. She knows I'm here,> Ness said.

Before he could say anything more, Ness eased out. Bess focused on Ness. For a moment worry crossed Bess's face, her tiny eyes closing to a slit and her mouth opening as if to start screaming.

"Easy, little one," Ness said aloud. "I'm not someone you have to worry about."

Bess's eyes shot wide open and she stared at Ness, her whole body visibly tightening. Then she softened and waved her fists at Ness.

<Marty. Melanie. May I touch her?> Ness asked.

Melanie glanced worriedly at Marty. <Too much virtual?>

He shook his head. <Kathy says she has a virtual presence. If so, we'd better start teaching Bess who and what is and isn't safe.>

<Okay, then.> Melanie's subvocals carried her ambivalence. <Slow and careful.>

<A tap.> Ness gently brushed against Bess's right hand.

Bess startled, throwing her arms wide and squeaking. Then she refocused on Ness, staring hard again.

<She's curious. Fascinated,> Ness reported.

<How do you know?> Melanie asked.

<You can't feel it? It's not words. Lower level.>

<No.> Melanie seemed hesitant.

<Show me,> Marty said.

<Me too,> Melanie said.

Ness took them both by the hand. <Look at her.>

Bess stared at them. Marty looked deep into his daughter's eyes. At first, nothing. Then a gentle mental touch, seeking. Questioning. No words, but interest. Excitement, rising. Recognition.

Warmth comfort contact.

"She knows who we are," he said aloud. "And she knows *you*, Ness."

"Oh my God," Melanie whispered. She slipped her hand free from Ness's touch. "How did she develop this understanding? Because I took her virtual?"

"I don't know," Marty said. "Ness?"

"She recognized me before then," Ness said.

"We don't tell this to anybody," Melanie said. <Will and Julia, yes. They don't have device access.>

"Your mother?" Marty asked.

Melanie shook her head. <Especially not my mother. Or Kathy.>

<You won't be able to hide it from Sarah,> Ness said.

<I don't care about Sarah,> Melanie responded. <I *want* Sarah to know. Sarah won't tell Mom.>

<Then why not your mother?> Marty asked.

<The gadget, and,> Melanie hesitated, clearly thinking through it. <The gadget. Mostly. But also because—my mother's long-term agenda is different from mine. Because of what happened at Charleston. Because—I don't know. There's something about the dynamic of Mom and Sarah from Mom's side that worries me.>

<She's turning into Sarah?>

<A little. But Sarah is becoming more reasonable.> Melanie shivered. <It's frightening that I think of Sarah like that. And yet, when it comes to the device, she *is* more—realistic.>

"Are you ready to talk to Conley?" he asked.

"Yes. Watch Bess while I get dressed."

"My pleasure." He pulled Bess close as Melanie got up, quickly mesmerized as Bess's unfocused stare briefly focused, her eyes meeting his. Then she whimpered.

"She wants to be wrapped back up," Melanie said. "She likes to be tightly swaddled, except when she's eating."

He wrapped the blanket around Bess and held her. She continued to look at him.

"Hey, little girl," he crooned. "Hey there." He kept up a reassuring patter of nonsense words, glancing away several times to watch Melanie as she slowly moved around the room.

"I am so out of shape after this pregnancy," she moaned, holding up a pair of black slacks in her regular size. "Will I ever be able to wear these again?"

"Honey, it's only been a few days. You'll get your figure and conditioning back."

"But I want it back now." She pulled on a pair of maternity tights and a tunic, both in forest green, then went into the bathroom to finish getting ready. Marty carried Bess over to the window, studying the mountains.

Melanie came out of the bathroom, wearing the frontpack, and took Bess from him. Marty helped her adjust the final fittings.

Melanie took a deep breath. "I'm ready."

They went to the kids' learning center, where the boys and Sophie had grown accustomed to meeting them for a late morning reading session. Sophie and Donnie settled in his lap while Alex curled up with Melanie and Bess. Time flew by quickly as he read out loud.

The door opened, briefly startling Marty before he remembered.

Conley's here now.

Helen entered, followed by Conley, Nik, Angela, and Karl.

Conley inhaled sharply.

"Auntie Dee, come see this book!" Donnie called.

Alex waved but turned back to Melanie. Conley winced.

"Auntie Dee, come on!" Donnie demanded.

Conley tightened her shoulders. She glanced back at Nik. He gestured her forward. Conley walked over to Marty and knelt beside them, Nik a ghostly shadow behind her.

"So, darlin', what's this book about?"

"May I show the book to Auntie Dee?" Donnie asked Marty.

Marty grinned. "Good job of asking, Donnie. You okay with that, Soph?"

Sophie nodded. Marty handed the book to Donnie. He slid out of Marty's lap to sit on the floor. Conley joined him as he pointed out the pictures and haltingly read a few sentences. She pulled him into her lap and he sagged against her with a sigh. Sophie signed a Security code to Angela. Angela handsigned back. Sophie went to Angela, leaning against her mother.

Melanie said something softly to Alex that Marty couldn't hear. Alex nodded and slid out of her lap, joining Donnie and Conley. For a brief instant it seemed like a quiet family moment.

Then Brenda entered, standing next to Helen. Sophie hugged Angela again and crossed the room to hug Nik before joining Helen and Brenda.

"Time to go," Sophie said to Donnie and Alex. Brenda took Bess and the frontpack from Melanie. Alex hugged Conley, then rushed over to Sophie and Helen. Donnie lingered, giving Conley a quick kiss before running to Sophie and Alex.

Brenda, Helen and the kids left the room.

Conley gracefully sprang up. Karl and Nik moved closer to her.

"I'm not going to do anything," Conley said tiredly, looking at the floor. She pressed her lips together, tightened her jaw, and glared at Nik and Angela. "Not that I'd want to. Not after seeing the boys like this. No stigma because of who they are?"

"None," Melanie said. "They're here because Sophie wanted to be with her parents, and they're part of her Security cohort in the crèche."

Conley let out a big sigh, tension flowing out of her body. "You're raising them as if they were your own."

"I *told* you we would do that," Melanie said.

"They *are* our own now," Nik said.

"Thank you," Conley sighed again. "Gina is probably mourning that they aren't being brought up in the true Freedom Army ways. But from me, yes. I'll thank you. They're good boys. They have good talents. They would have been nothing but weapons in Gina's hands, potential Netwalkers to avenge their father. Now, perhaps they have a future. Thank you."

Those boys as potential Netwalkers? What the—what? The Freedom Army looks at kids so callously?

Marty swallowed hard. The Freedom Army was worse than he thought.

Melanie flinched. "I don't understand why anyone consider them to be potential Netwalkers. They'd have to die first. I fought too hard to have my baby to understand how someone could think that way."

"You've forgotten what you know of Liam if that's the case," Conley said. "He would see them dead before he let you raise them. They were tools to him and Gina both. Trust me, those boys wouldn't have lived to see eighteen." She shivered. "I'd have been dead by then."

"I guess I didn't know him that well." A sick look crossed Melanie's face. "I made a lot of mistakes when I was younger. Liam was the biggest."

"Do you think you had a choice? You were targeted, by Francis Stewart himself."

"But he's dead!" Marty snapped.

Conley laughed bitterly. "That's what you think."

"So he's a Netwalker," Melanie said.

Conley shook her head. "He's more than a Netwalker—" She screamed and sank to her knees, clutching at her head. Marty rushed to her but Melanie was quicker.

"Karl, throw a secured hologlobe! *Fast!*" Melanie placed her hands on Conley's temples, holding steady as Conley shrieked. Convulsions wracked Conley's body and she flopped onto her side. The globe stabilized around them. Conley gasped for breath as her body stopped jerking.

"Breathe with me," Melanie said, still keeping her hands on Conley's temples. "Deep breath in." Pause. "Out. In. Out."

Conley's breathing settled. She rolled onto her back and looked up at Melanie. "You know," she moaned. *"You know."*

Melanie sat back on her heels, her hands dropping to her side. "It's the device. We can't talk. Much."

"I've—wanted—but—" Conley screamed again, jerking into a fetal curl.

"Karl! Marty!" Melanie switched to mindspeech. <Link in. Now. Ness! We need protection and fast! Damn it, this needs to be a Sarah job, I need someone who knows the gadget! It has a direct link to her—somehow—and it's trying to fry her brain! How the hell can it do that with her chip disabled?>

Melanie yanked them into virtual.

<I see it!> Ness pointed toward something Marty couldn't see. Blue light flared as Melanie brought it up.

<Ness, Sarah forms a black cloud around my blue light to help banish the gadget. Can you do something like that?>

<I can try.>

<I'll manifest it as a sword. You form around it. Then we'll see if we can cut that link.>

<What will it do to Conley?> he asked.

<If we *don't* do something, that damned device will fry her brain!> Melanie called up the blue light. It wavered between a saber and a rapier shape before settling into saber form. Ness dissolved into a gray cloud. A gray shadow formed over the blue saber.

<Back me,> Melanie ordered.

Marty put his hands on Melanie's left shoulder and Karl her right. Tied into Melanie and Ness, he saw the outline of the link as it ominously pulsed, throbbing faster and faster.

Melanie nodded, then stepped forward, raising her saber high. Brought it down hard on the link.

Bright white, red and purple lights flared around them. Sharp, jabbing pain sizzled through him.

Then it faded. He collapsed to hands and knees; barely aware he was back in his body. Melanie crawled to Conley's limp body. She shook Conley.

"Conley. Conley. Deirdre. DEIRDRE CONLEY!"

Conley jerked convulsively. She blinked up at Melanie.

Is she brain-fried?

Blood from her mouth.

"Get me a rag; she's bitten her lip," Melanie said.

Marty staggered to his feet and found gauze and gloves. Melanie took them and pulled the gloves on, then pressed the gauze to Conley's lip.

"Better lip than tongue." Conley took over holding the gauze. "Holy Mother of God. It was trying to kill me."

Melanie rocked back on her heels. "The connection's broken now. Not that I'd trust it to stay that way." She glanced over at Karl. "Please bring us pencil and paper. Nothing electronic."

<What's up?> Marty asked Melanie.

<You'll see.> Melanie took the pad and quickly wrote something, showing it to Conley.

This may give us limited safety, he read over Melanie's shoulder. *Don't mention the item directly. No common terms for it.*

Conley nodded. She rolled onto her stomach and took the pad from Melanie.

Thanks, she wrote. *Couldn't talk before. Joking and being rude briefly diverts. Cutting helped shut down the thing's voice. Not perfect.*

Melanie took the pencil from Conley. *Thought so. We have another Tim Conley item. Can you scan it safely?*

I think so, Conley wrote.

"Nik?"

Nik joined Melanie. He handed the chip reader to Conley. She fumbled through the thick mittens, growling when the reader wouldn't work.

"Help her take them off," Melanie said.

Once her hands were free, Conley quickly skimmed through the chip. At one point she shivered, then pressed her lips together firmly. Then she put the chip reader aside and reached for the pad and pencil.

This is the right Tim Conley. She shivered again. *His body may be dead, but he's uploaded as a Netwalker. And he is leading the attacks against you, ever since you captured me.*

Melanie took a second pad and pencil from Karl. *Why?* she wrote.

Complete the job I was supposed to do under the object's influence. Set it and Francis Stewart free. Conley winced and put down her pencil. "I'm sorry. My hands hurt. I can't write much more."

"There has to be a better way than this to communicate," Melanie growled. "This isn't fast enough." She wrote quickly, almost scrawling. *Does this mean Francis Stewart is part of the whatchamacallit?*

Conley flexed her fingers before writing slowly. *They're linked in something called the Shadow Chamber.*

<Ness, do you think a Netwalker-generated secondary secured globe will be enough protection for her to speak openly?> he asked.

<Yes. It will buy us about fifteen minutes,> Ness replied. <More than that and a warning goes out to the device.>

<Do it.>

The sting of the secondary globe seemed greater than ever. <Sorry. Can't modulate the bite like you can in the flesh,> Ness apologized.

"We have fifteen minutes to talk before a warning," Marty said.

"That's why Ness threw the second globe?" Melanie asked.

He nodded.

"Thanks. Deirdre, tell us more—quickly—about Tim Conley and Francis Stewart and Gizmo."

"Tim was Stewart's right-hand man, then Liam's. When I became Gina's surrogate and Liam's comfort woman, Tim turned abusive on me."

"Gina's surrogate?" Melanie frowned.

Conley took a deep breath. "The boys may be genetically Gina's, but I bore them." Bitterness colored her voice. "I was sterilized before I became Liam's comfort woman, so he wouldn't taint the bloodline by having a bastard with me. They wanted the bloodline but Gina didn't want to carry them. They're more mine than hers. She conceived them because Liam wanted them. I bore them. I raised them. Donny and Alex. Cuddled with me, even though they weren't supposed to. Looked to me, even though I was supposed to be teaching them contempt for women. Gina was unhappy that they cared for me. But she didn't want to spend time with the boys."

"Do you want more time with the boys? I can set that up," Melanie said.

"I'd like that. But you don't dare trust me with them."

"Why not?"

"I did their base conditioning. Not everything the Army would want them to have, but enough. I'd still have to watch myself. Have to train me out of it. They respond too readily to me."

"Training is something we can do," Melanie said. "What more can you tell us about Francis Stewart and Gizmo? Is he a Netwalker?"

"Not in the sense that Liam and your Sarah are. He somehow became part of that Gizmo thing. That's all we were told." Conley swallowed. "Water?"

Nik handed her a drink bulb.

Conley nodded thanks at Nik before she quickly sucked it dry. "There's something called the Shadow Chamber. I could only reach it with Liam. Stewart is there. Liam and Tim might be as well. It generates new forms so that it's difficult if not impossible to kill them as Netwalkers."

<This explains Liam's reappearance,> Melanie said to Marty.

<Very probable.>

"How accessible is this Chamber?"

"You can't get there without Netwalker guidance," Conley said. "And when you're there," she shivered, "you don't know what reality is. I went there once. With Liam. In his Netwalker form. They sealed me into him then—made me his host."

"How do we stop Tim Conley's attacks?"

Conley wrapped her arms tightly around herself, looking down. "You find his living host—which isn't me. Break the connection. Then you go to the Chamber to lock him up."

"Then that is what we will do." Melanie straightened up. "Enough for now. Ness, drop that secondary globe. Eight minutes so far." She exhaled. "Processes. Conley—is there something else we can call you?"

"Deirdre or Dee."

"Deirdre, you work with Marty, Ness and Nik to identify these likely hosts for Tim Conley. I'll plan to go into the Chamber, starting with fixing Sarah. She's the only Netwalker strong enough to do that. But I'm not going to mess with Sarah until Julia gets here with my father. Period."

Weather delayed Julia's arrival until late that evening. Melanie socialized with the new Enforcer teams for a little while, but she was grateful when it was time to leave.

"I'm in for the night," she told Marty. "Take charge for me?"

He stroked her face. "No problem, honey." He bent to kiss Bess, out of the frontpack for this gathering. "What about when Julia and your dad get here?"

"Contingencies set up with Angela."

"Good." He kissed her. "Rest, honey. Today was a hard day."

"Yep." She wasn't going to argue that at all. Nor did she object when he carried Bess up the stairs for her and used a forefinger for Bess to suck on while she prepared for feeding and bed.

He lingered while she fed Bess. It was a relief to have Marty burp, change and settle Bess for bed before he left to rejoin the others. Melanie gratefully assembled her fortress of pillows and lay back against them with a sigh. Even though she was tired, her brain still jangled from the day's revelations.

At least I can work in virtual now.

She called up a hologlobe. Reviewing contracts was a nice, steady task to calm her brain, unlike reviewing the Seattle events. Melanie settled into a steady rhythm of scanning clauses, delivery dates, and quality specifications.

<Mel, are you open for a visit? Angela said you wanted me to ask.> Julia's question startled Melanie.

<Yes,> she answered. Bess started whimpering. <If you don't mind watching me feed the princess,> she added.

<I was hoping she would be awake.> Her father's virtual voice brought quick tears to Melanie's eyes. Long distance communication with Netwalkers without being a host herself was still difficult, and she hadn't been able to talk to him throughout her pregnancy.

<She's waking right now.> Melanie saved her files and closed the globe before getting up.

A light tap pushed the door open. "Oh!" Reiko said. "I didn't think it was ajar. Sorry. Are you ready?"

"Absolutely," Melanie said. Reiko came in, a diaper bag slung over her arm.

"I didn't know—" Melanie started to say, then stopped abruptly as Julia carried a baby into the room, just a little bit older than Bess. "Whose baby?"

"Mine," Julia said. "Melanie, this is Zack. He's two months old."

"You didn't say anything!"

<We didn't want to, not until we knew how your pregnancy fared,> her father Will said, popping out of Julia's chip and twisting through a 360 before hovering a couple of inches above the floor. Melanie swallowed hard at the sight of her father in loose-fitting long shorts and a snowboard t-shirt. Nothing at all like the ill, fragile but driven man he'd been at his death.

Bess stirred and stared at Will, but she didn't stiffen or cry out.

"You must have used a surrogate," she said. "I can't imagine the difficulties sustaining a pregnancy as a Netwalk host."

Julia shook her head. "I didn't have your problems, Mel." She sank into an overstuffed chair and prepared to nurse Zack. "Kathy and I had regular conversations comparing progress. We both agreed it wasn't a good idea to say anything about my pregnancy until after you'd given birth. We didn't know what the implications would be if I suddenly developed problems. So far, Zack's been developing typically."

Melanie returned to her pillow fortress and began to nurse Bess. "What made my pregnancy so hard as compared to yours?"

"Your exposures." Will crossed his legs and serenely floated in the air, about four feet off of the ground. "Plus the poison pill."

"What about virtual sensitivity in the fetus when a Netwalk host is pregnant?"

Julia frowned thoughtfully. "So far, that's not been an issue with Zack. He's aware of Will, but that happened after he was born. No prenatal awareness that we can tell."

"It's a major issue with Bess."

"Tell us about it." Reiko settled into another chair.

Melanie quickly summarized Bess's first few days of life and the conversations she and Marty had been having, careful to edit out direct descriptions of Gizmo. "I'm still scared about having taken her virtual," she ended.

Will uncrossed his legs and zoomed over to Bess and Melanie. Bess stopped suckling and stared hard at him. He chuckled. "Good recognition of virtual entities at a young age," he said, voice tinny. Bess startled and whimpered. Melanie soothed her and got her back to nursing.

A tight black line *tapped* against Melanie's awareness. She startled, then recognized her father's touch.

What is this?

Her bewilderment must have communicated itself to Will. The touch widened and she recognized it as a private mindspeech circuit. Then it narrowed back down.

A means of circumventing Gizmo?

<I don't sense anything out of the ordinary from her when I scan her,> he said, his virtual voice stronger than ever. <Given your epigenetic and toxin exposures. She has a strong virtual presence.>

<Sarah accused me of putting an implant in her already!>

<It's the presence of nanos in her system.> Will dropped the private link.

<How do the nanos affect her?> she asked. <Will she need a chip later on?>

<Probably,> Julia answered.

<Undoubtedly,> Will said. <She will clear these nanos from her system over time. You have similar ones. Only there's a structure that's still feeding them to you—the poison pill. It's weakened but still present. There's gadget ties in it.>

<Why can you see this and Ness or Sarah couldn't?>

<We've been studying this because of my pregnancy,> Julia said. <Will's had unique access to me and Zack because I'm his host.>

<I'll show Ness the routes,> Will added.

<Should I keep nursing Bess?>

<I would,> Julia said. <Once she's weaned, those nanos will clear fast.>

<I'll keep track while we're here,> Will said. <I don't think many are crossing over into your milk, so her count may be declining.>

<Thank you. Dad—what about the whatchamacallit and its reaction to Bess?>

The link tightened again, excluding Julia. <That worries me. I

haven't been around it for years, but I don't trust it to keep on forgetting me.>

<I can't talk to Marty about it. We managed a very brief conversation with a secondary globe during the Conley thing, but the utility of that maxes at fifteen minutes. I wouldn't take it over ten, for safety's sake. How safe is this link?>

<Not safe enough. Good for a short time, about the same as the secondary globe.>

<What do you know about the Shadow Chamber?>

Nothing. Will's form changed shape from snowboarder to elder garbed in a shapeless robe. <Too much to risk talking about except under much, much higher security than this,> he said. <Why?>

<Deirdre Conley says that Francis Stewart is there. That Liam and this Tim Conley might be there. I have to go to the Chamber to take care of this. With Sarah.>

Will swiftly changed form from elder back to snowboarder, frowning. <Sarah would be the best choice. And this could explain a few things. But girl, that is not a place to go on a whim. Even with Sarah for support. Let me think.> He twisted through several 360 rolls, reminding Melanie yet again of the times she'd seen him riding through a snowpark, before he got so sick. He stopped. Once again, he extended the slender link. <You require more tools, girl, you and Sarah both, to take on the gadget in the Chamber. With your best secondary Enforcers to guard your back.>

<Marty?>

<Maybe. And—I need to run checks on your Bess. It worries me that the device went after Bess. You may need to have her with you as well, for her protection.>

Oh God.

<Dad—will Bess be all right? All this virtual stuff?>

<She doesn't feel any different from Zack.> Her father paused. <And if that thing has already targeted her, then the sooner she can orient in virtual, the better.>

<But she's just a newborn!>

<A newborn the big G wanted to attack. Girl of mine, that's signifi-

cant. It didn't like you very much as a baby, but it didn't want to attack you.>

<The gadget didn't like me?>

<Very definitely not at first presentation. Distress noises, backing away. Different from Andrew, different from any other child presented.>

<What can we do?>

<I'll talk to Marty. Meanwhile, keep her close. Help her orient to you and Marty. Julia kept Zack close the first few weeks. That makes a difference in virtual orientation.>

Marty came into the room. "Who's this?" he asked Julia, peering at Zack.

Melanie leaned back.

Questions. Always more questions.

At some point it would be nice to find some answers.

CHAPTER 18

GRIM DATA REPORTS OPENED THE NEXT DAY'S ENFORCER MEETING.

"This is the final casualty total—so far—from the Freedom Army attack in Seattle." Melanie projected the results on the hologlobe's screen.

Marty winced, even though he already knew the stats. Seeing them —like this—slammed the devastation home.

"One. Our strongest Netwalker temporarily disabled. Two. Ten non-Netwalk individuals injured and in various stages of recovery. Three. Three attackers, all dead. Uploaded? Marty?"

"According to data from Ness and Will, no new uploads. That's based on our current tech. I'm worried about how accurate that is," Marty said.

Deirdre Conley questioned those estimates after reviewing the data. *That* bothered him.

"I think we're probably safe," Deirdre said. "*This* time. None of the three who died had chips with sufficient power to support Netwalker uploads, either in your versions or Freedom Army." She stood. "But you have a bigger problem. May I?"

Melanie nodded. "Please do."

Marty watched closely as Melanie helped Deirdre adjust the headset that substituted for her chip, his fingers itching to make minor corrections. Melanie's setup technique was slower than his—but utterly necessary.

I need to do this, she had said this morning. *Show everyone that I accept her.*

"I want to introduce Deirdre Conley, our newest Enforcer recruit," Melanie continued, stepping back from Deirdre. "She is formerly from the highest levels of the Freedom Army and she brings us important data."

<Is this for real?!> Grady texted Marty in a bright red and orange flame font. <What the HELL is Melanie doing? Has motherhood made her soft?>

Melanie bowed to Deirdre, then left her alone in front, pausing to gather Bess from Mama Brenda before sitting next to Marty.

<For real,> Marty confirmed. <I stand with Mel. Been working to turn this one for some time. Good reasons to trust her support. Listen to her.>

<Hope you two know what you're doing.>

<She has useful data. Ness and Will confirm.>

<If *they* think it's all right…> Grady nodded. He started to clap. The others slowly followed his lead.

"Well. Right." Deirdre looked around. "To keep this short and sweet, your biggest problem lies in a difference between your National Security-slash-Do It Right Netwalk templates and the Freedom Army templates."

<Are you all right?> he asked Melanie.

<Just—tired. And worried about the data.>

He hugged her. <Me too.> He left his arm around her shoulders and she tucked in closer to him with a soft sigh.

"Here's an example," Deirdre continued. "It's more difficult to describe because we do not have a Freedom Army template Netwalker live and available. But your recordings are quite good." A brief grin touched her lips. "Better than I'd hoped. Let me demonstrate one of the major issues, and do forgive me if my narration's not always the best," she added in a lilting, half-mocking voice. "The incident displayed is a bit, well, on the personal side."

Her capture scene.

Melanie sat up and took his hand, clamping down hard as Deirdre ran the sequence until Liam fully manifested himself.

"That's enough for the moment. Several things I want to note," Deirdre said. "First of all, notice that the physical manifestation of Liam in this *authentic* incident is based on a physical, living, human body. In this case, mine." She turned to face the group. "Despite your experience with other varieties of Netwalk, here's the key difference between Freedom Army Netwalk and the others. *Our technology never developed the ability for Netwalkers to operate independently of a human body.*"

A murmur rose around the room.

Will shimmered into shape next to Julia. He bobbed next to her in a lotus pose.

"So why doesn't the Freedom Army Netwalk allow for such appearances?" Will asked out loud. "Is it a technology issue?"

"No. Philosophic. Freedom Army Netwalkers modify the appearance of their hosts. Generally, it takes special construction for them to manifest themselves independently of their hosts."

"But we see these appearances separate from the body," Melanie said.

Deirdre nodded. "Independent function is limited to specific Netwalkers. It requires using overlaid mixtures of Netwalkers, chained to a primary personality. This strengthens the Netwalker's modification of the host's appearance and can aid the host. The primary Liam manifestation had five overlays. I gained Liam's strength when he manifested. His voice. I was still myself, but with additions to my shape. I'm told that I moved like him."

"What's the purpose of this type of overlay?" Will asked.

"Control of hosts, plus limiting the possibilities of Netwalkers going independent." Deirdre looked down and then back up. "The other factor you need to consider is how the Army views women. Most Freedom Army Netwalkers are men. Most of their hosts are women they control."

Melanie flinched. "Are hosts always women they control?"

Deirdre sighed. "Mostly. Or young children."

"But not all the attackers in the latest Seattle incident or during

Assassination Day were women!" Karl objected.

"Not all those hosts were willing," Deirdre said, her voice suddenly dead. "Some of them are mindwiped. Or young. Very, very young." She gulped. "The Freedom Army Netwalker's host does not have the autonomy that your hosts do. I didn't when I was Liam's host. They also—um—bind you to—" She looked over at Melanie and Melanie shook her head slightly. Deirdre shrugged, leaving the sentence hanging.

Grady nodded. <So they're bound to the gadget?> he texted Marty.

<Yes. Less said about that the better.>

<Understood.>

"Are you saying they use *children* as Netwalk hosts?" Reiko's outrage sharpened her vocal tones.

"In some cases, yes. And as Netwalkers."

<Is that what she meant when she said those boys would have been dead before they were eighteen?> Marty asked Melanie.

Melanie nodded, her lips pressed together in a thin line.

"So how are we getting these appearances separate from the body?" Reiko asked.

Deirdre pulled on datagloves. "The key is in layers." She went to the video from her capture and tapped up electromagnetic signatures from herself, then Liam. Then she tapped out a third signature from Liam. "Here's the pure Netwalker." She pointed to the middle signature. "This is Liam and me together. Compare it to mine."

Murmurs arose. Julia stalked over to the signatures and walked around them, examining them closely, followed by Will. Marty got up to check the three signatures.

"Ours don't look like that," Will said. "I don't mix with Julia to that degree."

"How do you manage to know so much about this process?" Cat challenged.

"As Liam's host, as his comfort woman, as the surrogate who carried his children, I was considered safe enough to be Gina Jeffreys's lab assistant." Deirdre glared at Cat. Melanie cleared her throat and they looked away from each other.

"Then what happened in both Seattle incidents?" Melanie asked.

"No clear host or Netwalker there."

Deirdre acknowledged her with a crisp nod. "Let's look at the first Seattle incident." She snapped up the scene.

Melanie's hand tightened on Marty's as it replayed. Once the red and black cloud was free from the Netwalker host and headed toward Melanie, Deirdre paused it.

"So. Look at this comparison. In the first scene, there's a guise, but no body. That's not a characteristic of a *pure* Freedom Army Netwalk."

"Then is this not a Freedom Army Netwalker?" Cat asked.

"It's a Freedom Army Netwalker—Liam, all right. Details are good. But it's not completely him."

"How can that be?" Grady asked.

"Digital cloning." Deirdre tapped up a signature from the red and black cloud. Then she sorted it out into three more signatures. The last one she towed over next to the pure Liam signature. "Now this is the pure Liam signature. Note the differences."

Ness stirred. "Lots of holes. Not as complete," she said out loud.

"While an *individual* Freedom Army Netwalker cannot function independently apart from a host, without overlays, add in overlays and they can. But they prefer not to do so," Deirdre continued. "Soloing is not a typical behavior for a Freedom Army Netwalker. If one appears independently of a host, then they are made up of overlays." She turned back to the signatures and tapped the first one. "This pattern has at least three, perhaps four more signatures in it. Pieces of signatures, really. Liam is a part of it but not the primary signature—it's one of his clones. The primary signature adopted his guise. A guise within a guise, which also allows us to date it. The primary Netwalker in this signature died after Liam."

"Do we know who the primary signature is?" Melanie asked.

Deirdre swallowed hard. "Tim Conley. My ex-husband. He and Gina were the lead Netwalk researchers for the Freedom Army." She drew a deep, ragged breath. "As for the others, I'm not sure. I suspect that I know who Tim's host is. She's been close to Andrew Stephens, and was the Freedom Army contact in Stephens Reclamation for years. He may not know that. She's been under deep cover and is not under his control."

Melanie nodded. "Her name?"

"Ask, and you shall receive." A faint smile twitched Conley's lips. "Celina Mariskova."

Celina Mariskova? But she was Andrew's Head of Security before—

"Damn it!" Nik exclaimed. "*Her?* Then that means the device—" He stopped.

Deirdre's face was flat and dead as she looked at Nik. "Yes. Celina Mariskova was Tim's comfort woman. And more. There's a reason I was locked down like I was, because I know these things."

"How badly is Andrew compromised?" Melanie asked.

"I don't know." Deirdre drew in a deep breath. "I don't know anything about that part of the operation, beyond Mariskova."

"Is Do It Right compromised in the same way?" Melanie asked.

Deirdre shook her head. "Liam was the most successful incursion."

Data flashed across Nik's eyes. He and Melanie exchanged glances. He nodded, his face sliding into the tight blankness that went along with his black ops role, and left.

Marty shuddered. What had Mel just told Nik?

<What's up?> he asked her.

<Not now.>

"And the others in that signature?" Melanie asked.

"Some poor Army foot soldiers that Tim pulled a song and dance game with, I'm sure. Let's just say that Tim might not have been the most scrupulous of boys when it came to putting this matrix together."

"Can you find out who they were?" he asked.

"Give me a moment." Deirdre turned to the three signatures. "That one's Tim for sure. Dominant one. We already have Liam. And these other two—"

She dipped her fingers into the electromags. Frowned. Peered more intently at them. Moaned. Stepped back from the electromags, shaking her head.

"No. No. Not Robbie and Jerry! *Tim, you bastard! No!*" Deirdre dropped her head into her hands.

Melanie swiftly dumped Bess into Marty's lap and rushed to Deirdre's side, along with Julia and Kathy.

Deirdre looked up, tears flowing, her face tight with anger.

"They're my younger brothers," she whispered, the stark emptiness in her voice striking chills in Marty. *"Tim killed my younger brothers and forced their uploads.* The son-of-a-bitch *killed my brothers!"*

"That's enough for this meeting," Melanie said. "Take a break and come back this afternoon." Voices rose as the team broke into groups, chattering. Some went over to check out the electromags while others left. Grady was amongst the group examining the electromags.

Marty sat where he was, waiting for Melanie. Grady joined him, scowling.

"All right," he said. "I buy it. Melanie knows what she's doing. But damn it, Marty—"

"I didn't know this last," Marty said. "I don't think Melanie did, either." He jerked his head to where Julia, Kathy and Melanie still gathered around Deirdre.

"Pretty damned clear *she* didn't know."

Cat joined them. "Damned convenient that she's got dead relatives in those electromags."

Grady shrugged. "It's the nature of the Freedom Army, Catherine. They eat their own alive. We don't see it in Rio like they do here." He sighed. "Okay. Cat, that transfer you've been asking for? You've got it."

Cat raised her brows. "You find this simulation believable?"

"Given what I know about the Freedom Army, Francis Stewart and —the *thing*—yes." Grady rose, Cat following him. "I want you here because if it's left unchecked, sooner or later the fallout will hit us in Rio. Melanie needs you if these bastards are going this far." He nodded to Marty. "Marty, later. Cat, let's talk about what Trina needs to know to take over from you."

Convenient that it convinced Grady.

<Grady's releasing Cat,> he told Melanie.

<Really? Good. Marty, take Bess back to Brenda. We're going to be here a while. This is—pretty damn devastating to Deirdre. For fucking good reasons.>

<All right.>

<I need you to check on Mom and Sarah, then come back and

review this layering process in more depth with Dad and Ness. We *will* find a way to beat this.>

<And Andrew?>

<I'm—taking care of that. Gotta go.>

She shut off the connection. Marty waited for a moment, but there was no further response. He got up carefully.

Bess first, then Diana and Sarah.

But he had to wonder what *taking care of Andrew* meant this time.

ANGELA FOUND NIK PACKING HIS GO-BAG IN THE ARMORY. HE LOOKED UP at her from working the action of his preferred sniper rifle, face that studied blank he maintained before going out on a black operation.

"It's come to this," she said.

"Not what you think it is," Nik said, examining the action one last time before swiftly breaking the rifle down into travel components. "Mel can't file Contract on Andrew, and he can't file on her. Not while they're both on the Courts Exec." He fitted the rifle components into the compact bag, then picked up a blaster, checking the charge. "I'm supposed to bring Mariskova back. Alive. With as little collateral damage as possible."

"Do you know where she is?"

"Southern California. Something with Stephens, but no longer Head of Security." He packed the blaster. "My job to find out."

She knew better than to ask about his recon. "Alone or with support?"

"I'm taking Karl. I need an Enforcer." He sighed. "Ange, this is locked up in the Courts Exec issues. I can't bring any other support than Karl directly from DIR, because I'm not doing this for Mel. This job is from the Exec. Mel and Andrew were excluded from that vote because of their roles."

"Does that mean you get Exec support?"

He packed five stun poppers. "Can't answer that."

"I'll have a backup team ready to move on your call, just in case. Better to act first and beg forgiveness than pick up the dead."

How long will it take me to get them within close range of Stephens Reclamation in LA?

Angela sent a quick query about her current go-team statuses and locations.

Nik paused in his packing. "I know you will. Thanks."

Her data came back. "I can have a team close and ready within three hours." She sent the order to her closest team.

Nik securely closed the top seam on the bag with a stroke of his index finger. "Good. That should be perfect timing. Depending on what I discover, this could get one hell of a lot bigger. We're moving fast and silent."

"Does Mel know about this?"

"She's the one who informed the Exec about Mariskova's Freedom Army connections. And put me at their disposal. I'm going in under Zoë Wright's orders. Head Judge of the Corporate Courts counts for something."

"Be careful."

He bent to kiss her. "Always," he whispered. "Always and forever."

"Always and forever," she murmured back. "And do it right."

"I will."

One last kiss on her lips, a second on her forehead.

Karl knocked on the doorframe. "Skimmer's here."

"Right there," Nik said.

Karl left. Nik kissed Angela on her forehead again, then each eyelid. "Dream of me, and light a candle."

"I will. Don't forget to dream of me."

He half-smiled, and cupped her cheek. Then he straightened up and strode out of the armory.

Angela waited half a minute, not wanting to see him go.

If I don't see him go, he'll come back safe to me.

An old superstition of hers, but it had held true for over fifteen years together.

Angela shook herself.

Best get prepared for more trouble.

Nik might be going into Andrew's domain under orders from the

Corporate Courts Executive Council, but there was no guarantee that his actions wouldn't trigger a backlash against Melanie and DIR.

MELANIE SPLASHED WATER ON HER FACE AND RUBBED HER EYES, TRYING and failing to avoid looking in the mirror. She almost didn't recognize herself in the strained face still swollen from pregnancy.

What a day already. We still need to put Sarah back together.

And then the Chamber.

"Do you want Bess with me or with Brenda?" Marty asked, standing in the doorway, sleeping Bess in his arms.

"I'll take her," Melanie said. She slipped the frontpack on. Bess stirred as Melanie put her in the frontpack, but calmed with a reassuring murmur from Melanie. She kissed Bess's head.

"You going to be all right?" Marty asked.

Melanie leaned her head against his shoulder. "Yeah. Just—a lot today."

He hugged her. "A lot going on over the past few years."

"And no clear sign of a break ahead."

"We're making progress. Don't doubt that," he said.

"But every time we do something, more problems unfold. Layers within layers."

"I think we're getting to the bottom of it."

"I hope we are," she said. "I want to tackle Sarah tomorrow at the latest. Sooner, perhaps, depending on what happens with Nik's expedition."

"Kathy reports that your mother is showing good recovery vitals. She'll be ready for an intervention soon."

"Good. I want to get Sarah back as quickly as we can."

"I want you conserving your energy as much as possible," he said. "Little things. Floater to the meeting. Sit down when presenting. Snacking and hydrating. Mel, you've just had a tough labor and delivery, and now this. I'm worried—"

"I agree with everything you suggest," she said.

He pulled back, staring at her. "What have you done with my

Melanie? The queen of overdoing is *agreeing* with me? What happened?"

"Marty, I feel it." She sighed. "Having Bess—it changes things. Too much at stake for me to be stupid."

"*Good*. I have a floater on the way for you to take to the meeting."

"Thank you." She left the bathroom and pulled together her materials. Enforcer go-bag. Blinked up her links for the afternoon meeting. Checked Bess's diaper bag.

"Floater's here," Marty said. He took the bag.

She let him take control of the floater. It felt odd to drift down the stairs in the floater, though she had been doing that during the height of her pregnancy complications. But with Bess on her chest, even in a frontpack, what had been normal seemed scary. Melanie tightened her arms around Bess.

Outside, the weather was crisp and clear once again, smelling faintly damp from last night's snow flurries. No snow remained, even in the shadow of the lodgepole and Ponderosa pines, but the damp spots hinted where it had lingered late in the morning.

When they got back to the conference room, about half the staff were already there.

<Tell me what you need to have set up,> Marty directed.

Melanie sent him a schematic of the hologlobe setup she wanted and the brief agenda she'd devised over lunch. Marty settled her in a chair with water bottle, protein drink and energy cubes nearby. It had only been an hour since lunch, but she made herself nibble some cubes and sip on the protein drink.

<When Bess wakes, there's breast milk in a bottle in the bag,> she told Marty. <She doesn't like the bottle, but she'll take it.>

<Good.>

Julia came over to her. "Keeping Bess close?"

Melanie nodded. "For the first few weeks at least. Dad thinks it will help her orient to the differences between virtual and real world, and it feels right to me."

"I agree. Mel, you look exhausted."

"I am," she admitted. "But—" She shrugged. "There's not really an alternative."

"It gets better."

"Thanks."

Marty joined them. "Everyone who can be here is here," he said. "Paula from Rio is down with the flu, and in the infirmary with Diana. Deirdre's in the infirmary helping Kathy and learning more about Netwalk toxin effects. Kathy's linking in through hologlobe. Reiko has a team examining the electromags further."

And Karl's with Nik, somewhere in Southern California, to find Mariskova.

Melanie drew a deep breath. "Let's get started." She noted the attendees. Julia. Cat. Grady. Crispin, an Enforcer prospect who still needed an upgraded chip. Angela. Several new Enforcers from Nagano she didn't know well yet.

"We have a deep virus structure in Sarah that needs to be extracted. It appears to be tied to a certain manifestation we can't mention," she said.

"No doubt about it. It's linked," Julia said firmly. "Melanie, if I may bring it up?"

"Please do."

Julia rose and coded the hologlobe to fill the whole room. Bess stirred slightly as the edge of the globe passed through them.

"We can't do this for long," Julia said. "But Will and I have traced down the keys here—"

Red lights flashed within the globe.

<ALERT!> pulsed in flashing bright red letters. <INTRUSION. INFIRMARY. UNIDENTIFIED NETWALK HACK.>

Not supposed to be happening!

Melanie bolted from her chair. Marty grabbed her arm.

"Mel! Give Bess to me! Free you up."

Melanie paused. Then she slipped out of the frontpack, making herself move slowly and carefully despite her deepest instincts to *run run run now.* She made sure Bess was secure on Marty's chest.

"You and Julia *stay back*!" she ordered. "If this is a Netwalk hack, Netwalkers are most vulnerable. *Don't expose yourselves!*"

"We'll be careful," Marty promised. <*GO!*>

<Love you!> She whirled and ran.

CHAPTER 19

MARTY FOLLOWED CLOSE ON MELANIE'S HEELS.

Julia ran past him. "Julia. No. Netwalkers are vulnerable. Mel says stay back."

"Will wants to be in the middle of this."

"Ness doesn't." He wondered about that. Ness had been aggressive when they were tracking Sarah down. "She's being awfully quiet."

They walked toward the infirmary. Even with the *stay back* order, he was at least going to be nearby.

Bess whimpered. "Easy, there, little girl," he crooned. Her body arched as much as it could against the frontpack's fabric and her feet pushed surprisingly hard against his belly. Marty slowed his steps, and she whimpered louder.

"Julia. Look at Bess." His voice quavered as Bess squalled. <Ness?>

<She's acting like she's tuned into what's happening.> Ness sounded tentative, unsure of herself. <Marty, that hack's inhibiting me. Ask Julia about Will.>

"Speed up and see what she does," Julia said.

As Marty quickened his steps, Bess's wails faded.

"Slow down," Julia directed.

Bess shrieked.

Julia and Marty frowned at each other. They sprinted down the hallway.

"Ness says the hack's inhibiting her. Same for Will?" Marty gasped.

"Yeah."

Bess's screams escalated suddenly.

She knows something. What? Damn it, I wish she could talk!

"What is Will sensing from Bess now?"

"He doesn't want to mess with her. He says it's not something he's felt from Bess before."

"Little girl, what on earth is happening?" Marty muttered to his daughter.

An angry, high-pitched, full-throttle yell was her response.

Little girl, I hope this doesn't mean your mother's in trouble.

WHY THE HELL DO WE HAVE AN INTRUDER HERE! ANGELA OUTRAN MELANIE and her pack of Enforcers down the hallway. *Especially a Netwalk intruder. To hell with this No-Fence crap, if it's not going to be any more effective than this!*

Sounds of screaming, yelling, breaking and shattering noises came from inside the infirmary as she slid to a stop. She tried the door. Locked. Angela pressed her lips tightly together, quickly using her shortcut access codes while considering a list of possibilities.

If Conley did this—

She forced the door open and plunged in. Sergio, her Number Two in Nik's absence, followed. A screaming, unidentifiable fury reached for her.

Someone hit her hard mid-thigh, carrying her out of the reach of that *thing*, pulling her away as Sergio dodged in the opposite direction.

"That one's gone fucking *insane!*" Deirdre gasped as they rolled to a stop. "Been trying to keep her from escaping. Netwalker gone crazy in her!"

Angela focused on the enraged woman—Paula from Rio Bravo. She had been down sick from the flu. One of Grady's people that they hadn't had time to fully vet before the conference. "Freedom Army?"

Sergio was in full duck and dodge mode to evade her.

We can't do shit against this thing until Mel and her crew gets here!

"Yeah," Deirdre gulped for air. "Miller's protecting Diana. Got her in the back bathroom. She's not doing well. Sarah wants out. Miller's sedating Diana to keep Sarah from playing. Damn it, wish I had that implant. We need fucking Enforcers! Hey!"

Deirdre grabbed a piece of lamp that lay on the floor at her feet, then hurled it at the shrieking woman, hitting her dead center and distracting her from Sergio.

Good aim.

She turned on them.

"You've gotta keep throwing shit at her!" Deirdre yelled across the room at Sergio. "Distract her, keep her off of us!"

Sergio pulled out his weapon.

"*Don't!*" Deirdre screamed. "Miller tried that! Shooting her makes that thing in her worse! It just sucks up the energy!" She scrambled away from Angela and grabbed up another chunk of broken metal.

The woman focused on Deirdre as she slid under a bed. She dived on top of the bed and swiped at Deirdre underneath. Angela threw another chunk of lamp at the fury, distracting her long enough for Deirdre to skid out on the other side. The woman turned away from Deirdre and toward Angela.

The door slammed open.

"*Stop*!" Melanie paused in the doorway, using her full Enforcer voice. Cat slid in next to Mel.

The fury paused, Melanie's voice turning her away from Deirdre. It hesitated for a moment, studying Mel and Cat.

"You two get out of here once we're clear!" Melanie commanded. "Where's Kathy and my mother?"

"In the bathroom," Angela said, taking advantage of this moment to ease in that direction.

If I can help there—

"You need me *here*," Deirdre said. "I know what the hell this is."

"You don't have an implant. You'll just be in our way," Melanie said, focusing on the fury moving slowly toward her.

"Then get me something that'll work like an implant!" Deirdre snapped.

"We don't have one here!"

"Miller was getting ready to fit me with something!" Deirdre grabbed a chunk of metal, and hurled it at the woman, triggering another wild flurry of action as the woman lunged for Deirdre, chasing her around the room while Melanie and Cat jumped away from the door and into the room, slamming the door shut behind them.

We need Kathy out here.

Angela took advantage of the chaos to sprint the remaining distance to the bathroom. Locked. She tapped in her access code. The door gave way and she dodged in. Kathy slammed her against the wall, kicking the door shut as she shoved a blaster against Angela's head. Angela forced herself to freeze as Kathy stared hard while keeping Angela pinned against the wall.

"It's me!" she snapped.

Recognition softened Kathy's hard glare. She released Angela and stepped back.

"Sorry. No way to tell when you burst in."

"She okay?" Angela asked. Diana slumped unconscious against the wall. A purpling bruise marked one cheek. Scratches lined Kathy's face. "You okay?"

"Yes, and yes. She fought me. Sarah's trying to break out. Gotta keep Diana unconscious until we can deal with her." Kathy sighed and sagged against the wall, securing her blaster, dialing it back to *stun* from *kill*. "Diana got me." She tapped her face. "Not Sarah or *that* thing." She jerked her head toward the outer room. "No toxin."

"What the hell happened?"

"Dunno. I was preparing to fit Deirdre with a headset when Deirdre hollered that Paula was changing shape. Then Paula jumped Diana. Deirdre got them separated without getting scratched. I tried to shoot Paula with a stun charge. Didn't work. Just made her stronger."

"Yeah, Deirdre told us."

"Good. Deirdre started throwing things and distracting Paula long enough to let me get Diana in here." Kathy frowned. "I had to hit Diana to do it. Sarah was controlling her. Without Deirdre, there'd be a bigger mess."

"Mel and her crew are here now."

"Good. What the hell does she want us to do?"

"Mel wanted us out of the way, including Deirdre. But Deirdre's hollering for an external implant simulator. Says she knows what to do."

Kathy's eyes narrowed. "That's what I was getting ready to fit. I can get it. You stay with Diana, monitor her, make sure she stays unconscious. Sarah can neutralize the sedative, so Diana's gotta be kept sedated. I'll get the external to Deirdre."

"Wait a minute! What the hell are you asking me to do?"

"Not that hard."

"Damn it, I don't want to risk killing her!"

"Look," Kathy growled, "this isn't that bad. It's some of the stuff we're designing for space station work for anyone to use, damn it!"

"What the hell do I do, then?"

"Here." Kathy guided Angela to Diana's side. "Monitor her breathing. You can do that visually. Take this." She thrust a scanner into Angela's hand, and took hand and scanner and pressed it into the crook of Diana's elbow. "Keep it here, like this. That line—" she pointed to a blue line on the scanner's screen— "marks the sedative level. Don't let it go over that line—" she pointed to a red line. "That means she's had too much. Hit her with the red side of this—" she pushed an injector into Angela's free hand. "Then you'll have to monitor that the level doesn't go too low. That's this line." She pointed to the green line on the screen. "If and when the blue line goes close to or below the green line, you use the green end of the injector to bring up the sedative level. You may be dancing back and forth for a while, but for God's sake, don't let her wake up! You'll be fighting with Sarah!"

Angela nodded, gritting her teeth. "How much do I give her?"

"It's preloaded. Don't worry about it. Repeat this back to me—"

"No need. I've got it. If the blue line goes over the red line, use the red side on Diana. If it drops near or below the green, use the green end."

"Correct." Kathy slid out the door.

Angela focused on Diana, staring at the scanner's screen.

I hope to hell I don't end up killing her with this stuff.

DAMN IT, THERE'S TOO MUCH GOING ON TO THROW A SECURED HOLOGLOBE!

This Netwalker was like the one controlling the false Renee. That memory kept Melanie cautious as they jumped around the room, avoiding the constantly shifting Paula. She didn't need another dose of toxin.

At the moment, things were quiet as they warily eyed each other. No one was ready to brave the teeth and nails of *this* one. Sedation darts weren't working—yet. Why? Direct blows—Deirdre dodged in once to clobber Paula, hard enough that it should have knocked her out and freed her Netwalker.

That hadn't worked either.

Melanie wasn't certain, but she suspected that, from the way that Paula/the Netwalker were moving that the Netwalker was completely in charge of the body and Paula was gone. Dead? Unconscious?

No way to know until they could manage to subdue Paula/the Netwalker.

The bathroom door opened, and Kathy sprinted out, pulling the door shut behind her.

Must have left Ange with Mom.

Kathy's movement spooked the Netwalker/Paula toward Sergio. The dance of run, throw, duck, started up again as Kathy ignored them all, fumbling inside a compartment near the bathroom door, swearing loudly.

Then Kathy yelled triumphantly. "There! I *know* I dropped that damned thing in here when things went weird!"

What the hell is she doing?

Kathy backed out of the compartment with a fistful of wires and a headset.

The external implant for Deirdre!

Bess's screams echoed faintly outside the door.

Damn it, I told him to stay back!

Melanie threw something at the Netwalker/Paula as Kathy ran to Deirdre, then spent moments ducking her until Sergio got her attention.

"Stop." Deirdre's voice crackled with command as she broke away from Kathy, the external implant wired up. She walked toward the Netwalker/Paula, not wavering. "Leave her."

The Netwalker/Paula growled at Deirdre, but didn't move.

It's reacting to her. Sensitive to her tones? Something from Freedom Army Netwalk?

"Come out from her," Deirdre ordered. "In the name of the Prophet, I command you!"

Interesting.

The Netwalker didn't move as Deirdre approached. Melanie shook out the trap door chip from her sleeve pocket and activated it.

"Leave her, now!" Deirdre slapped the Netwalker/Paula. Bess's screams drew closer as Paula fell. A gray and red cloud rose from the collapsed body.

"Get back before it attacks you!" Melanie yelled at Deirdre.

As the cloud dove toward Deirdre's face, she crossed her wrists and raised them high to protect her face, not flinching back.

"In the name of Liam, I command you!" Deirdre snarled at it. "In the name of Joseph, I command you! Back!"

The cloud stopped short of Deirdre.

Code phrases. Very specific references to specific people. Wonder if this is a stock formula or if she has to see the Netwalker to know which names to use?

"Back!" Deirdre ordered, taking a step forward. The cloud retreated.

The door opened. Marty and Julia slipped into the room. The Netwalker shied away from Bess and Marty. Deirdre moved with the cloud, pressing her advantage.

Melanie caught Marty's eye and nodded toward Deirdre. He nodded back and moved into position, five feet away from Deirdre, matching her shoulder-to-shoulder so that the cloud was at the apex of a triangle between them. Melanie placed the cage behind the cloud, where the Netwalker would go if it kept retreating.

The cloud attempted to dart away from the cage. Deirdre herded it back. Finally, it was safely inside the chip. Melanie tapped the chip shut.

Bess stopped screaming. Melanie hurried over to Marty and Bess.

"She started howling about the time you would have gotten here," Marty said, an apologetic tone in his voice. "She pitched a bigger fit every time I slowed down. Julia saw it. And Will," his voice quavered. "Will felt what Sarah did about Bess. Not Ness. I don't know why."

"Give her to me," Melanie whispered. She wanted to hold Bess.

Bess whined as Marty eased her out of the frontpack, her eyes on Melanie, straining toward her mother.

"There, there, little one," she breathed as she wrapped her arms around her baby. "It's okay. It's gone."

Bess burrowed against Melanie.

What does this mean for our daughter?

Her legs wobbled underneath her. Melanie sagged against the wall, sliding to the floor and bringing her knees up to cradle Bess.

"Mel, we *have* to deal with that virus in Sarah, now," Kathy said grimly. "She's fighting too hard to get out. We can't take any more chances."

"I know." Melanie leaned her head back against the wall, still rubbing Bess's back. Her head felt heavy, so heavy. And it ached. "Can't do it right this second. I need rest. Plus I want Deirdre by my side, chip implanted."

"We can't wait long enough to implant Deirdre," Kathy insisted.

"Then tune up her external. I'm not doing this without Deirdre to help deal with that Freedom Army element in the virus."

And Nik's mission is likely to blow up on me at any moment now.

"We can rig up a reliable headset in five hours," Marty said. "Remember, the Nagano team is here. Between Julia, Reiko and Will, we have enough tech firepower to do it."

Deirdre limped over and dropped on the floor next to Melanie. "This external doesn't work as smoothly as I'd like. It kept cutting out."

"And you still went after her?"

Bold.

Deirdre shrugged. "What options did I have? We needed to take care of that Netwalker. Big bluff on my part, but it was right."

"The words?"

Deirdre nodded. "That Liam and Joseph invocation is good.

Joseph's always reliable with someone from the Army, and I went out on a limb with Liam."

"Who is Joseph?"

"An early aide of Francis Stewart. I don't know too much about him outside of Army stories we told the kids. He did some pretty amazing things during the Disruption, if any of it can be believed. Died a martyr, killed in Charleston."

Charleston again.

"I need to know more about Charleston," she said. "Sounds like I've messed up by not looking into it before now. When we're done with this, record it. Unless it's something I need to know right away."

"You'll be okay," Deirdre said. "There are moves that go with the invocations. It shouldn't take too long for you to learn them."

"Good." Melanie summoned the strength to push herself back up the wall until she stood, still holding Bess. "Get that headset tuned and tweaked. Rest for a short period after. And then we're tackling that virus in Sarah."

After that, we're shutting down Tim Conley and this Liam clone or clones.

No way was she going to present Bess to Gizmo before this business got settled.

It's all tied together. I know it.

CHAPTER 20

SHOWTIME.

Marty walked from Auxiliary Lab One to the infirmary.

Angela stood guard outside the infirmary, Sergio with her.

"Good luck," she said.

"Thanks," Marty said.

Inside, Kathy frowned at a screen showing Diana's vitals.

"Mel and Deirdre are right behind me," he said. "Mel wanted to pick up Bess."

Not something I agree with, even if Will and Julia think it's okay. But it wouldn't be the first time I'm wrong and they're right. And Mel could use any help from any source. Even Bess.

"How's Diana doing?" he continued.

"Better. Awake in forty minutes. We'll let Sarah out in thirty, before Diana's fully awake. Better to deal with just Sarah rather than the two of them together."

Marty nodded. "Sounds good to me."

Even before her soft <*love*> in feeling rather than words brushed his awareness, he sensed Melanie's presence on the other side of the door. Something new. When the doors opened, he realized she broadcast a defensive presence in virtual.

<Very wideband,> Ness said. <This *is* new.>

<Bess's presence, you think?> he asked

<Absolutely. Bess gives her more defensive strength. Could also be the augmented effect from Deirdre. They nick together nicely as cooperative Enforcers, better even than Mel and Cat.>

Good.

Melanie peered at Diana's monitors.

"Chip Deirdre as quickly as possible after we resolve this situation with Sarah," she murmured. "We need her functioning with a real chip as quickly as possible."

"We have to take her to the Mountain to do it."

"Any reason we need to stay here much longer?" she asked.

"Not really."

"So once we get Sarah dealt with, then we're going back home. It's time."

"I agree. What's your plan?"

Melanie nodded to Deirdre. "She'll lead in capturing the Netwalk virus once we get Sarah out of Mom. It appears to have a strong Freedom Army element. Deirdre *knows* those connections better than I can. It will take me a solid week of research to understand their complex mythology, and I'm never going to have the awareness of it that she does."

"All right. Give me the details, Deirdre," he said.

"We start by breaking out the parts from Sarah," Deirdre said. "The virus is a Freedom Army overlay on the National Security template."

Cat joined them. "Sorry for being late. Grady and Trina needed my help with a transition question."

"I'll brief you while Deirdre briefs Marty," Melanie said, stepping back and pulling Cat into a corner.

"What's the order of action?" he asked Deirdre.

"Melanie brings Sarah out. I'll peel off the viral overlay. Melanie puts Sarah back inside Diana's chip to recharge and rejuvenate. You'll work with Melanie; Cat works with me. We'll trap door it. Ideally, I'd be working with Melanie instead of Cat to catch that Netwalker. But Cat's not as strong with Sarah as Melanie is, and we need a strong Enforcer on Sarah. I need an Enforcer with me who's run trap door chips. We've tried it, and I can't manipulate the trap door chip with an external. So it's me and Cat to trap that Netwalker. Or at least hold it until you and Melanie are done with Sarah."

Kathy looked up from releasing the restraint field on Diana. "You're cutting it close," she said. "We need to start *now.* Diana's getting close to waking up and Sarah is *definitely* stirring."

<Ready?> Marty asked Ness.

<As ready as I'll ever be. Want me out?>

<Might be a good thing. Falcon guise.>

His shoulder tingled. Then Ness clutched his shoulder, in falcon shape.

Melanie faced Diana's prone body, raising a hologlobe to encompass the entire laboratory. Melanie took them virtual, smoother than she had earlier, but still abrupt.

One moment, things were quiet. The next, Sarah was *there,* in full predatory mode, a skeletal form with glowing red eyes and fingernails, white hair hanging lankly from her skull, shards of an old winter stealthsuit clinging to her body. Marty tensed. He spotted the shadowing of another form over Sarah, but couldn't make out the shape.

Deirdre stepped forward. Sarah screamed and swiped at her. Deirdre dodged Sarah's moves deftly, dancing away while chanting phrases Marty couldn't hear over Sarah's shrieking. They squared off, Deirdre focusing intently on Sarah, Cat at her side.

The shadow peeled off of Sarah. He heard Melanie gasp and focused more directly on the shadow. A faint visage of Liam sneered at Melanie.

Damn son-of-a-bitch, always popping up.

But there was an even wispier second shade, one that looked like a young teen whose face contorted in agony. This silhouette reached out toward Deirdre, moaning.

"Robin!" Deirdre groaned. "Damn you, Tim, Robin of all people! He didn't deserve this!" She gulped, then she and Cat moved in, blocking Marty's view.

Sarah has to be our priority.

His hand brushed Melanie's arm, drawing her attention back toward Sarah. Luckily, Sarah was immobile, looking confused and half her previous size, even though she still appeared in predatory mode.

"Sarah." Melanie's voice was calm, matter-of-fact, lacking any note of Enforcer compulsion. "You need to go back into the chip and recharge. Reintegrate."

"What's happened?"

"What's the last thing you remember?"

"Liam. Going after my host!" Sarah's eyes darted around the room, paused. Marty turned. The Liam guise capered around, evading the trap door chip being wielded by Cat.

She's not as adept as Mel at setting the trap doors. We need to practice that skill more.

"*No*, Sarah." The first notes of compulsion crept into Melanie's voice as Sarah bristled, focusing on Liam.

Ness stirred restlessly on Marty's shoulder. She let out a sharp, piercing cry that drew Sarah's attention away from Liam.

"Let *them* deal with Liam," Melanie commanded Sarah.

"I need to stop him!"

"You need to get back inside your chip!"

"He's got—"

"Nothing!" Marty snapped, moving up next to Melanie. Ness launched off of his shoulder, hovering between Sarah and Liam. "He gave you a virus through your last physical contact with him. *It's not the real Liam. It's a Freedom Army guise.*"

Bess bellowed a full-throated cry.

"What's *she* doing here?"

"She has an effect on you," Melanie said sharply. "And on those rogue Netwalkers. Damn it, you need to get *back inside*!"

"I *need* to help *you*!"

"Not like you are," Melanie said firmly. She crossed her arms over her chest, murmuring words Marty couldn't hear. Ness flew closer to Sarah. Her shape changed, back to her normal self, except for her shattered, bloody head.

Ness's original guise, the one she'd first formed after her death.

"*You* need to stop *this*!" Ness snarled at Sarah, inches from Sarah's face.

"Who the hell do you think you are?" Sarah growled.

"I was good enough to develop this Netwalk program for you

when we were both alive!" Ness yelled back. "And I'm telling you now, you've been contaminated! If you don't go back in, we'll have to kill this version and restore you from backups!"

"I don't *have* a backup right now!" Sarah retreated from Ness. "I'll lose it all and part of me will be in the Chamber!"

"Then get your ass back into that chip! We have to fix you, and reintegration is where it starts." Ness reformed into the falcon, keening threateningly.

"I need to touch him," Sarah whimpered. "I really need to touch him. Something's pushing me."

"You've been infected," Marty said. "That's a compulsion that must be part of the infection. Let us deal with the guise. Then we'll look at your pattern, after you've had a chance to reintegrate. Reintegration may fix things by itself."

"Sarah." Diana croaked. She raised herself off her bed onto one elbow. "Back inside. Do it. Now. Or I'll crawl off of this bed and rip your head off myself to force it!"

"You would, you bitch. All right, all right." Sarah slowly made her way back into the chip by the slowest method possible.

It wasn't until she winked out that Marty turned his attention back to Deirdre and Cat. Melanie now managed the trap door chip. Sarah's disappearance didn't stop Bess's shrieks. If anything, her screams had escalated. Did she recognize the Liam guise as a cause of trouble?

<I'd hold back,> Ness advised him. <If three Enforcers can't catch him, then we won't. They got the second shadow but this Liam guise is tougher.>

<You could chase him in.>

<I'd prefer to avoid contact. That's the infection source, not the other one.>

Melanie gestured to Deirdre and Cat. She sounded a high A tone. First Deirdre, then Cat, matched her tone.

The guise froze in place. Melanie deftly flipped the chip's cage over it. The cage contracted, slowly oozing back into the chip.

"And that is *that*," Melanie muttered, closing up the trap door and handing it off to Cat. "Put the chip in that safe over there. Marty, you have a lot of analysis work ahead."

"Don't I know it."

Melanie turned to Deirdre and Cat. "You *must* practice with that trap door. We can't have you dancing around like that. The movement has to be decisive and determined. Too damned many of these Netwalkers out there for you to take this much time trapping them. I want you doing twice-daily practice drills."

They nodded.

"Deirdre, was that a pure Liam guise?" Kathy asked.

"I'll have to see the electromag to be sure. I'm betting that this Liam appearance is just a guise for the overlay, an overlay over the actual overlay." Deirdre swallowed hard. "The actual overlay was a partial of my brother Robin. He had just enough of himself to give us a hand."

"I wonder if that Liam guise is the virus itself," Kathy said to Marty.

"It is," Ness confirmed.

Melanie looked up from comforting Bess, now out of the frontpack. "Agreed. That secondary shadow went into the trap door easily enough."

"He *wanted* away from that existence," Deirdre said. "God." Her voice caught and she buried her head in her hands.

Diana groaned from the bed. "What the hell is going on?" she asked tiredly.

Melanie handed Bess to Marty. "I'd better brief her on what's happening."

"Don't take too long. You need rest."

"I'm not sure I have the time."

"You do. You will. Brief your mom, then find me in your offices. I'll brief you with what I've found out, and then we are *both* taking time off. We've taken care of the immediate problem."

She studied his eyes, then nodded, slowly.

Plus there was the question of whatever Sarah's backup issue was.

It's tied into the Chamber. What exactly the hell is this Chamber?

All they knew about it so far was from what Deirdre Conley had told them. And vague hints from their Netwalkers that it was not a pleasant place. This latest revelation from Sarah made it even more worrisome.

Mel has to go to this Shadow Chamber to deal with the Gizmo-Liam-Francis Stewart link. With Sarah and probably Bess. What the hell is she going to find there? And how the hell does Sarah function without effective backups? Reset to zero? Have to fix that somehow.

I am going to do my damnedest to figure that out. I'm not letting any of my girls go in there with so little information.

To his surprise he realized he included Sarah in that determination.

"NO WORD FROM NIK YET," ANGELA SAID. "IT'S BEEN FOUR HOURS. AND our strike force isn't picking up anything unusual on their scanners. If it wasn't a Courts operation, I'd send them in closer to get more info. I'm afraid Nik and Karl have been captured. Can *you* get any information?"

Melanie sighed and shook her head. "I'm embargoed from any data on this op, Ange."

I don't like it. But no options, no choices.

"Wait a minute." Angela raised one hand. "Some sort of action. *Finally*! Our skimmer's just taken off from Southern California, under pursuit. Action at last! Sending our team in to watch their backs!"

URGENT. URGENT. URGENT, her screen flashed, ID blocked.

"I have a blocked ID message," she told Angela, quickly tracing the ID. "Andrew."

"The shit has well and truly hit the fan," Angela said.

"I'll link you in." Melanie popped it open, her gut tightening.

"What the fuck are you doing, Melanie?" Andrew shrieked, hair disheveled, eyes wild. "WHAT THE GODDAMN FUCK ARE YOU DOING!"

"Slow down, Drew! What are you talking about?"

"YOU KNOW DAMNED GOOD AND WELL WHAT YOUR PET ASSASSIN IS DOING! I WANT CELINA BACK! NOW!"

"Take a deep breath and calm down, Andrew! It's not my operation, it's fucking Zoë Wright's operation! The Courts are in charge!"

"And it's *your* hit man leading it," Andrew snarled. "I'm filing

Contract, precious sister of mine, I'M FILING CONTRACT UNLESS I GET HER BACK!"

"I CAN'T DO ANYTHING ABOUT IT!" Melanie screamed, projecting an Enforcer tone, enough to startle Andrew into silence. She took a deep breath, watching Andrew closely as he swallowed hard, shaking his head. "Andrew," she said. "The Courts conscripted Nik for this operation. *It's a Courts operation. It's connected to Seattle. She's the host of the Netwalker enabling these attacks.*"

"Mel, she *can't* be a Netwalker host." Andrew's voice cracked. "She's my consort now, not my Security. And she's pregnant."

Holy Mother of God, no wonder he's so angry.

"Drew, I'm sorry. We have evidence showing that she's been involved with the highest circles of the Freedom Army for some time now."

"Why—what—that can't be," Andrew spluttered.

"Direct from Liam's former host. Celina was Tim Conley's comfort woman and now she's Conley's host. Our source couldn't—wouldn't talk because the—thing—has direct linkages into them. I still don't entirely know how the hell it worked, but they were blocked down pretty tight and couldn't talk. Just like we are through the Exec, only worse."

Silence. Andrew stared at Melanie.

Deirdre was right. He didn't know. If he did he'd be all on offense, all bluster and anger, not a reaction like this. Have to get him on our side. Maybe we can use him to turn Mariskova. That's more data on the Army.

"The—*thing*—is involved, Drew. Somehow, the Freedom Army has managed to link into the *gadget.* Their Netwalk isn't like ours. It's something else. And it's bad. It's a breach that could blow up on all of us. I had to report it to the Exec and—well—you see the result. I'm not being told just how bad it is or what the Exec plans to do."

How much dare I tell him of what I do know?

From the sick look on Andrew's face, it was clear he understood the implications.

He deserves to know it. He's on the Exec too.

Melanie chewed on her lower lip, thinking it through.

"Charleston all over again. Only it's *me.*" Andrew dropped his head into his hands. "God, how long do I have before I'm the target? Mel, is it Mom *or is it the gadget doing this?"* He flinched.

"I don't know. I think what you just said is possible. That scares me. Drew, work with me. I can help."

Andrew looked up. He looked at Melanie, opened his mouth, then startled. "Just a minute." He leaned forward to toggle something out of sight and studied it. Then he sighed and slumped back in his chair, shading his eyes with his hand, shaking his head.

"I can help," Melanie repeated.

"I think I need it," Andrew said in a very small voice. "I just got a file from the Courts. Mel. Please. Tell me before I look. How bad is this? I know it's bad from the coding, the codes say that there's sanctions against me, but how bad is this? *Another woman connected to me that the gadget's exploited.* God, how is that damned thing getting its claws into me so that I keep hooking up with Freedom Army women?"

She knew the feeling well, too damned well.

"Drew, here's what I know. Celina is linked to a virus in Liam's guise that took Sarah down. The linkage—may not be entirely of her own volition. We're still trying to figure out how—the gadget—influences women with Freedom Army connections." Melanie swallowed hard. "Including me, because of Liam."

"That fucking deep?"

"Uh-huh. From our source's information, Tim Conley was a lead Netwalk developer for the Freedom Army, along with Gina Jeffreys. Conley's dead. Somehow he, Liam and Stewart have found a way to access a level in—*it*—called the Shadow Chamber."

"Oh God," Andrew groaned, resting his forehead on his hand, still shaking it back and forth slowly. He looked up. "Mel. I had no idea. Honestly. *I had no idea about either Celina or Renee."*

"I didn't know about Liam's Freedom Army connections either."

Andrew swallowed. "Point taken. Thank you. I don't know if anyone else on the Exec would have bothered to tell me straight. Not even our mother." He slammed his hand down hard on the arm of his chair. *"What the fuck do I do, Mel?* She's pregnant—this is real, I go to her appointments with her—and—well—I love her. Or at least I thought I loved her. If it's real and not a manipulation. And I thought she loved me. Now I wonder if it was love or if it was manipulation. Getting a handle on—the thing—through my biological ties. This—connection. That's not something to play with. *What the fuck do I do?"*

Think. This gives you a chance to mend things with Drew.

Melanie tapped her fingertips on her chair arm.

"Nik's taking her to the Mountain," Angela interposed. "Private message."

"Why there?"

"Diana. Her orders."

"What game is our mother playing?" Andrew asked. "Or—is the *thing* directing her? I've had some doubts about her behavior lately."

"Yeah. Me too." Melanie sucked in her lower lip. "She's not doing this with Sarah's advice. Not this soon after Sarah went in the chip to recuperate. That worries me. Ange. How fast can you get us moved to the Mountain with a full working lab staff? Not Corporate staff; that'll take too long and we don't need them immediately. That can be a standard transfer."

"Six hours for everyone."

"How about the Enforcer core?" Melanie scowled. "Damn it, I need Sarah. That means Mom as well. How can we transport Mom while keeping her from meddling?"

"Core group can be there in two hours. Puts us there just before Nik's skimmer. Transport your mother under infirmary protections."

"Who's controlling the Mountain, my staff or hers?"

Angela half-grinned. "Right now, it's her staff. That can change in twenty minutes."

"Make it happen. Put it out that we're going back to the Mountain because we're concerned about security here after the attack on Sarah."

"Your mother will wonder about the rush," Angela cautioned.

"Let her! I'll tell her on the way over. Secure the labs. Let's yank that Netwalker out of Celina and cage it. Then go after Tim Conley and Liam in the Chamber. Our labs, our staff, *our Netwalker skills,* can do it while keeping Celina and her fetus alive. We'll need Sarah's cooperation, at the minimum, and I hope we can get Mom's. If not—" Melanie shrugged. "We'll find a way."

"You're pulling a rebellion on *Mom? You?*" Andrew laughed bitterly, but he sat up, looking hopefully at Melanie.

I'm gambling on Sarah's response.

"This particular response on Mom's part doesn't make sense, unless she's operating under someone else's direction. It would make more sense to bring Celina to the Ranch and secure her here, where we're already meeting. We have experience with these situations."

"It must be the connection to—*it*—that has her spooked." Andrew leaned forward. "You said this was a Zoë Wright operation?"

"Yes."

Andrew nodded. "I had some dealings with Wright when Sarah was alive. I didn't know much about the doodah at the time, but Wright was very touchy about anything that came close to it. Mom tends to line up with Wright." He sighed. "They're all edgy about anything close to the thingamajig."

"As we learned in Charleston."

"We have control of the labs," Angela reported. "No big deal. Your mother's staff was covering for Courts Security, but they were happy enough to hand over authority with no argument."

"Then let's get with it," Melanie said. "Drew, I'll give you a timeline when I know what we're up against. I promise, we'll do our best to keep Celina safe—as long as she doesn't do something stupid."

"I'm worried about her doing just that," Andrew said. "Mel, she's ex-Federation military. That's why—well, I would never have thought of her as Freedom Army."

"Send us every bit of information you have on her."

"There's a few holes," Andrew cautioned. "Nothing unusual for anyone with her background in these times. Damn it, I should have checked her better."

"I didn't know Liam was married when he was engaged to me."

"He *what?*"

"Sarah knew. I thought you did."

Andrew shook his head. "Peter knew a lot he didn't tell me. Same with Sarah."

"And they pitted us against each other so we didn't have the time to compare notes to find things out," Melanie sighed. "Not that we'd have discovered this. Liam's secret was apparently kept safe at the highest levels of National Security."

Andrew shook his head. "This implication of the Freedom Army being heavily involved with—*it*—scares the crap out of me, Mel. You don't know—" He shook his head again. "I have to talk to Celina. Have to decide how close I'm keeping her if she's that tied to them."

"Until we break her linkage to Tim Conley, we might not know how deeply involved she is," Melanie cautioned. "Even at that it could take time." She considered and rejected telling Andrew about the Jeffreys boys and their connection to Deirdre.

Maybe later. Let's see how this shakes out.

But for now, she needed an ally against Gizmo and possibly the Exec. Andrew was her best bet, with her mother an uncertain player.

God, I've got to talk to Sarah. Privately. Maybe she knows Mom's game and the degree to which Gizmo is influencing things.

"Mel, when you get Celina in the lab, let me talk to her before you start working. It *might* keep her from fighting you too hard."

"If you think it will make a difference, then sure."

Andrew was quiet for a moment. "If she knows I'm aware that she's there and that I support what you do, it could help. Mel, remember she's ex-Federation military," he repeated.

"And Freedom Army. High level. I'll remember that, all right."

"Just—keep her safe. Keep the fetus safe. I need that child. You know why." Andrew gulped. "More than that—I need *her*." His voice cracked on the last three words.

"We'll do our best, okay? Drew, I need to go. We'll link you in once we get things started."

"Good luck."

"Thanks."

Andrew faded out of her screen, leaving only Angela, who raised her eyebrows at Melanie. Melanie raised a hand to stop her questions.

"Ange, I can't talk about it right now. The *thing* is an issue."

Angela pursed her lips, then nodded. "Agreed. Dealing with that has to be a priority."

"Get us to the Mountain in one piece, Ange."

"I can do that. And—there, there might be some other options. More later."

Angela winked out, leaving Melanie alone with her thoughts, staring at the hologlobe.

Is Gizmo Francis Stewart's tool or is it something else? And what does Mom know that she won't share?

"YOU'RE GETTING INTO BUSINESS YOU DON'T UNDERSTAND!" DIANA snapped.

How much do you know about Gizmo, Mom? Really?

"The only way to safely get that Netwalker out of Mariskova is with my help," Melanie said, keeping her voice level. "Our experience with Deirdre Conley shows that you're not going to get any useful information out of Mariskova until then."

"The Courts need an interrogation sooner."

"We're not getting in the Courts' way. We're making their job easier." Melanie hesitated. Dare she share Andrew's news?

Might make her more amenable to us working with Mariskova first.

"Your team isn't completely secure."

"Neither is yours, if Andrew's team is compromised at this level!" Melanie snapped. "Can you be sure of *everyone* on your team?"

Her mother hesitated, a troubled look on her face, enough to assure Melanie that she had made a point.

"Mom," she continued. "Andrew's frantic. Celina's pregnant with his child. She's his consort. We have to take this into consideration. He's fulfilling the Courts mandate for a biological heir—and she's the mother of his child."

"Are you sure?"

"Nik did a bio screen once his team secured her," Marty said. "She's pregnant. 97% probability that the child is Andrew's."

"Then that puts a different light on things." Diana scowled. "I wish he made a better choice." She leaned back. "He's introducing outside elements I'd just as soon not get reinforced."

Like Freedom Army bloodlines?

Deirdre Conley wasn't in this skimmer, but Melanie could imagine her wry comment. Further talks with Deirdre made it unequivocally clear that Francis Stewart had been seeking to breed specific traits in his descendants and followers, and left his program in the hands of multiple Freedom Army leaders.

And then there was the Gizmo Protectorate breeding plan. For lack of a better phrase, that had to be the motivation for demanding biological heirs from the Corporate leaders involved in the Courts.

Or is that really a Francis Stewart plan?

"Mom, unless the Courts lay out a detailed breeding plan and offer specific desirable mates, we can't pick and choose which consorts are acceptable." *And was this match with Celina Andrew's idea, Gizmo's idea, or Francis Stewart's idea?* "Quite frankly, if that is the case, I can't support it."

"You're right, when you put it in those terms. Melanie, I just wish you'd talked to me first. You're taking an awful lot upon yourself."

"I know," she said. "But when it comes to these situations—we're the experts. Not the Courts. Not the Exec. *Us.*"

"I'll give you that. But, next time? Don't go unilateral on me."

"I'll try not to do that," Melanie conceded. "But no promises."

Diana winced but said no more.

CHAPTER 21

Maybe this will be the end of the Liam mess.

Marty waited for Celina's arrival with Melanie and a Security squad. Nik was first out. He waved to the Security squad and sent them in.

How many people do they need for one woman? She can't be that bad!

Ex-Federation military, though. And she had been Andrew's Security designate for Gizmo.

Mel's taking this seriously.

That was sufficient cause for caution.

Melanie tensed up, then strode forward, suddenly pulling up every ounce of Enforcer presence that she could summon.

Then again, maybe this Celina is *that bad.*

A group of six Security exited the skimmer, clutching a writhing, screaming figure. The remaining Security held their weapons locked on her. Karl looked over at them and shook his head.

<She's been like this for the last hour,> he said to Marty and Melanie.

<Is she sane?> Marty asked Melanie.

<Damned if I know. I'm calling Andrew, *now.* If anyone can snap her out of this, it's him!>

Melanie snapped up a hologlobe.

"Mel, I don't know—" Nik said.

The hologlobe shimmered. Andrew projected in the screen.

"Cee. CEE!" he yelled.

Celina paused for a moment before continuing to struggle.

"I'm shoving you in her face," Melanie said. She grabbed the globe's tether and dragged it over to Celina.

Andrew yelled again. This time she stopped, twitching all over.

"Cee. Cooperate with them. They're trying to help."

"I don't believe it!" she yelled. "That's not you!" She tried to wrench free, but the team closed in tight around her, wrestling Celina still.

"CEE! Bankdagistan!"

Another stiff, twitching pause, followed by resumed struggle.

"That's the code word to override her programming!" Andrew groaned. "She's flooding with Berserker! I thought we pulled that implant!"

"Drew, what the hell is that?" Melanie snapped. "I thought—"

"Medical implant," Andrew growled. "Military issue. Proprietary to Stephens. Mel, it's *not a goddamn wireless.*" He gulped. "It's a drug implant. Standard Federation military issue. You can't do a damn bloody thing if it's overriding her programming. But it was supposed to have been pulled out of her six months ago!"

"Then what the hell do we do?" Melanie stepped back from the raging Celina. "Get her to the labs," she said to Nik and Angela. "Julia's ready for the prep. If she's got that damned drug flooding her system, who knows what it's doing to her!"

"Here's the file," Andrew sighed. "Mel, this is proprietary."

Melanie tugged on a dataglove and reached inside the globe, yanking the link directly from Andrew. He shied back and raised his eyebrows as she tossed it to Marty.

"Here you go. Get this to the labs. And Andrew, *that* ability is proprietary."

Marty missed their further exchange as he sent the data to Kathy and bolted for the lab. He skidded inside ahead of the team dragging Celina.

"Good God, this drug is a mess," Kathy said as he joined her. "Implant?"

"Andrew told Mel it was supposed to have been yanked. He used a code word on her that didn't work."

"I'm familiar with that class of med," Will said. "If she's blowing through a code word from a trusted associate, either she doesn't trust him anymore or else the implant is flooding her system."

Chaos erupted as the team hauled Celina in. Kathy tightened her lips and picked up an injector. "Just give me an opening," she snapped at Nik.

Nik nodded. He shoved between two Security, providing a steady backing for Kathy. Kathy darted in and out. Celina kept struggling. Then, suddenly, she sagged, collapsing against the hands holding her tight. Kathy gestured toward a gurney. As the team eased her onto it, Kathy and Reiko strapped Celina down. Marty joined them.

"That *might* give us five minutes," Julia cautioned, looking up from the screen she was scanning. "We have to pull that damned implant first."

"Don't just strap her. Use a blanket suppression field," Marty said.

"Have to pull the implant first."

"Then get it done," Nik said. "We've been feeding her sedatives like it was candy. She throws them off fast."

"We don't dare give her much more," Kathy growled. "She's way over what her tolerance should be."

"When she crashes it's going to be big," Marty said.

"If she doesn't freakin' *die*," Kathy said grimly.

Melanie, Deirdre, Cat and Diana joined them. Melanie wore her Courts blacks.

<Why the blacks?> he asked Melanie.

<Andrew's suggestion.> Melanie scowled. <He thinks Celina might react better if I have this on. And if the gadget's involved—I should have been wearing this when we broke Deirdre's links. It might have gone better. So what do we have here, Ness?>

<Ugly, ugly, ugly. I see almost a dozen overlays.>

<A dozen?> Melanie scowled. "A dozen?" she repeated out loud. "Deirdre, I thought you said the upper limit was six!"

"Obviously Tim's upgraded the tech," Deirdre said. "Or else those aren't true copies but viral copies."

"You'd better go work it out *now,*" Julia said. "Will, either sleep or go with them. I can't have you active around her. Reiko, let's pull that damned implant and figure out how soon it will clear her system."

"How many of us do you need here to help?" Marty asked.

"No Netwalkers. No hosts. Every damn Security I can get and at least one Enforcer."

"I'll stay," Karl said.

"You heard her," Melanie said. "Meet in Auxiliary Lab One to start with. I plan to pull a subgroup to Aux Two. Dad, you need to rest in my chip?"

Will switched to his snowboarder guise. "Only if I get stressed. You good with that?"

"Have to be," Melanie said flatly. "Come on. Let's switch to Aux One and Two."

"Julia, how long do you need?"

"Fifteen minutes. Maybe less."

"Okay. Everyone *out.*" Melanie caught Marty's eye. <You supervise Aux One.>

<Why?>

<I'm pulling Cat and Deirdre, maybe Dad, into Aux Two. The three of us are going to be the leads on this one.>

<Where's Bess?>

<Nursery, with Brenda.> Melanie frowned. <Bring her close, Marty. The feedback might set Bess off. And if—the thing—is targeting her, one of those overlays might be programmed to attack her. Keep her close for safety's sake.> She sighed. <I don't want to take her virtual again. But I'll do that if I have to, to keep her safe from a Gizmo attack.>

<Got it.>

But, like Melanie, he hoped it wouldn't come to her taking Bess virtual.

MELANIE GLARED AT THE ELECTROMAGNETIC SIGNATURES. TWELVE overlays, all Liam. All viral infections.

I still want to know why six was supposed to be the max when we've got twelve here!

A hand touched her shoulder. "Fascinating," Deirdre said. She traced a repetitive pattern on the screen. "That's an important piece right there. He's upgraded. That's why there's twelve overlays instead of the typical five. I didn't know that was fucking possible. Aha. The extras are Dialogue targets. Explains it."

"What are you seeing?" Cat looked over Melanie's other shoulder.

"Twelve overlays. Five targeted to Netwalkers, the remaining seven to Dialogues. That's how he's getting around the usual limit of six overlays. Sneaky bastard."

"How are we going to get this damned Netwalker locked into the chip and kill those fucking overlays without infecting us?" Melanie asked.

"Let me look at it," Deirdre said. "I'll need your seat, might have to manipulate the image."

Melanie slid out of her seat and let Deirdre focus on the electromag reading.

"Fuck!" Deirdre slammed the table with her right hand after only a few moments of scanning. "I can't believe it's so damned simple and we haven't seen it yet! We have to trap door chip each and every damned overlay individually. Not just Tim."

"Given the infection possibilities, we're gonna have to move fast," Melanie said. "Maybe faster than four Enforcers can move."

"Let me think," Cat said. "Can non-Enforcers work the trap door chips? That would give us Marty, maybe Julia and Reiko to help, and would cut down on the number of overlays apiece we have to chip."

"Chips have to be run by Enforcers," Melanie said.

Too bad because she's onto something. But it's a higher-level skill, not a Dialogue skill.

"If we could just peel them off, there's a way to do it, I know that's how Tim's been setting up his matrices." Deirdre chewed on a fingernail, then winced and dropped it from her mouth, wiping the blood from her cuticle on her jeans. "No. More I think about it, may not work. I don't have access to Tim's software. Okay. Hit Tim first. Then the copies. He's their brain. Take him out, they'll be easy to handle."

"But how do we keep them off from us and away from Tim without getting infected ourselves?" Melanie asked.

Deirdre snapped her fingers. "Can we run globes inside globes?"

"Well, yeah, that's how we're going to have to start out, because Celina's in that security globe—" Melanie's voice trailed off. It *could* work. "Globe the copies? That could work. But we have to move fast. Who's going to keep Tim distracted?"

"Marty, Reiko and Julia can throw globes, right?" Deirdre asked.

"So can Nik and Angela. And my mother," Melanie said.

"There we go." Deirdre nodded. "Get everyone we can in here to throw globes and englobe every damned one of those copies. Piece of cake. I'll take Tim on, with you and Cat as backup. Get Tim chipped, then we'll chip each overlay in its own globe."

Melanie shivered. She wasn't convinced that the process would be that simple.

"Have a solution yet?" Marty asked.

Melanie jumped. She hadn't heard him come up behind her. "We think we have a method." Briefly, she sketched their ideas.

Marty nodded. "Throwing globes right away can work. We'll have to move fast." He sighed. "Julia wants you to know that we need to get that Netwalker out of Celina as soon as possible. That Berserker drug has been augmented from the data Andrew sent us. Not a Stephens upgrade. Too crude."

"Deirdre, how likely is it that she's under her own control and not under the same sort of—*influence*—you were?"

"Can't answer that for certain until Tim's out of her and that tie is broken. Her link's likely to be as strong as mine was. It will try to push her into self-destruction."

"Five minutes," Melanie said. "Get what you need together, because this is going to be crazy."

And that is the understatement of the year.

THEY HEADED FOR THE MAIN DIALOGUE LAB. MARTY TOOK A DEEP BREATH before stepping inside.

Celina lay under a blanket suppression field like the one they'd had on Deirdre after her capture. She no longer screamed but glowered at them, muscles tense, fists clenched, still straining against the suppression field. Sweat trickled from her forehead, even though they kept the lab cooler than the rest of the building.

Julia was nowhere in sight.

Probably running blood tests.

Marty broke away from Melanie to examine what was in the infusion line and at Celina's stats.

The feed was a mixture of glucose, an anti-corticosteroid, and a quick-acting blood pressure medication. Marty checked Celina's stats. Sky-high blood pressure.

Drug effect?

"Marty." Julia came up next to him. "Good. You've seen what I'm doing. She's under the influence of a corticosteroid-based accelerant that jumps her metabolism way up high. That's why she was tossing off those sedatives. We'll have to watch for a crash in an hour, now that she's off that med. I'm doing my best, but I can't see any way around that."

"Touchy."

"Any idea of how we're fighting this Netwalker?"

"*She* has a plan." Marty jerked his head toward the other side of the lab, where Melanie contemplated the electromagnetic signatures that Julia's team had taken.

"Okay," Melanie said suddenly. She stepped back and turned, half-smiling as her eyes met Marty's gaze. "Everyone into Aux One. Briefing. Final plan, modified."

Brenda followed them into Aux One, Bess in the frontpack. Melanie pulled it on, securing it and tapping both datasuit and frontpack protections onto high.

"Here's the process," she said. "The whole room will be in a secured hologlobe. Datasuit protections set on high. Julia, Marty. Sleep Dad and Ness. Lock them down *hard*. Extra datasuits on you two."

"Already done," Marty said. Julia nodded in agreement.

"Mom," Melanie sighed. "I need Sarah's help. We have to go to the Shadow Chamber at some point, and I want Sarah at my back."

Diana shook her head. "You can't seriously be thinking of going there! Especially not with Bess!"

"She doesn't have a choice." Sarah popped out, in her younger guise. "I'm the only one who can safely take her there."

"That's a stupid choice!" The fear in Diana's voice sent prickles down Marty's neck.

Sarah shook her head. "Once I had the time to process, I put things together." She gave Melanie a sideways glance. "That virus is a nasty one. Your data worked quite nicely as an inoculant."

"Was I right about the location?"

"Yes."

"Good." Melanie looked away from Sarah. "I left an inoculant file available for Sarah to review once her recharge was done. It included questions I had about the Chamber, and the incidents at Seattle and the Ranch."

"Inoculant file?" Julia asked.

"Self-repair instructions," Sarah said. "As well as data. Embarrassing. I should have seen that I was being lured into the Chamber without safeguards."

"Part of the viral influence," Melanie said. "Hopefully the self-repair instructions helped."

"Combined with the data, they certainly did. I'm still cringing about losing that much control. It won't happen again."

"Do you think they managed to lure more Netwalkers in the Chamber?"

"Wild ones, possibly. Energy storage." Sarah grinned briefly. "Something I would have done for recharging, before I had a host. Only there's no way Stewart would have let me do it."

"Then it shouldn't be too bad."

"I wouldn't rush into that conclusion," Sarah cautioned. "There's good evidence that your blown Dialogues ended up in the Chamber, as well as the mindwiped Netwalker hosts like the Seattle attackers and that Paula girl."

"Wait a minute," Marty said. "Diana, what do *you* know about the Shadow Chamber?"

"Enough to know that I don't like anyone messing with it," Diana snapped. "Sarah, did you tell her where it is?"

"She knows," Sarah said. "She saw it when she first got sworn. Didn't you, Melanie?"

Melanie nodded.

Gizmo. The Chamber's in Gizmo.

Marty shuddered at the realization.

"Yes," Melanie said in a low voice. "I think you know too, Marty. The pieces fit together."

"So how the hell are we attacking it?" he asked.

"First, we evict Tim Conley from Celina. He'll bolt through virtual back to the Chamber. Sarah, Deirdre, Cat, and I follow him."

"With Bess?"

Melanie sighed. "I keep going over the scenarios. If the gadget wasn't involved, then she would be okay here. But the device—" her voice trailed off. She shook herself. "She's safest with me if something happens." Her voice quavered, then grew firmer and more confident. "She'll be more of a hazard than a help to you, and at higher risk from harm from one of those copies."

Marty wanted to object, but she was right.

Just—both my dear ones. Together, if something goes wrong.

"Okay. Get us set up," Julia said. "The faster the better."

They returned to the main Dialogue lab.

Melanie, Cat and Deirdre gathered around the head of Celina's bed. Celina watched Melanie warily.

Melanie half-closed her eyes, lips moving slightly. The blue light shimmered around her and Bess. She lightly rested a hand on one of Celina's, and the blue light flowed around the two of them. Celina's hand twitched in a futile attempt to pull away. A distressed expression crossed her face.

"Stand down," Melanie murmured. "Bankdagistan. Ultra."

Celina's eyes widened. Her body relaxed. She swallowed and tried to speak.

"Good girl," Melanie said. "Don't try to talk. Don't fight us. We'll get you out of this and back to Drew in as good a shape as we can."

Celina started to nod. Then, mid-nod, her body tightened. Her face twisted into a snarling rictus as her body slammed against the restraints. The blue light faded.

<Damn it! Fucking gadget overrode her will! She responded to the second-level code Drew gave me!> Melanie's lips tightened.

Deirdre adjusted her headset. Then she placed her hands on Celina's temples. Celina writhed and tried to look back at Deirdre, her upper body arching and straining against the restraint field. Her eyes widened.

Marty rolled globe generators into his hands.

"You'd better get back," Melanie said to Julia. "Who knows how fast these overlays are going to be moving? Hosts need to be further away. Less of a target."

Julia nodded and moved next to Marty. Like him, she had globes in her hands, ready to throw.

<Think we're safe?> she asked.

<Don't want to push it. Don't want those viral overlays in me,> he answered.

<Same here. Luck!>

"Out with you, Tim Conley and company!" Deirdre commanded, her voice acquiring a deep tone he hadn't heard her use before.

A scowl twisted Celina's face. Her features changed to those of a handsome blond man. She struggled harder than ever against the blanket field. Kathy whirled to adjust the controls.

"Damn it!" Julia snarled. "Look at those monitors! Deirdre, get him *out* of her or he'll kill her!"

"I know that!" Deirdre snapped back, keeping her hands snug against Celina's temples while the woman bucked and writhed. "Mel, Cat, I need help to push them out! They won't go!"

Cat edged in next to Deirdre and wove her hands through Deirdre's arms to place her hands over Deirdre's. Celina's body tightened and jerked against the blanket restraint. Incoherent babble poured out of her mouth. Deirdre and Cat struggled to keep their hands together on her temples, their bodies pressed tightly together as she writhed. A faint flash of blue light winked in and out, Melanie swearing softly as it failed.

"He's pushing her to crash," Julia groaned. "He'll kill her!"

Melanie slid in between Cat and Celina, keeping herself low. Then she placed her hands over Deirdre's and Cat's.

"Get *out*," Melanie ordered. Marty saw the flashes of Dialogue overlays in her eyes, mirrored in Deirdre's. Faint blue light shimmered around Melanie, Deirdre and Cat's hands. He tensed, ready for whatever could happen next.

"Tim Conley, out of your host!" The three chorused together.

The blond man's face faded into gray and blue clouds that rose from Celina. She sagged against the bed. Smaller blobs of red and black clouds spread from the larger gray and blue cloud.

Globe them! Now! Marty threw both of his globes, doing his best to aim them as precisely as possible. One of his globes missed, and he dove to the floor to retrieve it.

"Cat! Deirdre!" Melanie yelled. The secured hologlobe shimmered into place, cutting off Bess's screams. Marty froze.

Oh god, they're off and I can't help—

"Marty!" Diana bellowed. He twisted just in time to see the red and black globule heading for his face. He fumbled in his sleeve for another globe, but it wouldn't come loose. He batted frantically at the globule, trying to avoid its track, but it kept moving directly toward his temple.

A globe exploded around it. Karl tossed him another.

"Thanks!" Marty yelled back.

No time to worry about Mel.

But even as he spun to find another globule and englobe it, a faint undercurrent of worry pulled at him.

Trust Mel. You've got to trust Mel.

Except that Mel currently was trusting Sarah to keep her safe.

<This way!> Sarah led them after Tim Conley. Unlike their previous chase, there was no hesitation in the pursuit.

They flashed by the place where Conley disappeared the last time. He paused for a moment, but Sarah shoved Melanie and the shrieking Bess forward. Conley bolted off again as Melanie came close to him. Bess quieted.

<A portal into the Chamber,> Sarah snapped. <We don't want him to use that one. Some portals are weaker than others. That one puts him in a place of strength.>

Just what the hell is this place?

The virtual environment around them changed, background changing from primary reds and blues to paler pastels, magenta and blue.

Sarah braked as Conley picked up a wave of speed. <Too fast. He can zip in but we can't. It will attack us if we go in too fast.>

<How does that work?> Deirdre asked, pushing a compulsion tone.

<Modulate,> Melanie warned as Sarah started to react. <Sarah, tolerate. Deirdre, modulate. Too forceful.>

<Sorry.>

Sarah settled with a shiver, almost like a hen ruffling her feathers into place after dealing with an annoyance. <We zip into the Chamber too fast without the appropriate coding and it triggers automatic protective measures.> She pointed into the distance, as Conley disappeared into a pulsating magenta wall. <The fact that he can dart in like that is not good. Means he's native there. I've only seen Francis Stewart do that. Until now.>

<When?> Melanie asked.

<When I was still an independent Netwalker,> Sarah said. <We have to move very carefully. Be aware. It's very disassociating, Melanie. Your Courts blacks will help you orient. Trust them.>

<What about Bess?>

<I'll protect her.>

Something about Sarah's tone set Melanie on edge. <Sarah, you'd better not be playing games!>

<I'm not certain we can completely pull him out of Gizmo. But we can disable him, both him and Liam. That'll leave them confined in there, like Francis Stewart.>

<Just what the hell is that about?> Deirdre demanded.

<They can't escape as long as the Chamber is barricaded. That's the rationale for the Gizmo Protectorate,> Sarah said. <And it worked...until Stewart's followers started the initial attempts to rescue

him. Which led to the development of Dialogue and Netwalk. No time for details now.>

<So how do we proceed?> Melanie asked.

<I lead. Melanie, bring up your blue light as an offensive weapon. I'll keep Bess from blocking it. We'll walk up to that barrier and you'll touch it—and me—to the barrier. We'll trace an opening, then go in.>

<And from there?> Cat asked.

<We find Conley. Then Liam.>

<If we can trap door them, we'll trap door them,> Melanie said. <If not, Sarah, you've said we can disable them. How?>

<There's a code-based protocol. Whatever you hear in there, whatever you see, do not give consent to anyone other than me! Don't let them touch you. Melanie, focus on me. Cat and Deirdre, focus on Melanie.>

<Okay.> Melanie invoked her blue light. It wavered. She took a deeper breath, remembering to channel the light through her suit links. The light steadied, forming into a rapier. Sarah nodded, transformed into a black cloud, then settled on the tip of her rapier. Melanie looked back at the others, then patted Bess's frontpack.

Onward.

They stood in front of the magenta wall. It throbbed in a heartbeat rhythm. She reached forward and traced a line down it.

The world exploded around her.

Bess shrieked.

Melanie abruptly spun end-over-end, oriented only by the blue rapier with something tugging at it. It took both hands to hold on to the blue rapier.

<Deirdre! Cat!>

No response except a cacophony of hysterical laughter around her. Bess screamed louder. Faces flashed by, familiar faces including her father and Ness.

Why are they in here?

Melanie tugged harder at her rapier, fighting to get control back. It broke free from whatever tugged at it and she fell, endlessly fell. At least she could keep the presences back by brandishing the rapier.

<SARAH!>

<You don't need to shout. I'm here. Visualize a floor! USE YOUR SUIT CODES!>

<*Authenticate!*> Melanie subvocaled to her suit command channel. She landed hard, crouching on a marble surface reminiscent of the floor in the Corporate Courts meeting chamber. She rose slowly, turning in a circle. Netwalkers surrounded her, *hordes* of wild Netwalkers. One dared to swipe at her. She smacked it with the rapier and it zapped away, screeching. Bess screamed louder and louder.

Oh God, what is this doing to her? Wait. If I use a soothing tone on Bess—

She hummed. The Netwalkers encircling them backed away. Melanie became aware that Cat and Deirdre clutched at her ankles. As the Netwalkers moved back, Cat and Deirdre stood, moving in close, their shoulders touching hers.

<Now what, Sarah?>

<We can't do anything until we get rid of this mob.>

<How do we do that?>

<Like this.> The black cloud unwound itself from the tip of Melanie's rapier. Sarah took shape in her predator form. The Netwalkers scattered, malignly whispering as they retreated a safe distance.

<Follow me.> Sarah stalked off, not looking to see if Melanie and the others followed. They approached an opaque chamber. Sarah traced a complex circuit pattern on the door, then tapped out a code on the keypad that appeared in the center of the circuitry.

<You'll have to authenticate it for optimal entry,> Sarah told Melanie.

<What is this?>

<This is the Shadow Chamber itself. The only way to access it is with a Netwalker who has access to these codes. I didn't think anyone had the ability to jump in here without the codes except Francis Stewart himself. Obviously, I was wrong.>

<All that out there wasn't the Chamber?> Deirdre asked.

<Oh, it was. Just the outer Chamber.> Sarah fixed Deirdre and Cat with a stern look. <I can't protect all of you. Melanie and Bess only from here on.>

<Who's protecting them?> Melanie asked.

Sarah whistled. A fainter, shadowy version of herself twisted into shape in front of them. <My last adaptation.> She stepped forward and touched her hand to the shadow self. Teal lights flashed between them. The shadowy shape grew more distinct, but a black cap edged with teal rested on her head. <She's been briefed,> Sarah said. <She won't be reliable for long. None of the Shadows are. But that black cap tells you she's a copy and not my current version. As it starts to fade, though, *don't trust her*. Fading means the compulsion I put on her is going away.>

<Sarah, just what the hell is this?> Melanie asked.

<One of the failed copies of myself that got reset every time I have to reintegrate. I can't back myself up. This is the closest I can get—and I don't dare come here alone because my copies will take me over! That's the risk you take every time I reset. Now. Melanie. We don't have much time. Let's go!>

<You sure about this?> Deirdre asked Melanie, while Cat looked around them nervously.

<I don't see an option.> Melanie nodded to Sarah. <Let's do it.>

<Come on.> Sarah took her hand. <Like this. You have to authenticate it with your Courts links.>

Melanie rested her hand on the door, half expecting a Gizmo-like jolt. Instead, she felt a brief sting. The door slid open. Sarah took them through. Light changed abruptly from the brightness outside the Shadow Chamber to darkness, lit only by gelatinous forms that changed shape constantly. Melanie didn't realize she'd hesitated until Sarah yanked hard on her hand.

<*Don't look,* damn it!>

Melanie shook herself. <Thanks.>

They marched on, Sarah holding Melanie's hand. Melanie kept her other hand on the frontpack, murmuring softly to Bess, projecting warm, cuddling, comforting images. Bess's emotions were stronger than ever, fear predominating.

Mama's here, Mama's safe, Mama's protecting.

Bess echoed those emotions back, calming.

<Keep projecting those thoughts,> Sarah said. <Makes it easier for me to sort through the personalities.>

<Why are so many Netwalkers in here? I didn't think we had that many!>

<More of them than there was the last time I came in. Partials. Many, many partials. But close enough to complete versions that it's hard for me to sift. Someone's been dragging them in for recharging. Or making overlays. There's a lot of flaws.> Sarah stopped. <There.>

Melanie flinched as Liam's shape suddenly rose in front of them.

<How convenient for you to bring your baby, Melanie.> He expanded in size, laughing. The laughter distorted into funhouse echoes.

<Oh, knock it *off!*> she snapped, twisting the final word. <This is ridiculously beyond clichéd, even for you!>

Liam deflated. <Now Mel, I thought you'd appreciate this.>

Bess suddenly shrieked. Melanie whirled, dropping Sarah's hand, raising the rapier high just in time to deflect Tim Conley's grabbing hands. She slashed and lunged at him, driving him back. Conley grinned at her and she whipped around, expecting Liam to be sneaking up on her.

She was alone. No Sarah. And the other shapes began to press in. Melanie spun slowly, rapier at alert. She shook out a trap door chip. The next time she spotted Conley she flung the trap at him. He neatly deflected it, sending it spinning back at her, mouth open to gobble her up.

<Two can play this game!> he crowed.

She slashed desperately at the trap door. It disintegrated.

What the hell?

No chips, then. Something grabbed her and Melanie screamed as she swatted at the form wrapping around her arm.

<STOP THAT.> Sarah's tone verged on mild panic. <It's just me!> She took her predatory shape. <Your coat stings me when you react like that!>

<The chip doesn't work!>

<I saw that! Tones! Let's disarm them and get the hell out of here before Gizmo itself wakes up!>

The escalating panic in Sarah's voice triggered matching fear in Melanie, even as she felt a rumbling, stirring presence.

Gizmo.

She began a faltering high A.

Light flashed. Heavy rumbles vibrated through her head and body. Gizmo emerged, the size of a soccer ball. As the spiky sphere expanded, Melanie quavered, struggling to keep the note pure. Jagged red lines darted toward them, aiming at Bess's frontpack.

Melanie intercepted the red lines with her rapier. It exploded in her hand, white-hot needles of pain jabbing up her arm and throughout her body. She focused all of her energy on keeping the white-hot needles away from Bess, visualizing herself as a shield wrapping around her daughter.

Bess. Protect Bess. Mama. Bess. Protect.

<Get that tone back!> Sarah screeched. <Trust your coat, it's activated to deflect all but the worst. Get that tone back! *It's our only way out of here!*>

Melanie picked up the tone. Sarah vibrated it, augmenting the tone.

Tone. Tone. High A. She couldn't tell what was Bess, what was Sarah, what was her. Tone. Conley and Liam jerked back, diminishing until they were plastered against one wall of the Chamber, chains appearing on their wrists and ankles. The wild Netwalkers flowed toward Conley and Liam, surrounding them protectively.

<There. They won't get out of here very quickly. Hmm. I know of yet another trick.> Sarah plucked two buttons from Melanie's sleeve.

She glided toward Conley and Liam. The wild Netwalkers swarmed toward her, until Sarah flailed about her with a button in each hand. She brushed against three Netwalkers. They screamed, then disappeared.

Liam flinched as Sarah stuck a button on his forehead. Conley tried to evade Sarah but she shoved it hard into his face.

Sarah growled as she returned, spreading her black cloud over Melanie's right hand. <Bastards. Mess with *my* family, will you? That's the price you pay!>

<What did you just do?>

<A gamble. There's—more to this coat than you've been told. I

wasn't sure they had given you the full deal until now. We better get going. Move. Slowly.>

<What direction?> Melanie asked.

<Just move. I'll guide. Keep up the tone!>

Bess. She could identify Bess. But the alien awareness that was Sarah filled both of them. Melanie clung to Bess, doing her best to sort Sarah away from Bess. Step. Step. Step.

Don't look at anything. Move and let Sarah guide. Tone. Tone. Bess. Protect Bess.

<We have to close the door,> Sarah said. Melanie blinked, realizing they were outside of the inner chamber.

<How?>

<Tone. Let me guide your hand. Can you bring up the blue light again?>

Melanie tried. Nothing.

<No.>

<This'll have to do.> Sarah sounded resigned. <I should have expected it. They've tweaked the coat design from what I last knew. You lost just enough strength when I took those buttons—and Bess's blockage. Has to be the tone.>

This time the high A came easily.

Melanie traced marks on the magenta membrane. It throbbed under her touch—*Gizmo.*

<It's awake!> Sarah yelled. <It's hunting Bess. Have to get you two out of here!>

They hurried to rejoin Cat and Deirdre. Melanie jerked to a stop, unable to take one more step.

<You have to lead us back,> Cat said.

<I can't move.>

At least not without releasing my protection of Bess.

<She's maxed out her virtual energy,> Sarah told them. <You have to carry her back.>

Cat and Deirdre hurried to her side, lifting Melanie in their bridged hands. She sagged against Deirdre. <Which way do we go?> Deirdre asked.

Melanie looked around, unsure of herself.

Sarah clucked impatiently. <Hold out your hand.>

Melanie obeyed. Sarah changed into the black cloud and wrapped herself around Melanie's hand. <Point. That'll lead us where we need to go.>

Melanie pointed. But no sooner had they started to move than Bess stirred uneasily. A few more steps and Bess whined. Melanie dropped her hand, scanning around. She didn't recognize the data lines here.

Bess is right. That's not it.

She pointed in a different direction, only to find the same thing. On the fourth try, things finally started looking recognizable. Bess settled.

They finally returned to the familiar lab. Melanie slid into her body and made sure that Bess returned into hers. She gulped deep breaths of air. Tired. So damn tired. As she started to rise, her knees wobbled and she sank down hard on the chair, listing sideways.

Marty grabbed her. "That's it. You're down for the count."

Melanie shook her head. "Can't. Debrief. Too important. Where the hell is Sarah?"

<In the chip,> Sarah answered. <We're all drained.>

"Celina?" she asked Marty.

"Sleeping off the meds," he said tersely. "She's clear and lucid. Talked to Andrew. Karl broke her free of that Gizmo link, using what we discovered from breaking Deirdre free. Andrew will pick her up tomorrow."

"And the overlays?" Deirdre asked.

"Chipped. Karl handled it."

"Good." Melanie wanted nothing more than to curl up with Marty and Bess and go to sleep. But there were things to manage first. "We have one hell of a Gizmo problem, and we need to make damn sure that Andrew's on our side."

"But first you're going to rest."

Melanie shook her head. "Get me some Burnout. I need to talk to people. We need to debrief what happened."

"Mel—"

"*Bess is at risk from the gadget.* We *can't* wait."

"She's right," Deirdre sighed. "The device is stirring."

"I agree," Diana said. "Sarah showed me what happened. We can't wait."

Marty stood, lifting Melanie and Bess in his arms. "At the very least, we can finish this debriefing with Melanie in bed."

"That's doable," Melanie agreed.

"Fifteen minutes," Marty said firmly. "Give me time to get Mel settled and order up our dinner. Working dinner in our suite."

<And after that, you're going to sleep,> he said firmly to Melanie.

She laughed. <Dearest, no argument from me. But. Please. Bring every extra piece of electronic protection you can conjure up. I'm afraid we're going to need it.>

<Your father and I have already started. Celina told us enough to give us an idea of what's going on. Now. Rest.>

CHAPTER 22

It's taking longer than usual for the Burnout to kick in.

Melanie leaned back against her pillows, eyes closed, uncharacteristically quiet for having swallowed a Burnout tab five minutes earlier. Marty frowned, chewing at the inside of his cheek as he studied her.

<Okay to come in?> Kathy Miller asked.

He blinked up the time. Fifteen minutes on the mark. Still no food for Mel.

<Come on in,> Melanie answered, pushing herself up.

Kathy carried a tray. Julia and Diana followed her. "Security handed off the tray to me. Cat and Deirdre will be here shortly."

Melanie grabbed her sandwich and gobbled it.

Bess squealed, her eyes focusing on something to his side. Marty looked to identify the source of her focus. Will hovered nearby, wearing his Buddhist robes and gesturing. She waved her hands, motions mirroring Will's.

<Interesting,> Will commented to Marty, using the tightly focused link he'd demonstrated earlier. <She's reacting more quickly than Zack did. More virtual exposures earlier on, but she's not afraid of me. He was at first.>

<I guess that's good,> he said.

<May reflect her more extensive virtual experience.>

Deirdre and Cat entered the room. Both Enforcers had the same drawn look as Melanie.

Virtual effect of the Chamber?

"Sarah, it's time," Melanie said.

Sarah slid out. She wore the white stealthsuit but it was in one piece, and her features shared the same drawn, strained visage as Cat, Melanie and Deirdre.

"It's still looking for her," Sarah said. "Can't you feel it?"

Melanie tightened her lips. "Sarah, I'm so wiped out that Burnout's not working right."

"We have to stop it!" Sarah's voice rose to a tinny screech. "If it gets Bess, it'll have enough power to blow the Chamber safeguards!"

Melanie dropped her forehead into her hands. "My head's splitting—"

"That's the fucking gadget." As Sarah spoke, she shifted into predator mode, the white stealthsuit transforming into shredded bits as she spoke. "God damn it, Melanie, get that much-touted energy of yours up and running! Your baby is at risk!"

"I know it!" Melanie yelled at her. "I feel it pounding in me! Sarah, what the hell did we bring back with us? I thought we got rid of that virus!"

Marty's arms tightened on Bess, pulling her tight to his chest as a dreadful thought occurred to him. <Ness, is Bess clear?>

<It's not Bess.>

<How do you know?>

"Stop it!" Deirdre growled, pitching her voice carefully. "Sarah, pushing Melanie harder isn't getting us anywhere!"

Sarah's eyes flashed red. She transformed into a black spear hurtling at Deirdre. A forest green shield formed in Deirdre's hand, blocking the spear. It shattered into shards, scattering over the floor.

Sarah reformed in predatory guise.

Wow. And Deirdre is doing this with the headset, not a chip. My God, we've found someone almost as strong as Mel. What will Deirdre be like with a chip activated?

"You *will not* do that," Deirdre said in a low voice.

Sarah raised her arm and Deirdre crossed her forearms protectively across her chest, glaring at Sarah. She took one step toward Sarah, faint dark green shimmering around her hands. Black borders oscillated around the edges of Sarah's white stealthsuit and lined her glowing red eyes.

"*Stop.*" Melanie's voice rolled with authority. "Sarah, damn it, did we bring a virus back with us? Stop wasting time playing dominance games."

Sarah and Deirdre didn't move.

"*Sarah.*" Quicker than he expected, Melanie leapt between Deirdre and Sarah, one upraised palm thrust toward Deirdre, the other toward Sarah, pushing at both of them. She glowered first at Sarah, then at Deirdre. "Both of you. *Stand down now.*"

Sarah dropped her hand. Her shape softened into her normal formal guise.

Deirdre sighed. She uncrossed her forearms and stepped back.

"Thank you," Melanie said. She dropped her arms and sank onto the end of the bed. "We can't afford this crap. *No more fighting.*"

"Who the hell does she think she is?" Sarah snarled.

"She's an Enforcer!"

"She's not sworn—"

"She is to me." Melanie's voice brooked no argument. "And you are overreaching. Knock it off, Sarah. *Now.*"

Sarah bristled. Deirdre straightened up.

<The device is playing everyone to get an open pathway to Bess,> Ness told him.

Marty forced a cough. That drew three sharp glares from Melanie, Deirdre and Sarah. "Look, Ness just told me that the thingamajig is pushing all of us in order to get a pathway to Bess. So *stop the damn fighting.*"

Melanie sighed. "Thanks, Marty. Ness is right. Sarah. Deirdre. Look at it."

Silence. Then Sarah, softly. "She's right. Damn it, that thing knows just how to play me!"

Deirdre looked up. "I see it, too. Stupid stuff."

"It's pushing at me," Melanie said. "If it wasn't for my Courts blacks—" Her voice trailed off.

"Meanwhile, I'd like to know what happened," Marty said. "Did you capture Liam and Conley?"

Melanie retreated to her mound of pillows, pulling her knees to her chest. "No. We did not. But we locked them down. For the moment they're out of play. This problem is that damned gadget."

"What's going on with the gadget and Bess?" Diana asked.

"It's hunting Bess," Sarah said.

"And I'm feeling it," Melanie said in a low voice, resting her forehead on her knees. "One hell of a headache."

"Oh, no," Diana said. "That reaction from—the device—is *not* what we expected."

Melanie lifted her head wearily. "Then just what the hell *did* you expect from my child, Mother? God knows, you've been pushing me to reproduce for how many years now? *Why is my child so damned important?*" She hurled a pillow across the room. "I go through hell to bear this child, and now this fucking *thing* wants her for some sort of weird torture or power or what? Damn. It. And damn you, for *putting me through this without telling me everything I need to know first!*"

Marty shuddered at the bitterness in her voice. "Mel, you're giving into it again."

"I'm *tired.* I want to *rest.* I've just had a baby. I've been spending the entire time since she's been born protecting her. And now—'the reaction is not what we expected'—is *not* what I want to hear, not under the witches brew of hormones and gadgets and Burnout and exhaustion!"

Diana paled and backed away from the baleful glare Melanie gave her.

"Melanie—"

"What does take to keep my child safe?"

"I've been through this myself," Diana said in a placating voice. "Mel, you're not the only one who's had to go through this. I—"

"Don't give me that bullshit." Melanie's voice rose to a hysterical pitch. "*What does it take to keep my child safe from Gizmo*?" She moaned and clutched her head.

Marty slid close to her. Cradling Bess in one arm, he pulled Melanie close. She buried her head in his chest, shaking. Her tears dampened his shirt. Bess whimpered along with her mother.

"That's enough, Diana," he said firmly. "And you too, Sarah. *This is fucking enough.* How do we stop it?"

"We manage it, not control it," Diana said.

"That's failed," Deirdre said. "Tim showed us that. Liam showed us."

Melanie shuddered. She lifted her head, wiping her blotched and swollen eyes with one hand. Dampness clung to her cheekbones, giving them a faint sheen.

"We didn't completely fail," she said. "We did restrain Liam and Tim Conley in the depth of the Chamber. For now. But damn it, the device is now seeking out my baby. It's attacked Bess twice. Why? Is it Francis Stewart pushing a breeding plan or is it the thing itself? And *why won't anyone tell me why it's so damn important*?"

"We don't know—" Diana began.

Sarah bristled. "Stop that bullshit! You know better."

"We *don't* know," Diana insisted.

Sarah pulsed, changing shape yet again to a younger form. "Why are you lying to your daughter?"

"Stop it!" Diana lunged at Sarah, who easily darted away. "Stop it! You know that's not the case!"

"You're lying to her and you're lying to yourself!"

"STOP IT!" Diana awkwardly threw a globe. Sarah swerved to avoid it, but at the last moment the globe zipped around and swallowed Sarah. Diana jumped into the globe. The red shimmer of a locked globe—*not one of ours!*—rose around them.

Melanie groaned. Cat gasped. Deirdre flung herself against the globe.

"Not that way!" Melanie yelled. She leapt off the bed. "Get us gloves! NOW!"

Reiko broke out of the stunned frozenness that locked everyone else in the room. She grabbed two pairs of datagloves and handed one pair to Melanie, then helped Deirdre pull on the other pair.

<Guard Bess,> Melanie snapped at Marty. <Get Cat to help you. No time!> She grabbed Deirdre's hand. They pounded on the globe while

Melanie yelled codes. It cracked open and they jumped in, the globe seamlessly sealing shut behind them.

<Cat! Help me protect Bess!>

Cat shivered. <I froze! Marty, I froze!> She stiffly walked toward him. <I—I don't know what happened!>

<We need to protect Bess,> he repeated. <Globe us. You with me and Bess.>

<Okay.>

Marty shivered as the globe went up around them, wrapping himself around Bess.

I hope Melanie's okay.

He'd feel a lot better if Deirdre's chip was active. Headsets could always be pulled. Deirdre might be a talented novice Enforcer, but without that link to an active chip of some sort, even the most experienced Enforcer—*like Mel*—was helpless in virtual.

THE SIDE BLAST FROM A SARAH BLOW SENT MELANIE SPRAWLING AS SHE landed within the globe. Deirdre twirled around her, pulling Melanie into a reactive crack-the-whip snap in the lesser gravity of this globe.

Get grounded first.

She wasn't virtual, she was flesh in this one. Whatever her mother had done, this wasn't the typical secured globe.

Not our product. Not our issue.

Worrisome.

Who the hell gave her this one? And what abilities did they lead her to think she has?

If they got out of this situation whole, she was going to clamp down on these unauthorized virtual management tools from the Courts.

Bad enough we have to deal with the Freedom Army's crap without our own people doing this to us!

Diana and Sarah kept on fighting silently, intently, without acknowledging their presence. Her mother tried to grab for Sarah's head. Sarah dodged, throwing the occasional punch.

Diana crashed into the side of the hologlobe. She landed on hands and knees, shaking her head. Sarah stood back, not diving in for a kill like she normally would.

She's behaving defensively, not attacking. Why?

<SARAH!>

No response, as Diana charged at Sarah.

"MOM!"

Sarah ducked. Diana slammed against the globe's opposite side. This time, instead of going down, Diana used the globe's resilience to rebound back and grab Sarah around the waist. Sarah locked her hands around Diana's throat.

<Go virtual?> Deirdre asked.

Melanie blinked up codes to access the globe's settings. Her mother wasn't virtual. She quickly tweaked the settings for normal gravity, moving everything back to Do It Right specs.

The globe reset itself to her mother's settings.

God damn it, she's programmed an override.

<KEYPAD!> she commanded. If she had to reset it by brute force, she would. <Deirdre, *split them up* while I fix this damn globe!>

<Gotcha.> Deirdre dove toward Diana and Sarah.

The keypad materialized. As she typed in the codes, they streamed from the keypad toward the globe walls.

Activate.

The globe flashed red around them. Gravity pulled too hard at her.

Diana staggered away from Sarah as Deirdre shoved against her.

"KEY OVERRIDE!" Diana yelled, still not acknowledging Melanie or Deirdre's presence. Deirdre wrestled one of Diana's arms behind her but Diana broke free easily.

Too easily.

The globe flashed green. Weight lifted.

What the hell?

<SARAH!>

For the first time, Sarah noticed Deirdre and Melanie. She startled jerkily.

<Melanie? What the hell are you two doing here?>

<Stopping this. What are you two doing?>

Diana charged at Sarah, dragging Deirdre along with her. Melanie stepped between Diana and Sarah. Her mother brushed her aside. Sarah flitted away, darting high before zipping to the other side of the globe. Deirdre tripped Diana.

<It's got her. *IT'S GOT HER!*> Sarah keened.

<Get in my chip!> Melanie commanded. Now that she had seen the Chamber, she knew what Sarah faced.

<No! She's been hit with a poison pill! Yours is mostly deactivated and the coat gives you more protection. If I go in you your pill reactivates!>

How the hell did Mom get hit with a poison pill?

Blue light. She needed to bring up blue light.

Diana twisted, moving faster than Melanie had ever seen her react before. She pinioned Deirdre underneath her and yanked off her headset. Melanie screamed as jagged interference stabbed through her brain, turning everything white around her.

When the whiteness cleared, her mother's hands were tight on Deirdre's throat. Deirdre flailed and kicked wildly. Melanie flung herself onto Diana's back, doing her best to pull her mother off of Deirdre.

Diana shook Melanie off. Melanie hurled herself against Diana, yanking hard at one arm, trying to pry Diana's fingers off of Deirdre's throat.

<SARAH. DO SOMETHING!>

<It's blocking me out of her chip! I can't touch her.>

Suddenly Diana turned on Melanie, releasing Deirdre. Melanie had just enough time to grab her mother's hands before they closed around her own neck. It took every ounce of strength she had left to keep Diana at bay while Deirdre gasped next to her.

"MOM! MOM!" Melanie bellowed.

Her mother kept pushing relentlessly against Melanie's hands, eyes glassy and unfocused, face tight and unrecognizably twisted in fury.

<MOM.> Melanie projected as much command as she could.

Diana's grip momentarily slackened. "Oh *no*," she moaned, face softening, eyes widening in horror.

And then her face warped back into rage.

What the hell? Blinding white light dazzled Marty's eyes and brain. Ness shrieked deep inside his chip and Bess screamed. When the whiteness cleared, Cat straightened up from her doubled over position, hands tight against her temples.

No more protective globe.

Bess raged against him. Marty tried to soothe her. Every other Dialogue in the room shared Cat's stunned, dazed look.

<What's going on?> he asked Ness.

<Diana yanked Deirdre's headset. She's fried it!>

<How the hell can Diana do this?>

<It's not Diana, it's that damned gadget,> Will said. <It has a foothold in Diana! I got a scan before she ducked into that globe. Poison pill. Like Mel's. Probably planted by that same virus that infected Sarah.>

<We have to get them out of that globe!> Marty looked around wildly. <It'll kill them. All three of them! Cat!>

Cat straightened. "As soon as Karl gets here. I'm going in." She scowled, tightening her shoulders. "Karl and Nik will protect you against—it. But pray it doesn't come to that. Things might not work. Melanie's not had time to practice these theories she's been cooking up."

<They'll work.> Will's speech was shaky enough to give Marty pause as he rocked Bess in his arms. <Then there's the Ultimate Trick Melanie doesn't know about yet. You know what to do, Cat.> Will's tone gathered firmness as Karl and Nik came in. <You've had more practice with it than Melanie. Link with her. Get them back, Cat. Get them *all* back.>

Movement startled Marty's gaze upward. Angela and Brenda stood next to him, both armed. Angela nodded at him. Prickles ran up his neck as he recognized their weapons as modified to deal with robots or drones.

What the hell have they been doing?

Mel *had* been busy with theoretical Enforcer work during pregnancy. But what was this?

Or is this Will's doing?

Karl and Cat linked up. Julia attached a metal extension to Reiko's hand.

Has to be Will's work.

Reiko worked the extension's claws, then stepped between Karl and Cat. They rested their entwined hands on the extension's base.

Karl and Cat uttered codes. Then pure tones. The claws clamped. Reiko's extension plucked neatly at a dark spot on the pulsating hologlobe.

The globe faded away.

Deirdre lay in a fetal curl, hands clutching her temples, Sarah huddled next to her. Diana looked up from wrestling with Melanie, her teeth bared.

Behind them shimmered a faint silhouette of Gizmo.

Cat stepped forward. As she did, Karl waved everyone else over to the bed.

"Get Will and Ness in their chips, *now*!" He set four coppery discs around them, leaving enough space at the end of the bed for Security to stand.

"Osaka!" Karl commanded.

Marty blinked. A shimmering red line zigzagged between the discs, then rose to a translucent cube that surrounded them. Bess's wailing settled into hiccups.

"The Last Chance Cage," Karl announced. "One of Will's toys. Our Dialogues and Netwalk chips won't work while it runs. It's crude. It blocks all wireless activity. But it should keep Gizmo away."

BRIGHT RED LIGHT FLASHED AROUND THEM. DIANA RELEASED HER THROAT and fell to one side. Melanie gasped for air. She tried to blink up her Dialogue.

"Dialogue and Netwalk chips aren't working," Cat said. "We employed the Last Chance Cage from Nagano. It seems to work."

What about Sarah? She's probably back to one of the previous versions saved in the Chamber!

"What did you do with Sarah?"

"Safe." Cat gestured toward a small globe. Sarah sat quietly, knees curled to her chest.

Melanie rolled to her side. "Mom has a poison pill linked to the device." She pushed herself up and rolled onto her knees, squatting on her heels. "We have to deal with that. Sarah said she's locked out of Mom's chip."

"Like yours, only fully active," Cat said.

"Crap. So my pill is linked to that damned gadget."

"What condition is Deirdre in?" Melanie asked.

"Better with this—cage, you call it?—going." Deirdre groaned. "I feel like I've been drinking all night. Brain fuzz. Where's the fucking headset?"

"It's fried," Cat said. "And nothing works in here right now. Still, you can start getting oriented with this new one." She held out a new headset.

"Thanks." Deirdre took it, grimacing as she tapped it into connectivity. "Not that I can tell anything with the blockage."

"You'll be able to tell soon enough once we drop the barrier," Cat said grimly.

Melanie peered through the vibrating red barrier as best she could. "Where's everyone else?"

"In another cage. With vibrating weapons. No Netwalkers out." Cat handed Deirdre, then Melanie, bulky pistol-like weapons with ovoid-shaped barrels that had an opening half the size of Melanie's palm. "Here's your weapons." She knelt next to Diana, shaking her gently. "Are you conscious?"

Diana moaned, throwing one forearm over her eyes. "I'm—not safe."

"We know that," Cat said. "We'll sedate you when we drop the barrier."

Oh great. More fighting.

Melanie drew a ragged breath. Cat waved Melanie and Deirdre over to her. She showed them a small sphere, made of an ornate black and gold wire framework that contained an undulating yellow glow.

"Will briefed me on this. The Ultimate Trick, he calls it. It's the only tool left. But it's overkill."

"How?"

"It will blow this poison pill out of Diana. She can renew her Gizmo connection through Sarah and through her Courts coat. But it will also kill your link, Melanie. Permanently deactivates your coat. Fries your Executive Council links. You'll have to rebuild them."

"Never mind about that. Will it kill my poison pill?"

"We're less certain about that." Cat frowned. "I need a backup. We can try to extract Karl from the other cage before we drop this one and engage Gizmo—"

"No. Karl's better at Security and I want him there."

"But your Courts role—if he's here we might be able to preserve the basic linkage."

"Gizmo wants Bess. It can't have her. If blowing the poison pill in me and Mom removes that threat, then I'll gladly figure out what to do about the linkages later. So how do we work this? Drop the cage and set it off?"

"It's not that simple. The minute the cage drops Gizmo reactivates in your mother. Maybe in you."

"I'll manifest the blue light," Melanie said. "Put restraints on Mom."

Diana drew a ragged breath. "That might not be enough. When it runs through me, I don't have control. I'm sorry. It's been driving me for a while."

"I understand." *More than you realize, Mom.* Grim determination hardened. "Deirdre, you keep Mom at bay. Cat, you activate the Ultimate Trick. I'll manage Gizmo until we blow that link in Mom."

"You'd better figure out how to get Sarah back." Her mother sounded resigned. "I don't know which one you'll get back this time."

She knows what reforming does to Sarah.

Melanie's resolve firmed even more. "You know what the Chamber does to her."

"Melanie, this isn't the time—"

"It has something to do with Francis Stewart, doesn't it?"

Her mother sighed angrily, hissing through her teeth. "Melanie—"

"How much of this is Gizmo and how much is Francis Stewart's hatred of Sarah?"

Diana sagged against the floor as Cat and Deirdre bound her ankles and wrists. "I don't know. I really don't know."

"She's bound," Cat said.

Melanie nodded curtly. "Then let's get this job done."

Once again, she tensed, waiting.

The cage dropped. Immediately the rumbling tension from Gizmo vibrated through Melanie's body, angry, seeking.

She brought up the blue light as Sarah burst free. Cat screamed as neon green spikes struck at her. Diana strained against her bonds. Deirdre yelled and thrust a forest green shield between Cat and the jagged spikes.

<We have to back it off!> Sarah yelled. She wrapped herself as black cloud around the blue light spear. Melanie thrust it between Gizmo and Cat. Her arms quivered as electric shocks vibrated through them.

<Push it back,> Sarah directed. Melanie raised the spear high, pushing the spikes step by ever-more-challenging heavier step toward the Gizmo shadow. The Francis Stewart image appeared. It added orange spikes to the green Gizmo spikes, catching Melanie in the gut. She gasped, almost losing the blue light.

Then Deirdre was there. Forest green met orange. They shorted out. The Gizmo shadow rumbled threateningly, though a faint squeal underlay the sonics. Melanie and Deirdre brought up their weapons and fired. The Stewart visage faded away, stripping away the spiky façade covering Gizmo. Melanie and Deirdre stared at the unearthly entities writhing underneath. Not Netwalkers. Not human.

Francis Stewart's shape tried to form. Melanie shot. It disintegrated. Sarah reformed, momentarily wearing the shredded white stealthsuit before stabilizing into her older self. She popped between Melanie and Deirdre.

<Protect me.>

As yellow flared around them, she and Deirdre wrapped their arms around Sarah. Then Cat was there. They fell to their knees.

All four of them trembled together as Gizmo rumbled louder and louder, swelling as lines of yellow-red fire traced along its surface. Diana screamed and passed out as the Gizmo analogue exploded. Bits flew around them.

<*There,*> Sarah said. <*Look.*>

As the bits faded away to nothing around them, Melanie saw a final searing image of Stewart and Gizmo wrapped in a fiery, alien embrace, extending into dimensions she hadn't realized were possible, then disappearing.

<It's alien,> Sarah said shakily. <I never knew that for certain until now, but—it's alien.>

Melanie breathed deep and hard. Knowing this made her decision certain. She dropped her arms and tried to rise but couldn't. Cat rolled away from them to take care of Diana.

<I'm going back into the chip,> Sarah said. <I can help her best from there. At least until it finds another way to insinuate itself into her. It will, you know.>

"Yeah," Melanie said. She collapsed on the floor. "But if Gizmo's alien, what do we do to stop it?" She tensed, expecting a sharp mental jab sufficient to trigger a headache.

Nothing.

<Sarah, am I clear?>

<Yes. Until you decide to relink, that is.>

"I'm not going to do that," Melanie said.

The other cube dropped. Marty picked her up. She closed her eyes and leaned against his chest with her eyes closed, ignoring everyone else but him and Bess. He helped her ease off her coat, then settled her back in bed.

Finally, everything was quiet. As Melanie settled into sleep, she felt at peace for the first time in ages.

I made the right choice.

CHAPTER 23

GOD, WHAT A MESS.

Angela waited with Nik for Andrew's skimmer to land. Andrew had beaten the Courts interrogation staff here—they, unlike Andrew's pilot, worried about the Mountain's storms today. Or had Andrew pushed so that he could beat the Courts staff?

No matter. He was here first.

Andrew's Security staff exited, then Andrew, wearing a heavy raincoat and shrugging off offers of an umbrella.

"Classic Mountain weather," he said as he came up to Nik and Angela. "Where's Mel?"

"Still crashed from yesterday. A lot of stuff came down as a result of clearing those links out of Mariskova," Nik said.

Andrew nodded. "Can I see Celina?"

"Of course." Karl stepped forward. "I'll be your escort."

They dropped behind Andrew's party, following them to Mariskova's room in the infirmary.

<Where's Marty?> Nik asked. <I thought he was going to join us.>

<Going over last-minute details with Mel. He'll meet us outside Mariskova's room once Andrew's done.>

They stopped in the hallway by Mariskova's room.

Karl and one of Andrew's staff went in with him. The rest of

Andrew's staff stood stiffly at attention. Angela leaned against a wall, not feeling the need to keep up appearances. Nik caught the eye of one of Andrew's Security and jerked his head toward an alcove down the main hallway.

<A few details to cover,> he told Angela before walking off with Andrew's Security. Angela noted the rank, including the bars that indicated Courts clearance. Mariskova's replacement. The two men stopped out of earshot and talked quietly but intensely, Nik doing more of the speaking.

Angela shivered. Not having Courts clearance, she hadn't been privy to the discussions between Nik and Melanie. But she had a pretty good idea about what was soon to happen.

Mel, you are so going to upset things once more.

At last Andrew and Karl emerged from Mariskova's room. Andrew appeared more relaxed.

"She's in as good a shape as I could expect from what's happened. Maybe better. Can I talk to Mel or Marty?"

Marty came down the hallway, joining Nik and his counterpart, almost as if he'd been watching.

"Mel's still lying down," he said. "And your mother is completely exhausted. There's been—a number of complications. But Melanie wants to talk to you."

"And I want to talk to her." Andrew joined Marty. They plunged back outside for the short walk back to the family quarters. If anything, the storm was stronger than ever, whipping Angela's overcoat around her legs.

They stopped outside of Marty and Melanie's suite. Andrew nodded to two of his staff, one male, one female. The rest took up positions outside the door.

"Might I suggest your staff join our people in the family lounge?" Angela said.

Andrew paused for a moment. "Yes."

Marty waited until the Security was all gone, save for Nik, Angela and Andrew's two staff. Then he opened the door and stood aside. "Come on in."

A fire crackled loudly in the living room's fireplace. To Angela's surprise, Melanie sat on a stool next to the fire, Bess in a cradle next to her, a bathrobe wrapped around her. She rose stiffly as Andrew entered the room, the robe falling away to reveal her Courts blacks.

"Hello Drew." Her voice sounded tired and lacked her usual vitality as she offered her hand. "Forgive me, but I'm exhausted after what it took to clear Celina. She's all right?"

Something doesn't look right about Mel.

Andrew took her hand in both of his and to Angela's further surprise, kissed her on the cheek. "Better than I expected from Marty's report. Much better than I feared. Thank you." He stepped back to look down at Bess. "This is your daughter?"

"Yes." Melanie made no move to pick up Bess and Andrew didn't seem to expect it. "Excuse me for not showing her off, but she's exhausted after the past few days. It's been—a little stressful." She gestured to the chairs. "Let's sit." She dropped into her usual rocking chair. Marty stood next to her.

Andrew shook his head as he sat. "I don't know how you pulled it off. Taking on—the thing—like Marty said you did."

Melanie sighed. "I had help." She picked up a formal envelope from a small stack on the side table and handed it to Andrew. "Read this, please."

Angela tensed.

If what I've overheard is correct, now is when it hits the fan—

Andrew carefully broke the wax seal on the flap and eased the cream-colored paper out. He paled as he read. "Mel—you're joking!"

"Read the rest of it." Melanie's voice was firmer, but she looked more tense, drawn and haggard than she had when Andrew walked into the room.

Andrew glanced down. When he was done, he slid the paper back inside the envelope. It took several tries before his shaking hands succeeded.

"Mel. You can't quit the Exec and take Do It Right out of the Courts. *You can't.* What does our mother say?"

"You'll be able to hear it for yourself soon. She's on her way, along with Zoë Wright. Zoë is with her to spy out just what the hell's going on plus twist my arm about renewing my links. I sent them their versions of your letter only a few minutes before you came in."

"You can't do this."

"Legal says I can." Melanie straightened up. "Andrew. That damned gadget tried to kill me. It tried to kill my child. It will try once again to kill yours. I know—" she hesitated, her voice faltering, biting her lip as she looked at Bess. "As a result of what's happened, as a result of talking to Celina and Deirdre, I know too damned much about it. About what it wants to do to us."

Andrew's face tightened. "You mean Francis Stewart's legacy. His creation."

Melanie shook her head slowly. "The only damned thing Stewart did was make a connection with it, an unbreakable connection that he either drove insane or it drove him insane. It's not a human creation, Drew." She jumped up and began to pace. "*It's alien.* And Drew, how long before others like it get here? With what it knows about us, what it may have told them about us? About our defenses?"

Andrew sank back in his chair. "Now you're sounding like Sarah in her wilder moments before she died."

"Sarah pushed Ness to create Netwalk to counter the gadget. From what Ness says, Sarah went deep enough before she died to become aware of what I just saw in clearing Celina and getting its corruption out of Mom. Netwalk is our weapon against the device and its kind, Drew." Melanie stopped abruptly, turning to face Andrew, arms wrapped around herself, her eyes big and staring. "Tim Conley and Liam Jeffreys are betraying Netwalk's secrets to the gadget—which is hoarding partial Netwalkers and using them to fuel itself."

"What does leaving the Courts serve?"

"It keeps my child safe. It allows me to provide a newer, stronger, more effective Netwalker defense against the device and its kind. Not that I plan to publicize that. But I am taking Netwalk away from the Courts. Except for Sarah. Sarah is our inside guard." Melanie sighed and sat down again. "Drew. I don't expect you to join me, nor should you. Nor am I going to tell all of this to Mom."

"I doubt she'd believe you anyway. Mel, this is bizarre."

Melanie shook her head. "I don't dare present Bess to it," she whispered. "You saw what happened to me when I was presented. We blew all of that linkage away cleaning the poison pill it planted in Mom. What's it going to do to me on a second presentation—and what would it do to my baby? *Peter's* in it."

"You're sure?" Andrew's voice quavered.

"I'm positive. Here's something else for you to consider. What will it do to your son? Ask Celina what Stewart made it do to her. How it damned near killed her rather than let us pull Tim Conley out of her. Remember what they did to us at Charleston? We got too damned close to something they didn't want us to know."

"I've wondered about that."

Melanie nodded. "The big piece is that *Gizmo is alien.* And there may be more like it. I don't think the Courts are safe, especially not for me and those closest to me. I worry about Mom, but she has Sarah to keep her safe."

Andrew flinched. His eyes met Melanie's, almost as haunted as hers now. "What do I do? You know they'll want me to present my son. If he survives to be born."

"We'll figure something out to stall them. Drew, keep your kids away from it. It's scarred us. It wants something we have. One of our genetic markers."

<Incoming,> Sergio texted. Nik snapped alert, flashing handsign at Andrew's staff. Angela moved protectively toward Bess but Marty was quicker, striding over to sweep Bess up out of the crib and place her in Melanie's arms.

The door banged open.

"You can't do this!" Diana roared. "Melanie, just what the hell are you doing?"

"I'm protecting my child," Melanie snarled. "You saw what it did at the end! You went through its infestation! I am not handing Bess over like you did me and Drew!"

That stopped Diana cold. Zoë Wright entered the room slowly, carefully. "She can do it, Diana. Legal agrees that the wording is tight."

Diana shook her head. "You don't understand what you're triggering."

"Oh yes I do," Melanie whispered. She glanced down at Bess and her face briefly softened. "I don't deny the need for the Protectorate, Mom. Nor will I deny you Sarah. You need her protection against the gadget. But I will not be party to any further incursions it makes into our human genome. And I will fight its control to my dying day."

"And High Space?"

"High Space becomes my highest priority. The other is my Netwalker uprising. Netwalk is—and will be—*my* tool. Consider it an insurance program for when the Protectorate fails." Melanie handed Bess to Marty.

<Ange. Help me get this off,> she texted. Angela hurried over. Little prickles stung her fingers as she held the sleeves while Melanie eased first one arm, then the other, out. Melanie took the coat from her, gazing down at it for a moment, standing there in her white uniform blouse and black slacks. Then she slowly, carefully laid it across her forearms, letting the sleeves dangle free as she walked across the room and held it out to Zoë Wright.

"I surrender my coat of office," she said formally, dropping to one knee in front of Wright and raising her hands.

"Are you sure about this?" Wright's voice quavered slightly.

"For my daughter's sake," Melanie said firmly. "I'm certain."

"I accept your resignation," Wright said, taking the coat from Melanie. She handed it off to one of her own Security.

"How am I going to monitor Sarah, especially at the Courts? Or are you going to resume your role as consultant to the Courts?" Diana threw her hands up and wobbled slightly. Kathy Miller shouldered past Zoë Wright and helped Diana sit down.

Melanie shook her head. "I'm not returning to anything that puts me near that fucking device! But I'm assigning you Deirdre Conley as Enforcer. She's stronger than Cat and better able to deal with *its* quirks. I'll still be available for off-site consultation."

"I wish you wouldn't do this."

Melanie shook her head. "No. I have to protect Bess."

"It'll take a while to untangle all the ties."

"Not as bad as you think," Kathy Miller said.

"Will I still be able to see you and Bess?" Diana's voice turned pleading.

"Of course! Mom, I'm not completely cutting off ties. I just—I can't risk the device having links in me. Or in those closest to me. There'll be a research group available to work with you. We'll keep your chip upgraded and Sarah safe. But no other ties between the Protectorate and Do It Right."

Kathy Miller jerked her head toward the door. Nik signed to Andrew's staff and Angela. They withdrew.

"Time to leave the family alone," Nik said softly once they were outside.

"I don't think Diana's going to fully accept this decision," Angela said.

"Oh, she will," Kathy said. "Diana is nothing if not pragmatic."

I hope you're right.

Angela really didn't look forward to the possibility of warring against Diana. Unlike Sarah, Diana knew too much about their current operations.

That will have to change. As soon as possible.

She wasn't accustomed to viewing Diana as a foe—but stranger things had happened.

MELANIE STRETCHED, STUDYING HER BODY CRITICALLY IN THE MIRROR AS she moved through her exercises in the workout room. Not quite back to pre-pregnancy condition, but it had only been a week.

<Not bad,> Sarah said suddenly, taking the shape of her younger self.

Melanie startled but kept herself from reacting. <You're a long way from Mom!> Last report had her mother on the other side of the continent.

<Not this weekend,> Sarah settled on the barre. <The Courts meet. It's in the Rockies. Keep myself small, I can visit when she's asleep. Or, at least, this remote part of me can. It's not fully me. It's a remote message.>

<Didn't know you could do it.>

<I didn't either, not until I got things sorted out from our last little

sortie. She's still brooding, keeps me locked up. Sleep is my time to escape.>

Melanie sat on a bench. <So. Remote message. What is it?>

<Call it a thank you. I didn't realize how deeply the device had its claws into me. Your little Deirdre is going to keep me honest.>

<And my mother?>

Sarah frowned. <That I couldn't tell you. She's hiding herself more than ever.>

<Should we find you a new host? I hate to do it. Mom needs the protection, but maybe you'd be safer.>

<No. Not—yet. You need me where I am. Watch Bess. Keep her safe.> Sarah faded out.

Melanie stared thoughtfully at the mirror. Then she rose and pulled on sweats over her tights and leotard, heading back to their suite.

Marty looked up as she entered. "You're back early."

"I had a visit from Sarah." She described what happened.

"That's puzzling," Marty said. "None of that seems to be worth a message."

A green warning light flashed on her overlays. Melanie blinked it up.

<Here's the real message,> Sarah's text read. <Check this file. I managed to clip it from internal sources. Only way to safely deliver was to distract you and the device by the remote message while this one took the long way around. Not sure what it means. Send you more as I can. Plus there's a complete file on the specs for Courts coats. That way Marty and Will can create one of your own, free from the gadget's control. You'll need it.>

Melanie ran a quick check. The files looked clean. She forwarded it to Marty. He frowned thoughtfully, ran his own checks, then popped it open in a guarded hologlobe.

"It's data on the Disruption attacks," he said finally, his voice speeding up as he looked more closely at it. "It shows how the device replicates and spreads—Mel, this is a deep file. Folded upon itself. How the hell did Sarah manage to get it?"

"I don't know," Melanie said.

But I am glad she's on our side. For now, anyway.

She wondered how long it would be before more Gizmos appeared.
Not before Bess grows up. I hope.
The thought of her daughter brought a faint smile to her lips.
Bess will be the leader of my uprising.

THE END

NEWSLETTER

Like what you've read? Want to follow Joyce either through her monthly newsletter or through an email feed of her irregular blog posts?

Sign up for Joyce's newsletter here:

https://tinyletter.com/JoyceReynolds-Ward

Or follow Joyce's irregular blog posts on her Substack, here:

https://joycereynoldsward.substack.com/

BOOKS AND PUBLICATIONS

The Martiniere Legacy

First Meetings: A Martiniere Legacy Short Story

Inheritance: The Martiniere Legacy Book One

Ascendant: The Martiniere Legacy Book Two

Realization: The Martiniere Legacy Book Three

A Belated Christmas Honeymoon: A Martiniere Legacy Short Story

The Enduring Legacy: The Martiniere Legacy Book Four

People of the Martiniere Legacy

The Heritage of Michael Martiniere: A Martiniere Legacy Novel

Broken Angel: The Lost Years of Gabriel Martiniere: A Martiniere Legacy Novel

Justine Fixes Everything: Reflections on Mortality

The Martiniere Multiverse

A Different Life: What If?

A Different Life: Now. Always. Forever.

Goddess's Honor titles currently available (chronological order):

The Goddess's Choice: A Goddess's Honor Short Story

Beyond Honor: A Goddess's Honor Novella

Exile's Honor: A Goddess's Honor Novelette

Birth of Sorrow: A Goddess's Honor Short Story
Pledges of Honor: Goddess's Honor Book One
Return to Wickmasa: A Goddess's Honor Short Story
Crown Anniversary: A Goddess's Honor Short Story
Challenges of Honor: Goddess's Honor Book Two
Cleaning House: A Goddess's Honor Outtake Story
Unexpected Alliances: A Goddess's Honor Rough Draft Outtake Story
Choices of Honor: Goddess's Honor Book Three
Judgment of Honor: Goddess's Honor Book Four

Netwalk Sequence Author Preferred 2022 Editions

Life in the Shadows: Book One
Netwalk: Book Two
Netwalker Uprising: Book Three
Netwalk's Children: Book Four
Learning in Space: Book Five
Netwalking Space: Book Six

Bright Star Fair Witches

Becoming Solo: A Bright Star Fair Witches Novella

Non-Series Titles currently available:

Alien Savvy: A Western SF Novella
Klone's Stronghold
Beating the Apocalypse
Bearing Witness

Vella Titles:

Falcon of the Martinieres (part of *Justine Fixes Everything*)
Bearing Witness
Beating the Apocalypse
A Different Life—What If? An Alternative Martiniere Legacy Novel
Becoming Solo
A Different Life—Linda's Story: An Alternative Martiniere Legacy Novel
Federation Cowboy

Audiobooks Available:

Alien Savvy: A Western SF Novella

Released from other publishers:

"Queen of the Snows," in *Once Upon A Winter: A Folk and Fairy Tale Anthology*, edited by H. L. Macfarlane

"My Man Left Me, My Dog Hates Me, and There Goes My Truck," in *Black-Eyed Peas on New Year's Day: An Anthology of Hope*, edited by Shannon Page

"Lost Loves," in *All Worlds Wayfarer*

"The Wisdom of Robins," in *Whimsical Beasts: A Campcon Anthology*, edited by Joyce Reynolds-Ward

"The Cow at the End of the World," in *Well…It's Your Cow*, edited by Frog Jones

"To Plant or Pull Up Stakes," in *Pulling Up Stakes: A Campcon Anthology*, edited by Joyce Reynolds-Ward

"The Notice," in *Children of a Different Sky*, edited by Alma Alexander

ABOUT THE AUTHOR

Joyce Reynolds-Ward has been called "the best writer I've never heard of" by one reviewer. Her work includes themes of high-stakes family and political conflict, digital sentience, personal agency and control, realistic strong women, and (whenever possible) horses. She is the author of *The Netwalk Sequence* series, the *Goddess's Honor* series, and the recently released *The Martiniere Legacy* series as well as standalones *Klone's Stronghold, Alien Savvy,* and *Beating the Apocalypse*. Samples of her Martiniere short stories/novel in progress and her nonfiction can be found on Substack at either Speculations from the Wide Open Spaces (general, writing) or Martiniere Stories (fiction). Joyce is a Self-Published Fantasy BlogOff Semifinalist, a Writers of the Future SemiFinalist, and an Anthology Builder Finalist. She is the Secretary of the Northwest Independent Writers Association, a member of the Science Fiction and Fantasy Writers Association, and a member of Soroptimists International.

www.ingramcontent.com/pod-product-compliance
Lightning Source LLC
Chambersburg PA
CBHW020327120726
47904CB00002B/305

* 9 7 8 0 9 8 4 9 8 0 3 6 9 *